Praise for the novels

DOMINICK ABEL LITERARY AGENCY, INC.
146 West 82nd Street, Suite 1B
New York, New York 10024
(212) 877-0710

La Nouvelle Agence
7, rue Corneille
75006 Paris

THE OTHER EYE

JERRY KENNEALY

AN ONYX BOOK

ONYX
Published by New American Library, a division of
Penguin Putnam Inc., 375 Hudson Street,
New York, New York 10014, U.S.A.
Penguin Books Ltd, 27 Wrights Lane,
London W8 5TZ, England
Penguin Books Australia Ltd, Ringwood,
Victoria, Australia
Penguin Books Canada Ltd, 10 Alcorn Avenue,
Toronto, Ontario, Canada M4V 3B2
Penguin Books (N.Z.) Ltd, 182–190 Wairau Road,
Auckland 10, New Zealand

Penguin Books Ltd, Registered Offices:
Harmondsworth, Middlesex, England

First published by Onyx, an imprint of New American Library,
a division of Penguin Putnam Inc.

First Printing, October 2000
10 9 8 7 6 5 4 3 2 1

 REGISTERED TRADEMARK—MARCA REGISTRADA

Printed in the United States of America

PUBLISHER'S NOTE
This is a work of fiction. Names, characters, places, and incidents either are
the product of the author's imagination or are used fictitiously, and any resemblance to actual persons, living or dead, business establishments, events, or
locales is entirely coincidental.

For the Coffee Shop Gang
Dean Bagley, Hal Gevertz,
and Herb Kessler,
whose contributions to the preparation
of this book were nonexistent.
But they did pick up the check
every once in a while.

Prologue

New York City

"I don't like this place, Mark. It gives me the creeps," Denise Duval said nervously, looking out through the car's windshield as the wipers carved twin arcs out of the downpour.

"This won't take long," Mark Martel promised. Denise's high-cheekboned face was a mere silhouette in the dashboard lighting. "Ten minutes, then dinner at La Caravelle, and tomorrow morning we fly off to Mexico." He slowed down as they approached the riverfront warehouse that George Alvord had chosen for the delivery.

Truth be told, Martel didn't like the place either. He would have much preferred to make the exchange at Alvord's art gallery on Wooster Street, but when a man was paying you two hundred thousand dollars for a stolen painting, you let him pick the spot. He coasted to a stop in front of an eight-foot chain-link fence topped with barbed wire. Leaning out of the window, he pushed the button on the white plastic speaker and called out, "It's Martel. Open up."

There was a grunted reply, followed by the raspy grinding of mechanical devices as the gate slowly swung inward.

Martel drove toward the dark warehouse. He made a U-turn, pushed the gearshift into park, and adjusted the volume on the car's CD player. Soft music enveloped the interior.

"There, you've got jazz, a view of the World Trade Center on your left, New Jersey across the Hudson, and"—he reached over to her lap and scratched the floppy ears of Denise's miniature French poodle—"D'Artagnan to protect you."

Denise blew him a kiss as he exited the car. Martel retrieved a length of rolled-up carpet from the car's trunk, then jogged toward the gloomy outline of the warehouse.

Hollow flashes of lightning flickered against the leaden clouds, and rolling thunder rattled ominously over the Manhattan skyline.

A tugboat with long brown stains dribbling from its hosepipes bobbed in the dark river waters. Its diesel engine throbbed bronchially as Martel pounded on a corrugated-steel door.

"Come on, open up, damn it! I could drown out here."

The door swung open, and Martel quickly shouldered his way into the building.

"Where's Alvord?" he asked the jittery-looking young man holding the door.

"He's tied up at the gallery," Dick Brumback said, then cleared his throat with a cough into his fist. "Is that the painting?"

Martel waved the carpet. "Where's my money?"

"Follow me," Brumback ordered.

Martel didn't like the idea of George Alvord's not being there. Brumback was in his late twenties, with a prominent Adam's apple and an eternal five o'clock shadow. In Martel's mind, there was no reason why Brumback should even know his name, much less be involved in the transfer.

"Hold it," Martel said. "Is there anyone else here?"

"Just us," Brumback responded as he turned his back on Martel and started climbing a steep, reverberating wooden staircase that led to the upstairs offices.

The room Brumback guided Martel to was square, with a battered gray metal desk, a three-drawer wooden file cabinet with peeling varnish, and several mismatched chairs. Two bare lightbulbs surrounded by protective steel mesh dangled from the ceiling.

"Let's see the merchandise," Brumback said as he fell into a padded swivel chair with a thick-bodied thump.

Martel surveyed the room. There were three connecting doors. Rain flayed the lone window, sending jagged rivulets coursing down the glass. "I don't see the money."

Brumback grunted, then reached under the desk, dragged out a black canvas carryall, and dropped it on the desktop. "You show me yours, I'll show you mine," he said with a glassy smile.

Martel began gently unrolling the length of carpet, revealing Antonio Correggio's *Assumption of the Madonna*. The soft, delicate coloring showing the Madonna, cloaked in pale blue, surrounded by angels, her arms spread wide as she ascended into heaven, caused Martel to catch his breath.

Brumback wasn't as impressed. "Two hundred grand for that old relic," he muttered as he tossed the carryall to Martel, who caught it with both hands.

A door opened, and two men wearing ski masks and black raincoats stormed into the room. Each held a wicked-looking semiautomatic pistol in his outstretched hands.

One man was tall and lean, much like Martel. The other was short and stockily built. A thick, half-smoked cigar protruded from the short man's teeth. He worked the cigar to the edge of his mouth, then said, "Drop the money."

Martel followed orders, glaring at Brumback, who had eased himself back into the chair.

The short man approached the desk, stooping to pick up the carryall containing the money. Then he moved in close to Martel.

The cigar bobbed up and down as he spoke. "You punk. I hate punks like you. You must think you're some high-class fuckin' thief, huh? One painting for two hundred thou? Forget about it." He leaned over the desk. "I think you were right, Brumback. It is kind of an old relic."

A clump of ashes from the short man's cigar fell onto the painting. He reached over to brush them away.

"Don't do that," Martel snapped, reaching for the painting.

The short man pivoted and raked the barrel of the gun across Martel's face. "What'd you say?" he screamed, taking the cigar out of his mouth and throwing it at Martel. "You telling me what I can do?"

Martel blinked away the blood that was dribbling down into his eye. "That's a masterpiece. You can't—"

The short man slashed the gun barrel across Martel's face again, then yanked his mask off. His wide face tapered down to a narrow, arrogant chin. His dark hair was matted in spots, spiked up in others. Martel recognized him immediately. Victor Ganero, Jr., the son of the New York Mafia's boss-of-bosses.

"You ain't never goin' to tell me what I can and can't do, punk. You ain't never goin' to be able to tell anyone what to do!"

The chair made a squeaking sound as Dick Brumback rose unsteadily to his feet. "Vic, maybe I should leave now, and—"

Ganero wheeled around and casually shot Brumback three times, the ear-shattering blasts of the bullets echoing off the concrete walls.

Brumback was thrown backward into the chair, which began spinning around in wobbly circles before skidding to a stop when it hit the wooden file cabinet.

Martel edged toward the door, jerking to an abrupt halt when he felt a hard round metal object grind into his back.

"You're not going anywhere," growled the man who still wore a ski mask.

Ganero walked over to Martel and placed the tip of the hot gun barrel millimeters from Martel's right eye.

"You recognize me, don't you, punk? See what your big mouth did? Now I'm going to make sure that you—"

There were thudding sounds on the steps. Another masked man came barging into the room, his bulk filling the doorway. He stopped short when he saw that Ganero had removed his ski mask. "You okay?"

"I'm fine," Ganero declared with confidence. "Real fine."

"Martel brought someone with him. There's a broad in his car," the big man said.

Ganero jammed the gun barrel into Martel's eye socket. "A broad, huh? Whack her."

"She's got nothing to do with this," Martel protested. "Why don't you—"

"Shut up!" Ganero screamed. "Big Soup, bring the broad up here." He was breathing heavily, audibly wheezing. "We might as well fuck her before we whack her."

Martel tensed his fingers, then made a desperate lunge for the gun. Ganero pulled the trigger and smiled as Martel recoiled and dropped to the floor.

He leaned over the body, ready to deliver a bullet to the back of Martel's head, when he noticed the watch.

Ganero dropped to one knee, put the gun on the floor, and used both hands to pry the chunky gold watch off Martel's wrist.

"Not bad," he said when he got to his feet, holding the timepiece up to one of the bare lightbulbs.

The taller gunman sighed and removed his ski mask. Johnny Musso was forty-three, hawk-nosed, with a small, funnel-shaped mouth. His gray eyes were so pale his eyes seemed to have no pupils. Musso had worked for Victor Ganero, Sr., for fifteen years. He respected Big Vic. The son, in Musso's estimation, was an idiot. A dangerous, coke-snorting idiot, who was going to get himself into a lot of trouble. "You didn't have to shoot him, Junior. Your father is not going to be happy about this.''

"Bullshit," Ganero said in a self-satisfied tone. He stooped to pick up his gun. "Pop's going to get his precious painting *and* the two hundred grand back.''

Tony "Big Soup" Zarela took off his ski mask and mopped his face with it. Slightly older than Musso, he had worked for Victor Ganero, Sr., since he was eighteen. Like Musso, he thought little of Junior, but the boss had told Big Soup to take care of the kid, and whatever Victor Ganero, Sr., told him to do, he did. Without question. "I'll go get the broad," he said softly.

"Do it quick," Musso ordered, picking up the painting. "Then you two dump the bodies in the river. I'll deliver this and the dough back to Vic.''

"Hey," Ganero protested, toeing his shoe into Martel's body. "I ain't gonna lug this big bastard over to the river.''

Musso's voice turned frosty. "You made the mess, Junior. You clean it up.''

Ganero's face reddened. He spun the pistol around his index finger, like a movie cowboy. "Don't push it, Johnny. You don't tell me what to do.''

Musso stood his ground. "Put the gun away, or I'll take it away.''

Junior did an elaborate twirl with the pistol and slid it into the holster under his coat. The two men stared at each other for several moments. Ganero broke the silence when he heard footsteps coming up the stairs. "Why don't you stick around for a turn at Martel's broad?''

Chapter 1

"Okay, who's next?" the uniformed guard asked, knowing full well that the uptight prisoner who had been standing at attention in the hallway for the last half hour had been waiting for this day for a very long time.

"I think it's me, sir," Harry Vlad replied stiffly. "Number two-four-four-six. Vlad."

The guard narrowed his eyes and checked the roster. "Vlad. Harold J., right?"

"Right, sir."

The guard tugged a thick manila folder out of a foot-high stack of files on his desk. "Yeah. Here you are." He flipped through the file. "You've been with us awhile, haven't you, Harold?"

"Two years, five months, and three days, sir." Harry wanted to add, six hours and twenty minutes, you fatheaded prick. Give me my stuff and let me out of here.

The guard was in no hurry. The release desk was his favorite duty post. Keeping the prisoners waiting an extra hour or two was the highlight of his day. He glanced up at the clock on the wall. It was almost lunchtime. Should he keep this one chilling for another hour? If he did, he'd be late for lunch, and today was meat loaf. He loved meat loaf.

"Okay, Vlad." The guard pushed himself to his feet, crossed to the low-ceilinged room housing the prisoners' personal property and returned with a brown cardboard box. He used a pocketknife to cut through the cord securing the contents.

"Check it out," he ordered, flopping back into his chair.

Harry sorted through the wrinkled slacks, sport coat, shirt, and tie that he had worn in court the day he'd been sentenced. Stuffed inside one of his shoes were his wallet, cigarette lighter, and wristwatch.

The guard leaned back and studied Harry through half-closed eyes. "Anything missing, Vlad?"

The lighter was a Bic throwaway, not the one that Harry had stolen from right under the eyes of a beautiful blond saleswoman at Tiffany's. The watch was a cheap knockoff, not Harry's gold Rolex. "No. Everything's here, sir."

The guard smiled knowingly and thrust a thumb over his shoulder. "You can change in there. Hurry up. I don't want to be late for lunch."

That was one order that Harry followed willingly. He stripped himself of the drab gray prison jeans and shirt and quickly donned his old clothes, happy to note that the pants were still a perfect fit.

He felt like a new man. No, he decided when he returned to the guard's desk. He felt like his old self.

The guard tossed him an envelope. "There's a check in the amount of six hundred and forty-seven dollars. You can cash it at any bank in town." He eyed the wall clock again. "The bus comes by in an hour or so."

The guard pushed himself to his feet, and Harry expected him to extend his hand across the desk and wish him luck.

"So long, Vlad. For now. I bet we'll be seeing you again."

"You'd lose that bet, buddy," Harry forecast, testing his newfound freedom. No more sirs, or downcast looks. He drilled his eyes into the guard's. "You'd lose that big time."

A cold March wind blustered through the partitioned walls of the bus stop. The Shawngunk Mountain Range— the "Gunks"—shimmered in the background. A four-star climb site for the nutcases that got their guns off climbing mountains. Harry had often gazed out at the remote, jagged peaks from the iron-grilled windows of the prison workshop.

He jogged in place and rubbed his hands together as he waited for the bus. No climbing mountains for Harry Vlad. Fire escapes, drainpipes, elevator shafts, yes. But mountains, no.

Harry was now thirty-two. He was of medium height, his body well muscled. His hair was flaxen, the color of a nicotine stain. He considered himself handsome, his only flaw a toothpick-size gap between his upper front teeth. He had thought of having his teeth capped but had been talked out of it by a cocktail waitress who claimed the gap gave his face character.

Harry had fifty-eight dollars in cash and the check for six hundred and forty-seven dollars—blood money—earned by working in the prison's eyeglass-manufacturing plant for the princely sum of fifty cents an hour.

He had used some of the money he earned in prison to buy cigarettes for the guards and his fellow prisoners. Six cartons of Marlboros had gotten him an afternoon job in the prison library, which had enabled him to keep track of the outside world—at least the part of the world that he was interested in. Another three cartons of cigarettes had convinced the head librarian to add such magazines as *Architectural Digest, Art Faire, Town and Country,* and *Connoisseur* to the prison's subscription list.

Harry had pored through the magazines showcasing the rich and famous, their mansions and artworks, the way a college student studied SAT primers. The glossy photographs often exposed the front door, the roof, the nearest point of access, be it a beachfront or a country road. A burglar's blueprint. The addresses were never supplied, but it was a simple matter to trace the properties through public records.

He'd once done a job for a fussy old collector who

had used a red pen to circle the items he wanted from a Glen Cove mansion featured in a eight-page layout of *Art Faire*.

The real bonus for Harry had appeared in a piece in *Connoisseur* about an upscale wine auction at a San Francisco Hotel, the Fairmont. Hotels were Harry's favorite milieu—easy to get into, easy to get out of. One of the photos showed a crowded room, dozens of society-type men and women sipping from test-tube-shaped glasses. Harry's well-trained eye had scanned the crowd, checking their clothing, their jewelry, cataloging them as to their wealth and trying to pick out just who might be an undercover security guard.

One of the faces had jumped off the page at him. A tall, lean-faced man, caught walking in mid-stride, his arm slightly extended, looking as if he was carrying something in front of him. Whatever was in his hands was concealed by the crowd. He was wearing a button-down shirt, no jacket, no tie. His hair was much longer than Harry remembered, but there was no doubt in his mind who it was. Mark Martel.

Harry felt like he'd just hit a Vegas jackpot. He wondered if Martel was living in San Francisco or had just been on vacation and somehow had been captured by the camera's lens. He'd thought about this long and hard while lying in his prison cell bunk. Martel had been put into a federal witness protection program after he'd agreed to testify against Victor Ganero, Jr.

Somehow Martel had survived being shot in the head and dumped in the Hudson River. The would-be killer hadn't reckoned with the fact that Mark Martel had been narrowly beaten out of a bronze medal in the Olympics fifteen-hundred-meter freestyle.

Vlad had once watched Martel plow endlessly back and forth in the YMCA pool on Lexington Avenue. His hair was short, close to the scalp, then. Harry had tried to convince Martel to join him in a caper involving the theft of a Renoir from an upstate museum, but Martel had turned him down cold.

Harry remembered the meeting well. Martel, always a loner, was mad as hell that Vlad had approached him with the proposition, threatening to toss Vlad into the pool if he didn't stay away from him.

Harry Vlad always paid close attention to the competition. He had tried following Martel around New York City a couple of times, but was never able to stay with him for more than a few minutes. Martel was a very cautious man, which was probably why he had never been arrested. From what Vlad had learned, Martel was not only a thief but also a collector. George Alvord, the chiseling art dealer they both used as a fence, had told Harry that Martel had a Joseph Turner landscape and a couple of Gauguins in his private collection.

Harry had followed the Ganero trial closely. Junior Ganero's father, Victor, the don-of-dons, had put out a contract on Martel, promising to personally take out his other eye if he so much as showed up in court.

Victor Ganero, Jr.'s trial ended in a hung jury. Ten to two for conviction. The D.A. vowed to push for a new trial, but he never got the chance. Junior was found shot to death in an alleyway in Little Italy. One bullet through his right eye.

The word was that old man Ganero held Mark Martel responsible for his son's murder and that he wanted to take care of Martel himself, by plucking out his remaining eye with an ice pick before finishing him off. And Ganero would pay half a million dollars to anyone who could find Martel. Which meant that Martel would want to move far away from New York. As far away as possible. Someplace like San Francisco. Yes, the more Harry thought about it, the more sense it made. Frisco was one city where the Mafia had never really gotten a foothold.

So, Harry figured, all he had to do now was find Martel. Or get Martel to come to him. Then he could either make a deal with Martel or turn him over to Victor Ganero. Or both.

After his son's death, Victor Ganero had moved from New York out to some damn place in the Arizona desert. Rumors were that the move was made because of Ganero's health, which meant Harry had to find Martel before the old don kicked off.

Harry was tired of the snow and freezing weather. He decided that he would move west, too. To a healthier—maybe even a wealthier—climate. Somewhere fresh, where he wasn't known, where the cops hadn't heard of him.

The beeping of a horn brought Harry out of his reverie.

"Hey," the bus driver shouted through the open door, "are you coming, or what?"

"I'm coming," Harry responded cheerfully, bounding onto the bus.

Chapter 2

Mark Verre wasn't sure what woke him, the soft chirp of the burglar alarm or Gauguin's low, throaty growl. He rolled off the bed, quickly slipped on a pair of jeans, withdrew a pistol from the nightstand, and padded barefoot to the door.

"What's wrong, Mark?" Arlene Severi called from the bed, her voice drowsy with sleep.

"Nothing," he whispered. "Probably just a deer or a bobcat. I'll be right back."

Gauguin, a charcoal-coated, 130-pound Scottish deerhound—similar to an Irish wolfhound but sleeker and faster because of the greyhound blood in its past—was waiting for Verre when he opened the bedroom door. Gauguin's tail was wagging and his teeth were bared.

The dog had been trained never to leave his post during the night unless released by Verre. Mark gave him a silent signal—a quick snap of the fingers followed by an outthrust arm.

Gauguin leaped at the command, his feet clicking on the tiled flooring as he bounded down the stairs ahead of Verre. The dog was whining and scratching at the front door by the time Mark got there. He deactivated the burglar alarm. One blinking red light indicated that someone, or something, had violated the motion alarm near the front porch. He opened the door, commanded, "Get him," and the big dog let out a feral snarl and leaped into the night.

Mark heard the cough and the whining sound of a

small engine, followed by Gauguin's hearty barks. He ran outside as a single headlight pierced the darkness. A motorcycle, he correctly concluded.

There was a small package alongside the door. A common brown grocery bag. He picked it up carefully, his hands clasping the familiar shape of a liquor bottle. He opened the bag, withdrew the bottle, and cursed. It was Martel's XO cognac.

He put two fingers into his mouth and whistled sharply three times, the signal for Gauguin to abandon the hunt.

The dog came back minutes later, panting for breath.

Mark roughed his hair. "Good boy, good boy. Come on, you deserve a reward."

He led the way to the kitchen, set the 9 mm Sig-Sauer pistol on the table, and removed a slice of left-over veal roast from a terra-cotta pot. He gave it to Gauguin, who chomped at it greedily, licking the juice and gravy from Mark's fingers, before going to his water bowl and lapping up the contents.

Mark replenished the water, then shoved his hands into the back pockets of his jeans to keep them from shaking as he stared at the label on the bottle of cognac. Martel's. The bastards had found him.

"What was it, Mark?" Arlene Severi asked from the doorway. She was dressed in tan shorts and an orange T-shirt that bore the name of her restaurant, La Cucina. She was thirty-five, an inch or two over five feet tall, with coppery hair, a generous mouth, and espresso-brown eyes with oversized irises. Mark's first impression of her had been that she looked like a pint-size Sophia Loren.

"Deer or bobcat, I guess."

"I heard a motorcycle. Deer and bobcats don't usually drive them, do they?" she asked dryly.

"Why did you get dressed?" Mark sidestepped. "Let's go back to bed."

Arlene yawned and stretched her arms over her

head. "It's almost six. I want to get back to the restaurant."

"Stay. Just for an hour or two. Please. At least until it's light out there."

"What's the matter, Mark? You look nervous. Is something wrong?"

"No, no," he responded lightly. "I just don't want you to go. I'll fix breakfast."

"I'd like to stay, but there are some deliveries coming in this morning, and I have to get things ready for Carrie. She'll be home tomorrow."

Mark nodded his understanding. Arlene operated a gourmet restaurant in nearby Calistoga, and Carrie, her fourteen-year-old daughter, had spent the weekend with her father in San Francisco. "I'll walk you to the car."

Mark held out his arms for a hug, pulling Arlene to his chest, burying his head in her hair. She recoiled when she saw the pistol on the table. "Why the gun?" she asked.

Mark shrugged his shoulders and pulled her back to him. "I'm sorry the morning came so damn fast."

"Me, too." She raised her head and kissed him full on the lips, then stepped back. Something was wrong. He looked tense, frightened, but she knew he wouldn't confide in her.

She often wondered just what the deep, dark secret was that Mark kept to himself. Did it have something to do with his false eye? It had taken her a while to realize that his right eye didn't move in unison with his left. It had a dull, glassy look about it in certain lights. When she'd first asked him about it, he laughed it off. "Yes, it's glass. Hand-painted." But he'd never told her the circumstances of how he'd lost his eye, or how he'd gotten the nasty cluster scar at the back of his head that she discovered one night when running her fingers through his hair.

Rumors were that Mark had bought an interest in the Hatton Winery, though they were never substantiated and Joan Hatton wouldn't confirm it. The winery had been ready to go bust before Verre came on the scene. New equipment was purchased, along with more acreage, and then Mark constructed a small house on the vineyard property.

He had kept to himself until last summer, when he started going to parties at the neighboring wineries and frequenting local restaurants. That was where she'd met him, at La Cucina.

All she knew was that he was handsome, funny, hardworking, a marvelous swimmer, a talented painter, adored by her daughter, Carrie, and that she was in love with him.

"It's going to be another hot one," Mark said, draping his arm over Arlene's shoulders as he walked her out of the house and to her bright-red Alfa Romeo convertible. Gauguin moved silently by his side.

An orange-sherbet sun was chinning itself over St. Helena Mountain. September was just around the corner, which meant one thing in the Napa Valley. Harvest time was approaching.

"Am I going to see you tonight?" she asked, switching on the engine.

"No. I'm going into the city on some winery business and won't be back until late."

She grabbed his hand and brought it to her lips. "Then tomorrow. Carrie will want to see you too, and I'm preparing a special dinner for a party of ten— Moules à la Provencale and Thon en Chartreuse. Steamed mussels and tuna with vegetables and wine. I'll make sure there's enough left over for us."

Mark lifted her hand from the wheel and gently kissed it. "Drive carefully."

She promised she would, then gunned the motor. The sports car's wheels churned up a fountain of dust and gravel as she spun around in a tight U-turn.

Mark raced to his Jeep Cherokee, Gauguin jumping in beside him. He trailed Arlene's taillights as they left the winery property, turning right on the Silverado

Trail, heading toward Calistoga. He held back, following her from a discreet distance, making sure no one else was after her. Or him. After she parked and ran into her combination house-and-restaurant, he sat in the Jeep, a block away, slowly scratching Gauguin behind the ears, his thoughts on the cognac bottle left on his doorstep. Who had found him? Victor Ganero, or one of his henchmen? It seemed too subtle a gesture for them. They would have simply kicked in the door, shotguns and Uzis blasting everything and everyone in sight.

Whoever it was, Arlene, and her daughter, Carrie, as well as Joan Hatton, could be in danger too. He sighed out loud, drawing a sharp look from Gauguin.

By six-thirty, neighboring lights started popping on, car motors turned over. Cats and dogs were out on their morning hunts. Gauguin let out a low growl when he spotted a piebald cat stalking a blue jay.

"Let's go home," Mark told the dog. "We have bigger problems now, my friend."

Chapter 3

It was nearly ten o'clock, and the temperature was in the low nineties. Mark Verre took a bandanna from his back pocket and wiped the sweat from his neck. He swatted a fly away from his face and took a slow 180-degree look at the forty-seven acres of the Hatton Winery that spiraled down through the valley below him. The neighboring vineyards stretched for miles in each direction, a sea of lush green, marred occasionally by football field–size scars of autumn crimson, the dreaded red leaf disease that had cost Joan Hatton a good portion of her Merlot crop last season.

Mark loved everything about the winery—working in the soil, coaxing the grapes to ripeness, harvesting them, smelling the wonderful scents of the fermentation process, and, of course, enjoying the final product.

And a wonderful product it was. Hatton wines were winning prestigious tasting contests in which they were pitted against the very best in the Napa Valley, as well as the fine Burgundies of France.

He took no credit for the awards. Joan Hatton deserved all the applause. All he had done was provide the financing and some manual labor.

Mark watched as Joan, dressed in washed-out denim overalls and a floppy straw hat, cut back a row of Cabernet Sauvignon vines. She was a gaunt, narrow-shouldered woman, with a no-nonsense Midwestern face deeply tanned from too much sun. She plucked one grape from a dusty velvet cluster and bit into it, rolling the fruit around in her mouth for a few seconds.

Joan had been one of the first vintners in the valley to plant her vines on steep mountainsides, to limit production, thin the vines, cut back on growth, and concentrate on flavor.

She smiled at Mark. "Another two weeks. No more."

He nodded his agreement. Joan was a "smell and taste" vintner. No long-winded oenology experts measuring sugar and acid levels with sophisticated computer analysis for her. Just her own gut feeling from the taste and smell of the grapes.

"How are you?" Joan asked. "We didn't see you yesterday."

Mark had spent the day in his house, watching the road, waiting. He and Gauguin had slept in between the rows of vines during the night. There was no sign of anyone until early that morning when a black van pulled up near the winery entrance on the Silverado Trail and switched off its engine. It hadn't moved since seven o'clock.

Mark hated to bring up the bad news. "Joan. Did you see that van parked down by the entrance this morning?"

She turned and squinted down toward the Silverado Trail. "Van? No. Should I have?"

"I'm afraid so," he responded softly.

"Damn," Joan said harshly. "He's found you?"

Mark squatted down and dragged his fingers through the hard red-brown soil. "Someone has. A bottle of Martel's cognac was left at my door early yesterday morning."

Joan started to say something, then decided against it. She sank slowly to the ground, kneeling next to Mark. Gauguin took advantage of her position and came over to nuzzle her shoulder.

She raked her fingers through the dog's heavy coat. "You said it might happen one of these days."

Mark shrugged and jammed his hands into his pockets. Joan Hatton was the only person he'd confided in about the circumstances leading up to the murder of his fiancée, Denise, in New York, his testimony at the trial, and the contract that Victor Ganero, Sr., had put out on him. He'd told her after he approached her with an offer to buy in to the winery. Joan had taken a week to think it over, and Mark had thought he'd made a major mistake by letting her in on his problems. Then she'd called him at his apartment in Los Angeles. "Don't bullshit me," she told him bluntly. "Did you kill Junior Ganero?"

"No, Joan. I thought about it. But I didn't."

"What are the odds of this Mafia gangster finding you?"

"I'd say pretty low, if I stay in the background. Victor Ganero's in his mid-seventies now. He's no longer in New York. He may have cooled off. He may—"

"Maybe the bastard will die," Joan cut in. "Okay, Mark. You supply the money and I'll show you how great wine is made."

It developed into a good partnership. Mark learned the business slowly, from the bottom up, starting by washing out fermentation tanks, digging out rocks from the hillside, handpicking the grapes. He never butted in. Joan was in charge of the hiring, firing, and the producing of the wine.

He soon learned that being a vintner meant being able to jury-rig grape slides, cobble together makeshift presses, backhoe trenches, and stack barrels.

He had stayed close to the winery, not venturing past the front gates for more than a year; then Joan had eased him into the merchandising side of the industry, something she hated. He had designed new labels, replacing the stark black-and-white Hatton Winery hallmark with his own soft pastel abstract paintings of the vineyard. His first business-related trip was to the state of Washington to contract for new aging barrels. The price of French oak had driven the cost of a barrel into orbit, and the native California oaks were too gnarly. A bright young entrepreneur in Washington had solved the problem. Mark had been amazed when he'd visited the timber stand. Acres and acres of oak trees, all as straight and round as telephone poles.

Now he handled most of the sales and marketing, freeing Joan to do what she did better than anyone: make great wine.

"I'm not sure that Victor Ganero left the bottle of cognac, Joan."

"Then who, damn it?" Joan pushed herself to her feet and dusted off her hands. "Who's in that van down by the gates?"

"I don't know, but I'm going to find out. If . . . if it is Ganero, I'll have to move quickly. You shouldn't be in any danger," he said, trying to sound convincing.

"Hmmmph," Joan snorted. "Goddamn crooks. You do what you have to do, Mark. You've been square with me. I've got no complaints."

"I'm going to San Francisco. I'll have Pete drive me to Calistoga, and then I'll borrow a car. I don't want the van following me." He grabbed her hand in both of his. "I'll be back tonight."

"You better be," she warned. "We've a hell of a lot of work for you here."

Mark angled down the hillside toward a flat area where a battered old Ford truck was parked. It had once been a shiny red, but now it was faded to rusty pink, worn to the bare metal in spots. The headlights were fixed in place with an X of electrician's tape. A shotgun was racked against the rear window. Pete Altes, the winery foreman, often fired the weapon into the air to frighten birds away from the vineyards. Occasionally he would lower the sights to go after quail, or jackrabbits. The truck was shielded from the road by a twenty-foot hill, so even if someone in the van had binoculars, he couldn't zero in on it.

Altes was leaning against the truck's fender, en-

joying a cup of coffee. When he spotted Verre, he
pulled a thermos from the front seat. "Coffee, Mark?"

"No, thanks. I need a ride, Pete. Into Calistoga."

Altes, a broad-chested man in his fifties, with wind-
gnawed features, took off his straw cowboy hat and
scratched his head. "Sure. Something wrong with your
Jeep?"

"No. There's a black van down by the gate. It could
be trouble."

"What kind of trouble, *amigo*?"

"Nothing I want spilling over on you." Mark climbed
up into the truck's cab. Gauguin stared up at him with
pleading eyes. "Okay, come on, come on."

Altes carefully nursed the engine to life.

"Down," Mark ordered, as the truck began chugging toward the steep road leading to the Silverado
Trail. Gauguin reluctantly pulled his head away from
the window and sank onto the floorboard.

Mark ducked down alongside the dog. Altes stopped
for a moment at the gates, studying the van. It was
sheeted in dust. The dark-tinted windows blended in
with the vehicle's black exterior. Two small antennas
poked out of the roof.

"Get the license plate number," Mark whispered
from his crouched position.

"It's kinda covered with dirt. Maybe I should roust
him when I come back."

"No," Mark said sharply. "Don't go near it."

Tony Zarela dismissed the three women who came
each weekday morning to clean the house. "*Viate*.
Scram. You're finished for the day." Two were on
the wrong side of forty—thick-bodied Mexicans who
dressed in traditional flowered dresses. They griped
constantly about Zarela or Sineo following them
around the house while they went about their chores.
The third was a *figone*, quite young, a real beauty,
with smooth, tawny skin and a nice round butt that
she squeezed into frayed jeans. The boss's orders were

that the women were always to work together, so Zarela hadn't been able to trap the young one alone. Yet. He had to search them before they entered and left the premises, but today he waved them on out the front door, not bothering to check their purses.

"Mañana, señor," one of the older women called to Zarela.

"Yeah, yeah. Tomorrow." He shepherded them down the steps and to the garage area, where their beat-up jalopy was waiting.

A taxi was parked outside the sculptured iron gate. Zarela held up a hand to indicate to the driver to stay just where he was.

The sun was boiling through a layer of blood-colored clouds. The weatherman had predicted a temperature of 104 degrees. Zarela mopped his forehead with the back of his hand as he walked down the cobbled path to open the gate. The woman driving the jalopy tooted the horn and gave him a toothy smile as she passed by. The young one stared at him, a look of mocking amusement in her wide chocolate-brown eyes.

"You're going to get it," Zarela whispered, vowing to catch her alone in the house one day and slap some respect into her.

He jerked his thumb at the cab and Harry Vlad exited the rear door. Zarela waited until Vlad was alongside him, then told the cab driver to wait.

The cabbie pulled a face, and Zarela slammed his fist on the taxi's hood. "You're gettin' paid. You wait!"

He carefully locked the gate, then marched up the steps to the house, Vlad dutifully following behind him.

"You stay here," Tony "Big Soup" Zarela ordered, pointing a sausage-size finger at Vlad.

"I won't move a muscle, Tony," Harry assured the big man. He frowned as he watched Zarela lumber away. Big Soup could have been a retired NFL lineman whose muscle had melted into fat after leaving the game. He was dressed in a dark-blue double-breasted suit, white shirt, and narrow black knit tie, his enormous feet encased in shiny black brogues. He looked like an undertaker. New York clothes, not Carefree, Arizona, duds.

There was usually another goon hanging around with Zarela—Sineo, a greasy-haired hood with jug ears and a Buddha-like stomach. Harry wasn't sure if Sineo was his first or last name. Sineo dressed like Tony's clone: dark suit, dress shirt, and dark tie.

Harry was wearing a pair of light chinos, an Izod shirt with the alligator emblem near his heart, and sandals. No socks. It was too damn hot for socks.

He crossed the uneven stone patio and gazed out at the surrounding scenery. Vast canyons of gray-faced mountains and flat stretches of shadowy desert spotted with cactus and low-lying scrub took up most of the view to the north.

Harry was disappointed by the rock colors. He'd always imagined Arizona as being just like it was in the old John Wayne movies—rusty-red rocks sculptured by thousands of years of wind and rain. These looked just like those damn mountains near the Shawngunk prison.

The view to the west was entirely different. Huge mansions in flat, modern architectural styles, spaced an acre or two apart, half-mooned around an expanse of emerald-green grass and the too-blue-to-be-true lakes and ponds of a fastidiously manicured golf course.

While all the neighboring mansions had a look-alike newness to them, the home of Victor Ganero seemed as if the entire estate had been uprooted from another time, another place, and dropped into the middle of the Arizona desert.

Apricot-colored stucco walls capped with weathered tile roofing. What Harry didn't know was that the stones he was walking on were imported from a quarry in Italy, and that the roof sported ancient four-hundred-year-old "thigh tiles" that had been hand-crafted by laborers who molded each and every tile on their thighs. The architect had journeyed from Ganero's native land to assure that Casa Ganero resembled the home of Ganero's grandfather in Cosenza.

The full-grown olive trees had come from California, as had the bougainvillaea and citrus plants.

Harry Vlad heard Zarela's heavy footsteps clacking on the tile floor.

"The boss will see you," Zarela said grudgingly. "Bring the painting."

Harry scooped up the heavily wrapped package that he had toted in and fell in line behind Zarela. The interior walls were covered with red flocked wallpaper. The overstuffed furniture was of muddy-colored maroons and greens.

It was stifling inside the house. Harry couldn't feel, or hear, any sign of an air conditioner.

Zarela twisted his basketball-size head around several times to make sure Vlad was staying in line. He led Harry past a thirty-six-foot dining room table to a brass-rimmed door.

Zarela knocked lightly on the door, then leaned down to give Harry some advice. "Dress up next time, *checca*. You look like a fag beach boy. And don't keep the boss too long."

Chapter 4

The delicious aroma of freshly baked bread and sautéing garlic and onions set Gauguin off on a barking frenzy.

Arlene Severi wheeled around from the huge cast-iron oven, her hands cloaked in oversized potholder mitts. Her beige apron was speckled with flour. She pushed a lock of hair away from her forehead and smiled. "Mark. I didn't think I was going to see you until tonight."

"I need a favor," he said. "I'd like to borrow your car."

"My car?" Arlene's forehead wrinkled in puzzlement. "Sure. What happened to yours?"

"I'll have it back late this afternoon," Mark said quickly, dodging her question.

Arlene slipped out of the gloves and rummaged through her purse for the car keys. "I hope everything is all right. You seemed so—"

"Hi, Mom!"

Mark, Arlene, and Gauguin all turned to see Carrie dash into the room. She was a taller version of her mother, and at fourteen, her figure was beginning to blossom. She wore knee-less jeans and bright-yellow tube top. Her dark hair was drawn back in a waist-long braid.

Carrie ran over and kissed her mother, then hugged Mark to her chest, planting a kiss, which included a light, playful tickling of her tongue on his ear, before bending down to pet Gauguin.

"Hi, big guy," she crooned to the dog. "Are you hungry?"

"He's always hungry," Mark conceded.

Gauguin's tail beat a steady rhythm as he followed Carrie to the double row of stainless-steel refrigerators.

Arlene went back to her purse. She found the car keys and handed them to Verre. "Mark, something's wrong. What is it?"

The sound of someone coughing cut off his answer. "What's doing, babe?"

"Hello, Dan," Arlene said with little enthusiasm.

Mark had heard about Arlene's ex-husband, Dan Heller, but had never met him before. Arlene didn't want to talk about Heller, and he respected her wishes. It was Carrie who had filled him in on the fact that her father was a San Francisco police inspector. A homicide detective. Mark had often wondered if he would have allowed himself to get close to Arlene had he known that when they'd first met. Now it didn't matter. He'd thought of proposing marriage more than once. The only thing holding him back was the menacing shadow of Victor Ganero.

Heller was in his mid-forties and very tall, at least four inches over Mark's six feet, with a wide, ruggedly handsome face. His hair was more salt than pepper. His pale-gray eyes were canopied by barbed-wire eyebrows. He wore a baggy blue polo shirt over rumpled gray slacks. Mark could see the tip of a holster peeking out from under the shirt.

Arlene's voice turned frosty. "How was the weekend?"

"Great," Heller boomed. "You should have come with Carrie. We had a blast." He turned to Verre and held out a hand. His eyes searched Mark's face, as if committing it to memory. "You must be the painter guy that Carrie told me about."

Mark dropped Arlene's car keys into his pocket before shaking the policeman's hand. "I'm really not much of a painter."

"Don't let him kid you," Carrie called out over her shoulder. "He's terrific." She cut up some raw liver for Gauguin, then helped herself to one of the freshly baked croissants. "These are terrific, Mom."

Heller held on to Verre's hand as if reluctant to set it free. "Terrific. Everything's terrific when you're fourteen." He nodded in satisfaction when he identified Mark's glass eye. "You make wine, too, huh?"

"No. I just handle the books. Joan Hatton makes the wine." Mark freed his hand, then snapped his fingers, and Gauguin trotted over to him.

Heller reached out to pet the dog but jerked his hand back when Gauguin let out a low growl.

"He's suspicious of strangers," Mark warned him.

"Rough-looking animal," Heller said, shoving his hands in his pants pockets. "I've never seen one like it. What the hell is it?"

"A Scottish deerhound."

"What's it good for?" Heller pressed.

"Loyalty." Mark paused, then added, "And eliminating any leftovers."

"Gauguin's great," Carrie assured her father.

"I've never liked big dogs," Heller said in a stony voice. He zeroed in on Mark's glass eye. "Big dog, little man." He favored Verre with a patronizing smile. "I don't mean you, Mark. Just that it happens a lot, you know? I've run into some weird guys with dogs. The weirder they are, the bigger the dog. Kind of a crutch, you know what I mean?"

"I sure do," Mark answered solemnly, thinking of Denise Duval's miniature poodle, D'Artagnan. Denise's body had been dredged up from the river bottom by the Coast Guard. D'Artagnan had never been found. "He's a trained killer. Attack, Gauguin."

The towering policeman took a hurried step backward, but Gauguin remained motionless at his master's side.

"We're still working on that one," Mark grinned. "Sometimes he just won't obey."

Carrie broke the tension with a giggle. "He's kidding you, Dad." She dropped to the floor and began roughhousing with Gauguin.

"Very funny," Heller said acidly. "Carrie told me you're a barrel of laughs."

Mark held out his hand again and smiled. The last thing he wanted to do was make an enemy of Arlene's ex-husband. Or any policeman. "Good to meet you, Dan."

Heller kept his hands in his pockets. "Likewise."

Arlene followed Mark out to the carport adjoining the entrance to the restaurant. "That didn't go very well, did it?"

Mark began unsnapping the Alfa Romeo's tonneau and putting up the convertible top. "He seems like a good guy. Carrie obviously likes him."

"Yes. She doesn't know him like I do." Arlene gave him a hand securing the car's top. "Can I help, Mark?"

"You are," he assured her. "Thanks for letting me use the car. I'll be back in a few hours." He took a blanket from the Alfa Romeo's mini-trunk and spread it across the passenger seat.

Gauguin tilted his head to one side, as if to say, "You expect me to get in there?"

Mark snapped his fingers and Gauguin reluctantly planted his paws on the blanket, then hoisted himself into the cramped confines of the sports car.

Mark slid behind the wheel, turned the key, and stabbed the accelerator. He wished he had another choice, someone besides Arlene to borrow a car from. But, he rationalized, the person who had left the bottle of cognac at his door must already know all about Arlene.

She blew him a kiss and whispered, "Drive carefully."

Gauguin shifted uncomfortably in the bucket seat, finally maneuvering so that he could rest his head on Mark's lap.

Arlene stood motionless and watched until the convertible was out of sight. As she turned, she bumped into her ex-husband.

"Verre gets everything, huh?" Dan Heller said with a forced grin. "Including your precious sports car. That big dog is going to tear up the leather upholstery."

As Arlene pushed past Heller, he grabbed her shoulder lightly. She wheeled around, fists balled up as if ready to strike out.

"Arlene, I'm sorry. I wasn't prepared to meet Verre. I . . . I was hoping that we could . . . maybe have a few days together. Just take a drive, visit a winery, or—"

"Forget it, Dan," Arlene responded hotly. "You had Carrie for the weekend. We'll see you in two weeks." She turned on her heel and marched back into the restaurant's kitchen, head held high, arms swinging aggressively.

Dan Heller's jaw bunched. He kicked out at a good-size stone, sending it crashing into the trunk of the gnarled oak tree that sheltered La Cucina's outdoor dining area. Dummy, he chastised himself. He'd spent days working on a speech for Arlene—a "let's forgive and forget" speech—and now she wouldn't even talk to him. Verre. Carrie had told him that her mother liked Verre a lot. How much was a lot? Too much, apparently.

Heller walked slowly back to his car, his plans for the day now ruined. He might as well go back to work, he figured. Back to work and to do some checking on Arlene's boyfriend.

Johnny Musso poured himself a cup of steaming coffee from the elaborate brass espresso machine. He looked up when Tony "Big Soup" Zarela entered the kitchen.

"Who's the punk?" Musso asked.

Zarela removed his suit coat and carefully draped

it around the back of a chair, then went to the stove, lifted the lid from a five-gallon pot and stirred the mixture with a huge wooden spoon. Zarela had always kept a pot of soup going at Ganero's New York home, and he had continued the exercise since Ganero moved to Arizona. "Harry Vlad. He's been knocking off some paintings for the boss." He sampled the soup and smacked his lips. "Needs more parsley and salt."

Musso watched in amusement as Zarela, a man who had willingly pulverized the arms and legs of many an enemy of Victor Ganero's, padded delicately around the kitchen. Zarela's favorite weapon of intimidation was an aluminum baseball bat that had been filled with cement. Just the sight of Zarela walking into a room with the bat dangling from his hands was enough to make most men spill whatever secrets they had.

Musso had to admit that the soup was good. Very good—in New York. Not Arizona. He hated his bi-monthly visits to Carefree. Carefree. Even the name irritated him.

Zarela sampled the soup again and smiled. "That's better. You want a bowl, Johnny?"

"I'll pass. Tell me more about this Vlad punk."

Zarela rolled his massive shoulders. "He's delivering what the boss wants. Some more of them old religious paintings." He ladled soup into a bowl, then sat down at the kitchen table, the chair groaning under his considerable weight. "Vlad said something interesting. He thinks that Mark Martel is out here."

Musso's interest was immediate. "Martel is here? In Arizona?"

"No. On the West Coast. Los Angeles, or San Francisco, maybe." Zarela made slurping noises, then added, "I'd sure like to get my hands on that *minchia*."

Musso nodded his understanding. If Musso hadn't been able to bribe two of the jurors, Mark Martel's testimony would have landed Zarela in prison alongside Junior Ganero. Martel had heard Junior use the names "Big Soup" and "Johnny" that night on the waterfront. Every cop in New York knew Zarela's nickname, and they were equally sure that Musso was the Johnny on the spot.

Zarela had sweated out a few days in a holding cell in the Tombs, but he was released and never charged. Martel had made a threat against Zarela, outside the courtroom. His head and left arm had been heavily bandaged because of the gunshot wound and from having been bumped around the Hudson River, but he had managed to point a finger at Junior Ganero, vowing to "Get you, Junior." His finger moved to Zarela as well. "And you, you ugly son of a bitch." The court bailiffs and district attorneys had quickly moved Martel back into the safety of the courtroom.

Musso had skated by with a single, somewhat comical interview by the district attorney. Musso's attorney had pointed out that there were thousands of "Johnnys" in the New York area, including the D.A.'s own son.

Later, when Junior was murdered, one bullet in the right eye, Victor Ganero had ordered Johnny Musso to find out who was responsible, and Musso verified Ganero's suspicions that Mark Martel had been the killer. But so far, all of Ganero's efforts to find him had failed. It had been an obsession with the old man. "Get him! I want him!" The half-million-dollar contract was still out, but Don Ganero didn't mention Junior anymore, or Martel. The only thing he seemed interested in now was his paintings. And his immortal soul. One of Zarela's chores was driving the Mafia don to church several times a week.

Zarela finished his bowl of soup, then burped. "You're lucky, Johnny. Only having to come out to this shit hole twice a month. Man, I miss New York. There's not a single decent restaurant out here. Nothing like Puglia's, or Rao's. Not even a delicatessen. Next time, bring me a pastrami from the Carnegie Deli, will ya, Johnny? There's nothing here. No good food, no joints, not even any real broads. The whores all look the same—tall and blond, with silicon tits. It's like grabbin' a big Spaldeen." He swept a hand across his face as if brushing away insects. "The boss don't want no whores in the house. I got to smuggle them into my room—make sure they don't make any noise—or else nail them in the car."

Musso grinned sideways at Zarela's problems. The big man always made a lot of noise when he was with a woman. And so did the unlucky woman. He thought back to Mark Martel again. His girlfriend had gotten a real working over before she was whacked. Martel had been one lucky bastard. Junior couldn't even kill a guy when he had the gun in his victim's eye.

"Man, I miss the city," Zarela continued in a gloomy tone. "There's not even any real cabs out here. This Vlad punk took a cab from his hotel. He's got it waitin' 'cause it takes an hour to get one when you call."

Musso settled in on a chair across from Zarela. "Things aren't too good back home, Tony. I wish you were there to give me a hand. I need you. The feds are all over us. I've got snitches coming out of my ears. The Russian gangs are moving in on our garbage-hauling contracts. The lousy Jamaicans are cutting into the Fulton Street Fish Market. And the Indians, the goddamn Wahoo Indians. The government lets them open casinos all over the country. They'll be giving Manhattan back to them one of these days. The boys aren't happy." He nodded his head toward the back of the house. "Vic's living out here like a king, while we're having our brains beat out."

Zarela rubbed his temples with the heels of his hands. "I know, I know, but what can I do? The boss don't want to go back to New York."

"Times change, people change. You've got to be ready for it, Tony. Tell me more about Harry Vlad."

"What's to tell? He steals paintings the boss likes, the boss gives him some cash, then he goes out and steals more of the damn things. I figure he must—"

The tinkling of a bell cut Zarela off. He heaved

himself to his feet. "That's the boss. I got to pay
Vlad off."

"How much?" Musso asked.

Zarela rubbed his thumb against his index finger.
"Seventy-five thou." He shook his huge head slowly,
as if the movement caused him pain. "Seventy-five
large for a painting the size of a magazine. Crazy,
huh?"

"Crazy," Musso agreed. "Send the cab away. I'll drive
Vlad back to his hotel on my way to the airport."

Chapter 5

Calistoga still had a small-town feel about it, a turn-of-the-century main street crowded with beauty shops, grocery stores, one-man insurance and real estate offices, and coffee shops that still served regular coffee and donuts. The mud baths and hot mineral spas made it a mecca for the health-conscious, dating back to the time when only stagecoaches made the dusty two-day journey from San Francisco.

Mark motored slowly through town, then turned left on Highway 29. St. Helena was only eleven miles south of Calistoga, but its once rustic main street had been gentrified—upscale antique shops, espresso and cappuccino stands, Rodeo Drive–style clothiers, jewelry stores whose windows were cluttered with Rolex watches and Cartier bracelets.

By the time he entered the tunnel of elm trees signaling the entrance to the Berringer Winery on the outskirts of St. Helena, Mark was sure he wasn't being followed. He snuggled the Alfa Romeo into a parking lot jammed with Jaguars, BMWs, Mercedes, and overly wide Hummers whose owners, not satisfied with taking up two spaces, gobbled up three by parking at an angle to ensure that their macho machines wouldn't get scratched.

He parked close to one of the Hummers and, much to Gauguin's relief, put the convertible top down.

Gauguin barked in appreciation and held his head into the wind when Mark got the car back on the road.

Traffic flowed smoothly until they popped out of

the Waldo Tunnel in Marin County. The Oz-like view of the Golden Gate Bridge, Alcatraz, and the sun-dappled skyline of San Francisco usually inspired Mark to pull off to the side of the road and do some sketching. But not today.

The cheerful young brunette toll-taker made a crack about Gauguin's size when Mark handed her three one-dollar bills.

"You should put that guy in a trailer."

Mark forced a smile, then drove quickly into town, down Lombard, right on Van Ness, then left on Golden Gate Avenue.

The federal building was exactly as he'd remembered it. A dull, flat, gray monolith with gritty windows running all around.

He found an open parking meter, put what quarters he had into the machine, took Gauguin for a walk down to the park across from the recently restructured city hall, then returned to the Alfa Romeo.

Gauguin was reluctant to get back into the tiny car. "Go. Stay," Mark ordered. He fished in his pockets for more quarters. Finding none, he went to a corner coffee shop. The proprietor, a dark-faced man with eyes like polished marbles, refused to make change unless Mark made a purchase. He bought a tepid, muddy-looking cup of coffee, returned to the car, and waited, using the napkin and, when that was covered, the paper cup to sketch the passing pedestrians.

When Mark spotted Bill Rangel leaving the federal building, he fed four more quarters into the parking meter, stroked Gauguin's head, and crossed the street.

As soon as Rangel's feet hit the sidewalk, the Justice Department bureaucrat stopped to light up a cigarette. He inhaled deeply and let out a long stream of smoke, unmindful of the frowns and outright looks of contempt from nearby pedestrians. He took another pull on the cigarette, holding the smoke in as long as he could before releasing it.

San Francisco had some of the toughest antismoking

ordinances anywhere in the United States, and Rangel, whose office was on the thirty-fourth floor, didn't have a long enough coffee break to sneak out for a quick smoke during working hours, so he suffered longingly from nine till the lunch hour.

Bill Rangel had aged in the last three years. In his mid-fifties, he had a long and baggy face, and there were flabby pouches under his eyes. The silver-dollar-size bald spot at the crown of his cottony gray hair had expanded to the size of a softball.

Mark slipped back into the thick-pressed crowd, keeping his eye on Rangel's bald spot as he sauntered slowly down Golden Gate Avenue, stopping only to light another cigarette from the dog-end of his old one.

After two blocks, Mark knew just where Rangel was headed. He'd seen Rangel on a daily basis when they were working out a new identity for Mark Martel, and every lunch hour had been spent at the same restaurant, Original Joe's on Taylor Street.

It didn't seem that much had changed in the neighborhood, except perhaps that the ragged column of street people waiting in line for their turn at the tables of St. Anthony's soup kitchen seemed longer, the crowd less surly, more subdued, as if the fact that what once had seemed to be a few weeks' or a few months' predicament had settled into a way of life. Or death.

Rangel veered left at the boarded-up lobby of the Golden Gate Theater, stopping to light one more cigarette in front of a sex shop featuring grotesque, oversized rubber replicas of women in bikinis and short nightgowns. The stiletto-heeled hookers paid Rangel no attention, but one pint-size girl with taffy-colored hair hurried up to Verre.

"Wannadatehoney?" she asked, making the sentence a one-word question. A black leather vest, held together by dog-leash clips rather than buttons, barely covered her freckled breasts.

"I'm broke," Mark informed her, and the hooker did an about-face worthy of a marine drill sergeant.

Rangel's lunch routine had remained the same. Two whiskey sours at the bar, the first one consumed on a stool, the second carried over to a small banquette at the rear of the restaurant.

Mark slid in across from Rangel as he was about to give his order to the sad-faced waiter.

"He'll have the cheeseburger, medium, with the house salad, house dressing," Mark told the waiter.

"So, what else is new?" the waiter deadpanned. "You want something?"

"A glass of red wine," Mark said. He stared across at Rangel. "Hi, Bill. Long time no see."

"Jesus Christ."

"No. Mark Verre. Remember?"

Rangel took a hit on his whiskey sour. "Remember? Hell, yeah. I remember." He fidgeted in his chair and looked around the restaurant. "What are you doing here?"

"Someone's found me, Bill. I'd hate to think it was through you."

Rangel loosened his tie and took another pull on his drink. "Not me. I don't know where you are, what you're doing, nothing, for Christ's sake. And I don't want to know."

"Then who?" Mark pressed.

Rangel stared at his drink and frowned. "I don't know. Once I process you guys, you're out of my hands. Good-bye, good luck, and, in most cases, good riddance."

"You were the only one who was supposed to know my name change, about—"

The waiter bumped into the table as he went about the task of opening a bottle of wine. The label leaped out at Mark. His autumn-gold watercolor of the Hatton Winery.

"I only ordered a glass of wine," Mark said in a shaky voice.

"Yeah, I know, but this is on the lady." The waiter pointed to the bar with the cork before pushing it toward Mark. "She brought the wine, said she wanted to surprise you. Now, you want to taste, or you just want me to pour?"

"Leave the bottle," Mark said stiffly.

"What's going on?" Rangel said angrily. "Who is she?"

The woman smiling at them from the bar was long-legged, with silky black hair that hung ruler-straight down to her shoulders. She was wearing a short white accordion-pleated skirt and a gold V-necked silk blouse. She stood up, scooped a saddle-leather purse off the bar, and walked straight toward Mark with a strong, athletic stride. She stopped at the table and smiled confidently. "May I join you, gentlemen?"

"Who the hell are you?" Mark demanded.

"I'll take that as an invitation." She slipped into the booth across from Mark, causing Bill Rangel to slide over.

"Lisa Cole, Mr. Verre." She opened her purse and took out a black calfskin card holder. "I'm working for Boston Insurance," she announced as she passed out business cards to Mark and Rangel.

Mark studied the card for a moment before rolling it up into a ball and dropping it onto the carpet. He stared daggers at Rangel. "You know her, don't you?"

Rangel's glass shook as he drained the remains of his whiskey sour. "I never saw her before."

Lisa Cole said, "He's telling the truth, Mr. Martel— or I should say, Mr. Verre. That's the name you want me to use, isn't it? Mr. Rangel and the Justice Department haven't been of any help to us."

Mark stared at the woman for a long moment before replying. "What do you want?"

Rangel shifted his weight. "Let me out of here."

"Don't go—you may be of help to Mr. Verre. Or Martel. Which *do* you prefer to be called?"

The waiter came with two more glasses and began pouring the wine.

Lisa Cole waited until he had left before saying, "What I want is a few Old World masterpieces. A Caravaggio, a Veronese, and that Botticelli you picked up last week." She took a sip of the wine. "And any others that you might have hidden away."

Bill Rangel studied Cole's business card for a moment, then broke the stony silence. "Boston Insurance. That's where Charlie Dwyer works now, isn't it?"

Mark's head swiveled toward Rangel. "Dwyer's working for an insurance company?"

"Yes," Cole said pleasantly. "He got a little tired of the dull civil service life." She smiled at Rangel. "No offense, sir."

Mark sank back into the booth's rolled-leather upholstery. He felt a sudden jolt of relief at knowing that it wasn't Victor Ganero or one of his men who had left that bottle of cognac on his doorstep. Charles Dwyer had been the chief investigator for the Justice Department during the Ganero trial. The fact that Martel had no criminal record cut little slack with Dwyer. Once Martel supplied the details of how the Antonio Correggio painting had been stolen, Dwyer was convinced that Martel was responsible for at least eleven other unsolved major art thefts. Dwyer made no bones about not wanting to make a deal with an art thief, but without Mark's testimony there would have been no case against Junior Ganero.

There had been some tense moments, Mark threatening to recant his testimony, Dwyer threatening to throw him in jail for stealing the Correggio. Mark knew that any jail time was actually a death sentence. The Mafia would have no difficulty killing him in prison. The Correggio never turned up. Dwyer was certain that Victor Ganero, Sr., had it, but he had never been able to prove that fact. The painting had become a fixation with Dwyer. If he could have pegged it to Victor Ganero, his case would have been made—without Mark Martel's help.

Dwyer had eventually agreed to Mark's demands: all inquiries into past thefts terminated, all his bank accounts and personal property returned.

Dwyer had gagged when he'd seen Martel's bank statement. "You're a lousy art crook and you're worth half a million bucks!"

It hadn't been just the money that had driven Dwyer up the wall. There'd been a ring of keys found in Martel's apartment. Five keys: a spare for his apartment, one for the apartment of his fiancée, Denise Duval, two for Martel's Jaguar, and one that Charlie Dwyer had not been able to find a lock for in any storage facility, or bus, railroad, or airline terminal. A key he was certain led to a cache of stolen art, and more money.

After the Junior Ganero hung-jury verdict, Charlie Dwyer had promised to throw Martel out into the streets if he so much as thought of not testifying at the retrial. Junior Ganero's murder had done nothing to satisfy Dwyer's passion for what he considered justice. He wanted to go after Martel for Junior's murder, but the Justice Department's man guarding Martel reported that Martel was in a motel room in Jersey City at the time of the shooting. Dwyer still wasn't convinced. The district attorney didn't care if Martel had shot Junior Ganero. "If he did, I just wish he had killed the old man too," were his last words on the subject.

"You never should have gone back to stealing priceless paintings," Lisa Cole preached. "You broke your part of the bargain." She turned to smile at Rangel. "That was part of his agreement with the government, wasn't it? No more thefts?"

Mark swallowed hard and squeezed his eyes shut. When he opened them, he took a closer look at Lisa Cole. She was in her late twenties, maybe early thirties, with smooth skin and broadly arched eyebrows over wide-set brown eyes. Her long, dark hair fell around her face and she had a habit of hurling it back with a shake of her head. A slight accent. Texas? His eyes drifted down to her leather purse, which was lying on the table in front of her, the gold Gucci buckle undone, pointing directly at him. Mark stood up abruptly, rocking the table.

"I wouldn't leave if I were you," Cole advised him. "I haven't gone to the police. Yet."

Mark leaned over the table so that his face was inches from hers. "Come to my place tonight. Six o'clock. Alone. And bring your files on the stolen paintings. And a swimsuit."

"No way. If you think I'm going to—"

Mark stalked off, bumping into the waiter, who was delivering Bill Rangel's cheeseburger.

Rangel reached for the ketchup bottle. "Charlie Dwyer never should have given you Martel's new identity, Miss Cole. It's not right."

"Not right?" Her eyes narrowed, making crow's-feet. "Boston Insurance having to fork over three million dollars because he stole a painting is what's not right."

Rangel pounded on the bottom of the ketchup bottle with his palm. "Are you sure he's the thief?"

"Oh, I'm sure. He as much as left his fingerprints at the scene."

"As much as?" Rangel queried, stabbing a knife blade into the upturned bottle to help get the ketchup flowing.

"Verre, or Martel, whatever he wants to call himself, has a definite M.O. When an old master insured by Boston was stolen here in San Francisco, Charlie Dwyer became suspicious. He remembered the way Martel operated. And we know of at least two other thefts in San Francisco that Martel may be responsible for. He must have thought that moving from New York to California would make him invisible." She frowned as she watched Rangel spread ketchup over the enormous burger and platter of French fries. "Are you going to eat all of that?"

"Probably not. But I'm a bachelor once again. So I take home what I can't eat."

Cole sipped from her wineglass. "This is very, very good. Let's go halves. I'll share the wine, if you'll split the burger."

Rangel took a bite out of the burger and chewed slowly before replying. "Does Boston Insurance have you on an expense account?"

Cole did that shaking-of-her-head gesture again. Rangel liked the way the restaurant lights bounced off her hair.

"Actually, I'm an independent. Boston is just one of the companies I work for."

"Ummm. These paintings you think Mark heisted. How much were they insured for?"

"All of them? About nine million dollars."

"And you get what? Ten percent if you make the recovery?"

She lifted a French fry from Rangel's plate. "Five."

"And Boston is paying you some wages, right? And you have an expense account, right?"

"Right," she conceded, gobbling down the fry and reaching for another.

Rangel nudged the plate over toward her. "Then Boston Insurance can pay for lunch. I like screwing Charlie Dwyer out of something, even if it's only a burger. Are you going to see Martel tonight?"

She wrapped a napkin around her half of the burger. "Yep."

"He looked scared. Desperate. They say he killed Junior Ganero. It takes a guy with a lot of nerve to kill a Mafia don's one and only son."

"Martel has a damn good reason to be scared," Cole contended. "Victor Ganero still has a half-million-dollar contract out on him."

Rangel picked up the wine bottle. "What's with the

fancy wine? It shook him up when you sent it over to the table."

Lisa Cole reached into her purse and turned off the tape recorder. There was no sense wasting the batteries on Bill Rangel. "Martel's a man of expensive tastes. He might as well enjoy himself now, because if he doesn't turn over those paintings to me, I'm going to see to it that he ends up in jail."

Chapter 6

The limousine's air conditioning welcomed Harry Vlad with a chilled kiss. He voiced a loud "Howdy" to the back of Sineo's grease-slicked head in the driver's seat. Harry was relieved to be out of Victor Ganero's house. And glad to be rid of the stolen painting. He was even happier about the seventy-five g's that were nestled between his feet in a brown paper bag. He leaned back into the plush leather seats, wondering why Sineo didn't get the Cadillac moving.

Tony Zarela had told him that Victor Ganero had instructed him to have the limousine return Harry to his hotel.

His stomach contracted and he began sweating. A ride? A one-way ride? No, he assured himself. Old man Ganero had nearly wept when Harry unwrapped the package and removed the Botticelli. And Ganero wanted more. All that Vlad could deliver. Harry had a list of paintings and statues provided by George Alvord, so there was no reason—

The door to the limousine jerked open, and a dark-haired, well-dressed man with a hawkish nose climbed in. He leaned forward, rapped his knuckles on the smoked-glass partition separating the rear of the stretch Cadillac from the driver, and the car purred away from the curb.

"You know who I am?" the man asked.

"Sure, sure. Johnny Musso." Harry extended his hand. "Nice to meet you."

Musso kept both hands on his knees. "What'd you call me?"

"Ah . . . sorry, sir. Mr. Musso. I didn't mean to—"

"Where's Mark Martel?"

Harry shifted uncomfortably, his haunches making light squeaking noises on the leather. "Gee, I wish I knew, Mr. Musso. I was telling Mr. Ganero—"

Musso's hand shot out and slapped Harry hard across the face. "Where's Martel?"

Harry felt his rectum tighten, his bladder throb. He had a sudden, terrible thought that he would wet his pants and Musso would kill him for soiling the upholstery. "Honest, Mr. Musso. If I knew, I'd have told Ganero, and I—"

Again Musso's hand flashed out; this time his fist was closed. Harry tasted the blood that streamed from his nose to his mouth.

"That's *Mr.* Ganero, to you, punk."

"Yes, sir. I didn't mean any—"

"Martel! Where the hell is he?"

"I'm not sure. Some guy told me that Martel had moved out to the West Coast. L.A., or San Francisco, and I—"

"What guy?"

Harry reached for his pants pocket. "Can I?" he asked sheepishly. "A handkerchief."

Musso gave him a curt nod. "What guy?"

Blotting his nose gave Harry time to consider what to say. Sticking to the phony story he'd told George Alvord and Big Vic Ganero seemed the safest bet. "Nick Sharkey. A jewelry guy. Stole nothing but jewelry. Sharkey knew Martel. I think they used the same fence a couple of times. He told me he heard Martel was working the left coast."

"When did you talk to Sharkey? Where?"

"Last year. At Shawngunk."

"Prison? You were in prison last year?"

"Yes, sir."

The news seemed to please Musso. He slouched into a comfortable position. "What were you in for?"

"A heist. Not my fault. I was in the Frick Museum, on East Seventieth. I had my piece, a small Vermeer portrait that had been stored in the basement archives. All I was doing was waiting for the morning, so I could walk out with the regular customers, when bam, there's shooting and whistles. Three dummies had busted in, tripped the silent alarm, and tried to shoot it out with the guards. One guard caught a slug. I got swept up with the dummies. Not my fault." He blotted his nose with the blood-soaked handkerchief. "Bad luck, that's all. Real bad luck."

"It happens," Musso said indifferently. "Tell me about Sharkey."

"He was a pro. But a hype, you know? He got sloppy. Even in the slam, he got sloppy. Dealing with the Ho boys for drugs. A mean bunch. He ended up getting knifed. But before that, he told me about Martel. He figured me and Martel were in the same line of work, so, like, maybe I'd be interested."

"Exactly what did he tell you, Harry?"

Vlad heaved a sigh of relief. Musso calling him by his first name was a good sign. And he seemed to have bought the story about Sharkey. So far. "He said he heard that Martel had gone into the witness protection program and—"

"That's old news. You don't tell me something better than that, you're gone, Vlad."

Harry's left nostril spouted again. He jammed the handkerchief against his nose, wincing at the contact. The first-name basis hadn't lasted long. "Sharkey said he'd heard that Martel was in L.A. 'Gone Hollywood.' I pumped him about it and all he told me was that some guy he sold a job of diamonds to told him that Martel was in Hollywood and had pulled a couple of jobs in San Francisco." Harry gently removed the handkerchief and held his hands out in a mollifying gesture. "Honest, Mr. Musso, that's all I know." The dark scowl on Musso's face brought the pain back to his groin. "That was a year ago," Harry said quickly. "I got to thinking about Martel when I was getting close to serving my time, but Sharkey had bought it by then. He didn't come through on a drug buy, so the Ho boys got him. In the shower. Cut him to ribbons. You could see the bloodstains in the tile grout for weeks."

The limousine was cruising along slowly. Harry looked over Musso's head at a range of sand, tumbleweed, and cactus. He didn't remember passing that stretch of land when he'd cabbed to Ganero's house from the Phoenician Hotel.

"How did someone like you make contact with Vic Ganero?" Musso demanded harshly.

"Alvord. George Alvord. He's a dealer in—"

"I know Alvord." Musso leaned forward, pushed a button, and the partition glass hissed down. "The airport," he ordered, then pushed the button again and the window slid home.

The Cadillac slowed down, then made a sharp U-turn. Harry almost wet his pants again, this time in relief.

"The painting you just brought to the house. Where'd you scratch it?"

"San Francisco."

Musso steepled his fingers and glared at Vlad. Harry crossed his legs, praying that his bladder would hold.

"You're a New York guy, Harry. So is Alvord. What are you doing out here?"

Make or break time, Vlad figured. Either he believes me now, or the car turns back toward the desert. "Alvord told me that Mr. Ganero was still in the market. For certain paintings. Old masterpieces—Italian, religious stuff. A lot of them are out on the West Coast. Alvord has a part interest in a gallery in San Francisco, so he knows what's out here. What's available. He has a list of items that Mr. Ganero is interested in." He squeezed his legs together. "Alvord told me something else, Mr. Musso. That the contract on Martel was still out. A half a mil for Martel. I figured I maybe could kill two birds with one stone, you know? Score some paintings, and flush Martel out. I'm using his style. If he is out here, and the feds think he's back in business, they may turn him out. Or Martel may get worried. He'd know someone was using his style. And, I'm not blowing smoke, but there're not many guys could handle that. Me, maybe one or two others. He could come looking for me. If he did, I was going to turn him over to Mr. Ganero."

"And pick up the half million, huh?"

"Yes, sir," Harry acknowledged solemnly. "Nothing wrong with that, is there?"

A slight grin ticked up the corners of Musso's mouth. "No. Nothing wrong with wanting money, Harry." He reached out his foot and tapped the paper bag with a highly polished loafer. "How much?"

"Seventy-five grand."

Musso's hands flexed into fists. "For one piece of work? You're in the right business, Harry. I know guys who have killed two, three, maybe four guys a year and didn't rake in that much. How much does Alvord get?"

"A third."

"Take your money, Harry. I'll deliver Alvord's share to him." He reached over and patted Harry's knee. "That sound good to you?"

Vlad opened his mouth, then quickly clamped it shut. "Yes, sir," he mumbled, reaching for the paper bag.

"Where were you planning to go now, Harry?"

"San Francisco. There's a statue there that—"

"Give me your address and phone number." Musso tore off a piece of the paper bag and dropped it on Vlad's lap. "I'm going to talk to Alvord, and your story had better check out." Musso rapped on the partition window. "Sineo, pull over. I think Harry has to take a piss."

*   *   *

Inspector Dan Heller two-finger-typed the name "Mark Verre" into his desktop computer. He didn't think there could be too many Mark Verres in California. He was right. The green-on-black screen gurgled for a few moments, then the information popped up. One Mark Verre, in Los Angeles.

Heller clicked the right buttons, and in a few moments the printer kicked in and he had Verre's driver's license printout. Mark Verre. NMI. No middle initial. Thirty-nine years of age, born on March 11, six foot one, 185 pounds, brown hair, blue eyes. His current address was listed as a post office box in Los Angeles. The license had been issued three years ago. No accidents. No violations.

Heller ran Verre for vehicles and found nothing registered under his name. He switched to the CI&I database and again the results were negative—no arrests in California. He tried NCIC. No national criminal record.

Heller brought his hands together at chest level, fingertips to fingertips. His eyes drifted from the computer screen to his wedding ring. He'd never taken it off, not even for a day. He and Arlene had been divorced for six years. Heller knew damn well that he had made a dumb mistake. Just one mistake, a brief fling with an airline attendant whose husband had threatened to kill her. Nothing he did could convince Arlene to give him another chance. Nothing. She was so hardheaded. Heller felt he had an ace in the hole, though—his daughter, Carrie. Carrie was on his side. She wanted them to get back together. At least she had been on his side until Verre came on the scene. Now every time he was able to spend a weekend with Carrie, all she seemed to talk about was Verre. How good-looking he was. How smart he was. What a great painter he was. How much dear old Mom liked him.

Heller absentmindedly twisted his wedding ring, as if it were too tight, then exited the database. He reached for an information request form and wrote in Verre's name, date of birth, and postal address, then thumbed through the open-case folders on his desk. He had to have a file to post the database information request to. He selected a case involving a homicide victim, a visiting St. Louis businessman who had been stabbed to death while asleep in his motel room. Heller was certain that the victim had been killed by a hunky drifter whom he had met in a Castro Street saloon, but being certain and proving the case were two different matters.

He scribbled the case number on the form and walked over to the Information Center in room 400. As he strolled the marble-floored hallway, he thought of a television show he'd watched last week. A cop show, filmed right in San Francisco. The star, all five feet three inches of him, had used a computer to pull up a criminal record, a credit report, confidential Social Security data showing who the subject was working for, how much in earnings he had reported to the government, and, wonder of all wonders, unlisted telephone numbers, something that Heller had to subpoena to get hold of.

He pushed his way past the swinging door leading to the captain of inspectors' office. "Hi, Julie," he called to the division clerk. She was nudging forty, with fine-spun chestnut-colored hair, hazy green eyes, and a wide, pouty mouth. She usually dressed in form-fitting outfits that drew unneeded attention to her hourglass figure. Today she had on dark-brown slacks and a creamy-yellow cashmere sweater. Her looks, coupled with a soft, juicy French accent, had everyone, from the chief on down, cautiously flirting with her. She was happily married to a fireman, but good-naturedly went along with the flirting.

"Hello, Inspector. What can I do for you today?"

"Do you have time to run a TRW check on this guy for me?"

"Certainly," she said pleasantly. She used the count-

ertop computer to access a civilian database that the
department contracted with, and entered the information on Verre. The searches cost a minimum of seven
dollars each, and therefore were monitored closely by
the department bean counters.

"Here you are," Julie said, when she pulled the
credit check out of the printer.

The report showed the same data as listed on Verre's
DMV. The only additional information was a Social
Security number. The first three digits of the number
indicated the state of origin. Verre's were 556. California numbers. Carrie had told him that Verre had come
to California a few years ago, from somewhere in Canada. He had lived in Paris previous to that.

"Can you do anything more with the Social Security
number, Julie?"

She made an exaggerated Gallic gesture with her
shoulders, doing wonderful things to the yellow sweater.

Then she accessed a database that traced the number
through the three major credit reporting agencies for
current and past addresses. The same address showed
up, no listing for an employer. The date of origin for
Verre's Social Security number caught Heller's interest. March, three years ago. Verre had picked up his
driver's license and Social Security number at the
same time. To Heller there seemed to be only two
possibilities: Verre was using phony ID or he was in
some governmental witness protection program.

"Did you find something useful?" Julie inquired.

"Yeah," Heller confirmed. "I think we hit on
something."

She leaned across the counter and tilted her head to
get a look at the printout. "It's an unusual name, no?"

"What's unusual about it?" Heller wanted to know.

"Verre." She shifted some hair from her shoulders
to her back. "It's French. For 'glass'."

Heller hurried back to his desk. Even if Verre had
moved to the United States from Canada, there should
have been some old Canadian addresses on his credit

report. And Uncle Sam didn't just routinely dish out Social Security numbers to businessmen from across the border.

He rummaged through his desk for the stack of business cards he'd accumulated over the years. An inspector from the Royal Canadian Mounted Police had come to San Francisco last November to pick up a prisoner. Heller had helped the Mountie with the paperwork, then showed him the town. He found the Mountie's card and grinned as he reached for the phone. It was payback time.

Chapter 7

A covey of quail trooped leisurely across the road, causing Lisa Cole to slam on her brakes. Her right palm hovered over the horn, then she latched back onto the steering wheel, her fingers drumming an impatient beat as she stared in exasperation at the orderly, single-file march the family of birds seemed to be enjoying.

Which was nothing like her own life at the moment. Hectic and chaotic would be a good description of that. Charlie Dwyer picking her to go after Mark Martel-Verre had been a stroke of luck, which she planned to parlay into a bonanza.

The fact that Dwyer had once been married to her aunt had gotten her foot in the door. Now she had to kick that door wide open. If she could connive, threaten, bully, trick—whatever—Mark Verre into turning over the stolen Italian Renaissance painting by Botticelli, she'd be in for a big payoff. The finder's fee would allow her to buy a BMW and move to the Nob Hill condo she was mad for. She would rent an office, a real office, and stop working out of her small apartment on Potrero Hill. Hire a staff, and let someone else handle the legwork, the tedious day-to-day drudgery that consumed so much of her time.

Charlie Dwyer had given her a deadline. One month. Get Martel, and the paintings, in a month, or she was off the case, and one of Boston Insurance's in-house investigators would take over. She had already burned up one week of that time.

The quail disappeared into a thicket of scrubby fawn-colored brush. Lisa tooted her horn, in frustration, vowing to feast on a meal of stuffed quail soon, slipped the transmission into first gear, and took off, quickly bringing the six-year-old Toyota up to speed.

She spotted the row of yellow rosebushes that ribboned the front of the Hatton Winery.

The stakeout van she'd hired was gone. The subrosa cameraman had phoned her from the vehicle, his voice close to panic: "Verre's back, and that huge dog of his is chewing on my tires. He's going to puncture them. I'm getting out of here!"

The image of Verre's monster dog making a meal of the van's tires amused Lisa. She slowed down and turned onto the narrow road leading to Verre's place, listening to the *ping* of small pebbles under the car's fender as she steered toward the house.

It looked different in the early-evening light. It blended in beautifully with the surroundings, two staggered stories of cinnamon-stained wood, matching the color of the soil between the rows of grapevines. Two days ago, in the morning darkness, she'd pulled a swift hit-and-run, pushing the motorcycle the final hundred yards to Martel's house, leaving the cognac bottle, then coasting away. She'd kicked the bike's motor on when she heard Martel's dog barking. If the animal had an appetite for van tires, what would he have done to the motorcycle?

She rolled to a stop alongside the feathery branches of a weeping willow. She was about to beep the horn to announce her arrival when she spotted the big dog bounding toward the car.

"Gauguin, stay!" Mark Verre called, and the animal skidded to a stop.

"He's not going to eat my tires, is he?" Lisa yelled when she saw Mark stride into sight. He was wearing the same shirt he'd worn to the restaurant, a frayed blue oxford-cloth Brooks Brothers with a button-down collar, although the buttons were missing. It was now open to the waist, giving her a peek at a muscular chest and a washboard stomach. A pair of thigh-length dark-blue swim trunks had replaced the khakis she'd seen him in earlier. He had the confident walk of an athlete. A sexy athlete, Lisa conceded. His thick, dark hair was just barely tipped with gray at the temples. His face narrow, sharply lined, dark from the sun, darker than his chest or legs. A workman's suntan, not a pool lizard's. Gas-jet-blue eyes—or eye, she corrected herself. The glass one was a damn good match. She wondered if those creases in his cheeks turned into dimples when he smiled. If he ever smiled. His face was set in a scowl now.

"What happened to your motorcycle?" Mark said in a mocking tone.

Lisa unlocked the door, picked up her purse and briefcase, and climbed slowly out of the car, her eyes still on the dog. "Gauguin. I like the name."

Mark walked over, opened the car's door, and surveyed the interior. "Leave the purse, and the briefcase," he ordered.

Lisa slid the purse off her shoulder. "I need my cigarettes and lighter," she protested.

"Just the smokes," Mark said.

Lisa glared at him. "What are you so nervous about?"

"Are you telling me that you don't have a recording device hidden somewhere?"

"Would I do that?" she asked, tossing her purse and briefcase back into the car.

"Swimsuit?" Mark queried.

"I'm not here for a good time, Mr. . . . Mark. I guess I should call you Mark from now on, so we don't have to go through this Martel-Verre routine. I'm here for the paintings."

Mark shook his head angrily and turned on his heel. Lisa stood motionless for a moment, then followed him down a brick path bordered by more flowering yellow rosebushes, some still labeled with metal tags, then under a trellised archway thick with multicolored flowering morning glory.

Railroad-tie steps led to a concrete patio. A dark-blue tiled pool ran from a sliding glass door at the back of the house to a small rock-formation waterfall, where water heady with foam cascaded down, feeding the pool. A white plastic table shaded by a green canvas umbrella held a bottle of white wine in a sweating silver bucket and a tray of hors d'oeuvres: cut-up vegetables, crackers, and slices of cheese.

Mark pointed at the pool. "We talk in there or we don't talk, Miss Cole."

"God, you are paranoid." Lisa stretched her arms out wide. She was wearing a tennis-style white skirt and a mustard-colored scoop-necked cotton shirt that revealed some cleavage. "Just where in the hell do you think I'd hide a recording device in this outfit?" she challenged.

"If there's one thing I'm an expert at, it's electronic transmitting equipment," Mark said coldly. "And I can think of several places where I could find one on you, if you'd allow me to look. It's your choice. There are some swimsuits in the house. We talk in the pool, or you can leave. Now."

Lisa tapped her foot angrily on the patio. "All right. Get the suits."

She helped herself to a glass of wine—Hatton Chardonnay. It was good. Damn good, she had to admit. She was chewing on a cracker larded with Camembert when Mark returned with several swimsuits in his hands.

"You can change inside."

"Can I, now? How nice." Lisa snatched the garments, kicked off her sandals, and walked smartly past Mark, through the sliding glass doors and into the house. She paused at the door to survey the kitchen—white walls, beige limestone floor, honey-colored cabinets. Gleaming copper pots and colanders hung from black iron hooks over the sink, and there was a chop-

ping block situated in the middle of the room. Braids
of garlic and clusters of bright-red peppers decorated
the walls. Verre had placed a row of kitchen chairs
across the arched doorway leading to the living area—
as if to say, this far and no farther.

Lisa sorted through the swimsuits. Two were much
too small. The one that would fit was a banana-yellow
one-piece Speedo wide-strap, high-neck model manu-
factured for swimming, not sunbathing. She undressed
with one eye on the patio, wondering if she had time
to poke around the house before Verre would come
looking for her.

She leaned over the row of chairs. A high-ceilinged
living room, all white, a minimalist approach. No
paintings on the walls. An off-white couch and matching chairs. Even the door's hardware was white.

Mark was in the pool, effortlessly gliding back and
forth. He made a sharp, professional underwater turn
before navigating in the opposite direction.

Lisa walked out to the pool, then dangled a foot in
the water before quickly pulling it back.

Mark swam over to her. "Come on in. Let's talk."

She took a deep breath, then jumped. The icy water
caused her to gasp.

"Move around," Mark suggested. "You'll warm up."

Lisa took the advice, swimming in an awkward,
head-out-of-the-water style that kept her eye makeup
from getting splashed. "Satisfied?" she challenged
when she was abreast of him. "If I had any bugs on
me, they'd be shorted out. So can we talk now?"

"Who else knows about me?" Mark demanded.
"How many others are working on—"

"Just Charlie Dwyer and me. No one else. Yet.
Now, about the paintings."

"I haven't stolen a painting, or anything else, in
years, Miss Cole. My last episode was a painful experi-
ence. My fiancée was raped and murdered, and I lost
an eye."

The pool water was up to Lisa's waist. She began

running in place to keep warm. "Yes, Charlie Dwyer told me all about you. People don't change. They go back to their old habits." She gestured toward the house with her chin. "A new house, a winery. You live awfully well for an ex-thief."

"You and Dwyer are wasting your time. I'm not your man."

"The robberies in San Francisco were carbon copies of the way you operate, Mark. You were sloppy. You left your calling card."

"What calling card?"

"The chip-bugs. What do you think? You left them behind in the alarm box."

Mark scooped up water with his hands and splashed it on his face. "When were these robberies?"

"The last one was nine days ago. You remember. The Livingstons gave a big party Friday night. That's another one of your trademarks, isn't it? Using a party as a way to access the property. You like to use disguises, too. What was it this last time? Did you come in with the catering crew? Or did you just slip in as a guest? The Livingstons made it very easy for you. There was no security guard." Lisa was tired of the icy water, tired of moving around trying to get warm. Tired of verbally boxing with him. "Cut the innocent act and return the painting and you can go back to being a gentleman vintner. Otherwise . . ."

"Otherwise what? You'll tell Victor Ganero where I am? Or would you let Charlie Dwyer have that honor? Ganero will carry out the contract. On me, and just for fun he'll probably go after my partner, Joan Hatton, and a woman I'm friendly with, and her fourteen-year-old daughter, whose swimsuit you happen to be wearing." Mark waded close to her. "You could get us all killed."

"I don't want that to happen. I just want the paintings."

"I'm not your man," Mark insisted. "But maybe I can find out who is. How long do you have?"

Lisa frowned and waded over to the pool steps. "What do you mean?" she asked, picking up a thick white towel.

Mark stared up at her. "I checked you out. You're an independent. You've been licensed for seven years. Boston Insurance called you in because you're local. You had to be desperate to try that dumb trick with the cognac bottle on my doorstep. You're probably running short of time. Pretty soon Boston will let their staff have a go at it, and the more people involved in this, the bigger target I become."

Lisa buried her head in a towel for a moment. "You seem to know an awful lot about insurance companies."

"How much time do you have?" Mark repeated impatiently.

She stalled by slowly wrapping the towel, sarong-style, around her hips. "Three weeks."

"Who's working with you?"

"My regular crew," she lied confidently. "We've had you under surveillance for three days."

"Does your crew know who I am?"

"Just that your name is Verre. They don't know anything about what happened in New York. Dwyer and I are the only ones who know your identity, and this address."

Mark was ready to accept that. Cole would want to keep the information to herself, so she would be the one who cashed in on the finder's fees for the stolen paintings. "How'd you find me?"

"Charlie had one of his old cronies in Justice pull your file. It had your new name and Social Security number."

Mark placed his palms on the side of the pool and hoisted himself out of the water. "That still doesn't tell me how you found this address."

Lisa tugged at the bottom of her swimsuit. "I'm a professional. I'm not going to—"

"Tell me, or this conversation is over, Miss Cole. I pack and run like hell and you'll never find me."

"All right. I wasted a couple of days staking out your Los Angeles post office box. Your credit card order for some books from Amazon.com turned the trick. They were delivered to a restaurant in Calistoga. We sat on the restaurant. La Cucina. Simple as that."

Mark bit down on his lower lip. He had been careless. Damn careless. And it pointed out just how sharp Lisa Cole was. All of his ID addresses were listed to a Los Angeles post office box. His mail was forwarded to a private mail drop in San Francisco, and he drove to the city once every week or so to pick it up. He'd ordered the books for Carrie's birthday. He poured two glasses of wine and handed her one. "I may need some more time, but I'll find the thief for you."

"All I want is the paintings."

"You want the finder's fees. All I want is to be left alone." He held the glass up in a toasting gesture. "Do we have a deal?"

Lisa clinked her glass against his. "It's a deal."

"Good. Now, give me all the information you have so far on what was stolen."

"No, no." Lisa protested. "I can't do that. Dwyer would have my license yanked."

Gauguin snuck up and brushed his whiskers against Lisa's towel. Startled, she jumped away, losing her balance. Mark caught her with one hand as she was about to tumble into the pool.

"Dwyer will never know. Besides, if I was the real thief, I would already know everything."

Lisa bulged her lower lip with her tongue as she considered the request. There might be something in the files that could help him. But there was nothing that could hurt her. "Okay. The information is in my briefcase."

"I'll get it. Help yourself to some more wine."

Chapter 8

Lisa Cole leaned back in the chaise lounge, sipped her wine, and watched as Mark Verre trawled through her file notes. She spotted a change in his body language. The stern look on his face had faded, replaced by—what? Concern? Uncertainty? Maybe even fear. His chin dropped toward his chest, his shoulders slumped. Could he be telling the truth? Or is he merely a good actor? A successful thief would have to be a good actor.

Mark carefully scrutinized the reports and the photographs of the missing paintings, then took the tiny clear silicone miniature transmitting devices that had been left behind at the burgled homes and bounced them in his right hand. They were identical to the type of transmitter he'd used a dozen or more times. Colorless, able to blend into any background, and self-contained, they would transmit anything within a twenty-foot radius for up to ten days. All he had to do was set up a receiver and recorder within range of the transmitter, listen to the tape for the sound of the security alarm being set, then decode the alarm button registers.

Once he had the alarm code, he would simply wait for the house to be vacated. He needed only a few minutes to jimmy the front door and punch in the code during the thirty-second grace period the security alarm service set up to discourage false alarms.

Martel had never gone into an occupied home and had never been involved in any type of violence during the thefts. He had racked his brain trying to figure out who could have known just how he'd operated. There was one man who knew. Noel Field, who had taught him everything. But Noel couldn't be the thief. He was too old now, and he and Mark had been friends. More than friends. Unless Noel had a new protégé. But neither Noel Field nor anyone else knew where he was living now. How did the thief know to pick San Francisco for his targets?

"The reports aren't very detailed," Mark complained when he was through examining them. He slipped the transmitting devices into their envelope, shuffled the documents together, tapping them on the table to straighten the pages, then slid them back into Lisa Cole's maroon calfskin briefcase. "You see the pattern, don't you?"

"Yes. You learn the alarm code. You always take just one painting, no matter what other valuables are there for the grabbing. Don't you ever get tempted to take more? I know the Livingstons had a houseful of major artworks, as well as some expensive jewelry. A nice job, except that you left the bug behind. That was careless of you. I guess that comes from being out of practice for a while."

Mark rubbed his chin angrily. "That's not the pattern I'm talking about. Caravaggio's *The Agony*, Andrea dei Veronese's *The Coronation of Mary*, and Sandro Botticelli's *Christ on the Cross*. All paintings by Renaissance masters. Veronese was Michelangelo's tutor. And all featuring either Christ or the Virgin Mary."

"And all worth millions," Lisa Cole added dryly.

Mark sliced the air with his hands. "To the insurance company. But not to this thief. The most important consideration when stealing an old master is to have someone to sell it to. Unless the thief has it sold ahead of time, it's useless to him. Not one of those paintings could be unloaded for anywhere near its real value. They're unique. Most Renaissance paintings of that rare quality are in museums, not in private hands. And obviously, this thief hasn't tried to sell them back to the insurance carrier, so—he has a collector. Someone with an obsession for Italian masterpieces, with strong religious content. Catholicism. Doesn't that give you a clue?"

Lisa pushed herself to her feet. The towel around her hips had come loose. "No one I know. I . . . wait a minute. Victor Ganero? Is that what you're trying to tell me?"

"Consider yourself told, Miss Cole. When I delivered the Correggio to that warehouse in New York, I had no idea who the actual buyer was. I found out the hard way that it was Victor Ganero. He has a raging zealot's passion for those paintings."

Lisa placed her empty wineglass on the table. "How convenient. You finger the one man in the world that no one would believe you'd have anything to do with." A sudden gust of wind swept through the area, rippling the pool's calm azure water. She folded her arms across her chest. "No. I don't buy it."

"What if I can prove I'm not your thief?"

"How do you plan to do that?"

"Ganero built a Mediterranean mansion in Carefree, Arizona. My bet is that the paintings you're looking for, and a lot more, are entombed there in his private museum."

"You seem very up to date on Victor Ganero."

"Under the circumstances, I'd be foolish not to be. When I first came west, I settled in Los Angeles. I spent a lot of time in Arizona learning all I could about him. And his mansion."

A coil of damp hair fell in front of Lisa's eyes. She tossed it back with a shake of her head. "What have you learned?"

"Victor Ganero seldom leaves his house. His main body guard is Tony 'Big Soup' Zarela. Did Charlie Dwyer fill you in on Zarela?"

"Just the basics."

"He's Ganero's enforcer. I'm sure he's the one who killed Denise, my fiancée, after he, Junior Ganero, and another wise guy, Johnny Musso, raped her. Junior Ganero thought it made more sense to murder people rather than to fork over the money."

"You've been to Ganero's house? What's the address?"

"Seven-forty-two Blackhawk Drive. It's situated on a bluff, right above a golf course. Heavily gated, and it has a first-class security system." Mark's good eye twitched at one corner. "Don't get any ideas, Miss Cole. You could never get near the place."

"But you could. Is that it?"

"*I* could. I know the flaw in the security system. If you're thinking about that half-million-dollar reward for delivering me to Ganero, forget about it. You wouldn't see a dime of the money. He'll kill whoever turns me in rather than pay them off."

"If you could get into Ganero's house, you wouldn't actually have to take anything. Just a few photos of the paintings would be enough—"

"Enough to get me killed," Mark pointed out.

"I don't want you or anyone else hurt," Lisa asserted. "All I want is those paintings."

"Then help me, damn it."

"How?"

"Work with me. I'll find your thief."

Lisa rolled her eyes at him questioningly. "You know who he is?"

"No. But I know who he's working for. A New York art dealer by the name of George Alvord. He supplied Ganero in the past. My hunch is that he and the thief have done everything possible to implicate me. The thief wants me to come after him. Leaving those transmitting devices behind wasn't careless. It was done on purpose. To bait me."

Lisa made clicking noises with her teeth. "Didn't Hitchcock or someone make a movie like this a long time ago? Using one thief to catch another one?"

"To catch the real thief, I'll need your help."

"What kind of help?"

"I need to see the full reports. When I find out who is impersonating me, I'll want you to run some checks on him."

"Okay, Mark. If you turn up the paintings, the finder's fees are mine and you can go back to being a gentleman vintner."

"I'll find the thief. I can't guarantee the paintings. They're probably in Ganero's mansion right now."

"If they are, we could—"

Gauguin let out a menacing growl. Mark's head jerked around at the sound of a beeping horn.

"Were you expecting someone?" Lisa Cole asked crossly.

"No. I'll see who it is."

Lisa reached down for a towel. "I'm not dressed for company," she complained, bundling the towel to her chest and scurrying off toward the house.

Mark signaled Gauguin to move and the big dog bounded off, past the pool and out to the parking area.

Dan Heller was sitting behind the wheel of a dusty gray Ford sedan, both hands visible on the steering wheel, a broad smile stitched across his face. He eased the window down halfway when he saw Mark Verre come into sight.

Gauguin was standing alongside the car door, his eyes fixed on Heller.

Mark snapped his fingers and the dog retreated half a dozen yards.

Heller rolled the car window down the rest of the way and leaned his head out. "I thought I better beep, to let you know I was here."

"Good idea," Mark agreed. "What can I do for you?"

"I was hoping I'd find Carrie here. She wasn't at the restaurant, and I remember her telling me that you were teaching her to paint and swim."

Mark approached the car, leaning his hands on the

roof and bending over to face Heller. "No, she's not here."

Heller looked over at the dusty black Toyota parked alongside a white Jeep Cherokee. "You've got company."

"Yes. One of our sales reps." Mark straightened up and glanced at his watch. "Are you headed back to San Francisco?"

"No. I've some time off; I think I'll hang around here for a few days. I don't see enough of Carrie." Heller pushed his arm out of the window and adjusted the side mirror, then added, "Or Arlene. Carrie tells me you're from Canada."

"That's right."

"And before that, Paris. You don't have much of an accent."

The crunching sound of footsteps on the gravel caused both men to look over at Lisa Cole. She slung her briefcase strap over her shoulder and gave Mark a subdued wave. "I'll be in touch."

"Good-looking lady," Heller observed as Cole's beat-up Toyota rolled past them. He switched on the engine and smiled at Mark. "Well, nice talking to you. Maybe we can get together for a drink. Or lunch." The car edged forward, then came to an abrupt stop and Heller stuck his head out through the open window again. "Were you in the wine business in Canada, Mark?"

"No. Sales."

Heller's face registered confusion. "Sales, huh? Anything in particular?"

"Commodities." Mark signaled to Gauguin and the dog quickly heeled at his side. "Sorry to be inhospitable, but I've some work to do."

"Yeah, I bet you do," Heller said with a one-sided grimace. He backed the car around in a wide turn and drove off.

Mark watched a plume of road dust billow up into the air, momentarily obscuring the car from sight. He bent down and scratched Gauguin behind his ears, then hurried back to the house and began packing, selecting clothes he hadn't worn in some time: a tailored sport coat, slacks, dress shirts, ties. City clothes, what were once his working clothes. He'd grown used to the casual denim and khaki wardrobe of a vintner. Now he had to dress and think like a thief again.

He wondered where Dan Heller had gone. Would he follow Lisa Cole back to the city? Probably not. All he had to do was radio in the Toyota's license number to find out who she was and where she lived. He would soon find out that she was a private investigator, not a winery sales rep.

All those questions. Heller had obviously already done some checking on him and come up empty-handed. Good cops are never satisfied with empty hands, and Mark had no doubt that Dan Heller was a good cop.

He added his shaving gear to his luggage, along with a false beard he'd used as a disguise when he'd taken trips out of the area, then stood motionless for a few seconds, debating whether or not to take a weapon. He had guns hidden all over the house: one in the bedroom nightstand, one in the kitchen stashed behind a container of flour, another in the living room under the couch, still another in his studio, nestled among the half-empty tubes of paint, and one Colt snub-nosed revolver in the Jeep, lodged under the dash-board. Revolvers, semiautomatics, all purchased from private parties, at county fairs and gun shows before the loophole was closed, and none of them were registered.

He selected a two-shot derringer that the manufacturer claimed could be hidden inside an empty pack of cigarettes. Mark had never had to fire one of his weapons, and he seldom touched them except for an occasional cleaning—until two days ago, when Lisa Cole left the cognac bottle at his doorstep.

He took five thousand dollars in cash from the bedroom safe, checked to make sure he had his wallet, keys, and money clip, slipped the derringer into his coat pocket, then reached for his suitcase.

Gauguin's head was resting on the case, his sad eyes following Mark's every move.

"I'm going to miss you, too, boy," he assured the dog. "But look on the bright side. You get to stay with Arlene and go off your diet."

He made a tour of the house, set the alarm, and ushered Gauguin to the Jeep. The temperature had simmered down to a comfortable level. Blue jays were darting through the scrub, jabbering about their evening meal. A small squadron of chicken vultures circled slowly over a stand of misshapen oak trees. He wondered what had caught their attention. Some dead or dying animal: a squirrel, rabbit, raccoon, or perhaps a deer. Hang in there, he silently advised the vultures' target. I did. He took a long final look at the house and pool, then the neat rows of vines drooping under the weight of ripening grapes, wondering if he would be back.

He had enough money stashed away in San Francisco to make a run for it. Move to another area, start all over again. But now he had too much to lose. He had to see this through. Find the thief and see to it that Lisa Cole or Charlie Dwyer put him behind bars.

Cole said that Dwyer had given her three weeks to recover the paintings. Could he trust Dwyer? Could he trust Cole? Could he trust anyone? He opened the Jeep's door for Gauguin. He'd have to trust himself. There was no one else.

Chapter 9

Tony "Big Soup" Zarela pressed the bell at the side of the massive hand-carved door leading to Victor Ganero's private chapel. He fiddled with a large iron key. The lock clicked and the door swung open.

The blazing evening sunset radiated through ancient stained-glass windows, turning the chapel's stone walls and floor into a kaleidoscope of color.

The windows, depicting the Stations of the Cross, had come from a bombed-out church in Rome, as had the silver-trimmed altar. The two mahogany pews were the sole survivors of a fire in a monastery clinging precariously to a mountaintop in Aosta, near the Swiss border. The life-size figure of Christ on the cross had been hand-carved in the eleventh century and had once hung in a Venice cathedral.

All of these items had been purchased, legally and anonymously, by Victor Ganero. Everything else in the room had been stolen. The chiseled stone walls held a collection of Old World religious paintings, carefully hung in gilded hardwood frames that Ganero had made by a Milano master craftsman.

The only nonreligious painting was one of Victor Ganero, Jr., showing him full-faced, with a sad smile, his eyes wet with tears. Zarela had made sure that the artist portrayed Junior as a much more handsome figure than he was in life.

Victor Ganero was dressed all in black, the only splash of color coming from a thick gold cross dangling on a chain around his neck. The Mafia don's silk suit had once fit his body like a glove, but now the coat drooped on his shoulders and billowed out at his waist. The alligator belt girdling his waist bunched up his pants, which draped over the heels of his shoes and dragged along the floor.

Zarela placed the tray gently on the cloth-covered altar and poured a glass of wine from a cut-glass decanter into a gem-encrusted gold-and-silver chalice that reportedly had once belonged to Pope Leo XII.

Ganero sipped sparingly at the wine, patted his lips with a snow-white handkerchief, then smiled at Zarela.

"What do you think, Soup?" he asked, nodding at the painting lying on the altar, the painting that Harry Vlad had delivered earlier.

"Nice, Boss," Tony said and, as if to give emphasis, nodded his head slowly up and down. "Really nice."

Victor Ganero's breath escaped in a long sigh. " 'Nice,' the man says. He looks at genius, at an artist whose hand was actually touched by God, and he says, 'Really nice.' "

Zarela lowered his brow and kneaded his forehead. "Hey, Boss, I think it's great. Really great, you know what I—"

Ganero flicked his index finger across his lips to signal Zarela to silence. He gazed at the painting for a long time before turning his attention back to Tony Zarela.

"What did Johnny talk to you about in the kitchen?"

"The usual stuff," Zarela said, then cleared his throat with a cough into his large fist. The don looked old, sick, feeble, but his brain was as sharp as ever. Zarela gave an almost verbatim report on his discussion with Musso, leaving out only the part about his dissatisfaction with living in Arizona and smuggling whores into the house. *"La fregna che te ceca!"* the boss had warned him. Pussy will blind you.

Ganero took another dainty sip of the wine. "Johnny worries too much about the Russians and those *minchione* Jamaicans. He was interested in Harry Vlad?"

"Kinda. He said he'd give Vlad a ride back to his hotel." Tony shrugged his big shoulders. "I figured it was okay." He paused, waiting for Ganero to respond, becoming nervous as the time stretched out. "It was okay, wasn't it, Boss? I mean I figured—"

"You did the right thing, Soup." Ganero reached out and patted Zarela lightly on his hand. "I don't want Johnny, or anyone else, interfering with the business arrangement I have with Harry Vlad. *Capisce?*"

"I understand, Boss. I think Johnny was just curious, you know? Do you think Vlad is gonna help us find Martel?"

"Yes, I believe he will." Ganero gazed back down at the painting. "I will take care of you, Tony. Remember that. From the grave I will take care of you." His eyes suddenly darted up, boring into Zarela's. The milky fatigue was gone from Ganero's eyes. They were bright, dark, flinty, dangerous. Hunter's eyes. Killer's eyes. "But if you don't follow my plan, I'll come back from the grave for you, Tony. You believe that, don't you?"

"Absolutely, Boss. You know you got no problem with me. Hey, how about dinner? I made cannelloni, and I've got some melon with prosciutto, and—"

Ganero cut him off with a wave of his hand. "Soup. A cup of soup. Bring it here."

Big Soup nodded his agreement and backed out of the chapel as Victor Ganero genuflected in front of the altar and made the sign of the cross.

Zarela held his breath until he was safely out of the room. He hurried to the kitchen, dug a bottle of vodka out of the freezer, poured himself a stiff drink, and gulped it down.

What the hell was he going to do? The don was getting stranger and stranger every day. He hardly ate, drank only a single glass of wine a day, and never touched a woman. Tony poured himself another measure of the vodka, sat down at the kitchen table, and sipped reflectively.

Zarela had overheard Johnny Musso and Sineo talking in the kitchen. Musso said that Ganero was becoming a *rincoglionire*—old and losing his touch. The boss was dying. No doubt about that. But he was a tough old *bastardo*. He might last a couple of years, maybe more.

Big Soup didn't know if he could handle that much more time in Carefree, Arizona. He wanted to get back to New York in the worst way. He rolled the icy glass across his forehead. He'd just have to stick it out, and then do exactly what the boss wanted, and hope that the next don was someone like Johnny Musso. Johnny was trying to talk sense to Don Ganero, explaining that Soup was too valuable to just sit around in the desert as a cook and chauffeur. But Tony knew that Don Ganero was never going to let him go back home.

According to state records, Victor Ganero, Jr., was still buried in a Brooklyn cemetery. The boss had ordered Zarela to dig the coffin up and bring it to Arizona. It was one of the worst jobs Tony had ever pulled. A cemetery in the middle of the night. It was cold, raining. An owl flew out of a nearby tree and almost gave him a heart attack. He used two *nullitas,* nobodies just off the boat from Sicily, to dig up Junior's coffin and load it onto a truck. When the two men went back to fill in the hole, Tony shot them both, dumped them in Junior's grave, and replaced the earth.

Zarela was the only one to know about "the plan." He had taken a solemn oath, promising to tell no one that Victor Ganero, upon his death, was to be buried in the crypt under the chapel, right alongside his son.

It was a damn big crypt. It had to be, because the paintings, each and every one that was now hanging in the chapel, were going into the ground with the boss.

"Do this for me, Tony," Ganero had demanded,

"or I will have you killed, mutilated, your body scattered across your mother's grave. Swear! Swear you will do what I order!"

Tony Zarela had knelt before Ganero, like an altar boy bowing before a cardinal. "I will, Don Ganero. I swear to you, I will do it."

"God and I, and you, Tony, are the only ones who can share in this pleasure."

Zarela's share of the pleasure consisted of sweeping and dusting the chapel, since no one else was allowed entrance.

Big Soup didn't believe in God. He did not see how a man in his profession could believe in God, or any of that religious mumbo jumbo. He had never bothered keeping track of the number of men he'd killed on orders from Victor Ganero, but if pressed for an accounting, he would have estimated thirty or forty. The number would have to be doubled if it included those who had been beaten and maimed, left alive, their battered faces and bodies serving as a gruesome warning to anyone who might cross Don Ganero. So, no, Big Soup didn't believe in God. But he did believe in the devil, and he believed that if he didn't follow the boss's plan, Ganero would somehow get him.

Inspector Dan Heller felt as if he'd earned himself the right to a good meal—and what better place to enjoy it than his ex-wife's restaurant.

The night was warm but not humid. A slight breeze brought the scents of trees and rich earth, and the fragrance of bare skin coated with suntan lotion. Country smells, not city smells. Heller liked it. He wondered if he could handle country life on a regular basis.

There was a crowd on the street in front of La Cucina, a fifty-fifty mix of casually dressed men and women, some holding cocktail glasses, determinedly inhaling on cigarettes, scrutinizing each newcomer as if they were afraid someone might slap the smokes out of their hands.

Heller spotted Carrie at the back of the restaurant, holding down the reservation podium, her head bent in concentration. He smiled at the sight of his daughter. Carrie was beautiful. She had her mother's looks, and it appeared that she'd inherited his height. It broke his heart to think that boys were already after her. She needed someone around to protect her. Someone a lot bigger and tougher than her mother. Someone exactly like me, he thought.

The crowd at the bar was three-deep, and Heller mumbled a series of "Excuse me," "Pardon me" apologies as he threaded his way through it.

He tapped a forefinger on the podium. "Hey, who do I have to know to get a meal in here?"

Carrie looked up, her face breaking into a wide smile when she saw it was her father.

"Daddy! I thought you went back to San Francisco."

"I have some vacation time on the books, so I decided to take a couple of days off. I'm at the Carlin Country Cottages just down the block."

Her cheeks dimpled. "Wonderful. Do you really want to eat?"

Heller rubbed his stomach. "I'm starved, Kitten." He surveyed the crowd. "Though if it's going to be a problem, I can—"

Carrie reached out for her father's hand. "No problem at all. Come on back to the family table."

Heller followed his daughter out to the patio area, past an open window facing into the kitchen. He looked around for Arlene, but she was nowhere in sight.

Carrie led him to a large wooden table screened from the rest of the dining area by a lattice partition entwined with flowering jasmine. She was wearing snug-fitting blue jeans and a chile-red sleeveless silk blouse tied high enough at the waist to reveal her belly button. He couldn't help but notice the men's heads swivel around as Carrie passed, and he made a mental note to discuss the way she dressed with her mother. The kid was too young to flaunt herself like that.

Carrie promised to return with a menu and a bottle of wine "right away."

Heller settled into a rattan chair, leaned back, and enjoyed the view. The sky was ink-black, frosted with stars. Arlene had placed small star-shaped electrical lights in the trees shielding the patio, and they blended in nicely with the real thing.

All in all, it had been a decent day. Going to Verre's house had turned out to be a damned good decision. He'd run a DMV check on the woman driving the old Toyota. Verre had described her as a winery sales rep. The car was registered to Lisa Cole, with an address on Carolina Street in the Potrero district of San Francisco. Not the best of locations.

Cole had no criminal record, but she had applied for a private investigator's license. Telephone information listed her as a PI. So why had Verre said that she was his sales rep? Why did he need a PI? Or was she there for another reason? Maybe someone else was digging into Verre's background.

He'd made contact with the Royal Canadian Mounted Police inspector, and the results of a check on Verre would be in by tomorrow.

California DMV files listed the white Jeep parked in Verre's lot as belonging to the Hatton Winery. If Verre had access to the Jeep, why had he borrowed Arlene's sports car this morning?

"Chardonnay okay, Pop?" Carrie asked, settling an opened bottle, a glass, and a menu on the table.

"Great. Did you tell your mother I was here?"

"I did," Carrie said cheerfully, filling his glass to the brim. "She seemed surprised."

"I hope she didn't throw any pots or pans." Heller reached for the menu. "I'm in the mood for fish. How about—" He stopped in mid-sentence at the sight of Mark Verre's big dog trotting up to Carrie. "Verre's here?"

Carrie took a sip of the wine, then said, "He's in the kitchen saying good-bye to Mom. He asked me to take care of Gauguin while he's gone."

Heller wrested the wineglass from her hand. "You're too young for that. Did Verre say where he was going? Or how long he'd be away?"

Carrie leaned down and patted Gauguin's head. "No. You're not sorry he's leaving are you, Daddy?" she teased.

"I thought I saw a white Jeep Cherokee parked at Verre's house. Is that his car?"

"Yep. Mom's doing a great ahi tuna tonight. I'll get you that and a salad. Okay?"

Not waiting for an answer, Carrie turned on her heel and headed for the kitchen. She came to a halt and looked over her shoulder. "I'll leave Gauguin with you for company."

"Great," Heller grunted. He stared down at the big dog.

Gauguin settled on his haunches and stared back.

"I wish you could talk, you ugly mutt," Heller whispered.

Gauguin's lips pulled back from his teeth and he growled lightly.

"Same to you, fella," Heller muttered and reached for his wineglass.

Chapter 10

George Alvord jabbed at the telephone's redial button as he scanned the trio of TV monitors suspended from the ceiling that surveyed the activities in the gallery, one floor above his office. It was close to closing time and the gallery was nearly empty. A gaunt, smartly clothed woman in her seventies was leaning forward to examine the painting of a spirited palomino jumping over a whitewashed ranch fence. She donned a pair of glasses to view the discreet brass price tag attached to the frame. Alvord looked away as her elegantly wigged head pulled back in disbelief.

"Harry Morgan. Suite 818," he said when the phone was answered.

"I'm afraid that line is still busy, sir," the hotel's receptionist informed him. "I'll be glad to give Mr. Morgan a message when the line is free."

"Yes. Have him call George Alvord as soon as possible. It's very important."

He broke the connection and silently cursed Harry Vlad. The man was never available when you wanted him. Alvord had to admit that he was pleased with the jobs Harry had done on the West Coast.

Minutes later the phone rang and Alvord picked it up quickly.

"Hi, George," Harry Vlad said casually.

"I've been waiting to hear from you," Alvord fumed. "How did the delivery go?"

"Okay, I guess."

"What do you mean? The customer wasn't satisfied?"

"Old man Ganero was satisfied all right. He's as happy as a kid with his own candy store. The problem is with the money."

Alvord was confused. "He didn't pay you?"

"Oh, yeah. He paid, but Johnny Musso gave me a ride to the airport, and he took your share from me. He says he's going to deliver it to you personally."

Johnny Musso. Good God. Alvord would never forget his one-and-only meeting with Musso. It was right after Mark Martel had been found clinging to a pier in the Hudson River. The following day the bodies of Alvord's employee Dick Brumback and Martel's fiancée had surfaced. Musso and a huge monster of a man had come to Alvord's gallery and told him that he was to say he knew nothing about the missing painting, and nothing about Martel. That it was all his employee's—Dick Brumback's—doing. Alvord was quite happy to agree to that scenario.

Then Musso had ordered Alvord to "come along for a little ride." Alvord was escorted to a sedan and made to prostrate himself in the rear of the car, with the monster's foot firmly settled on the back of his neck, while he was driven to a warehouse in Brooklyn. His legs had shaken so badly, the monster—Musso called him "Big Soup"—had to literally drag Alvord from the car into the warehouse.

He'd been taken down a dark concrete staircase to a small, damp, evil-smelling room. Musso had snapped on the light and there, leaning against a gritty brick wall, was Correggio's *Assumption of the Madonna,* the old master that Martel had stolen, at Alvord's request, for Victor Ganero, Sr.

Musso then took a small can from his coat pocket and began squirting a clear liquid on the painting. It had taken Alvord a few seconds to realize what was about to happen. Musso was saturating the painting with lighter fluid.

"God, don't do that," Alvord pleaded, but with no

effect. Musso calmly took out a cigarette lighter and set the canvas ablaze.

Alvord had stood there with tears running down his cheeks as the flames licked through the ancient canvas, ravenously devouring the Madonna and her angels.

Musso then walked over to Alvord, held the lighter fluid over his head, and as the liquid drained through Alvord's hair and dipped down onto his forehead, said, "You never saw this painting. You never talked to Don Ganero. You don't know nothing. Understand?"

Alvord had seriously considered closing the gallery, moving somewhere, anywhere, far from New York. Then one day Victor Ganero himself came to the gallery and told Alvord how much he appreciated his silence and that he was still in the market for old masters. Ganero had even paid Alvord for his losses on the Correggio Madonna that Junior had stolen that night at the warehouse.

Harry Vlad's booming voice brought Alvord out of his reverie. "Hey, George. Did you hear me? Musso says he's coming to see you and that he wants me to let him know if Martel comes looking for me."

"Has he?"

"No, not yet, George. But we better hope Martel pops up soon, or I get the feeling that Musso is going to take it out on both of us."

The receiver nearly slipped out of Alvord's hand as the face of Johnny Musso suddenly appeared on one of the TV screens.

Vlad said, "Listen, the client wants more. Everything he can get. Those addresses you sent out the other day? Two of them are not so good. The one on Clay Street is impossible to get into. The one on El Camino Del Mar is okay, but the people never leave the damn house. What about the statue in Belvedere? Have you gotten any more information?"

A copy of the insurance evaluation had just been faxed to Alvord that morning. "Yes. The owners are Mr. and Mrs. Burwell, the address is 676 Beach Road.

I've got to go. Call me tomorrow." He rose to his feet and gave himself a once-over in the mirror. The man in the image was of medium height, fastidiously dressed, with wings of gray in his thinning brown hair. His pale, heart-shaped face was etched by a network of fine lines. He adjusted the knot on his tie and hurried up the stairs to greet Johnny Musso.

The gangster was standing in front of the painting of the horse jumping the fence. Musso was wearing a charcoal-colored chesterfield coat that was nauseatingly familiar to Alvord. It was the same overcoat Musso had worn the day he'd destroyed the Correggio. He held a common brown paper bag in one hand.

"Mr. Musso," Alvord greeted him cheerfully. "Good to see you, sir."

"How much for this thing?" Musso asked, nodding at the painting.

"Well, the retail price is twenty-six thousand, but I'm sure that if you're interested, I can negotiate with the artist." He showed his teeth. "And of course, I would forfeit my commission."

Musso's eyes were in constant motion, flicking around the gallery. "I saw Harry Vlad. He told me he's working for you."

Alvord stretched his neck and fingered his tie knot. "Not directly, but on a commission basis. You could say he works for me from time to time."

"You'll vouch for him, then," Musso said firmly. "If he doesn't come through, it's your ass, Alvord."

"Please, Mr. Ganero and I have had a long-standing association. I assure you—"

Musso jabbed his extended knuckles into Alvord's bicep, causing the art dealer to wince.

"You're talking to me now. Don Ganero is not here to look after you. I am. So any information you get from Vlad about Martel, you give to me, right?"

"Yes, yes, of course," Alvord agreed, his right hand kneading his bicep, certain that there would be a bruise.

"I want Mark Martel. I personally want him. Understand?"

"Perfectly, Mr. Musso. Perfectly."

Johnny Musso tossed the paper bag of cash to Alvord. "That's Vlad's money. He told me you get a cut."

Alvord looked nervously around the gallery, but no one was paying them any attention. "Well, I do provide the—"

"I think you're getting the short end of the stick, Alvord, but that's between you and Vlad. Anything you two find out about Martel, you tell me. No one else—remember that."

Alvord cleared his voice with a cough into his fist, then said, "Certainly, Mr. Musso. You can count on me."

Musso glanced back at the painting of the horse. "How long did it take the guy to paint this thing?"

Alvord was thrown off balance by the question. "How long? Oh, it's hard to say. A month, a few weeks, it all depends—"

Musso's hand dipped into his pocket and came out with a gold cigarette lighter. He snapped it on and off several times. "It only takes a few seconds to crisp it. Or you, Alvord." He tapped the lighter against the painting. "I've got a friend who likes horses. Wrap it up."

Mark Verre was in La Cucina's kitchen explaining his unexpected trip to Arlene when Carrie rushed up to them with the news. "Daddy just came in."

Mark took the information much better than Arlene did. He patted Carrie on her shoulder. "I'll be gone for a couple of days. Thanks for taking care of Gauguin."

"Sure," Carrie responded happily. "Where are you going?"

"Back east," Mark said vaguely.

Carrie waved goodbye as she left the room.

Arlene brushed back a strand of hair that had

slipped out from under her chef's hat. "Something's wrong, Mark. What is it? Tell me."

"It's something that happened a long time ago. I hoped I would never have to deal with it, Arlene, but now I have to."

"What is it?" Arlene insisted. "Tell me."

Mark slipped a hand around her waist and pulled her close. "I can't give you all the details now, but I will when I get back."

"It has to do what happened the other night, doesn't it?" Arlene said. "The alarm going off. Someone was prowling around the house. That's why you had the gun."

He tilted her chin up and looked into her eyes. "I haven't told you much about myself. You may not want to have anything to do with me once I do. There are some dangerous people involved. That's why I want you to be careful while I'm gone. Keep Gauguin close by."

"Tell me now," she insisted. "It can't be all that bad, and I want to know—"

He cut her off by kissing her full on the lips for several seconds. When he broke away, he said, "I'll tell you everything when I get back in a few days. Now be careful. And it wouldn't be a bad idea to encourage Heller to spend a couple of days visiting with Carrie."

He gave her a final kiss, whispered, "I love you," then hurried out the back door, pausing to look back over his shoulder. Arlene, spatula in hand, stood staring at him, her forehead creased in fear and confusion.

He started to say something, but instead turned and walked quickly out to the Jeep, considering it a stroke of luck that Dan Heller was still in Calistoga and hadn't followed Lisa Cole to San Francisco.

The big policeman was obviously still very much in love with his ex-wife. He couldn't blame Heller, but his timing couldn't have been worse. Heller butting into his private life at the same time that one of

George Alvord's thieves was heisting paintings for Victor Ganero, purposely using Mark's M.O., and the insurance people were after him.

He drove toward San Francisco, stopping at a gas station in Napa to call Lisa Cole. He had no doubt that Heller would contact her.

Her phone was answered by a machine, Cole's voice advising callers that she was out, but would return the call shortly, if they left a message.

"This is Mark. I have to talk to you. It's important—"

There was a click, then Cole came on the line. "I always screen calls at this time of night. What's up?"

"The man you saw when you were leaving my house. He's a policeman."

Cole's voice showed her concern. "A cop. I didn't get much of a look at him. Does he know who you are? Christ, if—"

"No. Not yet. He's the ex-husband of a friend."

"That's not too bright of you," Cole admonished. "Dating an ex-cop's wife. What kind of a cop is he?"

"A San Francisco homicide inspector. Dan Heller. Have you heard of him?"

"I haven't had a hell of a lot to do with homicide cops."

"I'm sure he'll be around to talk to you, so you better have a story ready. Say I was a witness to an auto accident, or whatever you think is best."

Lisa Cole's reply was slow in coming. "Me, Charlie Dwyer, and now a homicide cop. You're a popular man."

"Too popular. I'm moving out of the house. You can contact me by calling and leaving a message on my answering machine. I'm guessing you have the number."

"Tell me this, Mark. If what you say is true, if you didn't steal these paintings, then how did the thief happen to choose San Francisco? How did he know that you'd be around here to take the blame?"

It was a question that had been gnawing at Mark, and one he couldn't answer.

"I'll be in touch," he said, then broke the connection and walked back toward the Jeep. A black Cadillac stretch limousine cruised by close enough to cause him to pull up short, then coasted to a stop near the station's rest rooms.

Mark hurried to the Jeep. He opened the door, his hand groping for the snub-nosed .38 revolver taped under the dash.

The limo's back door swung open, and a young man with long straw-colored hair and a maroon-jacketed tuxedo lumbered out, clutching a champagne bottle by its neck. He was joined by another tuxedoed youngster, also armed with a champagne bottle. They laughed at something, clinked the bottles together, then staggered toward the rest room.

Mark slipped into the Jeep, blotting the sweat from his brow with the back of his hand while he looked out at the necklace of headlights streaming down Highway 29.

You can't jump at the sight of every black limo that comes close, he preached to himself.

His mind drifted back to New York, to the trial. He recalled the daily ritual of the polished black Cadillac pulling up in front of the courthouse. Tony Zarela had always been the first to exit the car, from the front passenger seat. He would scan the crowd, a snarl frozen on his face, then open the back door. Victor Ganero, Jr., would pop out, smiling at the thick-pressed assemblage lining the courthouse steps, waving at a familiar figure, giving a thumbs-up to a pretty face, acting like a rock star about to prepare for a concert.

Johnny Musso was next. His face was always stonestill as he checked the crowd, before ducking his head back into the limousine and advising Victor Ganero, Sr., that it was safe to come out.

The senior Ganero took his time. He walked in a stiff-shouldered manner, acknowledging no one, closely flanked by Musso and his son, following Zarela up the stairs.

Mark had watched the daily performance from the third-floor balcony of the courthouse, squinting, straining, not yet accustomed to having vision in just one eye.

He had no doubt that the Mafia don's threat to take out his other eye was still in play. He'd lived with that threat for three years now. The temptation to run, to just take off, was almost overpowering. He knew that Ganero would go after anyone he could find who was close to his enemy.

Mark reached for the car keys, surprised to see that the revolver was still tightly clutched in his hand.

Chapter 11

San Francisco International Airport was in the midst of an ongoing reconstruction project. The smells of freshly poured concrete and jet fuel were thick in the air. Mark wove his way through a series of barricades and confusing directional signs to the main parking garage and slotted the Jeep into a wide-open spot on the garage's roof, where it could easily be spotted by anyone who might be looking for him.

It was hard to believe that he'd been in the warmth of the Napa Valley just an hour or so ago. A cold, biting southerly wind caused the flags on the international terminal to shudder and snap. A stream of airplanes, their navigation lights dancing in the cloudless black sky, waited for their turns to land.

Mark watched as a 747 lumbered down the runway, gradually gained speed, lifted off with a tortured groan from its engines, and, once airborne, was suddenly transformed from a slow, bloated, ungainly piece of machinery into a swift, graceful instrument perfectly at home in the night sky.

He hunched his shoulders against the wind and made his way to the terminal. He scanned the flight departure monitors. United Airlines had a direct flight taking off for New York City in thirty-five minutes. He hurried to the departure gate and spotted his target—a young man slouched on the floor. He was using his backpack as a pillow; his baseball cap was tipped and resting on the bridge of his nose.

Mark tapped him lightly on the shoulder. The man jerked upward, knocking his cap off in the process.

"Sorry to wake you," he said. "Are you booked on flight 212 to New York?"

The man reached around and clutched his backpack to his chest. "Yeah. What's the problem?"

"I have to get to New York in a hurry, and the flight is booked." Mark slipped his wallet out of his pocket and began peeling off bills. "I'd be happy to pay you double for your ticket if you could help me out."

The young man rubbed his chin thoughtfully. "You gotta get there in a hurry, huh? How about kickin' in another hundred bucks?"

Mark agreed to the deal, and ten minutes later he joined the queue and was herded into a seat in the far rear of the airplane.

Once they were airborne, Verre closed his eyes and thought about his destination. Hemingway had dubbed Paris "a moveable feast." Mark couldn't argue with that description. New York was more of an ever-changing, energized junket. Images of the city flickered in his mind: the museums, the galleries, the restaurants, jazz joints, ethnic neighborhoods, his apartment on West Eighty-second Street. The ugly warehouse bordering the Hudson where he'd been shot and Denise had been brutally raped and murdered. The debris-strewn alleyway in Little Italy where Junior Ganero's body had been found. Ganero's killer had not made the same mistake that Junior had with Mark.

The doctors said it was a miracle Mark had survived. The bullet, a .22 long, had bored a straight, narrow hole, exiting behind his ear. A mere millimeter higher and to the right and he would not have survived. There had been extensive nerve damage, tremendously painful headaches that lasted a year, and on-and-off bouts with vertigo that still bothered him. Junior's executioner had used a .45, the cartridge's trajectory traveling upward, eradicating his eye and most of his brain cells before exploding through his skull.

He'd never thought he would return to New York City. Even the fact that Victor Ganero was living in Arizona did little to ease the nervousness in his stomach.

From what he had gleaned from the newspapers and the Web, Johnny Musso was in charge. Musso—Ganero's heir apparent and, he was sure, the third ski-masked man in the warehouse that fatal night.

Junior Ganero had been the one who had shot him, and Tony Zarela was a known killer, yet somehow Mark felt that Musso was the most dangerous of them all. It was the way Musso had acted at the trial—calm, dangerous, oily in his movements. A lone wolf who lets the pack take down its prey, then moves in for the final kill.

The Plaza Hotel desk clerk greeted Noel Field with a raised eyebrow and a firm "How are you feeling today, Mr. Field?"

"Wonderful," Field responded with his usual vigor, knowing full well that the clerk, and his employer, Donald Trump, would much rather hear that he was ill: a heart attack, incurable cancer, or some strange virus that would cause him to abandon his hotel suite.

One of the best moves he'd made in his entire life was leasing a suite at the Plaza thirty years ago. The archaic New York city lease laws had kept his monthly fees at a paltry sum. The hotel's lawyers had tried every means at their disposal to pry him out of his rooms, including offering a flat-fee settlement in six figures.

"Say hello to the Donald," he beamed as he slid his room key across the marble desk.

He exited the hotel, stopping to admire the ring of horse-drawn carriages waiting to trot sightseers around Central Park. The streets were teeming with tourists, shoppers, and the usual New York crowd, so Field paid no particular attention to the bearded man with sunglasses and a wide-brimmed felt hat who stood near the entrance to F.A.O. Schwarz.

Field had no set destination. He began walking through the park, in the general direction of the Metropolitan Museum.

Noel Field was sixty-six and could have passed for a much younger man, except for the way he carried himself. The arthritis in his left hip caused him to move slowly, in a flat-footed, plodding manner.

He was a tall, gaunt man with sloping shoulders and a broad, arched back. His thick, wavy brown hair was heavily frosted with gray, unlike the neat, dark pencil-line mustache under his prominent nose.

He felt a sharp stab of pain when he was forced to move quickly to avoid two teenage skateboarders zigzagging down the path. He sank down gratefully on a park bench, wondering just how much longer he could put off an operation to replace his hip.

A bearded man wearing oversized dark glasses sat down alongside him and said, "Hello, Noel."

Field's mouth dropped open for a second, then he regained his poise. "Mark Martel. What the devil are you doing here?"

"I need your help, Noel," Martel responded. "Someone is impersonating me. Using my technique. All the things *you* taught me about how to be a top-notch thief."

Field held up his hands and wiggled his misshapen fingers. "Well, it certainly isn't me, Mark. I have difficulty tying my shoes nowadays." He raised his feet. "I have to wear loafers." He laughed lightly. "It's hell getting old, son."

Field sighed and studied Martel closely. "You're looking well. Tell me more about the man who's impersonating you."

"He gains access to the house long enough to bug the alarm system. Goes back in when the house is empty and takes one item. No matter what's there, he just takes the one item."

"Yes, you always showed amazing discipline that way, Mark. I could never do it. There was always something else that I couldn't keep my hands off— another painting, jewelry, rare coins or books. You know, you don't have a patent on this technique, Mark. And imitation is a form of flattery."

"He leaves the transmitting chips behind, Noel. Right inside the alarm box, so they can't be missed. It's as if he hopes I'll find out about the thefts and come looking for him."

"Have the police made the connection?"

"Not yet. But the insurance company has. Charlie Dwyer's working for Boston Insurance."

Field winced at that bit of news. "Tell me more about what he takes."

"Strictly religious paintings. Christian, featuring Christ or the Madonna. Major artists. Old masters. All very rare."

Field smoothed his mustache with his thumb and murmured softly. "Ummmm. You think the buyer is Victor Ganero, don't you?"

"Yes. Is George Alvord still supplying Ganero?"

"There are rumors to that effect," Field certified. "Ganero is living out west now. You know that, I suppose."

"Carefree, Arizona. Yes, I know that, Noel."

"I've heard that some of Mr. Ganero's employees here in New York are becoming impatient with the old don. They don't cotton to him lolling around out west while they do all the sweating and toiling here." Field folded his hands and dropped his head to his chest as two uniformed New York policemen strolled by.

"The Mafia isn't what it was a few years ago, Mark. The black, Chinese, Japanese, Irish, Puerto Rican, and Filipino gangs are moving into its territories, showing it no respect. The word is that the boys want new leadership, but Victor Ganero is not willing to let go."

"I feel bad for them," Mark said dryly. "Who is Alvord using now?"

Field placed his hands on his knees and painfully leveraged himself to his feet. "Let's walk. I can't sit for too long."

Mark fell in alongside his old mentor. "Who is Alvord using, Noel?"

"George stuck his head in the sand after that episode with you almost being killed. He's careful now, more careful than ever. If he is involved with Ganero, he'll use someone from the old school. He wouldn't trust a newcomer. It would help if you could tell me where the thefts took place. It wasn't around here—I would have heard about them."

"The West Coast."

"That certainly narrows it down," Field said with a chuckle. "There are only a few cities on the coast that house the kind of paintings you're talking about: San Diego, Los Angeles, San Francisco, and Seattle, right?"

"There have been three jobs, all in one city," Mark certified, without revealing just which city.

"Judging from the color of your skin, I think I can eliminate Seattle," Field observed. "And those calluses on your hands. You didn't get those from painting. You've been doing some physical labor, Mark. Ranching? You always liked horses. Or farming? I can't picture you growing lettuce or cabbage. Wine? You loved your years in Paris, and the French countryside, and you often talked of someday buying in to a winery. That makes me think of California. Rudy Seimsen is living in Carmel. That's near San Francisco, isn't it?"

Mark had forgotten just how observant his old friend was. "Yes, a little more than a hundred miles south."

"He's opened a faux gallery. He sells pastiches of your choice: Van Gogh, Rembrandt, those awful Monet water lily things. Anything the customer desires. They'll even customize the colors to match your living room rug, I'm told. I hear he's making a fortune."

A young couple on a bicycle built for two buzzed by, narrowly missing them both. The girl on the backseat twisted around and yelled a smiling "Sorry" as they sped away.

"Who else?" Mark asked.

"Alex Gassiot, though I doubt if he'd move west. Jack Welz, but I don't know if Jack could resist the temptation of taking everything that isn't nailed down on a job. And Harry Vlad. You remember Harry?"

"Yes. He tried to recruit me to help him in a museum caper."

"Good thing you didn't," Field smiled. "Poor Harry was caught and sent to one of the government's crossbar hotels. I don't know if he's out yet."

"I have to find out who it is, Noel."

Field stopped and looked directly at Mark. "Take off those ridiculous glasses, please."

Mark complied with the request, and Field leaned close, examining Mark's face.

"Amazing. Not a sign of a scar. You were damn lucky, son."

"Yes," Mark agreed. "And I want to stay that way. That's why I have to find this thief."

"And what if you do? Will that solve all your problems?"

"It's my best bet. I find him, and the insurance company leaves me alone."

Field shuffled off slowly. "I've been worried about you, Mark. I wasn't sure if you were alive."

Mark nodded his head. He and Field had been close at one time, an almost father-son relationship in some ways. "I didn't want to put you in jeopardy, Noel. If Ganero had thought that you knew where I was, you know what he would have done."

"Yes. George Alvord took me to lunch a couple of years ago. That nice French place by his gallery. He told me an extraordinary story. Remember Correggio's *Assumption of the Madonna*?"

"I'm not likely to forget it. It cost Denise her life and me my right eye."

Field's forehead furrowed. He had known Denise Duval very well and had hoped to be the best man at Mark and Denise's wedding. "Well, Alvord told me that two of Ganero's thugs had whisked him away to some dungeon in Brooklyn. Correggio's painting was lying against the wall. They doused it with lighter fluid and set it afire. Can you imagine that?"

"No way," Mark insisted. "It had to be a fake. They'd never burn up anything worth that kind of money."

"I agree, but it certainly had an effect on George. He was scared beyond belief. He wanted me to join forces with him in tracking you down. We were to split the reward. Poor old George. He never was too bright." Field flashed a smile. "Ganero wouldn't have paid off." He tugged at Mark's coat sleeve. "What makes you think the insurance company will let you go back to whatever it is you're doing if you hand them the thief?"

"It's my only chance. I'm being squeezed hard, Noel. It may be that the thief wants me to come after him. To show myself. So he can turn me over to Ganero."

Field chewed that over in his mind for a moment. "Hmmmm, maybe Alvord isn't as dumb as I had imagined him to be. He has one of his hired help pulling these jobs. He collects his fees, and if you do pop up, he can claim the reward. There's one curious aspect to all of this. You realize that, don't you? How does Alvord know where you're living?"

"I don't know," Mark admitted.

"Then I suggest we find out. From George Alvord." Noel reached out and hugged Mark to his chest. "I'm glad you came to me for help. Very glad."

*   *   *

Harry Vlad tossed the bow anchor over the side of the boat, waited until the rope played out before tying the line off, then maneuvered the vessel into position and dropped the stern anchor. He went through the mechanics of baiting hooks with anchovies and casting out into the wrinkled cobalt-blue waters of Paradise Cove.

Then he set the butt of the rod into the holder at the stern of the boat and ducked down into the cramped cabin below the wheelhouse.

He rubbed his hands together in delight. If you had to pull a surveillance, this was the ideal way to do it— from a well-stocked boat fifty yards offshore. The target George Alvord had provided him, Walter and Mechelle Burwell, lived in a Moorish-style Belvedere mansion of hospital-white rough stucco, with pointed arches, turrets, and blue-and-white canvas awnings arched above the windows. Somewhere in the house was a miniature Lorenzo Ghiberti bronze of John the Baptist that old man Ganero was drooling for.

A gleaming white yacht, four or five times the size of Harry's rental, was tied up at a dock at the rear of the house. A rope-and-wood gangplank led up to the bulkhead protecting the property from the bay waters. Harry fished an iced bottle of Anchor Steam beer from a portable chest, took a long sip, then popped open the two starboard-side portholes and got to work. The long-range bionic sound-amplification device was mounted on a swiveling tripod. It looked to Harry like the type of weapon that *Star Wars* bad guys used to blow away the good guys: a heavy black-plastic rifle stock with a finger-shaped parabolic cone at the tip and a telescopic sight along the barrel. He slipped on the attached earphones, adjusted the sound, and focused in on the house, maneuvering the crosshairs slowly from the roof down, checking each window, settling on the rear deck.

He could see the diving board of a swimming pool, then the L-shaped pool. A dozen or more chairs were scattered around, all in the same blue-and-white stripe pattern as the awnings. He could hear a radio playing Latin music.

A tall woman with reddish-blond hair in a lime-colored bikini was going through a slow-moving exercise routine. She had her back to Harry. He zoomed in with the lens. "Nice, nice, nice," he said aloud to himself. Her bronzed skin glistened in contrast to the bright swimsuit. He wondered about tan lines. God, how he loved tan lines.

The woman swirled around, her arms akimbo, eyes closed in concentration. Harry recognized her from photographs he'd researched in the library's back issues of the local newspapers. Walter Burwell's wife, Mechelle. She pushed her hands out in slow motion, seemingly blocking kicks or punches from an opponent. Tai chi or one of the other fancy Asian martial arts, Harry guessed, that looked good in the movies but couldn't compete with a pipe across the throat in real life.

She rotated gracefully from side to side. Harry dragged the lens away from her supple body and scanned the deck. The woman wasn't alone. A heavy-set middle-aged man with curly, gorilla body hair was sprawled out on a chaise lounge, a thick cigar protruding from his mouth. He was languidly turning the pages of a newspaper. Walter Burwell in the all too abundant flesh. Behind Burwell was a sliding glass door leading into the house.

The plans Harry had reviewed at the county building permit bureau indicated that there were two security-alarm switches, one just inside the front door, the other near the rear sliding doors, conveniently situated so the Burwells could lock up the house on the way out to their yacht.

"Easy. God, I love it when it's this easy," Harry whispered to himself, taking his eye away from the lens long enough to take a pull on his beer.

When he looked back at the house, a young man with jet-black hair styled in a pompadour and wearing a white jacket was walking toward Mechelle Burwell, carrying a tray in one hand.

Harry adjusted the volume and heard the man say, "Iced tea, Mrs. Burwell."

She stopped her routine, reached out, and took a tall glass from the tray. "Thank you, Ray-Ray," she said in a husky voice.

Harry made kissing sounds. Mechelle Burwell's thank-you had sounded like she was thanking him for more than just the iced tea. She sauntered slowly toward the house, the boy with the tray following closely behind her.

Walter Burwell looked up from his paper. "Ray-Ray, bring me a gin and tonic."

Harry marked the date and time on a foolscap tablet, along with the notation "W.B. sunning, wife exercising, houseboy serving drinks."

Harry helped himself to another beer and moved out on deck. A slight breeze kicked up the water. Birds' wings flashed like knives in the sun. Sailboats fanned along the shores of Angel Island. A ferryboat, outlined against the Golden Gate Bridge, plowed through the heavier waters of Raccoon Straits, heading toward San Francisco.

It was, Harry had to admit, a beautiful day. He was a true New Yorker, born and raised there, and he missed the Big Apple's action. But he was getting used to Frisco.

He had his next job all set and ready to go in the city, the only problem being that the house was always occupied. If he couldn't tackle that one, he'd hit this place, then take some time off. Relax and travel around the area: Tahoe, Reno, Beverly Hills.

He went below and scoped in on the house again. Walter Burwell was still on the chaise lounge, his head tilted back, the cigar jutting up toward the sun, the newspaper draped across his ample stomach.

"Have a nice long nap, Walter," Harry urged. He inched the scope to the sliding glass doors, then up to the second-floor windows. "I wonder what your wife and Ray-Ray are up to?"

Chapter 12

Lisa Cole finished up a rough draft of notes on her meeting with Mark Verre. She took a sip of coffee and lit up her first cigarette of the day, then placed a call to Boston Insurance. She wasn't sure just how Charlie Dwyer was going to respond to her meeting with Mark.

"What have you got?" Dwyer asked bluntly when they were connected.

Lisa read the report directly from the computer screen. "He's either a great actor, Uncle Charlie, or he's telling the truth about someone else stealing the paintings."

"Knock off the Uncle Charlie jazz. Your aunt and I have been divorced for a long time. And I never really figured Martel for the jobs, Lisa."

"But, you said—"

"Look—Martel was a specialist, a real pro. He wouldn't be dumb enough to leave those transmitting devices behind. But, as smart as your loving aunt always said you were, you were never going to find out who did. So I figured we'd squeeze him."

"Mark is sure the thief is working for a New York art dealer. George Alvord."

"Mark, huh? Glad to see you two are on a first-name basis." Dwyer's voice hardened. "I think Alvord's involved, too. It all fits. But we have to prove it. Once we learn who the thief is, he'll give us Alvord, and maybe finally I'll be able to get something on Ganero. Keep the pressure on Mark. Tell him you talked to me and that he's got less than three weeks. That I'm running out of patience and he's running out of time."

Lisa blew a smoke ring that wobbled through the air and broke apart against the computer screen. "You already suspected that Ganero was involved?"

"Yes. That's why I set you onto Martel. He'll do anything to keep Ganero from finding him, so I figured why not let him find the thief, and the paintings, for us."

Lisa pushed the half-smoked cigarette into an ashtray and snuffed it out, breaking it in half in the process.

"Then Victor Ganero must have a museum full of masterpieces sitting right there in his mansion. Ours and who knows how many others. If I could just get in there, with a camera and—"

"Don't even think about it," Dwyer warned. "Ganero's boys would have you for lunch, and believe me, they'd enjoy the meal. But you wouldn't."

"I still think we should take a crack at Ganero's house," Lisa said quickly. "Just a static surveillance. Leave a camera set up there. We could spot who's coming and going, maybe catch the thief making a delivery."

"You've got the address?"

"I can get it," Lisa replied, not wanting Dwyer to know that she already had it. This was her case, and she wanted to run it her way.

"Okay, I'll authorize the surveillance. Keep me posted. But stay on Martel, Lisa. Ride him hard. Either he finds out who's been taking the paintings or I turn him over to Ganero. It's that simple."

"You dirty old man," Lisa said, once she'd safely cradled the receiver. Uncle Charlie had fewer scruples than Victor Ganero.

There had to be a way to get into Ganero's house. A couple of photographs of the stolen paintings would be all she would need. These photos would be worth millions of dollars in finder's fees.

She slipped her address book out of the desk drawer and found the number for Bonnie Nelson, an investigator in Phoenix that she'd worked with before.

"Bonnie. Are you busy? I could use some help on a case." Lisa explained the details, and the risks involved. "Don't get too close to the house. Just set up a static video camera to take a frame every fifteen seconds. That should do it. I'm interested in who's going in and out of the house. I can be down there by, oh, late tomorrow afternoon."

They exchanged beeper numbers, and Bonnie said that either she or one of her employees would pick Lisa up at the Phoenix airport.

"That's great," Lisa said. "What I really want is—"

The ringing of the doorbell interrupted her. "I'll fill you in when I get there."

Lisa went to the front window, pried apart two slats of the venetian blinds with her fingers, and sized up the man standing on her doorstep. Her eyes moved down to his car parked in the driveway. A sedan with twin spotlights and a whip antenna.

She opened the front door, still holding her morning cup of coffee, and smiled pleasantly.

"Can I help you?"

"Police," the tall man in a sport coat said, flashing a gold shield at her. "Inspector Heller."

He really didn't need the badge, she thought. He had cop stamped all over him. The off-the-rack sport coat, shirt open at the collar, shoes that hadn't seen a polish since they'd left the factory—and the attitude. Cocky, tough, jaded, cynical, but with seams of compassion around the eyes. He was certainly taller and better-looking than most policemen she'd met. She had the feeling that Mark Martel had definitely picked the wrong ex-wife to play house with.

"Mind if I come in, Miss Cole?" Heller asked, one foot already halfway across the threshold.

His voice had a soft, authoritative cadence.

Lisa kept one hand on the door frame. "What is it, Officer? Those parking tickets? I'm sure I paid them."

Heller frowned in annoyance. "It's Inspector, and no, it's not about parking tickets. You don't remember me?"

Lisa's face went through a charade of puzzlement. "No, I'm sorry. What's it about?"

"Your visit to Mark Verre yesterday afternoon."

"Oh, that," Lisa said, sounding relieved. "Come on in."

Heller scanned the apartment, a mishmash of office and living room furniture side by side. Green metal filing cabinets bracketing a chocolate-colored leather couch. A TV set on a desk alongside a fax machine. A rocking chair, the cane seat covered with boxed envelopes and stacks of telephone books. The framed prints on the walls were Thomas Kincaid country cottages.

He turned his attention to Lisa Cole. She was wearing a white body-skimming knee-length pencil skirt and a black scoop-necked silk blouse. She was a looker, all right. He wondered if she and Verre were an item.

"What's your interest in Mark Verre?" Heller asked, as Lisa set her cup down and tidied up the fan of books and magazines on the coffee table.

"What's your interest in my interest, Inspector?"

Heller frowned. "He told me you were a sales rep for the winery. Are you working for Mark Verre?"

Lisa settled down on the armrest of the couch. "Give me a good reason why I shouldn't ask you to leave, and if you refuse, call your chief's office and tell him I'm being harassed by one of his detectives."

"I know a lot of people in your business," Heller said with an ingratiating smile on his face. "They find that when they cooperate with me, I cooperate with them."

Lisa brought her knees together and smoothed her

skirt. "So, if I tell you what I know about Verre, you'll do what for me?"

Heller took a business card from his wallet and handed it to her.

"There may be a time when you need to know if one of your clients has been a bad boy, or just when he was released from jail, and for what offense. Things like that."

Heller's business card featured an embossed gold shield. She flicked it with her fingernail.

"I'm always appreciative of a little help, Inspector, but I'm afraid I can't tell you much about Mr. Verre, other than that he witnessed an accident at Grant and Union Streets. My client insured one of the vehicles. They wanted me to get a statement from him. It's as simple as that."

"When was the accident?"

"July fourteenth."

"What time?"

"A little after six in the evening. Why?"

"Was anybody seriously injured?"

Lisa shook her head and her hair swished back away from her face. "Yes. The driver of the car that our insured hit suffered a broken neck."

"How did you locate Verre?"

"He gave his address to both drivers." She took a sip of coffee. "A genuine good Samaritan."

"Did you take a statement from Verre?"

"No. He said our insured ran the stop sign. My client wouldn't want that on tape." She stood up and glanced pointedly at her wristwatch. "What's your interest in Mr. Verre, Inspector?"

"Did you run a background check on him?"

"No. Should I have?"

Heller broke out his most cordial smile. "It wouldn't have done you much good." He headed for the door. "Thanks for your time."

"You didn't tell me why you're interested in Verre," Lisa called to him.

"I'll be in touch," Heller said, then let himself out, gently closing the door behind him.

Lisa watched from the window as Heller slipped into his car and backed into the street. There was a look of grim determination on his craggy features. She didn't believe for a second that he had bought the witness-to-a-car-accident story. What was behind his asking if she'd run a background check on Mark? And adding that it wouldn't have done her much good if she had?

Lisa had run Mark Verre through every possible database she could find. It was as if the man had been born three years ago, the day he entered the witness protection program.

Obviously Heller had also been checking on Mark and hadn't found much. But he would keep at it. She somehow felt sorry for Mark. Just a short time ago he'd had it made—a new identity, a beautiful house, a winery, a girlfriend. Now he had Charlie Dwyer *and* the cops chasing after him.

Last night, at his house. Both of them in their bathing suits. Warm summer breezes. Wine. She wasn't above using her looks to help her get information, but Martel hadn't responded. Either he really was in love with Arlene Severi or she was losing her touch.

What was it about Severi? Mark was a hunk, and Arlene's ex-husband the cop wasn't too shabby-looking either.

She would have another crack at Mark, but she would have to work fast if she was going to earn the finder's fee before his time ran out.

Chapter 13

"Hey, I thought you were taking some time off," homicide lieutenant Keith Olsen said when he wandered out of his office and spotted Dan Heller sitting at his desk.

"Yeah, I am. I just stopped by to pick up some things, Keith."

"Get a life, find a woman," Olsen advised. "You're all but married to the job, Dan."

"Easy for you to say," Heller joked. Olsen had been married to his high school sweetheart for twenty-seven years.

Olsen ducked back into his office and came out with a paper in his hand. "This fax came in for you from Canada. What've you got going with the Mounties?"

"There's a possibility that a suspect in the case of the St. Louis man who was popped in the Castro fled to Montreal."

"Good a place as any," Olsen responded with a shrug of his shoulders. He dropped the paper onto Heller's desk.

"Hey, Lieutenant, have you ever had any dealings with the feds on the witness protection program?"

"I avoid the feds as much as possible. Does this involve the suspect up in Canada?"

"No. It's personal," Heller said, thinking that he might get a little more help from Olsen that way. "Some guy's been hanging around Arlene. She thinks he might be in the witness protection program."

Olsen rubbed his forehead thoughtfully. "I don't

even know who to ask for information, Dan. The Justice Department is worse than the FBI. You know that."

Heller waited until the lieutenant was out of sight before examining the fax. The Mountie had come through, but the report was negative. There were no records on a Mark Verre in Canadian criminal or motor vehicle filings. Verre had said he sold commodities, but there was no record of him having a license to do so.

Heller's fingers fluttered over the computer keyboard, like a pianist about to begin a concert, then he stood up, grabbed his jacket, and strode toward the door. He'd checked every database he could think of for Mark Verre. And his call to the Justice Department had been a waste of time. The lieutenant was right. They tell you nothing. He'd also checked for accidents at the intersection of Grant and Union Streets on the date that Lisa Cole had provided him and had come up with nothing. No police report on file. Then he'd called Central Station to see if they had any record of the accident and again received a negative response.

The city ambulance crews hadn't been called to an incident in the vicinity of Grant and Union Streets. Either Lisa Cole was bullshitting him or a guy had driven away from an accident with a broken neck.

Lisa Cole wasn't going to be any help. The only way he was going to ID Mark Verre was through his fingerprints. Which meant a visit to Verre's house at the winery. A glass, a bottle of wine, or one of his paintbrushes. Verre's prints would be all over the house. All he had to do was get into the place.

Heller's stomach soured as he wondered if Arlene had a key.

Mark Martel watched as Noel Field and George Alvord exited Alvord's art gallery on Wooster Street and started walking toward Alvord's favorite restaurant, Montrechet.

Noel was going to try and pry some information out of Alvord over dinner, while Mark broke into the gallery owner's office.

When they were out of sight, Mark wove his way through traffic. He spotted Felix, the gangly Latin who was the saxophone leader of a three-man street band Mark had found earlier playing for tips near Washington Square.

Felix and his two companions were milling around on the sidewalk just down from the gallery. Mark gave him a cautionary wave. Felix had his sax in hand. He was flamboyantly dressed in plaid trousers, a faded tuxedo jacket, and a deerstalker cap. Gold earrings rimmed both ears and dangled from his nostrils. His friends were equally as colorful.

"You ready, my man?" Felix asked.

Mark passed him two hundred dollars. Felix counted the bills slowly, then smiled, showing a keyboard of brilliant white teeth. "Just like you promised. Is it show time?"

"Right now," Mark said. "And again in an hour—don't forget that."

Felix bobbed his head in agreement. "And you don't forget the extra two hundred." He nodded to his two companions, each of whom had a set of bongo drums dangling from leather straps around his shoulders. They dance-stepped into Alvord's gallery. Mark hung back, watching through the window as a man in a dark suit approached them nervously. The drums started a calypso beat and Felix began singing in a deep bass voice.

Mark slipped in through the front door unnoticed and walked directly to the stairs leading down to Alvord's office.

The gallery consisted of three levels. The main floor and a mezzanine showcased a variety of artwork, while the lower level housed Alvord's office, rest rooms, and a small employee lounge.

It took Mark less than fifteen seconds to pick the lock. He scanned the office. It didn't seem to have changed much since his last visit, more than three years ago. Two maroon leather club chairs bracketed a Cuban mahogany desk. The forged Cézanne geometric landscape was still in its position of honor behind the desk.

He kept one eye on the trio of TV screens that monitored the gallery as he flicked through Alvord's Rolodex. One of the cameras was focused on the front door and caught Felix and his two friends as they were escorted out to the street.

There were no phone numbers or addresses for the four suspects Noel Field had listed as possibilities: Alex Gassiot, Rudy Seimsen, Harry Vlad, and Jack Welz. He moved to the file cabinets, and again struck out on those names.

He then began hunting through Alvord's files under the titles of the paintings, and then the artists, for the old masters that Lisa Cole had told him had been stolen. He found nothing. Nor was there anything under the name Ganero, which certainly didn't surprise him.

Frustrated at his lack of success and realizing that he had wasted twenty-five of his allotted sixty minutes, he searched through the desk drawers, again coming up empty.

That left the computer. He clicked the machine on and used the mouse to navigate his way through dozens of Alvord's directories.

Mark sifted through several of them, his frustration growing as time ran short. Felix and his buddies were due to return in twelve minutes.

He slid the mouse to Quickfinder and typed in the names Gassiot, Seimsen, Vlad, and Welz—no record. He then tried the artists' names and titles of the paintings—another frustrating no record.

He was certain that the information was there somewhere. His fingers hovered nervously over the keyboard, then he entered—"San Francisco."

The computer tracked through the files and within seconds posted the results: File name—Auction.

Mark opened the Auction file—there were two paintings and one statue with San Francisco addresses. Next to each painting was the name and street address of the owners. The notation alongside the statue stated: "Ghiberti—Belvedere???"

The works were all old masters, and Mark was fairly certain that none had been up for auction in years.

He spotted Felix and his saxophone on one of the TV screens and quickly jotted down the information from the computer screen. He snapped off the machine and hastily made his way upstairs.

Two of Alvord's employees were discreetly yet firmly demanding that Felix and his two companions leave immediately.

Felix tipped his horn as Mark passed by, then went into the opening bars of "The Girl from Ipanema."

"How was dinner?" Mark asked as he slid into the chair alongside Noel Field in the famed Oak Bar of the Plaza Hotel. The room was crowded, and there was a pleasant buzz of conversation over the clicking of ice cubes and popping of champagne corks.

"Splendid," Field responded enthusiastically. "They do a wonderful veal kidney in sherry sauce there." He waved a hand at the waiter, then circled his finger over his glass. "Two more martinis, please."

"George Alvord was not all that cooperative, however. He didn't seem too taken with my plight of needing a top-notch thief to help me on a job in upstate New York. George suggested that I was getting along. 'You're too long in the tooth for that anymore, Noel,' he lectured me. I explained that it was for just that reason that I needed help. I ran off the four names, but he claimed he hadn't had anything to do with the batch of them in years. 'Never touch the dirty trade anymore. I'm making too much money to fool with it,' was his story, which is the proverbial crock. I know the IRS is after him for back taxes, and he's having trouble paying his rent and keeping his chorus boys in glad rags."

The waiter came with their drinks.

"A perfect Oak Bar martini is one of life's *petit-tresors*," Field said, smacking his lips before sampling the fresh drink. "How did your little burglary go?"

Mark passed over the information he had copied from the computer screen. "Have any of these come up for auction recently?"

Field slipped on a pair of half-lens reading glasses and pressed his tongue against his teeth as he studied Mark's notes. "Not a chance, dear boy. Two paintings by Filippo Lippi and a statue by Lorenzo Ghiberti. Not a chance. You do have to admire George. He does come up with outstanding information on these things, doesn't he? He has wonderful contacts among the insurance appraisal companies and auction houses. I've always envied him that."

"These were the only items associated with San Francisco. My guess is that they're Victor Ganero's shopping list."

Field swirled the olive in his drink, making a small whirlpool. "I brought up Ganero's name during our dinner. George nearly gagged on his mascarpone. I mentioned your name, too. I told him that I wished you were around, because you were just the man I needed for my job."

"What did he say?"

"He told me to forget about you. That you were probably dead."

"Wishful thinking," Mark replied dryly.

"What's your next move?"

Mark picked up the sheet of paper. "I'll check these out."

"Carmel is close to home, is it?" Field suggested softly.

"You don't want to know, do you, Noel?"

Field popped the martini olive into his mouth, chewed, and swallowed before responding. "Yes. I do want to help, Mark. I'll ask around and see what I can find out about Seimsen and the others."

"If you had to bet, which one would you pick, Noel?"

"Seimsen, first. He's the smartest of the group, then Harry Vlad," Field responded.

"I never met Seimsen. What's he like?"

"Intelligent. Calculating. In his late forties. Small of stature. I think he had visions of being a jockey in his youth. A rather decent forger in his own right."

"Why Vlad?"

"Because he and Seimsen worked together in the past. And Harry had rather an obsession with you. He realized you were the best, Mark. He was always pestering me about you, your technique, your style. I may have told him too much."

"I thought you said Vlad went to prison."

"Yes. He wasn't the perfect student that you were. I'll check and see if he's been released. I haven't visited my daughter, Dorothy, in years. I think I'll pop out to Los Angeles and see how my grandchildren are doing. While I'm there, I might take a trip to Carmel."

"You've done enough," Mark cautioned. "I don't want you getting hurt, Noel."

Field flicked his mustache and smiled. "Life has been pretty dull lately, Mark." His face sobered. "I want to help you. I want to do that very much. Don't take away an old man's chance at redemption."

Mark knew that Field somehow felt partially responsible for what had happened at the warehouse that night, even though his only participation in the burglary had been to scout out the house before the painting was stolen.

"Okay, Noel. Go see Seimsen in Carmel. But then you come back to New York. Okay?"

Field's eyes traveled slowly around the dimly lit cocktail lounge. "Believe me, I'm not abandoning the Plaza until Saint Peter makes the request."

Chapter 14

George Alvord was mulling over his dinner conversation with Noel Field as he strolled back to the gallery. He stopped to admire himself in a store window. He brushed back the hair over his ears and wondered just what the old scoundrel had really been after. Field had supposedly retired from the art game. He'd salted away enough money to live comfortably for the rest of his life, especially since he was living damn near for free at the Plaza.

Alvord reached his gallery near closing time, nine o'clock. Gerald Nerbert, his manager, rushed up to greet him. Alvord could tell by the beads of sweat along Nerbert's toupee that something had happened.

"We had three street ruffians come into the gallery, sir. I didn't think it was worth disturbing you. I booted them out, but they returned about an hour later. I threatened to call the police, and they finally left."

"Was anything taken?" Alvord demanded. "Did they damage anything?"

Nerbert shifted uneasily on his feet. "Nothing was taken or damaged. They were street musicians, that's all."

Alvord stalked around the gallery to assure himself that Nerbert was telling the truth.

"They were playing this terrible music," Nerbert said as he followed in Alvord's wake. "A saxophone and bongo drums."

"And you say they came back an hour after the first visit?"

"Yes, sir. An hour. Almost to the minute."

Alvord pinched the bridge of his nose as if he had a sudden headache. "The street musicians were probably a diversion, Gerald. Something's not right. Don't leave until I dismiss you."

Alvord hurried to his office. Nothing seemed to have been disturbed. He flopped into his chair and used the remote control to rewind the TV monitor tape. The reel-to-reel tapes recorded roving sequences, moving from one camera to another. After twenty-four hours the tape simply began recording over the previous day's recording.

Alvord couldn't remember when he had last checked the machine. Though its main purpose was to record any criminal activity in the gallery, he found it much more useful as a tool to keep track of his employees.

He pushed the stop button, then fast-forwarded to a scene of three garishly dressed black men storming in the front entrance. Nerbert approached and waved his arms at them, but they paid him little attention.

Alvord watched intently as the men began moving through the gallery. He used the sweep hand on his watch to measure the time from when they came in to when Gerald Nerbert herded them back to the street. Two minutes, thirty-four seconds.

He rewound the tape, this time focusing on the others in the gallery. There were eight customers, most with looks of disgust on their faces as they viewed the commotion. An exception was the fleeting appearance of a tall man with a full beard, wearing a felt hat and dark glasses.

Alvord fast-forwarded the tape until the musicians appeared again. It was a replay of their first visit, bongos being thumped, the saxophone waving around like a live animal in the hands of the man who seemed to be the leader of the group.

Gerald Nerbert and another employee arrived,

more agitated than before, and Alvord could read Nerbert's lips as he threatened to call the police.

Just before Nerbert herded them toward the exit, the same tall, bearded man hurriedly emerged and ducked out the gallery door.

Alvord picked up the phone and ordered Nerbert to come to the office. He showed the manager the video sequences. "The man with the beard and sunglasses. What did he want?"

Nerbert peered intently at the screen. "I don't recall seeing that gentleman, sir."

Alvord groaned out loud. "He was here for an hour, and you have no recollection of him?"

"No, sir," Nerbert responded meekly.

"Go," Alvord said disgustedly. "Close up and go home, Gerald."

Alvord got to his feet and paced nervously around the room before settling back into his chair and reviewing the tape again. He studied the images of the mysterious man in the beard. He was six feet or more in height, and he walked like an athlete. Dark hair. Straight nose. Somewhere between thirty-five and fifty years of age was Alvord's best estimate. The glasses, hat, and beard were an effective disguise.

Alvord felt a sudden sharp pain in his chest. Noel Field. Was Field somehow involved in this? Was that why Field had offered to take him to dinner? The pain sharpened when he remembered how friendly Field and Mark Martel had been.

He went back to the videotape. Could it have been Mark Martel? Here, in New York? Would he risk that?

He looked slowly around the office, as if searching for a bomb. A recording device? That was one of Martel's specialties. He would have to call an expert in the morning and have the whole gallery electronically swept. He fingered the computer keys. He turned the machine on and entered "Auction." The three San Francisco addresses were there. Would Martel, or whoever it was, have been smart enough to find the Auction file? It would take longer than an hour to search all the data on his hard drive, and first Martel would no doubt have checked the file cabinets and the desk.

Everything relating to the deals with Victor Ganero had been verbal; the money was paid in cash and was now resting in his safe-deposit box.

Alvord leaned back and breathed slowly for a long time, pulling in oxygen, trying to calm himself.

Should he tell Harry Vlad about the mysterious visitor? What if it was Martel? After all, the game plan was to get Martel to surface.

The more Alvord thought about it, the less likely it rang true. Martel would never risk coming back to New York. Still, it wouldn't hurt to have the office checked for bugs.

Chapter 15

Lisa Cole wound some fettucini around her fork and smiled at Dan Heller.

They were seated at a window table at Fior D'Italia, the oldest Italian restaurant in San Francisco, situated at the corner of Grant and Union Streets in the heart of the North Beach district.

"This is very good," Cole said, slurping in the pasta. "I don't think I've ever had a policeman buy me dinner before."

"Who said anything about buying?" Heller asked, blotting up the sauce from his veal *picatta* with a hunk of sourdough French bread. "I just said let's have dinner."

"Ah," Lisa said, reaching for her wineglass, "chivalry really is dead."

"Chivalry dates back to when the knights of old protected helpless women. You're not helpless, and you lied to me." Heller twisted around to look over his shoulder at the street corner. "There were no accidents at Grant and Union on July fourteenth. Not a one all day."

"Maybe none that were reported to the police," Lisa countered.

"No ambulances responded to assist a man with an injured neck, Miss Cole. You told me a man had broken his neck, remember? Now quit bullshitting me. What's your interest in Mark Verre?"

Lisa sipped at her wine to stall for time. Heller certainly was a thorough policeman. "It's an insurance case. He's a witness. I can't go any farther, I'm afraid." She licked her lips slowly, then added, "Client confidentiality."

"Do you know where Verre is now?"

"No. Do you?"

Heller hoisted his wineglass and took an audible sip. "I know where the white Jeep Cherokee he drives is parked. On the roof level of the garage at San Francisco International Airport. But no one named Verre has booked a flight out of the airport. Do you speak French?"

"Not a word," Lisa replied, wondering where that line of questioning would lead.

"Verre. It's French for 'glass.' Clever, huh? A man goes into the wine business and changes his name to Verre."

"Verre changed his name?" Lisa nursed a pause, then said, "Why? From what?"

"Why do men usually change their names? I want—" Heller cut himself off when the waiter came by to top off their glasses and ask if everything was all right.

"Everything's wonderful," Lisa said, "but could I trouble you for separate checks?"

The waiter nodded his agreement and gave Heller a raised eyebrow. He wondered if this had been a blind date and the man had said something to upset the lovely young woman.

"I'm buying," Heller insisted. "You just better start coming across with some honest answers."

Lisa concentrated on her fettucini for several moments, letting her temper cool down. She wiped the plate clean, then finished her wine. "Honest answers, huh? How about some honesty from you, Inspector? This is an excellent restaurant. I was in another good restaurant in Calistoga. La Cucina. Your ex-wife, Arlene, owns the place. Does she have anything to do with your interest in Mark Verre? I hear that she and Verre are good friends. Are you doing a little private investigating on your own? Is that why you're giving me a hard time?"

"Who told you about my ex-wife?" Heller asked.

Lisa waved her fork in the air. "I mentioned the restaurant to Verre. He told me that he knew the owner and that her ex-husband was a policeman. He thought I might have heard of you."

Heller leaned back in his seat and folded his arms across his chest. "You can do better than that, Miss Cole. I'm interested in Verre because I don't like a man in the federal witness protection program hanging around my family."

"Is Verre in the federal witness protection program?" Lisa asked innocently.

"Yes, and he's an ex-con, too."

Lisa Cole turned her head away. Heller had pushed his story too far. She knew for certain that Mark had never been arrested, much less convicted of a crime. So Heller was just fishing. He'd scored a hit on the witness protection program, but struck out badly with the "ex-con" charge.

Heller screwed up his napkin. "Am I going to have to get a search warrant and go through your files, or will you start cooperating?"

Lisa stood up abruptly, plucked a twenty-dollar bill from her purse and let it flutter to the table. "That should take care of my dinner, Inspector. You do whatever you think you have to do." She turned on her heel and stalked off in the direction of the exit.

Heller watched her progress. Nice legs. And in such a hurry. To go where? He hadn't expected much information from Lisa Cole, but he'd gotten enough. Her reaction to his calling Verre an ex-con meant he wasn't. And she knew it. And her story about mentioning La Cucina to Verre and him telling her about Arlene made no sense at all. Cole had to have worked pretty hard to come up with the relationship between Arlene and Verre. Her accident-witness story was a phony. So what the hell was her real interest in Verre?

"Will that be all, sir?" the waiter asked.

"Yeah, sure. Put it all on one check."

He sipped at the wine, wondering what his next move would be. Lisa Cole certainly wasn't easily intimidated. The threat of a search warrant hadn't fazed her a bit.

The waiter presented the bill in a leather folder. Heller cursed under his breath as he withdrew a credit card from his wallet. Eighty-three bucks. He picked up the twenty-dollar bill Cole had left to cover her half of the dinner. Don't get mad, he advised himself. Get even.

Mechelle Burwell peered over her husband's burly shoulder at the wallpaper. Blue, she decided. An ice blue. She was tired of the pigeon gray. She made soft murmuring sounds and arched her back. "Oh, baby, hurry, hurry," she whispered huskily into her husband's ear, while she leaned out toward the edge of the bed to survey the carpeting. White, poodle-dog white, thick and long, or maybe—. She let her eyes glide back to Walter. His bald head bobbing up and down, his mouth fastened on her left breast. He was getting ready to climax, thank God. She scratched her fingers lightly across his back and increased the tempo of her hips. "Now, baby, now. I want—"

The wailing of a burglar alarm caused Walter Burwell to pull back.

"Shit," he bellowed, crawling clumsily out of the bed. He stumbled around for a few moments, hands outstretched, like a blind person feeling his way.

Mechelle leaned over to the nightstand and clicked on the light as Walter parted the bedroom drapes and glared out at the street.

"It's Jim Ballinger's Mercedes. Someone broke the damn window." He continued to watch as his neighbor ran out to survey the damage.

Mechelle shook her head at the sight of her husband's profile. His belly was a solid mass the size of a beach ball. "Slipped muscle," as he liked to say. His penis was still erect and swollen. That damn Viagra. It was so much better when Walter had blamed his lack of sexual interest on his work. Now he took a Viagra pill three times a week.

Burwell padded back to bed, one hand lightly stroking his penis. "Unfinished business, baby." He reached out with one hand, tangling it in her long hair, pulling her face to him. "Finish it, baby. Finish it now."

Mechelle opened her lips and closed her eyes. Goddamn burglar alarm. Goddamn Walter. Goddamn Viagra.

Harry Vlad noticed that the light was now on in the upstairs room of the Burwell residence. There were lights popping on in half the houses on the street, just as he'd hoped. They had all heard the car's alarm go off. If the Burwells' house alarm went off when he broke in, it probably wouldn't be a big deal to them; they would assume it was just another car alarm.

He slouched back in the seat of the rented Jaguar, checked his watch, and waited to see if the local police had been called. After fifteen minutes he switched on the car's engine and motored slowly down the street. A man in slippers and a Burberry trench coat was sweeping up the glass on the street. The Mercedes was now covered with a tarp. He barely glanced up at the Jag before going back to his sweeping.

Harry was set now. Earlier that morning there had been three contractors' pickup trucks parked in the driveway, one belonging to an electrician, one to a cabinetmaker, the third to a painter. Harry had watched the workmen troop in and out. The dominant overall color was white, so he purchased a pair of white overalls and a white cap and simply strolled unnoticed into the house. The controls of the security alarm were right where they were shown to be on the building permit plans. He slipped a transmitter into both of the units, the one at the front door and the one near the sliding door leading to the back deck.

Burwell had set the alarm an hour or so ago, and the recorder in the Jag's glove compartment had captured each and every beep. Harry ran it through a decoder and came up with the code: 3562.

Now he would wait for Walter Burwell and the beautiful Mrs. Burwell to go sailing, shopping, or whatever, then snatch the Ghiberti statue. It didn't matter to Harry how long that would take—he still had the job in San Francisco ready and waiting. It made little difference to him. Whichever came first.

He didn't relish another trip to Arizona. Maybe he could talk George Alvord into delivering the statue. Let Georgie Boy go through that pat-down search from Tony Zarela.

Harry chuckled at the thought of Alvord's being pawed by Big Soup. He made an abrupt left turn and pulled into an open parking spot in front of Sam's, a waterfront saloon where he'd had lunch. They had a dock for bayside customers, and Harry had taken a break from his surveillance chores. A low fog rolled down the street, making the pavement Vaseline shiny. The red neon bar sign gave off an eerie glow, like blood seeping through a bandage of fog. There had been women all over the joint during the lunch hour. Maybe they came out at night, too. He figured he'd earned himself a couple of drinks. And maybe a couple of girls.

Chapter 16

After the flight back from New York, Mark Martel
stopped long enough at the San Francisco airport to
retrieve the snub-nosed revolver and the derringer
from the Jeep, then took a cab and had the driver
drop him off at Union Square in San Francisco.

It was two in the morning when he found a room
in a small hotel on Post Street that accepted cash. He
signed the register with his left hand, under the name
Jim Smith. The hotel clerk had false teeth and lisped
when he talked.

"Are you just going to be here the one night, Mr.
Smith?" he asked in a tone that suggested he had no
interest in an answer.

Mark woke at eight, showered, dressed, and took a
walk on the bustling downtown streets, stopping for
breakfast at Sears Fine Foods Restaurant on Powell
Street.

He ordered the house special, silver-dollar pan-
cakes, and handed the waitress his check with the
exact change and a ten-dollar bill.

"Give me five dollars worth of quarters, and the
rest is your tip," he told the waitress.

He crossed the street to the Sir Francis Drake
Hotel, the coins jingling in his pocket. The doorman,
resplendent in his authentic Beefeater Royal Guard
uniform, directed him to the bank of pay phones.

Arlene Severi answered the phone with a sharp
"Who is it?"

"It's me."

Arlene wedged the phone between her chin and shoulder while she wiped her flour-coated hands on her apron. "Mark. You're back. Why don't we—"

"I'm not home yet," he advised her. "But soon. Is everything okay? Are you taking good care of Gauguin?"

Arlene looked over at the door leading to the outdoor patio. Gauguin was parked there, his head resting on his paws, staring back at her. "I can't sleep and he won't eat, Mark. Can you believe that? He hardly touches anything."

"I'll be home in a couple of days. How's Carrie? She should be able to get him to eat."

"Oh, she's fine. Her father's been pestering her. She's off with him somewhere now."

"Heller's still hanging around, then," Mark said, with a mixture of relief and concern.

Arlene took a few seconds to respond. "Oh, yes, Dan's been around. He's becoming a bother."

"He still loves you."

"He thinks he does," Arlene said, her voice suddenly very serious. "Are you all right?"

"I'm fine. A few more days, then I'll be back and explain everything."

Arlene's voice dropped to a soft, childlike whisper. "I miss you."

"I miss you, too. Has there been anyone around asking for me?"

"No. Oh—Joan Hatton came by. She didn't seem to be her usual self."

"Did Joan mention anyone coming to the winery asking for me?"

"No. Nothing like that. She was just . . . worried about you."

"Joan's concerned about the upcoming harvest. Take care of Gauguin. And yourself," he added before breaking the connection.

His next call was to his home number for messages. There was one call.

"Hey. That policeman is being a real pest. Call me."

Lisa Cole's voice. Mark pushed the button to erase the call, then immediately dialed Cole's number, getting her answering machine. He said, "Hello, it's me," hoping that she was there, monitoring her calls. After a few seconds' wait, he hung up. "That policeman." He wondered just what Dan Heller was up to.

Mark nursed a cup of coffee while waiting for Dunhill's to open its doors, all the while worrying about the thief and how he'd tracked him to San Francisco.

The tobacco salesman greeted him cheerfully as he purchased a twenty-five-count box of Partagas double coronas, paying in cash. He then made his way into the private humidor room. The walls consisted of floor-to-ceiling personal cigar lockers. Mark's locker was the largest size available, three feet by four feet. He stood on an oak stepstool and used a small key, quite similar to the key that had frustrated Charlie Dwyer. That key had belonged to a locker in a private humidor room in Dunhill's Manhattan store.

There were more than a dozen cedar cigar boxes neatly stacked inside the locker. He gently removed one of the boxes, cradling it in his hands for a moment before lifting the lid. It had been more than three years since he'd had any reason to open that box. Inside was a variety of oddly shaped tungsten lock picks, a clear plastic matchbook-size box holding a series of tiny silicon chips, and an envelope-size electronic receiver.

Mark slipped the box into the bag the salesman had provided, then climbed up on the stool again and removed another box. It was stuffed with cash—a mixture of twenty-, fifty-, and hundred-dollar bills, all neatly rubber-banded in packets, each packet totaling five thousand dollars. He pocketed four of the packets, then ran his hands over two baton-size aluminum cylinders before closing the locker. One cylinder contained a Matisse drawing, the other a Degas charcoal. He'd purchased both in Paris some fifteen years ago.

They were all that was left of his collection. The rest he'd sold when Joan had accepted his offer to become a partner in the Hatton Winery.

He glanced at his watch when he was back out on Post Street and thought of calling Lisa Cole again. Was it too soon to tell her about the information he'd picked up in New York City?

A man had spread a ragged gray blanket on the pavement next to a street-side flower stand. The contrast was startling. The rainbow profusion of roses, carnations, daisies, and mums, and the beggar squatting Indian-style on the blanket. He wore a San Francisco Giants baseball cap that was too big for his narrow skull and practically rested on the rims of his ears. His skin was gray as putty, and his wrinkled flannel jacket at least two sizes too large.

He held a Styrofoam cup in one hand and asked in a reedy voice, "Got something for a Gulf vet?"

Mark dropped a few dollars into the cup. The man's rheumy eyes caught his.

"Thanks, pal. Wouldn't have a smoke, would you?"

"Matter of fact, I do." Mark tugged the box of just-purchased cigars out of the Dunhill's bag and dropped it on the soiled blanket.

Next, he found a branch of Radio Shack and purchased a cell phone with a built-in pager. As soon as he left the store, he used the phone to call Noel Field at the Pine Inn, in Carmel. Field was out, and Mark left his new pager number, then dialed Lisa Cole and left the same message on her answering machine.

Mark did some more shopping, picking up binoculars and a dark-blue jacket and cap at Eddie Bauer, then a camcorder at a camera shop on Kearny Street, and finally, a rental car.

He drove the new shark-gray Ford Taurus away from the rental agency, taking it on a trial run out to Golden Gate Park. He stopped in a grove of towering eucalyptus trees, removed the car's front license plate, and smeared mud over the rear plate. Then he sat in the car and studied the addresses he'd found on George Alvord's computer. It was time to begin the hunt.

The first address, 2850 Larkin Street, was a tall, narrow high-rise apartment with balconies on all four sides. The entrance gate was manned by a security guard. Mark used the binoculars and spotted another guard at the building's main door. Unless he wanted to scale the exterior, the thief would have to slip by the two guards, and once inside the building there would be a honeycomb of apartments with people coming and going throughout the day and night. An alarm going off for even a few seconds would penetrate the walls of neighboring apartments and alert nervous tenants.

He would never have attempted a burglary here, and, he reasoned, since the thief was imitating him, neither would he.

He drove west, out toward the ocean, curving through the upscale residences in Sea Cliff, past the California Palace of the Legion of Honor. The museum was featuring a Picasso exhibition, and the trails and parking lots were jammed.

The second address on the list, 999 El Camino Del Mar, was much more promising. So promising that Mark worried that the thief might be somewhere in the neighborhood now, on a stakeout. It was the last residence on the street, before the road ventured into the Lands End portion of the Golden Gate National Recreation Area. The front of the home appeared modest enough, a neatly trimmed box hedge fronting a one-story Spanish villa with a tile roof.

It was only after you drove past the house and observed it from the west side that you could make out the four floors descending toward the jagged rocks hugging the coastline. A cantilevered staircase bordered the house, ending in a hook-shaped deck that hovered over China Beach.

A possibility, he judged. Access from the front, the

side, and, if a man didn't mind dangling out over a hundred-foot drop to those jagged rocks below, the rear. The wooded park area provided a dozen havens where the thief could observe the house with little fear of being noticed.

Mark then drove to Belvedere Street, the third address on Alvord's list. Why hadn't Alvord posted a number for the house? Was it too dangerous? Or perhaps he just didn't have all the information yet.

Belvedere was a nine-block stretch of attached, wood-frame buildings that dated back to the turn of the century, starting at Haight Street and climbing up toward Twin Peaks. There were still some remnants of the flower children on Haight Street, sallow-faced young wanna-bes in sixties fashions, a few young women with wilting flowers in their unkempt hair, and mostly middle-aged men with cloudy eyes and scraggly beards.

Mark parked and walked the entire distance of Belvedere Street. There were a few well-maintained homes, but none that looked like they could afford to accommodate a Ghiberti statue.

He stopped for lunch at Bill's Place on Clement Street, doodling sketches of the El Camino Del Mar house while waiting for his cheeseburger, putting himself in the thief's skin, planning an assault on the property.

It was an inviting target.

Mark parked a good mile from the El Camino Del Mar residence and hiked through the woods, finding a perch in a cypress tree just up the road from the house. A cold, gusty wind, tinged with moisture from the Pacific Ocean, rattled the tree branches. Nightfall slowly blotted out the sky. Lights were on in the target house, and Mark could see shadowed outlines of a man, two women, and a couple of young boys through the backlighted curtains.

He focused the Sony camcorder he'd paid $860 for on the house. The salesman had guaranteed him that the NightShot camera could take clear video pictures in total darkness. He never explained just who would want to film something in total darkness. The 72X-definition lens showed a ghostly outline of the house and the surrounding shrubbery.

He was chiding himself for not bringing a thermos of coffee along when he caught sight of a rustling shadow moving off to his left. A man, hunched over, edging into the shrubbery, merging with the darkness, no more than twenty-five yards away.

Mark couldn't make a move without alerting him. He fought back a sneeze, jamming a gloved hand against his nose. Fifteen minutes. Twenty minutes. Twenty-four minutes, and the shadow moved off in a hurry. He tried picking the man up on the camcorder without success, then shimmied down the tree. His footsteps made crunching sounds in the leaves as he advanced slowly in the darkness. The shadow had moved south, up the street toward where Mark had parked his car.

He quickened his pace at the sound of a car door slamming shut, then broke out in a run when he heard the angry rasp of an engine turning over.

Headlights cut a path through the night air, and he caught a quick glimpse of twin red taillights before they disappeared around a curve.

Mark pounded a fist into his palm in frustration. He hadn't gotten a decent glimpse of the man, or the car. It could have been Gassiot, Seimsen, Vlad, or Welz. Whoever it was, the people in the house had scared him away. Would he come back? That was the question.

Chapter 17

Noel Field's first impression of Carmel by the Sea was of how small it was. The main drag, Ocean Avenue, was chalk-line straight and ran on a downward slope for a mile or so before bumping into the Pacific Ocean.

The streets crisscrossing Ocean were narrow affairs crammed with commercial buildings, the majority of which were pixilated, oddly shaped one-story shops and art galleries. The green-and-white clapboard Pine Inn was a positive skyscraper at three stories. Farther down the streets were quaint flower-bordered cottages with wave-shingle roofs.

Field wandered in and out of several of the galleries to get the feel of the place. The paintings on display appeared quite amateurish to him, but he was prepared to take off his hat and applaud if the dealers were getting anywhere near the affixed price tags.

He searched in vain for a bar for nearly thirty minutes before finding a small cocktail lounge tucked between an Old English tea shoppe and a store that specialized in custom-designed wind chimes.

Fortified by a Bloody Mary, he made his way to Rudy Seimsen's gallery, Faux-You. The too-cute name had him wondering if Rudy was having an early bout with senility.

The front window featured an array of oil reproductions of the more commercially popular works of artists such as Rembrandt, Whistler, Renoir, and Salvador Dali.

The gallery's interior consisted of white ceilings and walls and highly polished hardwood flooring. Soft, nonthreatening classical music was piped through invisible speakers.

There were a dozen or more customers, most of them clustered around a wall slathered with faux Van Goghs. Noel had an overpowering urge to touch one of them to see if the paint had dried yet.

"Wonderful, aren't they?" a slim woman with a sharp-boned nose and wine-black hair done up in a bun remarked. "Van Gogh is one of our most popular artists."

Field nodded at the group standing nearby. "Cut off your ear and they shall come, eh?" he said with a grin.

The woman managed a pale smile in response. "Is there something I can help you with, sir?"

"Yes. I'm an old friend of Rudy's. From New York. Is he in?"

"I'll find out," she promised, stopping to chat with the sham Van Gogh worshipers before disappearing through a beaded curtain at the rear of the gallery.

Field was examining a copy of a Piet Mondrian abstract, royal-blue squares bounded by black outlines, when Rudy Seimsen came out to greet him.

Rudy had aged, Field thought, but then, who hadn't. Seimsen's once-red hair had turned a sandy-gray color. He had a long-chinned face, and shaggy brows canopied the sockets of his eyes. He was wearing a black cashmere turtleneck sweater and neatly pressed jeans. Carmel chic, Field assumed. He didn't look at all like the chain-smoking, hard-drinking thief he'd once known.

"Noel. What brings you to Carmel?" Seimsen asked. All traces of his New York accent were gone.

"I was visiting my daughter in Los Angeles and thought I'd motor up to San Francisco. I couldn't pass by without stopping to see you, Rudy." Field turned his attention back to the Mondrian abstract. "Am I mistaken, or is that shade of blue a little brighter than the original?"

"You're correct. The buyer is a University of California alumnus. He brought me his old football jersey to match the shade just right."

"Good heavens," Noel mocked, his nose wrinkling in disgust. "Come, let's go somewhere for a drink."

Seimsen upturned his palms. "I've given it up. Come on in the back, and we can have tea."

Noel followed Seimsen through the beaded curtain, past a chain of cubicles, each outfitted with a desk, computer, telephone, and young woman seemingly hard at work.

"I do a big catalog business," Rudy explained, holding apart the beads of yet another curtain for Field.

The room into which he was led was a small lounge, complete with stove, refrigerator, and microwave.

"Sit, sit," Seimsen said, waving his hand at the padded chairs surrounding a round Formica-topped table.

"You seem to be doing quite well," Field said as he gingerly lowered himself into a sculptured plastic chair.

"It's fantastic, Noel. Fantastic. I wish I had met Linda years ago."

"Linda?"

"My wife. You spoke to her in the gallery." A mischievous grin appeared on Seimsen's features. He placed a cup of herb tea in front of Field and sat down across from him. "What do you think of the place?"

"Beats stealing, doesn't it?"

Seimsen let out a deep, throaty laugh. "Indeed." He sipped tea and eyed Noel through the steam. "And what of you, old friend? Have you given up the game?"

"Almost. I've been contacted by a client who has a keen interest in a certain item. Unfortunately I'm no longer capable of completing the transaction by myself, Rudy."

"You're crazy," Seimsen scoffed. "It's not worth it at this time of your life."

Noel took a sip of the tea. It tasted like warm orange juice. "I've made a few investments that haven't quite panned out, so I'm afraid I do have to go back to work."

"You're still at the Plaza?"

"Oh, yes. Most definitely," Field assured him.

"That might be the only thing that would bring me back to New York. Your hotel suite, Noel. But surely you don't think that I would come back to—"

"No, no. Of course not. I was just wondering if you knew of any able young men who might be in the need of a job."

"Me? I've been gone too long. You must still have connections, Noel."

Field settled his cup on its saucer. "I spoke to George Alvord the other night. He says he's out of the game too."

"Alvord will never go straight," Seimsen contended. "George screwed me out of more than my share of money, I can tell you that." He got to his feet and poked his head through the beaded curtain, then sat down, scuffing his chair close to Field's.

"A week or so ago I had another visitor, Noel. Harry Vlad."

"Really? I heard he was in prison."

"He's been out since early in the year. He looked prosperous, though. Very prosperous. Gold watch, tailored clothes, fifty-dollar haircut. Driving a jazzy new Jaguar convertible with dealer's paper plates. 'Champagne-colored,' he told me it was. Knowing Harry, he probably leased it with a phony credit card."

"Yes, that certainly sounds like Harry. I wonder where I could reach him?"

Seimsen waved his hands in front of him, like an umpire signaling the slider safe. "I don't know, Noel. And I really don't want to know."

"You didn't happen to notice the dealer's name on the Jag's plates, did you, Rudy?"

"No," Seimsen said firmly.

"Too bad," Field said, shifting uneasily in the chair. "Harry might be just the man for my job."

Mark was back at the El Camino Del Mar house at eight the following morning. At twenty after the hour a silver Mercedes sedan glided out of the garage and turned north.

It was close to noon when the hum of his pager caught Mark off guard for a moment. He saw that the incoming number had an 831 area code. Carmel. Noel Field.

He phoned the number and Noel answered cheerfully.

"Harry Vlad's your man, son. I'm sure of it. He was down here in Carmel flaunting himself at Rudy Seimsen a week or so ago."

"You're sure that Rudy isn't just pushing this off on Harry?"

"Positive. Rudy is raking in an unbelievable amount of money with his wonderful little faux art scam. It's positively disgusting, and it's all actually legal. Rudy said Harry is looking fit and prosperous. He was salivating over his brand-new Jaguar convertible. Champagne-colored—that's Harry, all right."

"Did Rudy have any idea where Vlad is?"

"No. I don't think Rudy really appreciated Harry's visit. Or mine, truth be told."

"Thanks, Noel. I really appreciate your help."

"I'm coming up there, Mark. San Francisco. I know Harry better than anyone. I'll help you find him."

"No," Mark protested. "You've stuck your neck out far enough. I don't want—"

"I'm coming. I take it as a personal affront that Harry is using information I gave him to go after you. I'll be there in time for dinner. Pick a place where we can meet."

Mark had forgotten how stubborn Noel could be. "All right. Louis', on Point Lobos. Six o'clock."

*   *   *

Noel Field examined the plastic menu with raised eyebrows. "I had heard that San Francisco had a reasonable number of gourmet restaurants." He looked at Mark over the top of the menu. "This, I hope, isn't one of them."

"Stick to the omelets," Mark suggested. "It's more of a breakfast place, but it's close to where I want to be tonight."

He slid some maps and diagrams he'd made of the house on El Camino Del Mar across the table to Field. "This was on Alvord's list. I was there last night. Someone showed up. I just caught a glimpse, not enough to recognize him."

"It was Vlad," Noel asserted.

"Whoever it was, he didn't stick around long. The house is occupied by a big family. I was there today, too. There were two kids running in and out. A woman in an apron hollered for them to come in for lunch."

Noel scrutinized the drawings. "That must be driving Harry crazy. What is inside the house? I've forgotten."

"A Lippi oil of the Crucifixion."

"What does Victor Ganero see in all these morbid things?" Field asked, rubbing his mustache. "Does he think that somehow his sins will be forgiven him because he collected the paintings? What was the name of the thief on the cross next to Jesus?"

"Dimis," Mark supplied.

"Then Ganero must see himself as Dimis. I do believe he's in for a shock when he gets to those pearly gates.

"Harry doesn't dare make a move while there are people inside, does he?"

"Not if he wants to continue impersonating me."

The waitress, a short, smiling woman with hair dyed raven-black, who must have been in her eighties, came over and took their orders.

"My word, she makes even me feel young," Field observed when the waitress had shuffled out to the kitchen. "So what are our plans? We wait for Harry to make a move, catch him, and turn him over to the authorities?"

"No. If Harry suspects I'm onto him, he tells Alvord or Ganero."

"What, then?"

"There's a private investigator, working for the insurance company. Lisa Cole. What I'd like to do is set her up, let her film Harry when we know he's about to go in."

"And is this Miss Cole joining us tonight?" Field asked.

"I haven't been able to make contact with her." Mark reached for the maps. He tapped his finger on a circle of trees. "I'm going to be here again, in these trees, tonight. If I catch sight of Harry, maybe I can follow him."

Field shook his lionesque head slowly back and forth. "Harry isn't anywhere near as good as you, Mark, but he's not a fool. If you get too close, he'll know you're there."

"I know that. All I want to do is spot him and follow him to where he's living now."

"Forget spotting Harry," Field suggested. "Find the Jaguar, Mark. Follow the car, not the man."

Field held his silence when the elderly waitress delivered his cheese omelet. He tested the eggs with his fork. "Mark, this is all well and good, but what if dear Harry doesn't make a move on this house tonight? Or tomorrow? Or next week?"

"I don't have much time, Noel. If something doesn't happen soon, Charlie Dwyer will throw me to the wolves. He wouldn't care a bit if I went to jail for these thefts, even if he knew I wasn't the thief. I've got to hope that Vlad makes an appearance. I don't have much else to go on."

Mark edged into the branches of the gnarled cypress tree. The poker-red glare of the sun had been swallowed up by the ocean a half hour ago. He was in the middle of the tree, some fifteen feet off the ground, with a perfect view of El Camino Del Mar. The branches formed a loosely thatched canopy around him.

The target house was well lit again, and he could see people moving from room to room. An hour later the fog had rolled in, like mist on a mirror at first, then thickening so that it blotted out everything beyond twenty-five yards. The woeful blast of the Mile Rock lighthouse foghorn soon got on his nerves. He hunched his shoulders and did isometrics to keep warm.

There was a sudden flick of movement to his left. A Jaguar convertible cruised gently past the house. It rolled to a stop by a cluster of pine trees and was quickly shrouded by the fog.

Mark slipped silently down from the tree and moved cautiously through the trail to where he'd parked the rented Ford Taurus.

Noel Field was sprawled across the front seat, a thermos in hand.

Mark yanked the door open. "Harry just drove by the house!"

Noel gulped down the coffee and capped the thermos. "I didn't see a Jaguar. But in this soup a battleship might have cruised by and I'd have missed it."

Fifteen minutes. Half an hour at the most, Mark estimated, before Harry decided that there was no way to get into the house tonight.

Mark switched on the ignition key and nursed the engine to life.

"What if Harry leaves by a different route?" Noel asked.

"Then we're screwed. But if we pull out now and he sees us, he'll vanish."

"I always hated the waiting," Noel said tightly. "Always hated that the most."

Mark nodded almost imperceptibly. "Me too."

They both recognized the outline of the Jaguar convertible as it sped past them.

Mark slipped the transmission into gear. "Here we go."

Harry Vlad slammed both feet on the brake pedal to avoid the trunk of a towering pine tree that suddenly emerged from the fog. The Jaguar skidded out of control briefly, then straightened out.

He leaned forward, his chest touching the steering wheel as he maneuvered along the curving, dew-slick road. It had been a waste of time. The bloody people *never* left the house. All that work down the drain. He'd gained entrance to the house six days ago. Decked out like a telephone repairman, he'd first cut the phone line, then simply knocked on the front door. The moon-faced maid had been suspicious at first, but once she picked up the phone and verified that the line was out, she let Harry in. The alarm-system box was right where it should have been, within six feet of the front door. Harry had positioned the transmitting device, then he went outside and reconnected the telephone line. It worked perfectly, and he had the code that same night. But they just goddamn *never* left the house. There was always someone there: the owner and his wife, or their maid, the *au pair,* and the damn kids.

He felt frustrated. The only reasonable thing to do was forget about that job for a week or two and concentrate on the Belvedere house. That thought didn't do much to relieve his frustration. Some good coke and a big-titted blonde was what he needed.

Mark followed the Jaguar through the park in the fog with his lights off. Once the wheels of the Taurus went off the road, and Noel Field let out a frightened yelp before the wheels caught in the gravel and propelled them forward.

The Jag took a right on Twenty-fifth Avenue, and Mark blew a long blast of air between his lips in relief.

If Harry had turned left into the wooded Presidio, he doubted that he could have kept him in sight.

He flicked on the Ford's headlights and mimicked Harry Vlad's path.

"If we can keep up with him, we've got it made," Noel Field assured him.

"That's a big if," Mark contended.

"Harry must be feeling poorly," Noel reasoned. "He no doubt thinks that he was cheated out of a chance at the Lippi painting. Knowing him as well as I do, Harry will drown his sorrow in gin or cocaine. And a woman."

The Jaguar slowed for a stoplight at Geary Boulevard and Mark pulled to the curb, fearful of getting too close. He got a clean look at the driver's profile as the Jaguar turned east on the green light. It definitely was Harry Vlad.

The Jaguar continued on the ribbon-straight boulevard at a leisurely pace, heading downtown. Vlad took a right on Polk Street, throttling down to loitering speed as he approached O'Farrell.

"That's Harry's idea of a good time," Noel Field observed, pointing to the garish purple building on the corner whose marquee advertised CONTINUOUS NAKED WOMEN. LAP DANCING! PRIVATE BOOTHS.

"I wonder what the devil lap dancing is?" Field mused. "It certainly sounds painful."

The Jaguar took off again, crossing Market Street, then turning left on Folsom. Harry Vlad pulled in behind a string of double-parked cars sitting in front of a three-story brick building. A red, white, and blue neon sign featured a scantily clad cowgirl riding bareback on a steam-snorting stallion. The words "Winky's Den" flashed over her head every few seconds.

Harry alighted from the Jag, tossing the car keys in the air before handing them to a white-jacketed parking attendant, then strolled past a restless, thick-pressed queue of young men and women waiting to gain entrance to the nightclub.

Harry ran up the canopy-sheltered steps and disappeared.

Noel Field cupped his ears with the palms of his hands. "Good Lord, that music! If it's that loud on the street, how can they stand it inside?"

"Let's hope Harry doesn't stay too long." Mark circled the block, parking in front of a fire hydrant, giving them a view of the club's entrance.

They didn't have to wait long. Harry Vlad reappeared before the attendant had the opportunity to move the Jaguar. Harry's arm was draped over the shoulders of a statuesque brunette in a jagged metallic mesh mini-dress scooped low in front.

She tottered on high heels as Harry tipped the attendant.

"Go to your place, not hers, Harry," Field prayed.

The Jaguar took off in a squeal of burned rubber, fishtailing to a stop at the first red light. The brunette's head dipped from view until the light turned green and didn't pop up until Harry turned into the garage of the Bay Tower Apartments.

Noel Field closed his eyes and massaged his temples. "Mark, my boy, I think this calls for a damn big drink."

Chapter 18

"Lisa, are you sure you still want to go through with this?" Bonnie Nelson asked as she guided her van to a smooth stop on Blackhawk Drive. Less than two hundred yards away, around a wall of flowering oleander, was the gated entrance to Casa Ganero.

"Absolutely," Lisa Cole responded, checking the rear-view mirror to make sure that the cleaning crew's old jalopy had pulled in behind them.

A lance of sunlight bounced off the windshield of Nelson's stakeout van. Lisa tilted the mirror and examined her makeup. It would have to do. The Minox camera was nestled in her hair, which she'd swept up on top of her head and covered with an Arizona Diamondbacks baseball cap that she'd borrowed from Bonnie.

"I still think you should have a mike on you, so I can monitor what's going on in there," Nelson said.

"Nothing's going to happen," Lisa assured her. "They're not going to do anything to three cleaning women." She glanced over at Bonnie, who had fluffy white hair and a chunky body. The desert sun had turned her face into a road map of wrinkles. She was nearing sixty and looked every day of it.

Lisa rested her hand on Bonnie's shoulder. "If I don't come out by one o'clock, think of something."

"Think of something," Nelson scoffed. "You're going into the dragon's cave, and I'm supposed to pull a rabbit out of the hat if you get into trouble."

"I'll be fine," Lisa assured her, then added with a wink, "but don't go too far away."

She hopped out of the car and strode back to the bird-bombed 1982 Pontiac. The car brought back memories of her father. He'd had an identical Pontiac when he was an army colonel stationed in Lubbock, Texas. He'd pulled rank and had a private assigned to clean and polish the car daily.

The Spanish that Lisa had picked up in Texas helped her communicate with the owner of the Pontiac, Dolores Gonzales, her sister Carmela, and niece, Maria, who worked four hours a day, five days a week, cleaning house at Casa Ganero.

Bonnie Nelson had spotted them on the first day's surveillance film and followed them to their home on Cody Street in South Phoenix.

The two Gonzales sisters spoke very little English and at first didn't volunteer much information, other than that they cleaned and did laundry for Señor Ganero.

Maria spoke some English and was happy to fill Lisa and Bonnie in on the layout of the house and just who was usually there. There were times when a guest arrived, and they were ordered to leave right away.

Señor Ganero was seldom seen. If he did happen to come across them, the women were told to look at the ground and remain silent until he left their presence. Victor Ganero was described as *anciano,* an old man.

There were two men who followed them around while they went about their chores. One, *el hombre grande,* was named Tony but was called Sopa Grande by the other man, whose name was Sineo.

The Gonzales sisters hated having a man watching over them all the time—so much so that they were planning to quit soon.

Maria gestured, laughed, and spoke in Spanish so rapidly that Lisa had to have Bonnie Nelson translate much of what was said. Tony Big Soup was constantly trying to lure Maria away from her aunts. Maria pretended not to understand any English and delighted in hearing the big man swear in frustration when she refused to go with him.

Lisa's story that she was a reporter and wanted to get a look at the inside of the mansion was greeted with suspicion, but Maria was not at all hesitant to accept two hundred dollars to take the day off and let Lisa go in her place. Dolores and Carmela Gonzales argued at first, but each agreed to accept a like amount. After all, if they were getting ready to quit anyway, why not?

Lisa opened the door to the Pontiac and said, *"Buenos dias"* to the Gonzales sisters.

They greeted her coldly, and Lisa felt sure that they now regretted their decision to take her along. She gave Bonnie a thumbs-up as they passed her van.

The old Pontiac's brakes squealed shrilly as Dolores Gonzales bucked the car to a halt in front of the iron gates protecting the entrance to Casa Ganero. She beeped the horn three times.

Minutes later a man in a dark suit came into view and used a key to unlock the gate.

"Es Sineo," Carmela Gonzales whispered softly.

The Pontiac bumped and heaved its way slowly through the gate, stopping alongside a serpentine brick wall. Nearby was an algae-streaked marble fountain, featuring a statue of a muscular man in a toga spilling water from a jar over his right shoulder into a series of oval-shaped pools. Citrus trees, heavy with lemons and oranges, covered a sloping meadow that led down to a stand of olive trees.

The man jogged over and peered into the car's windows.

"Who the hell is she?" Sineo demanded, pointing at Lisa. "Where's the other one?"

Dolores Gonzales climbed laboriously out of the

car. *"Maria es enferma."* She patted her ample stomach. *"Influenza."*

"Get out," Sineo ordered, walking to the other side of the car.

Lisa had been warned that she would be searched, and she held out her purse. Sineo sifted through it, his eyes blinking in annoyance. Big Soup wouldn't like this, the good-looking one being sick. Maria. Hell, maybe she didn't have the flu. Maybe Tony had knocked her up. He was always saying how he was going to nail her one of these days. He handed the woman back her purse and ran his eyes over her body. She wasn't that bad-looking. Her jeans weren't as tight as Maria's. A baggy gray T-shirt stretched down almost to her knees. He wanted to find out what was under that shirt.

"What's your name, Dolly?" he asked as he lightly ran his hands over her shoulders, down her back, and around front to cop a feel. *"Como se llama?"*

"Rosa," Lisa said, pushing his hands away from her.

"Hable English? Well, my little flower, you stay real close to the old ones, okay?"

Dolores Gonzales scuttled between them. *"Trabajo,"* she said. "We go to work."

Lisa fell in between the Gonzales sisters and started up the cobbled stairway leading to Casa Ganero, or the dragon's cave, according to Bonnie Nelson.

Mark had to approve of Harry Vlad's choice of living quarters. The Bay Tower Apartments was a modern, fifteen-story complex of rough concrete, the exterior textured by hammers and drills and still showing the marks of the wooden framework. The windows were nothing more than rectangular holes in the walls.

What it lacked in looks, it more than made up for in location—Front Street, near the Embarcadero—providing easy access to the Bay and Golden Gate Bridges and within walking distance of Pier 39 and trendy restaurants along the city's waterfront. Parking spots were for the most part nonexistent, so keeping tabs on the apartment entrance or the garage was going to be difficult.

He had dropped Noel Field off at the Mark Hopkins Hotel last night, after they had followed Vlad to the apartment building. Noel had complained right away that it wasn't the Plaza, but it would have to do.

Mark had hurried back to the Bay Tower, slumping down behind the steering wheel, dozing off and on during the night.

He managed to sneak into the garage at daybreak. The Jaguar was in its parking stall. He was tempted to get inside the Jag, but Harry no doubt had booby traps on the doors and trunk.

He called Lisa Cole several times but always got her answering machine. Lisa had been all over him for a week, and now that he needed her she was nowhere to be found. Where the hell was she?

Lisa Cole was panting and out of breath. Keeping up with the Gonzales sisters was harder than she'd thought it would be. Both Dolores and Carmela had chided her for not moving fast enough and for leaving streaks on the windows. They hurried through their tasks of vacuuming, dusting, and polishing the furniture.

Lisa and Bonnie Nelson had obtained a good description of the house from Maria and made a rough diagram. There was only one room in the house that the women were never allowed to enter. The *capilla,* chapel, which was located just down the hallway from the kitchen.

They were in the kitchen now, Dolores on her knees scrubbing the floor, Carmela wiping down the stove and refrigerator.

Sineo had stuck to them like glue for most of the morning. Now he was gone, and Lisa decided that this was her chance.

She slipped through the kitchen door and into the

hallway. She took a deep breath as she approached
the door to what should be the chapel. She had moved
the Minox camera from her hair to her pants pocket
an hour ago, and she'd been able to take several photographs of paintings that hung on the walls in the
living and dining rooms. They were all landscapes and
in no way matched the photographs or descriptions of
the stolen masterpieces. Without bringing the camera
to her eye, she clicked off several photographs of the
massive chapel door. She was reaching for the cross-
shaped brass door handle when suddenly her left arm
felt like it was being wrenched from its socket.

"Where the hell are you going?" Tony Zarela
roared, tossing her across the hall like a rag doll.

She bounced off the wall and fell to the floor, one
hand desperately trying to slide the camera into the
back pocket of her jeans.

Zarela pounced on her, knocking her hat off and
picking her up by the hair, his snarling face inches
from hers. "What are you doing here?"

Lisa twisted her head away and screamed, *"Ayuda
me!"* at the top of her lungs.

The Gonzales sisters burst into the hallway. Carmela ran directly to Lisa and wrapped stout arms
around her waist.

"Hey, Big Soup! What happened?"

Zarela turned to face Sineo, his hand still holding
on to Lisa's hair. She was standing on her tiptoes, one
hand desperately fumbling for Carmela's apron.

"Did you let this bitch in?" Zarela shouted at Sineo.

"They said Maria is sick," Sineo answered. "What's
she doing out here?"

Zarela released his grip and Lisa sank to the floor,
her right hand dropping the camera into Carmela's
apron pocket.

Zarela yanked Lisa by the hair again. "She was trying to get into the chapel."

Both Carmela and Dolores were screaming at him
in Spanish.

Zarela pushed Lisa against the wall, his left hand clasping her throat while his right roughly probed her body.

It wasn't the soft search that Sineo had performed earlier. Zarela's fingers poked and prodded, and he cupped his palm over one breast, then the other, squeezing so hard that Lisa gave a muffled cry of pain.

"Tony, for Christ's sake, let the *battona* go," Sineo said. "We got more important things to think about. The mail just came in. Take a look at this."

Zarela shoved Lisa to the floor and snatched the mail from Sineo's hand. "What the fuck's so important?"

"It's a postcard. Some guy wants to know if the don is still interested in—"

"Shut up," Zarela growled, cutting Sineo off. His eyebrows merged in irritation as he read the card.

Lisa was on her knees. Her mouth was wide open, gasping for breath, her hands massaging her throat.

She was able to see the front of the postcard, which displayed a photograph of the Golden Gate Bridge.

Zarela tore his eyes away from the postcard and stared daggers at Lisa. "Get this bitch out of here and don't let her come back." He turned to face the cowering figures of Dolores and Carmela Gonzales. *"Va a farti fottere!* You're all fired!" Carmela helped Lisa to her feet. Lisa tried to say something, but all that came out was a croak.

Zarela bent down until his eyes were level with hers, then he pulled his head back and spat in her face. "If I ever see you again, I'll fix you good, *battona!"*

Tony Zarela followed the three women out to their car, screaming an order at Sineo to shoot the car's tires out if they weren't gone in two minutes.

He stormed back into the house, stopping at the kitchen for a shot of vodka before approaching Don Ganero. What the hell was that woman doing that far from the two older ones? Maria, the hot-looking number, never strayed more than a few feet from her aunts. No matter. They were gone now, and he was gong to have to hire replacements.

He examined the postcard again. In simple block letters was a message: ARE YOU STILL INTERESTED IN MARK MARTEL? IF SO, LEAVE A NUMBER AT 415-555-6214.

He pressed the bell, then used the heavy iron key to gain entrance to the chapel. Victor Ganero was kneeling in front of the altar. The room was sound-proofed, so Don Ganero had heard nothing of the commotion in the hallway. Ganero scowled over his shoulder at the interruption.

"What is it?"

"Boss. Look at this."

The Mafia don rose unsteadily to his feet and snapped the postcard from Zarela's hand. The scowl on his face faded; his eyes narrowed. He squeezed his lips together and breathed heavily through his nose as he read the message. He looked at the top-right corner. It was postmarked San Francisco.

Ganero marched out of the room, Zarela at his heels. He went to the telephone in the dining room and stabbed in the numbers listed on the postcard.

"After the tone, please leave a message," a cold, computerized voice said.

Ganero let out a string of curses in Italian, slammed the phone back onto its base, then immediately picked it up again and dialed the operator.

"Area code four-one-five. Where is that?"

"San Francisco, sir."

Ganero replaced the phone gently this time. His sunken chest heaved, as if he'd been running.

"We're going to get Martel, Tony. We're finally going to avenge my son's death. Call Johnny Musso. I want him back here right away."

Chapter 19

Mark melted into the shadows as Harry Vlad gave the Jaguar a thorough going-over. The tall, handsome brunette Harry had picked up last night tapped her stiletto heel impatiently as she watched him.

"Are you going to give me a ride home, or what?"

"Relax, baby. You had a good time, right? You got paid, right? So stop bitching, or call a cab."

Harry held the door open for the woman, giving her butt a light tap as she struggled into the small car.

Vlad goosed the engine and took off, affording Mark a good look at him as he sped by. Harry looked as if he'd had a rough night.

As soon as the Jag was out of the garage, Mark climbed the stairs to the eighth floor, a cup of now-cold coffee clutched in one hand. He examined the lock on the door of suite 818. The majority of the hotels in the United States had switched from the standard metal key to a plastic, electronically coded key-card. The lock's code was changed after each checkout, the plastic key-card disposed of in a shredder. The Bay Tower Apartments had followed suit. The computerized key-card was also used to monitor access to the room. Each time the door opened and closed it registered on a computer, allowing the management to clock the amount of time the maids spent on each room. Another win for Big Brother, another loss for mankind, and, more important, for Mark at the moment. It would signal a red light for the project if Vlad became suspicious enough to check with the desk to learn if anyone had entered his room while he was gone.

He knelt at the door, lifted the cap from the Styrofoam cup, and spilled the coffee out slowly, making sure that the liquid spread under the doorsill.

He then went back to the stairwell and used his cell phone to call the front desk.

He grasped his throat with one hand and put a little New York into his speech. "Hey, this is suite 818. I spilled a cup of coffee at the door as I was leaving. You better send a maid up there right away."

He switched the phone off before the desk clerk could reply. His watch ticked off four and a half minutes before a heavyset woman in a white uniform and baize green apron, her tightly kinked hair streaked with gray, came down the hallway, pushing a laundry cart.

He watched as she first knocked on the door to suite 818, then used her passkey.

He heard her call out a "hello"; then she took a spray bottle and wet towel from the laundry cart, knelt at the threshold, and began cleaning the stained carpeting.

The maid looked up as Mark approached. A plastic name tag was attached to her apron.

He smiled apologetically. "Good morning, Sheila. I'm sorry about the spill. It was clumsy of me. I was in a hurry to get something from my car and the cup slipped out of my hand." He offered his hand, a ten-dollar bill tucked between his fingers.

"That's not necessary," the maid replied. "This is my job."

Mark edged past her into Vlad's room. "But I made your job a little harder. Take it. It'll make me feel better, really. I have some work to do this morning. Do you think you could come back in about an hour to clean the rest of the place? I'm expecting some visitors later."

He moved to the bathroom. The tile floor was littered with towels, the sink gritty from Vlad's morning shave. He rummaged through the medicine cabinet until he heard the maid call out, "All finished for now."

Vlad's suite was nicely furnished. The walls were covered in beige grass paper, the carpet a shade darker. Teak chairs and three small tables were sprinkled around the room. A large-screen TV dominated one wall. The adjoining bedroom was larger than the sitting room. A king-size bed, a wall of shutter-door closets. Half of the room was filled with office furniture: a teak desk, computer, fax machine, black matte halogen swivel lamps.

The bedsheets, pillows, and blankets were tangled together and spilled to the floor. He could see blots of lipstick on one pillowcase. A Lucite ice bucket held two upended bottles of champagne, which stood quietly in the water from the melted ice.

Mark pulled on a pair of latex gloves and carefully began exploring, starting with the closets. Vlad's coats and slacks bore no labels, but the material and cut were obviously of top quality. The drawers were filled with neatly folded underwear, cashmere sweaters, and stiffly starched dress shirts.

He flicked on the computer, saw the ever-present Windows logo, and after a few minutes of fiddling with the program, gave up. Either Harry Vlad hadn't used the machine or he'd hidden his correspondence well. A cassette telephone-answering machine was positioned next to the computer. He pushed the play button and a computerized voice informed him, "You have no new messages."

He scanned the in-house directory alongside the telephone. The services included an itemized billing to be faxed to the room before checkout.

He punched the front-desk button on the phone. "This is suite 818. Could you fax me a bill right away?"

"Will you be checking out this morning, Mr. Morgan?"

"No, but I need an accounting of my expenses to date."

"I understand, sir. Give me ten minutes."

Mark smiled knowingly at the selection of magazines stacked on the nightstand: *Architectural Digest, Town and Country, Connoisseur.* He flicked through them, hoping to find a layout of a house in the San Francisco area that might be a target for Vlad.

He was disappointed, until he noticed that the issue of *Connoisseur* was more than a year old, while the other magazines were current. He sat down on the bed and began turning the pages. There was a dog-eared crease at the corner of one page. Mark's eyes widened, and his mouth suddenly went bone-dry when he saw the featured article on a wine auction at the Fairmont Hotel. There he was, barely recognizable in the crowd! He remembered the event well. Joan Hatton had called up to the winery asking him to hurry down with several more cases of Merlot for an afternoon tasting. He focused on the photograph again. Vlad had to have been damn lucky to have picked him out of the crowd. Unless he had been studying the magazine with the intention of pulling a job at the hotel. The photograph had to be why Harry picked San Francisco to—

The ringing of the fax machine startled Mark. He jumped to his feet, the magazine dropping to the floor.

He reassembled the magazines while the fax spewed out two pieces of paper. In the last eight days, Vlad, using the name Harold Morgan, had run up quite a bill. The suite went for $275 a night, and there were a dozen or more room service charges.

What caught his interest was the list of telephone charges. Five to a New York City number that he recognized as George Alvord's gallery. There was also a page of local telephone calls made in the 415 area code.

Mark folded the fax papers and slipped them into

his pocket, making sure he left everything in place. The photograph of him in *Connoisseur* had been enough to give Vlad ideas. Harry Vlad was crafty and resourceful, a fairly successful thief. But he was just dumb enough to believe that Victor Ganero would pay off on the reward for locating Mark. Had he passed any information along to Ganero yet? Or were he and Alvord working together, hoping to spook Mark out into the open, then go to Ganero and claim the half-million reward?

There was a knock at the door. Mark pulled the revolver from his belt and peered through the peephole.

The smiling face of Sheila the maid peered back at him.

"Do you need a hand with that?"

Lisa Cole dropped her suitcase and whirled around, hands out in a clawlike position.

"Jesus Christ!" she rasped when she saw Mark Martel standing at the bottom of the steps leading to her apartment. "You scared the hell out of me."

"What happened to you?" Mark asked, picking up the suitcase. He squinted to study Lisa under the light. Her face was puffy, and she was moving awkwardly.

"Come on in. I need a drink."

Mark spotted the bruising on her throat as she foraged in her purse for her key. He waited until they were inside and he had deposited her suitcase on the carpet before questioning her again. "Where have you been? I've been trying to get hold of you for two days."

Lisa held a finger to her lips and said, "Sssshhhh." She padded into her kitchen and came back holding a bottle of Wild Turkey bourbon and two glasses.

"Usually I'm a red wine drinker, but tonight I need something stronger," she said in a hoarse voice as she poured two drinks. She took a sip of hers before handing Mark his glass.

"I ran into Tony Zarela this morning."

Mark's glass slipped out of his hand momentarily, but he caught it before the liquid spilled to the floor. "You what?"

"Sit down," Lisa suggested. "It's a long story."

She had to stop several times to swallow more of the whiskey. Her throat was throbbing and her whole body ached. She told Mark how she had hired a Phoenix private investigator, then gained entrance to Victor Ganero's house, and the story that Maria had told her about the chapel being off limits. "That has to be where he keeps the paintings. I was able to take some photos of paintings in the living room, but they were landscapes. And I took some pictures of the hallway leading up to the chapel door."

"It was crazy for you to try something like that!" Mark said angrily.

The Wild Turkey bottle clattered against her glass as she replenished her drink. "There's just two bodyguards at the house, Zarela and a guy called Sineo. When I was right at the chapel door, Zarela came out of nowhere. I thought he was going to kill me, and then Sineo came along—"

"What the hell were you thinking of?" Mark shouted. "You know what they did to my fiancée!"

Lisa held back an angry response. She took another hit on the whiskey, letting the liquid swish around her teeth before swallowing. "I thought Zarela *was* going to kill me for a moment. He called me something in Italian. *Battona*. Something like that."

Mark was fluent in French and had picked up enough Italian when he was in Europe and on the streets of New York to understand the language. "It means 'whore,' " he informed her as he paced back and forth.

"He fired the Gonzales sisters and kicked us out of the house. Thank God," she added with another sip of whiskey.

She pushed herself painfully to her feet. "No more

I-told-you-so's, okay? Listen. There's more bad news. Your policeman friend, Dan Heller, stopped by to see me. I gave him a story about you being a witness to an accident here in the city. He didn't believe me." She rolled her neck, wincing at the pain. "I didn't handle it well. I gave him a date and location for the accident. He checked the records and found nothing, so then he invites me out to dinner, to a restaurant on the same corner where I told him the accident had taken place. He came on real strong. He told me he was checking into your background because he didn't appreciate having someone in the witness protection program hanging around his family."

Mark continued pacing. "Did he say anything about New York?"

"No. He was fishing, because then he told me that you were an ex-con."

Mark stopped pacing. Heller *had* been on a fishing expedition. "What else did he say?"

"Oh, he started to act tough. He threatened to get a warrant and search my files if I didn't cooperate."

"And what did you say?"

"Nothing. I walked out on him. Listen, I'm tired, and I need a bath and about twenty-four hours of sleep. So, if you don't mind . . ."

"You're sure Zarela doesn't know who you really are? There's no way he can trace you back here?"

"No way," Lisa assured him. She opened the front door. "Call me tomorrow. I may be able to talk better and make a little more sense."

"If Zarela ever sees you again, Lisa, he will kill you."

"Thanks for reminding me." A spark came into her eyes. "You said I couldn't get near Ganero's place. You were wrong about that."

"Almost dead wrong," he said as he started down the stairs. "Be available tomorrow morning. We've got to talk."

Lisa double-bolted the front door and checked to

make sure the windows were locked before heading for the bathroom. While the tub was filling, she stripped and looked at herself in the bedroom's full-length mirror. There were bruises on her neck, both breasts, and her right thigh. She gingerly touched one breast and winced. She turned around and peered over her shoulder at her back in the mirror. Both buttocks were bruised.

At first, when Bonnie Nelson had heard what had happened, she wanted to drive Lisa to the police department and have her file charges against Zarela. But it hadn't taken long for the two of them to realize that once charges were filed, Zarela would know Lisa's real name and address. She shuddered at the thought of another go-round with Zarela.

Lisa carried the Wild Turkey bottle into the bathroom. She let out a soft moan as she inched her way into the hot water.

Mark was right about one thing. She had been lucky—damn lucky—to get out of there. She leaned forward suddenly, thinking she should have told Mark about the postcard with the picture of the Golden Gate Bridge. The one that Sineo had come running in with. What was it he'd said? Something about the card being from San Francisco, and the guy wanted to know if the don was still interested in—in what? Or who? Could it be Mark? She rested her head back against the cool porcelain and let the hot water work on her battered body. She'd been too scared to pay much attention to the postcard at the time.

Lisa turned the hot water back on and edged the tub stopper loose with her toes. Who would send Victor Ganero a postcard? Why not a phone call? Or E-mail? No one sent postcards anymore. Unless they were on vacation. Who, then? And were they after Mark? And would they turn him over to Ganero before he was able to deliver the thief to her? Or maybe the postcard had nothing to do with Martel, and he was the thief, and all this running around was doing nothing but getting her into trouble.

She sank up to her nose in the water and pictured Mark. There was no offer of tea or sympathy when she told him about her meeting with Tony Zarela. No attempted hugs or kisses or kind words of condolence. He was angry. All business. Well, if that was the game he wanted to play, she could play it too. And if he got hurt, or ended up in jail, that was his problem.

Chapter 20

Early the next morning Mark Martel was back at the Bay Tower Apartments, waiting for Harry Vlad to reappear. A jumble of discarded sketches littered the floor of the rented Ford Taurus—some of the apartment house, others of Vlad, and several of Lisa Cole.

Cole's visit to Victor Ganero's mansion had him worried. She seemed like a sharp, intelligent woman, but that move was just plain stupid, and he wondered how much he could trust her from now on. If Tony Zarela had started questioning her, she would have told him everything she knew, and then he'd have killed her. That was another thing that troubled him— why had Zarela let her get out of the mansion without questioning her?

Mark had called all the local phone numbers on the faxed charges to Vlad's room. Nine of the eleven calls had been answered by sexy-voiced young women working for escort services or massage parlors. The two calls that interested him the most were to neighboring Marin County. The county recorder's office and the Windjammer Yacht Harbor in Sausalito.

He dropped the sketch pad when Vlad's Jaguar sped past and drove into the Bay Tower garage.

After a nervous twenty-minute wait, he saw the Jag reappear. The convertible's top was down, and Harry was alone, his hair blowing in the wind.

The Jag made a left on Embarcadero, stopped briefly for a signal, then snarled west on Bay Street.

Mark kept a good half-block behind as Harry maneuvered the Jag through the heavy traffic. When they reached Marina Boulevard, Mark was pretty certain of their destination. The Golden Gate Bridge. The bridge was veiled by a thick fog. Only the tips of the towers were visible.

The six-lane southbound bridge traffic was bumper to bumper with commuters coming into the city. The two northbound lanes moved at the speed limit. Mark had a worried thought that maybe Harry wasn't going to the Windjammer Yacht Club in Sausalito—maybe he was heading up to the wine country. To Calistoga!

He relaxed when Harry took the Sausalito turnoff. The sun had broken through the fog. Harry turned into the yacht club's parking lot and secured the convertible's top before strolling in a leisurely fashion toward the docks.

Mark watched through binoculars as Vlad boarded a small white cruiser with *The Jakester* scrolled on its hull. Harry had the boat away from the dock in minutes.

Mark followed the boat's wake through the binoculars until it was a tiny speck in the gunmetal-gray bay waters.

Victor Ganero looked down from his balcony to the lush green fairways of the golf course. It amused him that men, rich men, would waste their time chasing a small white ball around for several hours in the heat of the day.

He handed the postcard to Johnny Musso. "Go to San Francisco. Talk to this man. Find Martel. Bring him here." He tapped a finger on the wrought-iron railing. "Here, to me. Understood?"

"Yes," Johnny Musso answered softly. "I understand." He examined the postcard. "You spoke to the man who wrote this?"

"Yes, yes," Ganero said impatiently. "He sounds greedy. A *merdata*," he said, using the Sicilian word for someone of no importance. "Pay him off." He coughed into his hand. His voice was dry—like cracked leather. "Get the information, kill him, and bring me back the money."

"Did he give you his name?"

"No. He's not that stupid."

Musso nodded his head. "I'll leave this afternoon. Alone. I won't need any help."

"No! Take Big Soup with you. Sineo will stay with me. You started it. I want you to finish it."

Musso bit back a response. Ganero still blamed him, not his precious son, for what had happened at the warehouse. "It will be done," he promised. "Your cough. It sounds worse. Are you sure you're all right?"

Ganero turned his back to Musso and gazed at the golf course. "Don't bury me yet, Johnny. Bring me Martel. That will be the best medicine. Go. Tell Tony to serve my dinner before you two leave."

Musso turned on his heel and headed for the kitchen. Tony Zarela and Sineo were sitting at the table, playing a game of gin rummy.

"Take a walk," Musso advised Sineo, who immediately folded his cards and left the room.

Zarela grinned at Musso, "Thanks. I was losing."

Musso hooked a chair around with his foot and sat down. "We're going to San Francisco."

"I figured that," Zarela said, gathering the cards.

"Vic says he called this guy who sent the postcard. From where?"

"Right from here," Zarela said sheepishly. "I tried to stop him, Johnny, but you know how he is."

"That wasn't smart. How many times did Vic call him?"

"Three. That I know of. All he got was an answering machine. The don left this number, and the guy called back. Were you able to get a fix on the number?"

"It's a phone company answering service," Musso said. "I can't trace it to the bastard."

Zarela shuffled the cards and began dealing a hand of solitaire. "The boss says he wants two hundred and fifty grand."

"So we give it to him. For about ten minutes."

Zarela slapped a black ten on a red jack. "What about the boss? I don't like leavin' him alone."

"Sineo will stay here."

"I still don't like it. Maybe we should get some guys—"

"Vic wants it this way, Tony. He wants you and me to finish up what we started."

Zarela fanned the cards across the table. "He's still pissed at us, ain't he?"

"At *me*," Musso corrected. "You're okay. He likes your soup. Bring him his dinner, then we can get going. I've got a plane waiting. And bring along your baseball bat. We'll use that little prick Harry Vlad to set this guy up," he said, waving the postcard.

Zarela smiled widely. "It'll be good for Vlad to do some real work for a change."

Dan Heller clapped his hands together several times, then called, "Nice dive, Kitten," as his daughter surfaced in Mark Verre's swimming pool. He watched with pride as she began swimming laps. She moved gracefully, her hands and arms barely disturbing the water, her face appearing briefly for a gulp of air, her feet propelling her effortlessly.

Carrie paused at the far end of the pool, shaking water from her hair. "Come on back in, Dad."

"I will. But I'm going to use the bathroom first. I'll bring out the sandwiches and Coke."

Heller skirted Gauguin, who, while he hadn't accepted him as a friend, at least didn't growl at him all the time. He entered the house through the sliding glass doors leading to the kitchen.

Heller had persuaded Carrie to come to Verre's place by telling her he wanted to see how her swimming lessons were progressing. "Besides, it'll be good for Gauguin. He's probably getting homesick."

He had been right about Arlene having a key to Verre's place. The key and the security alarm code. But he didn't have to trouble Arlene, because at the start of the summer Carrie had been given a key and the code also. She was in the habit of bicycling to Verre's house and using the pool and the studio when he was away or working in the vineyards.

Heller went to the sink, hoping to find an unwashed dish or glass from which he could pull Verre's prints. Both the sink and the dishwasher were empty. He hurried into the living room, his eyes searching for anything that would have Verre's prints on it. Nothing. He tried the first door he came to and found himself in Verre's art studio.

A skylight flooded the room with bright sunlight. There were dozens of brightly colored canvases stacked against the wall, lying on tables, in various states of completion on easels.

A brush, he thought. All I need is one of his paintbrushes. But Verre was instructing Carrie. What if he took the wrong brush and all he got were Carrie's prints?

He slid open a cabinet and pawed through cans of paint and turpentine, grumbling at the fruitless efforts of his search so far. His fingers were brushing over unopened boxes of paint tubes when they inadvertently came in contact with cold metal. He carefully picked up the gun between his thumb and forefinger. It was a serious weapon. A fully loaded four-inch-barrel Colt Python .357 Magnum revolver with a ventilated grip and target hammer.

Heller brought the gun up close to his nose, inhaling the scent of gun oil. He held it up to the skylight and smiled when he saw the outline of several fingerprints along the barrel.

Chapter 21

"Lisa. Over here."

Lisa Cole spun around and put a hand to her forehead to cut down on the glare of the sun. She spotted Mark on the balcony of Gilleran's Tavern. He was wearing a tan fisherman's hat with an extended bill and a flap that dropped down in back to cover the neck area. A pair of binoculars dangled from a cord around his neck. He had a sketch pad in one hand, a pencil in the other.

Gilleran's Tavern was an attempt at duplicating an Irish waterfront pub. The balcony flooring was unvarnished pine, the railing crisscrossed two-by-fours. A Guinness Stout umbrella topped each of the redwood tables. Accordion-dominated Irish tunes blared from the speakers. A canvas banner proclaiming BEST IRISH COFFEE IN THE WORLD SERVED HERE hung over the entrance.

The tavern perched over the yacht harbor and provided a panoramic view out to Alcatraz and the Bay Bridge. The dozens of docked boats in the scene ranged from impressive yachts, their sails neatly rolled and tied, to small power cruisers and tiny rowboats that bobbed on the water like bathtub ducks.

The only other person on the balcony was a distinguished-looking older man with thick gray hair and an old-fashioned movie-star mustache. He raised his wineglass in a courteous salute, then went back to reading his newspaper.

"What's so important that I had to rush over here?"

Lisa asked, her voice hoarse and raspy. She wore a dark-blue silk bandanna over her hair and a matching scarf around her neck. She moved her canvas-backed captain's chair into the shade. "God, I could use a drink," she said in a voice loud enough to carry inside the tavern.

A redheaded waiter in Levi's and a chambray shirt buttoned at the neck came to the table and, in a thick brogue, asked Lisa for her order.

"Irish coffee. No sugar."

Mark put his hand on the neck of his bottle of Guinness. "I'll stick with this. I found your thief," he said once the waiter had left.

Lisa's eyebrows rose in surprise. "Really?"

"Really. His name is Harry Vlad." He handed her the sketch pad. "This is what he looks like."

Lisa examined the drawing, which showed the face of an attractive man with a gap in his front teeth.

"Where is he?"

Mark pointed out to the bay. "Somewhere out there. His car is parked in the lot over to your right." He unslung the binoculars from his neck and handed them to her. "A Jaguar convertible near the pier leading to the dock."

Lisa located the Jaguar. "Nice. You crooks do live the good life. How did you find him so fast?" The waiter arrived with her drink and she twisted awkwardly in the chair to focus the binoculars on the Jaguar again. Mark spotted two thick bruises along the side of her neck that her scarf failed to conceal. It was obvious that she was still in pain from her encounter with Tony Zarela.

He removed the Bay Tower Apartments fax bill from his jacket pocket and passed it to her.

"Vlad's going by the name Harold Morgan. The New York telephone calls were to George Alvord. He's the go-between for Vlad and Victor Ganero. I was able to run down a few of the local numbers."

Lisa frowned at the penciled notations alongside

several of the numbers. "Centerfold Escorts, Victoria's Ultra Secret Massage, Kinkie's Spa. A man of great culture and refinement, your Mr. Vlad."

"Yes," Mark agreed. "What interested me was the Sausalito calls to this yacht harbor. I followed him here. He's sizing up his next job."

"From a boat?" Lisa asked, a note of skepticism in her voice.

"Yes. It means the target can be hit from the water. Harry's going to steal a Lorenzo Ghiberti."

"Am I supposed to know just who and what that is?"

"Ghiberti was a master Renaissance sculptor. He specialized in Christian bronzes. Usually they were life-size or larger. I'm guessing this is one of the miniatures he made to show to his client as a sample before getting the nod to go ahead with the major statue."

Lisa took a sip of the drink, then ran her tongue over her lips to lick away a trace of whipped cream. "How do you know what Vlad's planning to steal?"

"Someone managed to overhear George Alvord mention it. And that it was in Belvedere. I thought he meant Belvedere Street in San Francisco, but it's the town of Belvedere." Mark pointed out to the bay. "Over there in Marin County. Across from Angel Island."

"I know where Belvedere is," Lisa answered irritably. "So, I guess you want me to put a surveillance team on Harry Vlad."

"Like the one you had at the Hatton Winery? No. Harry would spot a tail like that in minutes. I'll find Harry's target."

"You have a pretty high opinion of yourself, don't you?"

"I was good at what I did, Lisa. Harry's good, too."

Lisa took a healthy swig of the Irish coffee, then said, "Tell me the truth. Didn't you ever feel rotten about doing a job? Sure, the people were insured, and no one has any sympathy for an insurance company, but still—"

Mark scratched his thumbnail across the beer bottle label. "I wasn't Robin Hood, stealing from the rich and giving it to the poor. But every painting I took had been stolen before, sometimes dozens of times." He tapped a finger under his glass eye. "Take the painting that cost me this and my fiancée her life. *Assumption of the Madonna.* Antonio Allegri Correggio painted it in 1530. He was forced to sell it to a local duke, then it passed through several unknown hands until 1796, when Napoleon Bonaparte's army stole it from Pope Pius VI, who had taken it from the Grand Duchy of Tuscany to settle a land claim. Napoleon was the world's greatest art plunderer until Hitler surpassed him. The Correggio went to France, was stolen by Italian partisans, smuggled back to Italy, disappeared several times, then turned up in a private German collection in 1910. It was then sold for a very low figure to an Italian collector, who was reportedly a high official in the Mafia. The Mafia official died and the painting disappeared. It turned up at auction in Canada and was sold in 1991 to a Swiss banker, who in turn sold it for an undisclosed amount to a Mr. Antoine Brovosky. The word on the street was that Brovosky had accepted the painting as part of his fee in a bond deal that netted him more than twenty million dollars and cost the American taxpayers at least twice that amount."

Lisa wasn't going to let him off the hook. "So, you think all that justifies what you did?"

"No. I'm just saying that the art world is full of people you like to call crooks, from the artists on down. An artist might peddle a work to a dealer for ten thousand in cash, yet the dealer tells everyone the price was much more so that he can up the ante and the artist's next work will bring a higher price. You take me to any museum of your choice, and I'll show you dozens of forgeries. There's an old joke in the art game. Of the seven hundred paintings produced by Jean Baptiste Cort, eight thousand of them are in the United States.

"The auction houses sell works that they know have been stolen, and quite often they rig the bidding to drive the prices up."

Lisa Cole finished her drink and held the empty glass up to catch the waiter's attention. "Do you think Victor Ganero still has the Madonna painting?"

"Yes. He's a fanatic. Possessing these paintings makes him feel immortal." Mark picked up the binoculars again and scanned the bay. "Ganero didn't pick his new home just for the weather. You can bet he's got all kinds of connections with the local cops and the D.A. So don't think about trying to get into his place again."

Lisa's hand went to her throat, her fingers fiddling with the scarf knot. "I spoke to Charlie Dwyer this morning. He's not a happy camper. He says he's getting a lot of pressure from his bosses. He hinted that I might not have much more time on the case. If Harry Vlad is the thief, maybe I should approach him and try to make a deal. I could—"

"Harry will vanish if you do that. You have nothing on him yet. He's passed the stolen paintings along. You'd just scare him off."

"I figure once we get Vlad, I can get the paintings."

Mark managed a pale smile. "Get them back from Victor Ganero? No. Our deal was that I find the thief for you."

"You haven't given me any proof that Vlad is the thief," Lisa admonished, scrounging in her purse for cigarettes and lighter.

She lit up a king-size menthol and spoke through an exhalation of smoke. "Charlie Dwyer isn't going to believe any of this without proof."

"Did you tell him about your visit to Ganero's house?"

"Hell, no." She poked around in her purse and

came out with a packet of photographs. "There's something I didn't tell you last night, Mark. It occurred to me after you'd left. While Tony Zarela was slapping me around, Sineo ran up to him, holding a postcard, and he said someone wanted to know if the boss was 'still interested in—'; then, before he could finish, Zarela told him to shut up and grabbed the postcard. There was a picture of the Golden Gate Bridge on it. At least it got Zarela interested enough to stop beating on me."

Mark's face scrunched up. "What the hell are you telling me? That someone mailed information about me to Victor Ganero?"

"He didn't mention your name," Lisa apologized. "I don't know what was on the postcard. I guess I should have brought it up last night, but I was beat and—"

"You're damn right, you should have," Mark fumed. "Sineo. What else did he say?"

"Once Zarela told him to shut up, he shut up." She bit down on her lower lip when the waiter set a fresh drink in front of her.

Mark tore his hat off and tilted his face up to the sun in frustration. What the hell was it all about? he wondered. A postcard. The Golden Gate Bridge. Was it someone in San Francisco who knew who he was? Or was it something else? Harry Vlad notifying Ganero of a stolen painting?

Lisa spread the photographs across the table. "These are the photos I was able to take before Zarela stopped me."

Mark picked up the photos one by one. "These paintings in the living room and dining room aren't worth anything." He paid close attention to the layout of the house. "Is this the hallway leading to the chapel?"

"Yes, that's it," Lisa said, once again reaching into her purse and coming out with a folded sheet of paper.

"This is a diagram of the house. The cleaning women helped me with it."

The diagram was neatly done in red and blue pencil, and showed the entire first floor, including the kitchen and three bedrooms. The chapel door was marked with a big red X.

"There are more rooms," Lisa explained. "Victor Ganero's bedroom is upstairs, and there's an entertainment center with a large-screen TV and Ping-Pong table downstairs, along with the bedrooms where Zarela and Sineo sleep. I never got that far."

Mark continued examining the photographs. The final shot was a blurred image of a man's shirt, tie, and suit coat. He waved the photo at Lisa with one hand, pocketing the diagram with the other.

"I must have snapped that one just before I slipped the camera into the apron pocket of one of the Gonzales sisters," Lisa explained. "That's Zarela pushing me around." She took a swallow of her fresh drink, then said, "So what's the plan now? Are you going to just sit here and wait for Vlad to come back?"

"The wait's over. There's Harry. In the small white powerboat pulling up to the dock alongside that black-hulled schooner."

Lisa waited impatiently for Mark to relinquish the binoculars. It took her several moments to find the right boat. A muscular man with flaxen hair jumped onto the dock. His shirt was off, revealing a sunburned body corded with muscles. His face bore a strong resemblance to Mark's sketch.

Lisa tracked Vlad as he walked toward the harbormaster's cabin. "He's stopping to use the phone."

"Let me see," Mark said anxiously. Vlad was shoveling coins into the pay phone. Sunglasses were perched on top of his head. His lips were pursed, as if he was whistling. Then his body language changed dramatically. His back stiffened, and his jaw firmed, jutted out, as if he was expecting to be slugged and had no way of stopping the punch. He slammed the phone down, ran back to the boat, jumped aboard, and emerged moments later, pulling a knit shirt over his head as he jogged toward the parking lot.

"He's suddenly in a big hurry," Lisa pointed out.

"Yes. He didn't put a lot of money into the phone. It had to be a local call."

Mark kept the binoculars trained on Vlad until he was in the car and the Jaguar was out of sight.

"What now?" Lisa asked, dropping her cigarette to the deck and squashing it with the sole of her shoe.

"Now you become an apprentice burglar."

Lisa Cole watched closely as Mark squatted in front of the door leading below to *The Jakester*'s cabin. He had donned plastic gloves and was running his fingers lightly around the door frame. He then slipped a wallet-size pouch out of his jacket and extracted what appeared to be one of those round mirrors that a dentist uses to explore for cavities.

Mark leaned back on his haunches and selected a slim steel device from his pouch. Again, it looked like a dentist's tool to Lisa, the one used to scrape tartar off of teeth.

There was a clicking sound, then a satisfied grunt from Mark. He stood up, motioned Lisa away from the door, then used a boathook to nudge the door open.

"Is all this drama for my benefit?" Lisa asked. "Or are you just trying to make it look harder than it really is?"

Mark ignored her, waving the boathook in front of him as he advanced toward the door. He dropped to one knee and hurled the boathook, javelin-style, into the cabin. It fell to the floor with a loud clatter.

"It should be safe to go in now."

Lisa stood her ground. "Did you really think that Harry Vlad might have booby-trapped the door?"

Mark ducked down and stepped into the cabin area. "It's what I would have done."

The cabin was compact. A tiny stove and refrigerator. Two bunk beds. An open door exposed a pint-size lavatory.

"Dare I touch this?" Lisa asked, pointing at an odd-looking contraption lying on one of the beds.

"It's not a bomb," Mark informed her. "It's a long-range telescope and bionic amplifying device. It will pick up a conversation from a thousand yards away under the right conditions."

A foolscap notepad was jammed into the seam between the bunk and the wall, under a porthole. Mark tilted his head to read the neat printing:

10:55 MB SUNNING AGAIN
11:20 WB COMES OUT—SWIMS—
11:45 WB BACK INTO HOUSE
12:22 RAY-RAY COMES OUT WITH LUNCH
1:17 WB INTO HOUSE

Lisa's head peeked over his shoulder. "You were right. Vlad's been watching someone. MB. WB. And Ray-Ray. I'd sure like to know who they are."

"Let's go," Mark said. "We're not going to learn anything more here." He carefully closed the cabin door, then stopped at the wheelhouse to examine the cluster of gauges set behind the wheel. He made a mental note of the odometer reading: 24699.

"Where to now?" Lisa wanted to know when they were back on the dock.

"You're going to rent a boat," he informed her.

Harry Vlad slotted the Jag into a spot in the Bay Tower garage and ran for the elevator.

The telephone message Johnny Musso left on his answering machine had him worried: "Vlad. I found Martel." Harry hated the thought of losing the half a million that Ganero had posted on Martel. Where had they found him? And how? If Martel had surfaced because of the art thefts, then Harry figured he was

due some money. Maybe not the full half-mil, but
something. After all, he was the one who told them
Martel was out on the West Coast. The rest of Musso's
message: "I need you." For what? Shit! Did Musso
think he was holding out on him?

Harry opened the door to his suite and stopped with
one foot hovering above the carpet. The TV was on.
He knew it hadn't been on when he'd left that morning.

"That you, punk?" a thick, heavy voice called from
the bedroom.

Harry edged forward. Tony "Big Soup" Zarela was
sprawled on the bed, reading a magazine. Jesus, it was
Connoisseur! The one with Mark Martel's photograph.

Vlad tried to keep the panic out of his voice.
"What's up?"

Zarela casually flipped a page of the magazine. "We
got a job for you, Harry. Some guy here in San Francisco sent the boss a postcard. He says he knows a lot
about Mark Martel. We're waiting to hear from him."

Harry's stomach gurgled as Zarela turned another
page.

"What . . . what do you want me to do?"

"I'm gonna turn over some dough to this guy after
he tells me what he knows about Martel. And you're
going to trail him, or heist his wallet. We don't care
what you do, or how you do it, Harry, but we gotta
know who he is and where he lives. He's probably
gonna play some dumb game, pick some crowded
place for the meet, then try and get away. We can't
let that happen."

"Sure, sure," Harry stammered. "But what if I
can't—"

Zarela stared at Vlad over the top of the magazine.
"You let the guy get away, then Johnny's going to be
pissed. Real pissed—you know what I mean? Pack a
bag. My car's in the garage. You're spending the night
with me."

Harry was about to ask where, but he wisely decided not to.

He hurried to the closet, one eye on Zarela as he paged through the magazine. He had to distract Tony, to stop him from seeing Martel's photograph. "I could use a drink. How about you?"

"You got vodka?"

"Sure. The mini-bar by the TV. Help yourself."

Zarela elbowed himself into a sitting position, then stood up, the magazine still clutched in his meaty paws.

"Did you see this story?"

Harry was shuffling clean underwear into his suitcase. Under the pile of clothing was an orange plastic tool called the safety hammer. It was sold primarily to police and fire departments for use in breaking into wrecked vehicles. On one end were two sharp steel points, either of which would easily shatter a car's window. It worked equally well on sliding glass doors. It was Harry's favorite entry tool, and it also made a damn good sap. He wondered what effect it would have on someone like Zarela. "What story's that?"

"The one on Italian restaurants. They got one listed here in Frisco that they say is as good as any in the country. The Stinking Rose. You ever try it?"

Harry exhaled and released his grip on the sap. "Yeah. Good joint. But you better love a lot of garlic." He zipped his case closed. "I'm all set."

Zarela tossed the magazine onto the bed and headed for the bar. "How about broads? This town good for hookers?"

"Terrific," Harry asserted. "Just terrific."

Chapter 22

Mark knelt to retrieve the candy bar wedged behind the front wheel of Harry Vlad's Jaguar.

Noel Field had attempted to follow Vlad from the Sausalito boat dock yesterday afternoon, but Vlad's speedy driving had left Field in the dust. Then Noel drove directly to the Bay Tower Apartments, where he found that Harry's Jag was in the garage. Field had placed the candy bar under the tire after Mark arrived on the scene.

They both staked out the garage until after midnight, but there had been no sign of Harry.

It was morning now, a little after nine o'clock. The candy was firm and solid, which meant that the Jag hadn't moved from its spot during the night.

Noel Field was in his hotel room, which was just where Mark wanted him. Field had taken too many chances already. It was time he went back to New York.

Mark retreated to his car. He peeled the wrapper from the candy bar, took a bite, and began chewing slowly. Cold coffee and candy bars were becoming staples of his diet.

Lisa Cole was waiting on the boat she'd rented in Sausalito, two docks over from where Vlad's boat was moored. The plan was for Mark to follow Harry, and once he was certain Vlad was heading for Sausalito, pass him and meet Lisa on the boat first, get away from the dock and cruise around nearby until Harry had *The Jakester* under way, then follow him to the site of his next theft.

Mark continued to chew on the candy as he racked his brain trying to figure out who had sent the postcard to Victor Ganero, and why. If it was someone who had information on him and was after the reward, why a postcard? Why not a phone call?

Harry Vlad or George Alvord would have made direct contact with Ganero if they had any solid information.

Certainly not Joan Hatton. He'd bet his life on that. He smiled wryly when he realized that he had already done that when he'd told Joan who he really was. And Lisa Cole said that Sineo told Zarela that "some *guy* wants to know if the don is still interested . . ." Interested in what? Him? Or something else? It was possible that Ganero had another thief supplying him with stolen art. It could have nothing at all to do with me, he thought hopefully.

Bill Rangel? Rangel knew his new identity, but that was all. And why would Rangel contact Ganero now? He'd had three years in which to turn the information over.

Dan Heller, Arlene's ex-husband? Heller wanted him out of Arlene's life, he knew, but the big policeman wouldn't go through the likes of Victor Ganero to accomplish that. Or would he? Was that a way of turning him in without Arlene knowing he was responsible?

Then there was Charlie Dwyer, who had worked for the Justice Department and was now an insurance executive. Dwyer had made it clear during the trial that he had no love for Mark. Maybe Dwyer had gotten fed up with waiting for Lisa Cole to come up with something and had decided to turn up the heat.

Or maybe there was a joker in the deck, someone he knew nothing about, who had stumbled upon his identity.

Noel Field said that Harry Vlad had done some

recent jail time. That might explain how Harry had come across the photograph in *Connoisseur*. He would have had a lot of time to catch up on his reading in jail, and that was just the kind of magazine that would interest him.

Come on, Harry, he urged silently. Come on, let's get on with the job.

Harry Vlad would have loved to be on board *The Jakester*. He would have loved to be back in New York. Other than Shawngunk Prison, he couldn't think of any place he would rather *not* have been than standing alongside Johnny Musso at the Montgomery Street Bay Area Rapid Transit station.

All around him people of every age, stripe, and color were rushing back and forth en route to and from their jobs.

Tony Zarela was positioned some fifty yards away, in front of the newsstand, just as he'd been instructed by the man who'd called his hotel room at ten minutes after seven in the morning, a little more than an hour ago.

Harry had spent a very uncomfortable night camped on a narrow couch while Big Soup had shared the king-size bed with a hooker Harry had called in from a massage parlor.

The room was littered with wine bottles and food wrappers. Zarela's snoring had kept Harry awake most of the night. The hooker had dragged her sore and sorry butt out of the room a little after two in the morning.

According to Zarela, Johnny Musso had taken the adjoining room, but Harry hadn't seen him.

Zarela's snoring had stopped abruptly at the first ring of the telephone.

He grunted his name, then a series of "uh-huhs."

The directions had been simple enough. Tony was to bring the money to the newspaper stand at the

Montgomery Street BART station at eight-thirty. He was to hold a bouquet of flowers, red roses, which he was to purchase at the flower stand at Montgomery and Post Streets.

Johnny Musso pulled his coat sleeve back and looked at his watch. "Any time now, Harry. The guy's probably watching Tony, so be careful. You know what will happen to you if you lose him."

Harry didn't know for sure. He didn't want to know. He had purchased a twenty-dollar BART ticket, more than enough to take him anywhere on the system if the man picking up the money went through a turnstile and down to the train platform one level below.

Musso was wearing a business suit, and he had a newspaper tucked under one arm. Harry had the uncomfortable feeling that there was a gun inside the paper. Musso drifted away, blending in with the crowd.

Harry moved toward the escalator leading from the station to Montgomery and Market Streets. A flight of stairs paralleled the escalator.

Harry joined the jostle of people riding the escalator, then circled back, taking the stairs down, watching the throng pass by. He stepped away from the stairs and turned his collar up. No one seemed to pay him any attention.

Zarela was shuffling around in a circle, scarcely lifting his feet. He looked ridiculous holding the bouquet of flowers in one of his big mitts and the shopping bag filled with cash in the other.

A disheveled middle-aged man with a bald spot on the back of his head walked toward Zarela, deliberately and without hurry.

Harry's muscles tensed, then relaxed as the man continued past Zarela. Then the man stopped short, snapped his fingers as if remembering something, and turned around.

Zarela said something to the man, then dropped the flowers to the ground and stooped to pick them up.

That was the signal to let Musso and Harry know that the transfer was taking place.

The man spoke rapidly, and after several moments Zarela, seemingly reluctantly, handed over the shopping bag.

The man's head was swiveling back and forth, and he appeared ready to bolt at any minute. He briefly opened the shopping bag, handed Zarela an envelope, then turned and scurried off toward the escalator.

Harry took the stairs and got a good look at the man's profile when he came abreast of him on the escalator. Close to sixty, thin, a beef-and-bourbon complexion, gray hair, gray suit. His scuffed black wingtips rattled on the escalator steps as he wove his way through the rush hour commuters.

Once the man hit the sidewalk, he started off at a half jog, which was fine with Harry. It made him that much easier to spot. Harry's one concern was that his quarry would hop into a waiting cab or a parked car and he would lose him.

The man darted across Market Street against a red light and disappeared into the lobby of the Palace Hotel.

Harry was nearly clipped by a UPS truck as he navigated through the traffic. By the time he entered the Palace Hotel lobby, there was no sign of the man. Harry didn't think that he'd had time to exit through the rear entrance. He checked the famed glass-roofed Garden Court dining room, then began to sweat. He'd lost him!

Where the hell did he go? Had he booked a room? A bellman wheeling a cart of luggage trudged by and Harry asked him for the location of the rest room.

It was down an out-of-the-way staircase, so as to discourage use by the homeless and street people peddling their wares on Market Street.

Harry opened the rest room door slowly. It appeared empty. He turned on a faucet, then dropped to the tiled floor on his hands and knees. A pair of scuffed black wingtips could be seen under the door to one of the lavatory stalls.

Harry straightened up, washed his hands, and smiled at his reflection in the mirror. He returned to the hotel lobby and waited, laughing when the man reappeared. An amateur, Harry judged. He'd donned a houndstooth cloth hat, a dark-blue parka, and sunglasses. There was no sign of the shopping bag, so the money must be in the parka's pocket or strapped to his body. He still wore the scuffed wingtips. A real amateur's mistake. You always change shoes after a job.

Harry followed him to the hotel's Montgomery Street exit. The uniformed doorman whistled up a cab from a long queue, and the man ducked into the taxi without giving the doorman a tip.

Harry slipped in front of a Japanese couple and passed the doorman a ten-dollar bill. He jumped into the first cab in line, a creased twenty-dollar bill in hand.

"That cab that just took off. I want to know where he's going."

The driver swiveled around. His cynical, lined face broke into a grin. "You want me to follow him?"

"No. I want you to listen to the dispatcher, find out where they're headed, and beat 'em there." He offered another twenty-dollar bill. "Can do?"

The driver turned up the dispatch radio and grinned again. "Can do, buddy. Can do."

Mark was in danger of dozing off. He hadn't had more than four straight hours of sleep since that last night in Calistoga. With Arlene. He dug his fingernails into the palms of his hands and wondered why Harry Vlad wasn't making a move. It could be that Harry had the job set up for later tonight and was taking advantage of the time by sleeping in. Or—Mark's worst fear—maybe Harry had decided to take a few days or weeks off.

"The troops have arrived," Noel Field said, opening

the passenger door. "With refreshments." He set a cardboard tray with two cups of steaming hot coffee and bakery rolls on the seat.

"I thought you were going back to New York," Mark said, reaching gratefully for one of the coffee cups.

"I'm starting to enjoy this town. I may stick around for a few days. Any sign of our boy Harry?"

"No. His car is still in the garage. It hasn't moved."

"Is your Miss Cole waiting in Sausalito?"

Mark nodded his head, then sipped at the coffee.

"She looks like a bright girl," Field said, having spent some time studying Lisa from behind the pages of the *Wall Street Journal* yesterday at Gilleran's Tavern. "But from what you tell me about her visit to Ganero's house, I wonder."

"She has more guts than brains, Noel. And like you always told me, guts get you in trouble and brains get you out of it." Mark yawned widely, his mouth snapping shut when he saw Harry Vlad emerge from a taxicab and hurriedly make his way into the apartment building.

He picked up his cell phone and called Lisa Cole, who was waiting on board the rented boat in Sausalito.

"He just came home," Mark informed her. "In a cab."

"Good. I'd just about given up on you."

Twelve minutes later the champagne-colored Jaguar snaked out of the apartment garage and turned left on Embarcadero. As it approached the Golden Gate Bridge, Mark called Lisa again. "He's on the road. Heading your way."

"What's my part in the action?" Field said.

"Cover my back, old friend. Lisa and I will follow Harry with the boat. You stay by the dock." He reached over and squeezed Noel's knee. "When this is over, we'll celebrate. In style."

*   *   *

Water burbled against the sleek hull of Walter Burwell's sixty-four-foot yacht. Harry waited until the vessel had rounded the western tip of Angel Island, then heeled the *Jakester*'s bow over smartly, guiding his boat to the Burwell dock.

He had watched as Walter and Mechelle Burwell loaded at least a dozen of their friends aboard the vessel. The thick pompadour of Ray-Ray was seen moving between the house and the yacht as the houseboy loaded baskets and trays of food. All undoubtedly for a nice on-the-water cocktail party. Harry didn't know exactly where the yacht was headed, and he didn't much care. No one carried that much food or that many passengers for a speedy loop around the bay. They'd be gone for hours, and all he needed was twenty minutes.

Harry secured the boat, then ran up the dock, past the pool, to the glass patio door. He pounded on it with the butt of his fist to make sure that no one was left behind, then studied it, searching for that nearly invisible seam in the top quadrant of the glass.

The manufacturers loved to show pictures of would-be burglars swinging axes that bounced harmlessly off their glass products. What they didn't show the customers was what happened when someone used a sharp-pointed object, like an ice pick, or Harry's safety hammer. He slammed the tool's sharp steel point against the glass, and it fragmented around his feet. The security alarm buzzed and Harry hastily stepped inside and entered the code. He stood perfectly still, welcoming the majestic silence, the palms of his hands sweating inside the plastic gloves. His chest was heaving, and he could feel the surge of blood coursing through his veins. It was always like this during a job. The adrenaline rush got him higher than cocaine or any of those home-brewed drugs he'd sampled in prison.

He located the Ghiberti statue upstairs, nestled between two ornate icons. He briefly stroked the icons, then decided against taking them. The Russian mobs had flooded the market with phonies.

Since this was going to be Harry's last job for Ganero, and Alvord, and since Ganero had found Martel, there was no longer a need for him to mimic Martel's style. He combed through the rest of the house, selecting the pick of the litter from Mechelle Burwell's jewelry cases, then pulled a painting out of its frame in the master bedroom. A Picasso, from the artist's cubist period. Certainly nothing that would be of interest to Victor Ganero, but Picassos were an easy sell.

Harry felt a tremendous sense of relief. Johnny Musso had been happy as hell when Harry told him he'd trailed the old man from the Palace Hotel to a house on Forty-sixth Avenue, out by the ocean.

"You done good. You'll be rewarded," Musso had promised.

Rewarded. The cheap Dago would probably toss him a few grand. He wondered how much money had been in the shopping bag Zarela had turned over to the man Harry trailed to the house out by the ocean. It didn't really matter. Harry would deliver the Ghiberti statue to Victor Ganero, peddle the Picasso and jewelry on his own, then take off for Mexico. Or Brazil. Somewhere far, far away from Ganero, Musso, Big Soup, and Mark Martel. Screw Mark Martel. Whoever the guy in the scuffed shoes was, he must know a hell of a lot more about Martel than I do, Harry reasoned. And his reward would be a going-over from Big Soup, so there was no sense in Harry pushing his luck. He now considered himself damn lucky to be out of that deal.

He rolled the Picasso up carefully, then headed back toward the boat, checking his watch as he moved. He'd been in the house eighteen minutes and picked up at least a hundred thousand dollars' worth of goodies. Not bad. Not bad at all.

*   *   *

"I wonder if Boston Insurance carries the policy on this house?" Lisa Cole said as she lowered the video recorder from her eye. Harry Vlad's boat was several hundred yards away, cruising back to Sausalito. She coughed lightly. Her throat still felt like it was lined with sandpaper.

The wind had kicked up, and Mark widened his stance as he turned the boat around. "Did you get all the footage you need?"

"Oh, yes. I've got your friend Mr. Vlad breaking into the house and coming out with his hands full. It's more than I need."

A wall of fog was streaming in from the Pacific Ocean, and the high clouds were blotting up the last of the day's sunshine.

Martel could just make out the wake from Vlad's boat. "That finishes it, then. For me." He looked over at Lisa. The wind fanned her hair out behind her. The bruises on her neck were darker than they'd been yesterday. "Our deal was that I find the thief for you."

When Lisa didn't respond, Mark cut the engines. "I fulfilled my part of the bargain. I expect you to do the same."

"Okay, okay." She shivered and wished she'd brought along a heavy sweater. "You're off the hook." She turned her back and lit a cigarette, scorching it halfway down in length, cupping the flame against the cold wind, and wondered whether Charlie Dwyer was really going to let Mark go back to being a winemaker.

Chapter 23

"If I was ten—no, five—years younger, I would certainly try to make the lovely Ms. Cole's acquaintance," Noel Field said as he watched Lisa hurry off to her car. "She looks quite happy. Almost as happy as Mr. Vlad did about twenty minutes ago."

They were sitting on the deck of Gilleran's Tavern again. Field had ordered a bottle of champagne in anticipation of a celebration.

"She filmed Harry breaking into and coming out of the house in Belvedere, Noel. He'll have to make a deal with her to stay out of jail."

"Then you should be as happy as she." Noel leaned across the table to catch his friend's eye. "You're off the hook now, I presume."

"I'm not sure," Mark responded gloomily. He topped off Noel's glass and told him about the Golden Gate Bridge postcard that Lisa had seen before she was tossed out of Victor Ganero's house.

Noel sipped his champagne reflectively, then said, "That doesn't sound good. Of course, it could have nothing to do with you, but it is a worry. If it was about you, who do you suppose could have sent it?"

"I have a few suspects, but nothing definite."

"So what's the game plan?"

Mark rocked back gently in his chair. "I have to figure that out. There are . . . friends at home. Friends I'm worried about."

Noel swallowed some champagne, then said, "A woman?"

"Yes. A wonderful woman. And her daughter. And my business partner."

"Does this woman know about your past? Who you really are?"

"No. My partner does. I don't want any of them hurt."

Field watched a thin line of bubbles rise through the pale golden wine. "I imagine not," he finally said. "I don't like to ask this of you, Noel. You've done enough already. But I was hoping that you could . . . sort of keep an eye on them for a couple of days."

"Are they here? In San Francisco?"

"No. But close by."

Noel raised his glass and clinked it against Mark's. "Of course I'll help." He grimaced as he shifted his weight in the chair. "Of course, I'm not the man I was a few years back. I'm going to have to do something about this damn hip."

"Maybe a mud bath would help," Mark suggested.

Frank Sinatra was singing one of Bill Rangel's favorite tunes, and in Rangel's estimation Sinatra was putting the young punk he was singing with, some rock-and-roll jerk that he'd never heard of, to shame. It was Sinatra's *Duets* album, and Rangel turned it into a trio, his wobbly, whiskey-slurred words sounding just fine to him. Not as good as Frank's, but better than the rock-and-roll jerk's.

Rangel couldn't remember being this drunk and this happy in a long, long time. He'd been as drunk often enough, but not as happy.

He snapped his fingers along to the music, wondering what Freida, his soon-to-be ex-wife number three, would think if she were here now. Freida didn't like his drinking, didn't like his music. She didn't even like his house, though it looked like she might take possession of it in the property settlement. His attorney had told him that she would no doubt get a good slice of his pension also. He had hoped to retire in a year, but

Freida's divorcing him had changed all that. And that was the reason he'd decided to turn Mark Martel in to the Mafia. During all the years he'd worked so hard at processing rapists, murderers, and drug dealers through the system, he'd never once thought of leaking their new identities.

Of course, none of those losers had a half-million-dollar bounty out on them like Mark Martel did.

Martel hadn't seemed like a bad guy. Rangel actually liked him. It had taken a long talk with his good friend Jack Daniel before he wrote that postcard to Victor Ganero. He wouldn't have even thought about Martel if he hadn't shown up at the restaurant like that, with the private investigator, Lisa Cole, reminding him of the reward. That was a stroke of luck.

Five hundred thousand dollars. Rangel hadn't asked for it all. Just half. A quarter of a million dollars. After all, he didn't know where Martel was. Just his new name. Half of the information that Ganero wanted. So he asked for half of the bounty. Chicken feed to someone like Victor Ganero.

He took a long sip of his drink and stared at the pile of money spread across the kitchen table. There was a phone book on the table, opened to the travel section. He'd called several travel agents earlier that day, inquiring about Europe, South America. Places he'd never thought he would see, and now he was going to see them all.

Rangel had counted the money over and over, every so often holding a bill up to the light, looking for imperfections, worried that they might be counterfeit or marked in some way. But they were real, and there were no visible marks. Good old dirty American cash.

The music softened. A lone piano. Sinatra's aged voice croaking out "One for My Baby."

Rangel was turning the volume up when he heard someone knocking on the front door.

He put his drink down and edged over to the door.

Peering through the peephole, he saw the distorted features of a man wearing a hat.

"What do you want?" he called through the door.

"Sorry to bother you. But is that your Chrysler parked in front of the house? We were visiting next door, and my wife backed into it. I'd rather not turn it in to my insurance company. I'll pay you for the damage."

Rangel opened the door a crack, but kept the latch chain in place. "You hit my car?"

"My wife did," the man smiled. He reached for his wallet. "Maybe we can come to an arrangement. Like I said, I don't want to bother my insurance company."

Rangel slid the chain free. "Hey, don't—"

Johnny Musso crashed the door into Rangel's face. He kicked him out of the way and entered the house, gun in hand.

Tony Zarela thundered up the stairs, slamming the door shut behind him. He jabbed the end of an aluminum baseball bat into Rangel's stomach, then grabbed him by the belt buckle with one hand and rapped his knees with the bat.

"Who else is here? Answer me!"

"No . . . no one," Rangel responded weakly. Blood was frothing between his teeth.

"Bring him in here," Musso yelled from the kitchen.

Rangel's shoe tips dragged across the carpeting as Zarela hauled him into the kitchen. Big Soup's face wrinkled in disgust at the sight of the room—the greasy stove, sink full of dirty dishes, half-empty TV dinner trays, overflowing ashtrays. Several cigarette butts had fallen onto the grimy linoleum. A tray of melted ice, an empty Jack Daniel's bottle, and a phone book sat on the kitchen table, surrounded by stacks of money. The whole house reeked of stale tobacco smoke.

Zarela shoved Rangel into a chair and bound his hands behind his back with a damp kitchen towel.

Rangel started to cry.

Musso bent down and pulled off one of Rangel's shoes, then one sock. He cruelly forced the sock into Rangel's mouth.

"Here's the rules, pal. When I take the sock out, you talk. You talk good, or I'm going to cut off your prick and stuff it in your mouth." Musso walked over to the sink and selected a kitchen knife with a serrated blade. He pulled the sock free, then said, "Where's Mark Martel?"

"I don't know," Rangel blubbered. "Honest. I know he's using the last name Verre. That's all I know."

Musso jammed the sock back into Rangel's mouth and tore at his zipper. "Don't bullshit me! Where is Martel? That piece of paper you gave us has his name, but no address. Where is he?"

Rangel felt like his eyes were going to pop out of his head as he watched the knife move closer to his exposed genitals. He struggled to say something, but the sock made it impossible to talk.

"Last chance," Musso said, pulling the sock free. He turned to Zarela. "Turn the music up."

"Honest, please. Martel came to me and said someone had found him, and—"

Musso shoved the sock into Rangel's mouth, stepped back and signaled to Zarela, who brought the knob of the baseball bat down on Rangel's shoulder.

Rangel tried to scream; his teeth bit through the sock and cut his tongue.

Musso waited until Rangel had stopped sobbing, then withdrew the sock and rested the blade of the knife on Rangel's nose. "Martel came to you? Why? Who are you?"

"I'm with the Justice Department," Rangel gasped. "I helped set up his new identity. I—"

Zarela leaned over and bounced the bat lightly off Rangel's head. "Then you gotta know where he lives."

Rangel started sobbing again. "I set Martel up with his new name, a Social Security number, and a driver's license. He was using a post office box in Los Angeles."

He shrank back into the chair as far as he could as the knife moved from his nose to his groin. "Honest. I don't know where he's living, but she does."

Musso upended the knife blade and drew the blunt end across Rangel's testicles. "She? Who is 'she'?"

Rangel spoke rapidly, telling him of their meeting at Original Joe's restaurant. "Her name is Lisa Cole. She's a private investigator here in San Francisco. She's working for Charlie Dwyer, at Boston Insurance Company. Dwyer left the Justice Department. He's an insurance executive now and—"

Musso slapped Rangel with his free hand. "Dwyer? Does Dwyer know where Martel is?"

"He must. He's in Boston. He thinks that Martel is back to stealing paintings, and he hired Lisa Cole to find him. She knows where Martel lives."

"You're sure of that?" Musso said.

"Yes. She was going to meet him at his house." Rangel sighed deeply as Musso dropped the knife to the floor. "He told her, Martel did, to bring a bathing suit. He was mad. Really mad that she'd found him."

"And you suddenly got the bright idea to contact Victor Ganero, huh?"

Rangel turned his head to the side and spat blood. He watched the drops speckle the floor near the knife.

"She . . . Cole mentioned the reward, and I . . . I thought that . . . "

Zarela grabbed Rangel by the hair and yanked his head up. "This broad. Cole. Where does she live?"

"Carolina Street. She's—" He swallowed blood and started to cough, spraying blood onto Johnny Musso's shirt and tie.

Musso reacted by forcing the blood-soaked sock back into Rangel's mouth. He grabbed the phone book and thumbed through the pages while Zarela began shoveling the money into a plastic garbage bag.

"I've got her, Tony. Lisa Cole, private investigator. Five-forty-five Carolina Street." Musso dropped the directory to the floor. "Let's go."

Zarela nodded his agreement. "It looks like the money's all here."

"Finish him," Musso ordered. "I'll wait in the car."

Bill Rangel tried to move his lips, but every movement only forced the sock deeper into his throat. He watched in horror as the big man slipped the bat under his arm, went to the sink, and washed his hands.

Zarela carefully dried his hands on a towel, then moved to the CD player. He jacked up the volume. Sinatra was doing "New York, New York."

Zarela placed a towel over Rangel's head, then smiled widely as he raised the bat over his shoulder. "Man, I love that song."

Gauguin's ears stiffened and his head jerked up. He sniffed the air for a moment, then leaped to his feet and began barking loudly.

"Shush," Arlene Severi said. "You'll frighten the customers away."

Most of the customers were already gone. There were just a couple of stragglers at the bar. One was Dan Heller, hoping to talk to her again. God, how she wished he would go back to San Francisco and leave her alone.

It was near closing time, and she was exhausted. Arlene sometimes thought that she had taken on too much. She loved most of what it took to operate a top-notch restaurant: the choosing of the foods, the preparation. Her mother had long ago instilled in her the joys of cooking, shopping, growing her own vegetables and fruits—so much so that Arlene preferred the rows of cabbage, parsley, zucchini, and basil in her garden to the many roses that Mark had surrounded his house with.

It was the management—bookkeeping, salaries, taxes—that was getting her down. She thought that if she could hang on long enough, Carrie would take over that end of the business. But that would not be for four or five years, and Arlene wasn't sure she could wait that long.

She'd talked to Mark about it several times, hoping to persuade him to take on the job, but he'd shown no real interest. She understood. The winery was a full-time job, but still—

Gauguin began barking again. He was at the back door, his nose pushing into the mesh screen. This time Arlene's voice was firm. "Quiet!" She went over and opened the door. "Go out and—"

"Are you beating up on my dog, lady?"

Gauguin bounded up to his master, his paws reaching Mark's shoulders, his tongue licking wildly.

Mark roughed Gauguin's hair with both hands, then ordered him to sit. He reached out to Arlene, pushing her chef's hat off her head, running his hands through the silky sheen of her hair, his lips moving from hers to the hollow of her throat.

"Thank God, you're back," Arlene whispered. "Is everything all right?"

"I think so," Mark responded with more certainty than he really felt. "Why don't you close up, and we can go to my place and talk?" He kissed her again, slowly at first, then harder, his hands bending her into him.

"Carrie's here," Arlene said when she'd broken free. "I can't spend the night." She unfastened her apron and tidied her hair. "Give me ten minutes to clean up." She stood on her tiptoes and kissed him again.

Mark reluctantly let go of her, then strolled out to the restaurant bar, Gauguin happily padding along beside him. Dino, La Cucina's bartender, was polishing glasses while waiting for the lone customer to finish his drink and leave. He smiled when he spotted Mark.

"Hey, what can I fix you?"

"A brandy would be fine." Mark slid onto the stool next to Dan Heller. "How's it going?"

"It's been better," Heller responded, his voice thick

with bourbon. "How was your business trip?" he asked sarcastically.

Mark rolled a finger at the bartender to indicate he was buying Heller a drink. "Not bad."

"Did you go back to Canada? That's where you say you're from, isn't it? Funny, I was talking to a friend of mine. Of the Royal Canadian Mounted Police. I thought he might know you, but he didn't." Heller held out his glass to the bartender, who added a hefty measure of bourbon. "He said he'd never heard of you," Heller added pointedly. "Said no one'd ever heard of you."

"I like to keep a low profile, Dan."

Some of Heller's drink went down the wrong way, and he began coughing loudly, his face turning red. Mark patted him on the back, but Heller peevishly pushed his hand away. "Low profile? Hell, man. You're underground. Deep underground." He lurched to his feet and threw a wad of bills on the bar. "A mystery man, that's what you are, a real goddamn mystery man." He knocked back the rest of his drink in one gulp, then ran a hand across his mouth as if he were wiping away a bad taste. "But that's my job. Solving mysteries."

Mark watched Heller head toward the door, walking on his heels, looking like he might fall backward at any moment.

"I don't think that guy likes you," Dino said, scraping up the pile of wet bills and coins that Heller had left behind. "But I'm glad to see you're back. Arlene's been a terror since you left."

Gauguin nudged his nose against Mark's leg, and he reached down and patted the dog's head. He swirled the pale liquor in the balloon snifter before taking a sip. Finding Harry Vlad and turning him over to Lisa Cole had seemed a victory at first, but now that he'd had time to think about it, the victory was damn hollow.

Lisa had seemed satisfied, but her boss, Charlie

Dwyer? How satisfied would he be? Was Harry Vlad enough? Or did Dwyer still want Ganero? He wondered how Harry would react. Dwyer would threaten Harry with jail if Vlad didn't dump on Alvord, or Ganero. Even if Vlad kept his mouth shut, jail was a certain death sentence. Ganero wouldn't take the risk of leaving Vlad alive. So Harry would spill his guts, do anything to keep from going back to prison. Vlad might end up in Bill Rangel's office, in the witness protection program.

There was still the question of the postcard sent to Victor Ganero. Mark worried that it was a foolish decision for him to come back to Calistoga so soon.

The image of his fiancée, Denise, when he'd viewed her body at the morgue in New York, was something he'd never forget. The Hudson River couldn't wash away the evidence of what had been done to her before she was murdered.

Arlene touched his shoulder lightly and whispered, "Let's go home."

Gauguin barked happily, as if he understood Arlene's message.

Chapter 24

Charlie Dwyer pointed at the TV screen. "You say Mark Martel was on the boat with you when you filmed this?"

"Yes. He was there."

"How cozy," Dwyer said. He leaned back in his chair and began straightening out a paper clip. "You don't look too good. And you sound terrible." He tossed the clip into the wastebasket. "Did you catch a cold?"

"Yes," Lisa said, one hand going to her throat. A black turtleneck sweater concealed her bruises. She'd taken the red-eye flight from San Francisco to Boston, on Dwyer's orders.

When she'd phoned him about the videotape, he sounded very excited and ordered her to bring the tape to Boston right away.

"I feel like I'm getting seasick," Dwyer complained. He pushed the VCR slow motion button.

"I think it's damn good footage," Lisa protested. "Look at that zoom shot. You can see Harry Vlad's face perfectly."

Dwyer grunted a neutral response. The camera had caught Vlad running out of the rear entrance of the Burwell mansion, a black bag over one shoulder and a rolled-up canvas in the other hand. The shattered glass door could be seen in the background.

Lisa said, "Does Boston insure the Burwells?"

Dwyer picked up a briar pipe and tapped the stem against his teeth. "Nope. Safeco Insurance has that pleasure. Vlad made off with a statue by some Italian guy I never heard of—"

"Lorenzo Ghiberti, a major early Renaissance sculptor. Most of his works are life-size bronzes."

Dwyer scowled at the interruption. "Well, this was a miniature, about a foot long. Vlad also took five diamond rings, an emerald brooch, two pearl neck-laces, and a Picasso. He's going to be pissed about that. The Picasso is a copy. The jewels and the statue are the real McCoy."

Dwyer started the videotape over, all the while sucking on the stem of his unlit pipe.

Lisa studied him over the rim of her coffee cup. Uncle Charlie had put on weight and lost some hair since she'd last seen him. He had compensated for his baldness by growing bushy white sideburns and a weedy mustache. Her aunt would be pleased about that. It hadn't been an amicable divorce.

Dwyer certainly seemed to have done well since leaving the Justice Department. His office was a cor-ner suite on Tremont Street, with a breathtaking view of Boston Common. The floor-to-ceiling windows caused Lisa to feel a slight wave of vertigo as she peered down at the Central Burial Ground.

She wished Dwyer would light his damn pipe. She was dying for a cigarette, but there were No Smoking signs posted all over the building and there didn't seem to be an ashtray anywhere in the room.

"Are you going to turn the videotape over to Safeco and the police?"

"Not yet," Dwyer said, combing his mustache with his fingernails. "First we put the squeeze on Harry Vlad. And we keep squeezing Martel."

"Mark thinks he's completed his side of the bargain, Charlie. I have to agree with him. He found Vlad for us. I don't think you—"

"That's your problem, Lisa," Dwyer criticized. "You're not thinking. So we have Vlad on video. Whoop-de-doo. He breaks into a house and comes out

with an armful of goodies." Dwyer swiveled around
in his chair and pointed the pipe at Lisa as if it were
a gun. "Why an armful? Why not just the statue, if
that's what he was stealing for Ganero? Why the jewels? The painting? That's not Martel's M.O."

"Who knows?" Lisa responded wearily. "Maybe
Vlad had buyers for those too. Maybe he just couldn't
resist."

Dwyer scratched his temple with the stem of the
pipe. "And maybe Martel set Vlad up on this. Suppose for a moment that the Burwells were Martel's
next target. And that he dropped it right into Vlad's
lap so it would get him off the hook."

Lisa dug a menthol cough lozenge out of her purse.
"No. I don't buy that."

"I'm not asking you to buy it," Dwyer flared. "I'm
telling you it's a strong possibility. The videotape
doesn't do a hell of a lot for Boston Insurance unless
we can persuade Vlad to rat out Martel or Ganero,
so we can get our paintings."

Lisa unwrapped the lozenge, slipped it into her
mouth, and rolled the wrapper into a small ball, which
she threw toward Dwyer's wastebasket. "I think I'm
entitled to the finder's fee for the statue and the Burwells' jewelry, Charlie."

Dwyer scooted his chair over and popped the videotape out of the VCR. "You're working for me. Not
Safeco. I'm going to make a copy of the video and
have somebody hit Vlad hard."

Lisa nearly swallowed the lozenge. "What the hell
do you mean—*somebody*? That's *my* video, damn it.
If anyone is going to slam it over Vlad's head, it's
going to be me."

Dwyer held up his hands in mock surrender. "Calm
down. Do you think you can handle Vlad? I've seen
his rap sheet. He's a pretty tough customer."

Lisa bit down on her lower lip to keep from swear-
ing. Tough customer. If Uncle Charlie wanted to meet

a real tough customer, she'd introduce him to Tony Zarela.

"I can handle it," she insisted.

Dwyer balanced the videotape in one hand, as if assessing its weight. "And Martel. Can you handle him as well, Lisa?"

"Yes. I can handle Mark."

Dwyer pushed a button on the desk to summon his secretary. "Mark. Yeah. I forgot you two are on a first-name basis. What else did you two do on the boat?"

"Screw you," Lisa responded calmly.

Dwyer sucked on his empty pipe for a moment. His secretary knocked lightly on the door, then entered. She was short, dark-haired, and very attractive.

Dwyer tossed her the videotape. "Have two copies of this made right away. I want them ready by the time I come back from lunch with my niece."

The secretary gave Lisa an appraising look before saying, "Yes, sir" and backing out of the room.

"Why do I have the feeling that she doesn't believe I'm your niece, Charlie?"

Dwyer smiled widely, his tobacco-stained teeth blending in with his gold molars. He put his pipe into his coat pocket.

"Come on. I'll take you to the Locke-Ober Company. I understand they didn't allow women inside until 1972. Ah, the good old days."

Harry Vlad hesitated before picking up the phone. It was probably George Alvord, and Harry was in no mood to talk to him. The platinum-blond hooker he'd found in a South-of-Market watering hole at closing time was snoring lightly. Harry leaned over her to grab the phone, noticing that her makeup was smeared, making her look like a raccoon. The sheet was down around her waist. Her breasts pointed straight up, like upended ice cream cones.

"Yeah," he croaked into the phone.

"I got another job for you."

It took Vlad a few seconds to recognize the voice. Tony "Big Soup" Zarela.

Harry struggled to his knees, the phone cord dragging across the blonde's face, causing her to stir.

"Listen. I followed the guy right to a house by the beach. What else do—"

"This is something different," Zarela said. "I'll meet you in the lobby in twenty minutes."

Vlad dropped the phone on the hooker's stomach and lunged out of the bed, sprinting toward the bathroom.

"Hey," the girl yelled. "Where the hell are you going in such a hurry?"

Harry stopped at the dresser, checking to make sure that his wallet and money clip were still there. Had he paid her or not? He fished two hundred dollars out of his wallet, crumpled the money up, and underhanded it toward the bed.

"You better be out of here in ten minutes, baby, or a big ugly bastard is going to come up here and make you give him a freebie."

The girl watched as Harry disappeared into the bathroom. She rolled out of bed, picked up the money, and hurriedly slipped into her clothes. Harry had already paid her last night. She never got in bed with anyone unless the money was in hand. She caught sight of herself in the mirror and winced, then donned a pair of dark sunglasses. She opened the bathroom door. The air was thick with steam. She pulled back the shower curtain, stuck her tongue out at Harry, and said, "I thought you were the big ugly bastard."

Chapter 25

Arlene had been hurt, confused, and more than just a little frightened by his confession last night. They'd been lying in his bed, both damp with sweat from their lovemaking. Arlene had rolled over onto his chest, her legs clamped tightly around his hips. "Now tell me just what the hell is going on," she'd demanded.

Her first response was that she didn't believe that he could have been a thief.

"Why?" she had asked in a disappointed voice.

"It wasn't planned, Arlene."

"You're a stranger to me. Is your name really Mark Verre?"

"Martel. Mark Martel. I was born in New York. My father had an art gallery in Greenwich Village. A small, not very successful art gallery. He helped out all kinds of painters, poets, sculptors, writers whom he liked, or, if he didn't like them, he liked their work. Several of them became famous, but they never seemed to get around to paying my father back. I was blissfully unaware of this. I did a turn in the Marines and was discharged in France. A few years in Paris, then bummed around Burgundy, toured Europe. I would come back for a few weeks in the summer, then hop back to Europe. The last time I came home I found my father sick and in hock up to his neck. I stole a small Matisse charcoal from an uptown gallery. I just walked in, slipped it under my sweater, and walked out. I sold it to a fence for enough to put my father back on his feet. Seven months later Pop was in the hospital. Leukemia. That's a damn expensive disease, Arlene. I stole another painting, then another. My father died, leaving behind an ocean of debt.

"All those friends of his, the artists, the other dealers, they picked his bones dry. I was broke. I couldn't make a living as an artist. One of my father's old friends found out about the stolen Matisse. He was a professional thief, an expert. He explained to me just how lucky I'd been. He took me under his wing."

"Some friend. He made you into a thief."

"I'd had a head start, Arlene. I can't blame what happened on Noel. He's here. Helping me. You'll meet him tomorrow."

"What about your mother?"

Mark plucked at the mattress buttons. "She died shortly after I was born."

"That's a sad story," Arlene conceded, "but there's no excuse for doing what you did."

She slid off him and headed for the shower. She didn't say a word until she was fully dressed. "What are you going to do now, Mark?"

"I don't know," he admitted.

She stood at the window, arms folded across her chest, her profile silhouetted on the wall by the streaming moonlight.

"I'm concerned about Carrie. I don't want her around here if there's a chance she's in danger."

"I agree. What about your ex-husband?"

Arlene's face registered surprise. "Dan? What about him?"

"He's been checking up on me. I'm not sure how much he's learned." Mark put his hands lightly on her shoulders, hoping she wouldn't shake him off, or run out of the house. Instead she leaned into him, burying her head on his chest. She started to sob.

He felt her nails digging into his back. "I'm sorry I came back. I shouldn't—"

"No," she said adamantly. "I don't want you running away again." She tilted her head to one side and looked up at him. "Dan loves Carrie. He's going to be furious when he finds out who you are and what's at stake."

"He loves Carrie," Mark agreed. "And he loves you. He looks like a good man to have on your side when there's trouble. Maybe I should fill him in, before he finds out for himself."

Arlene looked up at him through tear-filled eyes. "Can . . . can you still go to jail for what you've done?"

"No. I was given a clean bill of health from the police," he said, then added, "unless they think I'm active again."

"But won't the videotape prove who the real thief is? That should satisfy everyone."

"Yes," Mark said, staring out the window at the harvest moon. "It should."

The poker-red glare of the morning sun filtered through the shutters of the Calistoga Coffee Shop.

Gauguin chomped on a stale donut as Mark and Noel Field read through the San Francisco and Marin morning papers. There was no mention of Harry Vlad's burglary. Neither of them was surprised. Residential art thefts rarely made the newspapers. The insurance companies didn't want the publicity, and neither did the homeowners, fearing that a copycat might come for the rest of their valuables.

The waitress set a platter of home fries and a steaming cheese omelet in front of Mark, then said, "Can I give Gauguin another donut?"

"Sure." Mark was amused at people's reactions to the big dog. They seemed to want to feed him, as if they thought he wasn't getting enough at home.

"Gauguin," Field said softly. "Somehow the name doesn't quite fit this magnificent creature. Perhaps Rodin. He looks like one of the figures from *Gates of Hell*."

"He seems to like it," Mark said amiably.

He watched the early-morning crowd milling along the town's main street. Vacationing families were already waiting in line for glider trips, balloon rides, and mud baths.

A young woman wearing shorts and a halter top herded a pair of towheaded boys toward the table next to Mark. She skidded to a stop at the sight of Gauguin munching on the donut.

"He's harmless," Mark assured her.

Apparently his assurances weren't enough. She grabbed the boys by the hand and led them out to the street.

"I'm costing you customers," Mark said when the waitress came to clear his table.

"Ummmph," she snorted. "Some customer. They were here yesterday. She left a fifty-cent tip."

After breakfast they took a stroll over to La Cucina. They found Arlene in the kitchen, boning chickens.

"Arlene, this is Noel Field, the old friend I told you about last night."

Noel smiled cordially and extended his hand.

Arlene pointed the tip of the boning knife directly at him. "You're the man who taught Mark to be a thief."

"To my eternal sorrow," Noel responded solemnly. "I'm devoting what is left of my life to repentance." He paused dramatically and added, "And to keeping Mark from harm."

Arlene frowned, hesitated, and for a moment seemed to be searching for words.

Mark jumped in. "Noel's going to be dropping by to keep an eye on you and Carrie, Arlene."

Arlene tilted her head to one side as she sized Noel up. "I don't want him getting in the way," she said, then went back to boning the chickens.

Mark gave her a quick peck on the cheek, then waved Noel outside.

"She does not appear to be overly impressed with

me," Noel observed as they walked the short block back to the center of town.

Mark had left the rented Ford parked in a shady spot near the glider port. The Jeep was still sitting in the lot at the San Francisco airport. Gauguin barked merrily as a biplane towed a silver glider down the small runway and up into the cloudless powder-blue sky.

Noel rubbed his aching hip. "I think I'm going to take you up on that mud bath. It can't hurt."

Mark gestured his friend over to the car, where he took the Derringer out of his pocket and handed it to him.

Noel shook his head vigorously. "No, thanks. Never had any use for guns."

"Take it. Just in case you have to fire it in the air as a warning."

"All right," Noel said, thrusting the weapon into his pants pocket. "When will you be back?"

"Tonight. I want to see what Harry Vlad's up to."

Field gave him an exaggerated military salute, petted Gauguin, and limped off down the street toward Arlene's restaurant.

Mark kicked the engine over and drove off. Lisa Cole had told him she was taking the videotape to Boston. She wouldn't be back in San Francisco until later tonight.

Gauguin barked loudly, alerting Mark to the fact that his mind had been wandering and he'd driven past the entrance to the winery. He patted the dog's head gently. "We're going to San Francisco. Looks like I'm putting you through the wringer, too."

Dan Heller thought work would help keep his mind off his ex-wife for a while. He arrived at the homicide detail with a hangover and a bad attitude, grunted a hello to the secretary, and used the blackboard eraser to take off the "TC" alongside his name. TC was the department's abbreviation for time coming, days off accumulated from working overtime.

He chalked in "OD" to indicate he was back on duty.

Of the fourteen homicide inspectors, there were only five others with an OD tag alongside their names. The rest were marked as VAC for vacation, DP for off with a disability injury, SP for sick with pay, or, in the case of his partner, Diane McQueen, FL for family leave.

Diane had given birth to a daughter four months ago and was going to stretch her time off to a full six months, which meant that Heller was on his own until November.

He slumped behind his desk and flipped through the recent case log. In the last three days there had been just one homicide, a fourteen-day-old baby girl who'd been left in a dumpster to starve to death. Heller shuddered inwardly, thinking about his partner and her new baby daughter. About Carrie when she was born. How the hell could anyone—

"Hey, Heller," Lieutenant Olsen called from his office. "Weren't you asking me about the feds' witness protection program the other day?"

"Yeah." Heller leaned against the lieutenant's office doorjamb. "No one over there would talk to me."

Olsen gave a sour grin and waved an assignment sheet in front of his face as if it were a fan. "Well, here's a guy that's not going to talk to anyone, ever. An hour ago a woman walked into her ex-husband's house and found him beaten to death. The victim's name is William Rangel, and he worked for the Justice Department. In the witness protection program." He folded the assignment sheet in half and sailed it toward Heller. "I take it you're back on duty."

"I am," Heller responded, stooping to pick up the paper.

"Then it's your case. Be careful. The feds will be looking over your shoulder."

There were no federal agents looking over anyone's shoulder when Dan Heller arrived at 1153 Forty-sixth Avenue, only a black-and-white patrol car, the coroner's wagon, the crime lab van, and a bottle-green Porsche roadster sitting in the driveway.

The patrol car's red light was spinning in the luminous fog. The smell of the Pacific Ocean, two blocks to the west, was heavy in the air.

There was the usual string of gawking neighbors. They gave him hard, suspicious looks, as if it were his fault that their daily routine had been interrupted.

Heller double-parked alongside the coroner's wagon. A heavyset uniformed policeman strolled out to meet him. Heller recognized him, but couldn't remember his name.

"You guys must be busy," the cop complained. "I've been holding the fort for over two hours."

The grumpy cop's name came to Heller. Tyson, like the heavyweight fighter. "That's what you get paid for," he said with no sympathy. "What have we got?"

"A white guy, tied to a chair, his head squashed like a three-week-old Halloween pumpkin." Tyson aimed a beefy thumb at the Porsche. "That's his ex-wife's car. Her name is Freida Rangel. She came over to pick up some things. She thought he'd be at work. She found him in the kitchen and called nine-one-one. That's about it." He glanced pointedly at his watch. "You still need me? 'Cause I've got a lot of—"

"I need you. Don't take off unless someone's here to relieve you."

Freida Rangel was in the living room, talking to one of the medical examiners. She was a short, shapely woman with silvery-yellow hair, wearing a rhinestone-studded denim blouse and designer jeans. She twisted her head around when she heard Heller approaching. Her face was carefully made up. Pushing fifty, Heller guessed, but pushing away from it as hard as she could.

He introduced himself, and the first thing she did

was to apologize for the condition of the house. "It was never this messy when I was here, believe me."

For the next twenty minutes Heller conducted his standard witness interrogation. The Rangels' dissolution had been finalized three weeks ago. Freida had returned to pick up some "personal items" and found her husband in the kitchen. "Lord, somebody really beat his brains out. It must have been a burglar."

Heller had noticed the front door dead bolt and chain lock. Neither was damaged, but there were sprays of blood on the floor near the door. Rangel had let his killer into the house.

He watched from the front window as Freida Rangel slithered into her tiny Porsche. What is it about divorced women, he wondered, thinking of Arlene's Italian roadster. As soon as they dump the old man, they buy a sex machine.

Heller recoiled when he entered the kitchen and saw the victim. Freida had been right. Someone had literally beaten William Rangel's brains out. The top of his head was a messy pulp of dried blood and mangled bone, barely recognizable as having once been part of a human being. His pants were undone, his genitals exposed; there were dots of blood on his pant legs. One milk-white bare foot stuck out at an awkward angle. The other foot was encased in a shoe and sock. The second shoe was under the chair.

"Where's the other sock?" Heller said.

"In his throat," one of the medical examiners informed him. "His possessions are on the table. His wallet and a ring of keys were all he had on him."

The wallet and keys were encased in a Ziploc bag. Heller fingered through the wallet. Twenty-four dollars in cash, a tarnished Saint Christopher's medal, his driver's license, federal ID card, a Visa card, a lottery ticket, and two business cards, one for a chiropractor on Sutter Street and the other for a private investigator. Lisa Cole.

Heller whistled loudly between his teeth, causing the medical examiner to give him a sharp look.

"You find something interesting, Inspector?"

Heller held up the lottery ticket. "I was just thinking, it would be a shame if he won now, wouldn't it?"

Chapter 26

Harry Vlad could smell beer. It wasn't someone drinking beer, nor was it coming from broken bottles in the street. This was the smell of beer in the making.

He'd grown up in Brooklyn, two doors away from the old Piels brewery, and it was an odor he would never forget.

"There's a brewery around here," Harry said to Tony Zarela.

Zarela's arms were folded over the steering wheel and his forehead was resting on them. He opened one eye and squinted at Vlad. "You want a beer?"

"No. I said there's a brewery around here. Can't you smell it?"

"All I smell is that sissy cologne you're wearing," Zarela growled. "Keep an eye on the door."

Harry was beginning to think he was spending all too much time in Mafia cars. This time it was a Lincoln. Zarela had been waiting for him in the lobby of the Bay Tower Apartments with the news that "Johnny Musso wants you to break into a house, so get your tools."

Harry had made a stop in the garage, taking his set of lock picks and a pry bar from the Jag's trunk, then was driven to a part of San Francisco he'd never seen and that wasn't featured in any travel brochures.

The place Musso wanted him to break into was a three-story Victorian on Carolina Street, olive green with lots of gingerbread trim and a roof studded with dormer windows. The once-graceful house had been divided up into several units, each with its own separately numbered entrance.

There was a grass-and-concrete park down the block where gangs of kids played basketball and baseball. Four of them had hiked up the street to get a closer look at the Lincoln, hands in their jacket pockets, baseball caps on backward, smiling and jiving with each other, no doubt talking about how much money they could get for the Lincoln at a chop shop.

Zarela had rolled down the window, pointed the end of a baseball bat in their direction, and in no uncertain terms informed them what he'd do to them if they so much as leaned on the car. The kids sauntered away, stopping to give Zarela the finger, then laughed before running back to the playground.

Zarela chuckled as he closed the window, but Harry wouldn't want to be parked around there after dark, even with Zarela and his baseball bat for company.

Harry yawned and focused in on the entrance to 545 Carolina Street. He didn't like the layout. There were eight steps, going up to a small vestibule. The front door was easily visible from the street.

There was a locked iron gate on the side of the building, leading to a narrow alleyway. Anyone walking by, or the adjacent neighbors, could spot someone monkeying with either the gate or the door.

After all the good work he'd done lately, all those beautiful, well-planned jobs, Harry sure didn't want to be busted because some nosy neighbor called the cops.

"Maybe the guy's inside, sleeping or something," he suggested to Zarela. "Maybe we should come back."

"It ain't a guy. It's a broad." Zarela took a small flask from his jacket, tilted his head back, and swallowed loudly. He burped, then said, "A private eye by the name of Lisa Cole."

"Then maybe she's inside," Harry said tightly. The big gorilla could have offered him a drink. He needed a drink.

"This is her office. We been phoning since last

night. Nobody's there. Just an answering machine."
Zarela grunted as he turned to look at Harry. "She
knows where Mark Martel is. I think it's time you go
in, Harry, and have a look around."

Vlad noticed the "you" not "we." "I thought the
guy I followed for you was supposed to know where
Martel was."

Zarela took another swig from the flask and wiped
his hand across his mouth. "He didn't. This broad
does. Check it out, see if you can find anything that
pegs where Martel is. He's using the last name Verre
now." Zarela spelled it out slowly for Harry, then said,
"You don't find nothing, then I join you and we wait
for the broad."

Harry was about to ask, "Then what?" But he
caught himself in time. He didn't want to know what
was going to happen to the private eye, just like he
didn't want to know what had happened to the schmuck
he'd followed home in the taxi yesterday.

"You're sure she's not in there, huh? Maybe she's
just not answering her phone."

"Go find out," Zarela ordered.

Harry scanned the neighboring windows as he
walked briskly across the street. He examined the
brass padlock on the gate leading to the alley and
decided to try the front door first. A private eye. Shit,
the place probably had a security alarm. There were
no visible alarm company stickers, which was a good
sign. People who installed an alarm liked to advertise
the fact. The splintered wooden stairs creaked under
his feet as he climbed the steps.

He pressed the doorbell as he inspected the front
door. Solid wood, painted black, the paint a recent
job, by the look of the glossy finish, so any jimmy
scratches would show up. He kept an ear close to the
door as he tried the easy way first, wiggling a strip of
celluloid with shaved edges into the doorjamb. The fit
was tight, and the thin plastic buckled in his hand.

Next option, Harry told himself, glancing over his

shoulder before focusing his attention on the Yale single-cylinder classroom deadbolt. It was a lock he was familiar with. He had tutored a trusty at Shawngunk on how to pick the very same model, which happened to be on the door of the warden's private dining room. Harry's reward had been a bottle of the warden's expensive brandy.

Ninety seconds, he bet himself, as he closed his eyes and eased a diamond-head pick into the cylinder plug.

Harry was a "feel-picker." He maneuvered the pick directly under the lock pins, then with his free hand wormed a finger-length torque wrench into the lock and began lifting the six pins to the shear line, one at a time. He smiled when the lock clicked free, then hurried inside, shut the door behind him, leaned against it, and listened intently.

Silence. Blessed silence, except for the soft purring of the refrigerator. He made a quick survey: two rooms, one had a desk and computer, the other an unmade bed. There was a dinky kitchen and bath. The Cole broad must not be a very successful private eye—she was living in her office. Relieved to find the apartment empty, Harry checked for a back exit. There was none, other than the narrow kitchen and bathroom windows overlooking the alleyway.

He rubbed his hands together as he approached the file cabinet. The manila folders were arranged alphabetically, but there was nothing for Martel or Verre.

There was a small pile of snapshots on top of the cabinet. Harry flipped through them. They all featured one girl, a pretty brunette. She had a nice smile. Harry slipped two of the photos into his pocket, then searched through the desk, again not coming across anything that ID'd Martel. Or Verre. He knew that if he didn't find something on Martel, he would have to sit in the apartment with Tony Zarela until the woman came home. A PI. Hell, she probably had a gun or two in her purse. He'd have to—

The ringing of the doorbell froze Harry Vlad in place.

The bell rang a second time. Harry moved silently, gently putting down one foot, then the other.

He split the blinds a bare inch—and noticed that Zarela's Lincoln had disappeared.

A big man wearing a tweed sport coat was on the landing. The doorbell rang again, then a fist hammered on the door.

Harry shrank back. The bathroom window. He should have opened it! He'd lose precious seconds opening the damn thing now, and—Jesus Christ! He held his breath. The guy was shaking the door. Who the hell was he? And where was Zarela?

"Lisa. Open up, damn it!" a harsh voice shouted as the door rattled again. "Bill Rangel's dead! Did you know that? Open the damn door!"

Harry slipped off his loafers and backpedaled toward the bathroom, cursing under his breath as the floorboards squeaked.

There was another loud bang on the door, then heavy footsteps pounding down the stairs.

Harry raced back to the window and saw the man in the tweed sport coat stop at what had to be an unmarked police car: spotlights, a long whip radio antenna that looked like it would have been of use to NASA.

Get in the car, Harry pleaded silently. Get in the fucking car and get out of here!

Dan Heller flopped down on the hood of the car and glared back up at Lisa Cole's apartment. Where was she? Somewhere with Mark Verre? And what was her connection to William Rangel?

After leaving Rangel's house, Heller had stopped at the federal building. He'd been greeted coolly, until he revealed the news that William Rangel had been murdered. Then one young muscle-headed jerk told him that the department would "take care of their own."

Heller had blown his top and threatened to haul the muscle-head in for obstructing justice. Sloan Taylor, a scholarly-looking man of sixty with horn-rimmed glasses, a Justice Department legal officer, had calmed things down. He promised "full cooperation in all important matters of the investigation."

Heller had been ready and willing to pass along the name of Mark Verre to Taylor until Taylor and Muscle-head started playing "good-cop, bad-cop" with him. It had ended with vague promises of cooperation from both sides.

Heller had learned more from Rangel's ex-wife than he had from the Justice Department. According to Freida Rangel, her husband's job title was "asset relocator." The assets were the crooked politicians and gangsters that Rangel supplied with new identities. Dan was willing to bet his pension that one of the assets Rangel relocated was Mark Verre.

He slid off the hood of the car and walked around to the driver's side, pausing to give the street a long look. No one was paying him any attention. There'd been a stretch Lincoln Town Car parked up the street when he arrived. It had moved off in a hurry. This was not the neighborhood for a limousine. A funeral car? Someone must have died. Of natural causes, he hoped. He wanted to put all his energies into finding William Rangel's killer.

Lisa Cole dragged herself up the front steps to her apartment. She was still hurting from the roughing-up she'd taken from Tony Zarela, and now she'd added a serious case of jet lag to her list of ailments.

She was about to insert the key into the lock when she heard footsteps coming up the stairs behind her. She wheeled and crouched, ready to use the suitcase as a weapon.

"Take it easy," Dan Heller said.

"Jesus," Lisa exclaimed. "You scared the hell out of me. Stop bothering me, will you?"

Her hand was still shaking as she slid the key into the lock.

"We have to talk," Heller said.

Lisa dropped her bag and turned to face him. "I've had it with you, Inspector. Go away."

Heller held his ground. "Do you know a man by the name of William Rangel?"

Lisa was completely caught off guard. She turned on her heel and moved toward the desk. "The name's unfamiliar to me. Who is he?"

Heller slammed the door shut, causing Lisa to spin around abruptly. She ransacked her purse for a cigarette to stall for time. "I don't remember inviting you in."

"You never met Mr. Rangel?" Heller pressed.

"I just told you, the name is unfamiliar. Look, I'm tired. I just want to go to bed. Please leave."

"Not until you tell me about your connection to Rangel."

Lisa grimaced and reached for the phone. "I'm calling your supervisor and telling him that I'm being harassed by some goddamn cop who—"

"Mr. Rangel was a United States Justice Department employee. He was murdered. His killer cut him with a knife, then jammed a sock down his throat before beating him to death. The coroner believes the murder weapon was a lead pipe or a baseball bat. Whoever used it was a damn strong man."

Lisa lowered the phone to its cradle, then picked up her abandoned cigarette and rotated it nervously between her thumb and index finger.

"Your business card was in Rangel's wallet, Miss Cole. Can you explain that?"

"When . . . when was he killed?"

"Why are you interested? You claim you don't know the man."

"Look. You caught me at a bad time. I just flew to

Boston and back in twenty-four hours. I'm exhausted. Can we talk about this tomorrow?"

"Nice try," Heller said with a hint of admiration in his voice. "All tuckered out from a business trip, huh?"

"It's true," Lisa insisted. "I'll talk to you tomorrow. Not tonight."

Heller chewed on the side of his cheek as he considered the request. "All right. Be at my office at nine o'clock tomorrow morning."

"I'll be there," Lisa promised. That would give her plenty of time to call Charlie Dwyer in Boston.

"You'd better be," Heller threatened.

After Heller left, Lisa poured herself a stiff drink and carried it to the bathroom. She needed a hot bath and a good night's sleep. She had a feeling that sleep wasn't in the cards, but the bath would help. She shivered suddenly, wondering if she was coming down with a cold or the flu, then she spotted the wide-open window over the tub. She was sure it had been locked when she left for Boston. She always locked up before leaving home, and she'd never opened it that wide, ever.

The tubes of shampoo and bubble bath that normally rested on the windowsill were now stacked on the top of the toilet tank. The glass slipped out of her hand and shattered on the tile floor.

"Jesus Christ, someone's been in here," she whispered to herself.

Chapter 27

Lisa Cole's first guess was that Mark Martel had broken into her apartment. She cursed him wildly, noticing that the desk drawer was open. The contents were in their normal state of disarray, so it was impossible to determine whether or not anything had been taken.

She switched on the computer and checked the file directory. Everything seemed to be in order.

What was Mark after? Her report to Charlie Dwyer? There wasn't much in it that he didn't already know. Or was he after a copy of the videotape? Maybe Charlie was right, maybe Mark was involved with Harry Vlad, or he had set Vlad up.

The digital call counter on her answering machine indicated that fourteen calls had come in while she was away. She drummed her jittery fingers on the desk as the tape rewound.

Three of the most recent calls were from Mark, his voice abrupt. "Are you there? Pick up the phone."

The other calls were either short communications: "Hello?" or long silences followed by a grunt and the sound of the phone being slammed down. The "Hello?" voice was unfamiliar.

She dialed Mark's pager number, left a curt message, then immediately punched in the number of his home at the winery and was surprised when he answered in person.

"That was pretty goddamn stupid of you," she said hotly.

Mark untangled himself from the twisted bed linens and struggled to a sitting position.

Gauguin stared up at him with anticipation, his tail wagging frantically.

"Lisa. What are you talking about? What did Dwyer—"

"I'm talking about you breaking into my apartment, that's what! Who do you think—"

"Hold it," Mark said forcefully. "I didn't break into your place."

"Oh, sure. You expect—"

"Listen! It wasn't me. Where are you now?"

"At home. And I—"

"Call the police. Nine-one-one. Tell them you've spotted a prowler. When the cops show up, get the hell out of there."

Lisa stared at the computer screen. If it wasn't Mark, then . . . "Did you know that Bill Rangel was murdered?"

"No! Get out of there right now. Call me as soon as you're safe."

Lisa hesitated for a moment, then went into action. She dialed the police and told them a prowler was at her door, then scooped up her purse and her travel bag, which held the videotape and her reports. She peered out the window. There didn't seem to be anyone hiding in the shadows. When she heard the sirens approaching, she ran down the steps and jumped into her Toyota.

The night sky was cloudless. There was hardly any traffic. She stopped for a red light at the intersection of Sixteenth and Potrero Streets. The car behind her was inching up closer, its bumper almost touching hers. She couldn't make out the driver in the rearview mirror.

Lisa slipped the transmission into low and punched the accelerator. The small car jumped forward, its wheels hydroplaning briefly as she ran the red light.

She drove straight for several blocks, then took a

right turn, not sure what street she was on, just happy that no one was following her.

Mark motioned for Gauguin to follow him downstairs. He tuned the radio to an all-news station, put a pot of coffee on the burner, then tossed a few biscuits to Gauguin.

Lisa's call had rattled him. Bill Rangel murdered. Rangel must have been the one who sent the postcard to Victor Ganero.

The phone rang, and he snatched it up.

"I'm in my car now," Lisa informed him. "I didn't see anyone outside my place, except for the police."

"Tell me about Bill Rangel."

"He was beaten to death with a pipe or a baseball bat, according to Dan Heller."

"When did it happen?" Mark wanted to know.

"Hold on," Lisa said, dropping the cell phone to her lap and lighting a cigarette. She picked up the phone again. Her hand was shaking.

"Heller must have been waiting for me. He came up the stairs as I opened the door."

"When was this?" Mark asked impatiently.

Lisa pulled to the curb and took a deep drag on the cigarette before responding, her eyes focused on the rearview mirror. "About half an hour ago. He said he was by a couple of times during the day, looking for me. It was after he left that I saw the bathroom window was wide open. That's how I know *someone* broke in."

"Was anything missing?"

"I don't know," Lisa responded irritably. "There isn't much of value there, except to someone like you."

Mark stretched the phone cord so that he could pour himself a cup of coffee. He tried to remember Cole's apartment. It was situated over the garage. He would never admit it to her, but he'd actually thought of breaking into her place himself while she was gone.

An alleyway bordered the building, with apartments along it. Lisa's bathroom window was ten to twelve feet from ground level.

"Maybe you left the window open," Mark suggested.

"No way." Lisa pulled out into the street again. "I always lock it, and I never open it all the way like that. My shampoo and bubble bath bottles were removed from the sill and put on the top of the toilet tank."

"A pro isn't likely to climb through a window where he could be easily spotted. He'd come in the front door."

"Let me take a guess. You're blaming this on Harry Vlad, too."

"Lisa. If someone came in through the window, the shampoo bottles would have fallen on the floor."

"So, you're telling me what?"

"I'm just guessing. You said that Dan Heller told you he was by during the day. Maybe someone was in your apartment when he rang the bell, and Heller scared that someone into leaving through the bathroom window."

"And maybe that someone was you. Harry Vlad doesn't know that I exist."

"But Bill Rangel did. The day you barged in on us at Original Joe's restaurant, you gave each of us one of your business cards. His killer could have found the card. Or made Rangel talk. Did Heller say where and when Rangel was killed?"

Lisa's legs turned rubbery. God. She *had* given Rangel one of her cards. "Heller just said that he was cut up, had a sock shoved in his mouth, and was beaten to death."

It took Mark several seconds to respond. He had gone to the city that day, to check on Harry Vlad. Vlad's Jaguar was sitting in the garage at the Bay Tower Apartments. Then he'd stopped at Original Joe's. Rangel wasn't there. "You better find a place to spend the night, Lisa. Do you want to come up here?"

"No," she answered hurriedly. She still thought that it might have been Mark who'd broken into her apartment, and though she wanted to believe him, it was possible that he could have figured that Rangel was the one who'd sent Ganero that postcard and killed him.

Until she was certain that Mark hadn't murdered Rangel, she wasn't going to get near him.

She rolled down the car window and flipped her cigarette out into the dark street, watching it spark as it hit the pavement.

"Dan Heller expects me to meet him in his office in the morning," she said. "Nine o'clock. Or else."

"Are you going?"

"He's no dummy, Mark. He's going to put the pieces together."

Gauguin nudged Mark's leg, silently begging for another biscuit.

"Lisa. Was there anything in your apartment that would lead to me? Reports? Photographs?"

"No. I took everything with me to Boston." She searched her purse for another cigarette. "The file's still on my computer hard drive, of course."

"How do you know that whoever broke into your place didn't pull the file off the computer?"

"The file is coded to an insurance claim number, not a name."

That wasn't good enough for Mark. Someone could take the computer and run through all the files. "Is Charlie Dwyer satisfied that I wasn't involved in those art thefts?"

"Charlie's never satisfied," Lisa sighed wearily. "He thinks it's possible that you did the earlier jobs, then set Vlad up on the house in Belvedere."

"That's ridiculous," Mark protested loudly, startling Gauguin. "What about the videotape? When are you turning it over to the police?"

"That's Dwyer's call, not mine."

"Lisa. I didn't break into your apartment, and I didn't

murder Bill Rangel. Tony Zarela is known to bludgeon people to death. With a baseball bat. If it was Zarela, and he finds you, he'll kill you."

If Mark was trying to scare her, he was succeeding. She felt goose bumps prickle her arms. "I'll be in touch."

Mark injected a quick "Be careful," before the line went dead.

Chapter 28

Big Soup held the two photographs that Harry Vlad had taken from Lisa Cole's apartment up to the hotel room's ceiling light. "That's the same broad!" he exclaimed. "The one who came to clean the house!"

"What are you talking about?" Johnny Musso growled. "What broad?"

"She came to the boss's house with the two old cleaning women. Usually there's a young one, but she was sick." He snapped a finger against the photo. "So this broad came instead."

Harry Vlad edged toward the door. "Listen, Mr. Musso, I don't think you need me anymore, so I'll—"

"Don't move, punk!" Zarela yelled. "Take me back to the apartment. I want this *battona*."

Vlad looked at Musso in disbelief. "The cops could be there staking the house out." He turned to Zarela. "You took off and left me there when the cops showed up."

"Just one cop," Zarela scoffed. "And all he did was knock on the door."

"What was the cop's interest in Lisa Cole?" Johnny Musso asked softly, as if he was talking to himself. He examined the photos. "Maybe Rangel was closer to her than he told us, Tony."

"I'll find out," Zarela promised.

Harry pleaded with Musso. "Listen, I did everything you asked me to do. I found out where the guy at the BART station lived. I broke into the PI's apartment.

But I don't want to go back to her place again. I just got out of the joint. One more time, and they'll—"

Musso cut Harry off with a chop of his hand. "Quit whining. You'll go back with Tony. Later. Two, three in the morning. Tony will make sure there's no cops around. You open the door, then you can take off. Okay?"

"Yeah, okay," Harry mumbled, adding, "Mr. Musso," when the gangster's eyes narrowed.

Musso said, "Soup, you get the broad, but I want to talk to her before you whack her."

"Sure, sure," Zarela agreed readily. "I ain't gonna be in a hurry to finish her."

Harry's stomach rolled over, and for a moment he thought he was going to vomit on the rug. The two of them were planning a murder right in front of him. And they were going to make him an accessory.

He jumped when Johnny Musso tapped him on the shoulder.

"You're doing good, Harry. I take care of people who help me. Remember that."

Dan Heller stuck his head out the door of the homicide detail and scanned the hallway. It was twenty-five minutes past nine and Lisa Cole hadn't shown up yet.

He went back to his desk and phoned Cole's apartment, hanging up when the answering machine message came on.

He was about to call a judge to apply for a search warrant when Charlotte, the detail secretary, yelled out that he had a visitor.

Heller was ready to chew Cole out for being late. He lunged half out of his chair, then flopped back when a man in his fifties with slicked-back gray hair and wearing a pin-striped suit approached his desk. He was broad faced, with small, rimless glasses that cut into his flesh.

"Inspector Heller?" the man asked, setting his scuffed leather briefcase on the edge of the desk. He took a business card from his breast pocket and handed it to Heller. The card identified him as attorney Lawrence Arnster, with an office on Montgomery Street.

"What can I do for you, counselor?" Heller asked.

Arnster sat down uninvited and leaned back in the high-backed wooden chair as he scanned the office. "I haven't been in the Hall of Justice in years. Haven't done any criminal work in ages. I kind of miss it." He sighed and focused on Heller again. "I specialize in civil defense now, Inspector. I'm representing Boston Insurance. I believe you had an appointment with one of their representatives this morning."

"I have an appointment with a private investigator by the name of Lisa Cole. It's regarding a murder investigation, Mr. Arnster. Where is she?"

"Boston, I'm afraid. The home office. An emergency of some type. We regret the inconvenience. Perhaps if you could tell me the details of just what it is you want from Miss Cole, I could be of some assistance."

"I saw Lisa Cole around midnight last night. She had just come back from Boston. She was exhausted. I find it hard to believe that she flew back again this morning."

"Well, I'm told that's exactly what happened," Arnster said. "I understand it's regarding an important case and that Miss Cole's presence was needed."

"Who's the boss at Boston? Who ordered Cole out of town?"

Arnster smoothed his tie with his hand. "The claims department called me at home this morning and advised me to meet with you. I'm afraid I can't tell you much more than that, except that Miss Cole should be returning home in a day or so."

"Mr. Arnster. An employee of the United States Justice Department was brutally murdered, and Lisa Cole is an important witness. Either I talk to someone at Boston, or I sic Justice on you. It's your choice."

Arnster uncrossed and recrossed his legs, letting his eyes drift to the ceiling. "Perhaps I should discuss this with my client."

Heller picked up the phone and handed it to the attorney. "Why don't you do that right now?"

Arnster walked his fingertips across his briefcase. "Is there somewhere where I could have a little more privacy?"

Heller ushered the attorney into the lieutenant's vacant office, then walked over to the coffee machine and poured a cup for himself and one for Arnster.

The attorney had made himself comfortable, leaning back in the lieutenant's chair, his feet propped on the wastebasket.

"Yes, yes, I understand," Arnster said, squinting up at Heller. "In fact, here he is."

He passed the phone to Heller, who first asked, "Who am I speaking to?"

"Charlie Dwyer, Inspector. I hear you've got a bug up your ass about one of our people."

"I want Lisa Cole, Mr. Dwyer. I want her right now. This involves an investigation into the murder of a federal agent, and I—"

"You're talking to an ex-federal agent. I'm sorry about this agent's death, but you can't think that Lisa Cole had anything to do with it."

"I'll be the judge of just what she can do for the investigation. Where is she?"

Lawrence Arnster sampled the coffee, then stood up.

There was a pause, then Dwyer said, "I'll see what I can do about finding that out. What's your telephone number, Inspector?"

Heller gave him the number, then added, "I want to talk to Cole this morning, get it? This morning."

"Give me ten minutes," Dwyer responded, then hung up.

Arnster offered his hand. "I don't believe you'll be needing me any longer, Inspector."

"I don't think so either, counselor."

Heller waited impatiently for almost forty-five minutes before he called Boston Insurance. Charles Dwyer's secretary informed him that Mr. Dwyer was "in conference, and unavailable for the rest of the day."

Heller smashed the phone into its cradle and cursed. Lisa Cole was playing hide-and-seek. Why? What was she frightened of? And where the hell was she? He had a strong hunch that wherever she was, it was nowhere near Boston.

"You look like hell," Bonnie Nelson said, handing Lisa Cole a glass of fresh-squeezed orange juice.

Lisa took a sip before saying, "Thanks. For the juice. Not the description."

They were seated in Nelson's kitchen. The windows overlooked a small garden crammed with orange and lemon trees.

"I'll set up the static surveillance on Ganero's house, Lisa. But I won't be a part of your returning there, so if you—"

"Believe me, Bonnie, I have no intention of getting near the place," Lisa promised. "I just want to know who's going in and out."

"All right. Now, you get some sleep."

"Thanks, Bonnie. It's nice of you to take me in."

Nelson started for the garage. "If you want more juice, just go to the yard and pick some oranges. The electric squeezer is by the stove."

Lisa waited until she heard the garage door close, then walked out to the yard, sat down on the steps, and lit up a cigarette. She was hoping that Bonnie's cameras would capture Harry delivering the Ghiberti statue to Ganero's house.

Vlad would want his money. She wanted to hit him with both videotapes—the Belvedere burglary and the drop-off to Ganero. Then she'd have him, and the finder's fee.

She inhaled and coughed, then flicked the cigarette

into a clover-shaped fish pond. The menthol smoke irritated her raw throat. She picked an orange from one of the trees and wondered how Uncle Charlie would react to her hiring Bonnie again.

He hadn't been happy when Lisa called from the airport, waking him a few minutes after five in the morning, Boston time, and informing him of Heller's visit, Bill Rangel's murder, the break-in at her apartment, and her phone conversation with Mark Martel.

She was puzzled by his calm response. "Stay away from the police," he cautioned. "I'll check with some friends at Justice and see what they know about Rangel's murder. You find a nice safe place for a day or two. And don't go anywhere near Martel. Don't even talk to him on the phone until I sort this out."

A nice safe place. Somehow she didn't believe that Charlie Dwyer would think that being within ten miles of Victor Ganero's house was all that safe.

Chapter 29

Tony Zarela was fed up with waiting for Lisa Cole. He'd been there since three in the morning, and now it was close to noon. There was nothing to eat in her apartment but crackers, dry cheese, and an assortment of canned spaghetti, ravioli, and chili beans.

The liquor cabinet was nearly as bare as her refrigerator. He'd finished off the meager remains of a fifth of Wild Turkey, and was halfway through a bottle of red wine.

While the *battona* didn't spend much money on food, she did okay with clothes. Tony had pawed through her wardrobe and picked out a black see-through negligee that he imagined would look terrific on her.

Johnny Musso wanted Cole alive, but that didn't mean Tony couldn't have some fun with her. He had fantasized about taking her, hard and quick, then bringing her back to Arizona for a real workout.

Cole was gutsy, he had to give her that, coming to the house with those Mexican cleaning women. If he ever saw those *boiatas* again, he'd pay them back good.

Zarela's stomach was growling. He had just decided to open a can of chili beans when he heard footsteps coming up the front steps. He rubbed his hands together like someone preparing for a gourmet meal and tiptoed over to the door.

* * *

A man walking a dog is less likely to be noticed than a man walking alone, according to FBI statistics. Mark had made a point of studying FBI crime reports during his years as a thief.

He wasn't sure if a dog as big as Gauguin would fit into those statistics. A gang of street kids, their heads covered with identical red bandannas, crossed to the other side as Mark and Gauguin strolled down Carolina Street.

A baseball game was being played in the park. There was a lot of screaming and loud mixed-lyric rap music spilling from an assortment of boom boxes.

Mark had been watching Lisa Cole's apartment for more than an hour and was certain it wasn't under surveillance. He ran up the front steps with Gauguin at his heels, shaking his head at Lisa's choice of a door lock.

He made quick work of the lock and stepped inside.

Gauguin's growl saved him from serious injury as he ducked out of the way of a roundhouse right hand.

Tony Zarela snarled and kicked the door shut. His eyes widened and his mouth formed an obscene smile.

"Well, look who we got here. Martel!"

Mark tried to block the next blow, but Zarela's fist caught his shoulder, sending him skidding across the room.

Gauguin leaped at Zarela, his teeth going directly for the big man's groin.

Tony screamed in pain and dug his fingers into Gauguin's neck.

Mark got his breath back, pulled a revolver from his pocket, and shoved the barrel between Zarela's eyes.

"Freeze," he ordered.

Zarela responded by kicking Gauguin in the ribs, while his elbow punched into Mark's stomach.

The gun fell to the ground. Zarela stooped to pick it up and Gauguin jumped him again, his teeth ripping at Zarela's buttocks.

Mark picked up the nearest object, a brass lamp, and smashed the base over Zarela's head.

Zarela rocked back, falling to his knees, and once again Mark smashed the lamp over his head. Big Soup twisted around, grunting wildly as he tried to scramble to his feet, then fell to the floor with a thud, his face smacking into the hardwood.

Mark stood over him with the lamp, ready to land a final blow, and Gauguin jumped over and clamped his jaws around Zarela's neck.

Mark waved the dog away. He groped for Zarela's carotid artery. His pulse was slow and steady.

Those heavy blows to the head would have killed a normal man, but Zarela was anything but normal. Mark increased the pressure on Zarela's neck, pushing his thumbs into his blubbery flesh, thinking of his fiancée, Denise, of Lisa Cole, of all the times he'd dreamed of having this opportunity.

Zarela made a deep gurgling noise and Mark pulled his hands away, wiping them on his pant legs. He was disgusted with himself, though he wasn't sure if the disgust was because he wanted to kill the man or because he didn't have the courage to actually do it. He rolled Zarela over onto his back and went through his pockets. There was a wallet crammed with money, mostly hundred-dollar bills, an ID, credit cards, a telephone calling card, a smattering of coins, and a ring of keys.

Mark pocketed the money, then picked up his snubnosed revolver. He ordered Gauguin to guard the body, then checked out the rest of the apartment.

The bathroom window was wide open, and he wondered if it had been that way since Lisa Cole ran off. There was no way that Tony Zarela could have climbed through the narrow opening, so how had the big man gotten into her apartment?

Lisa's clothes were strewn around the bedroom floor. The bedspread was pulled back and a sheer black nightgown lay neatly positioned on the pillows.

Mark fashioned a makeshift rope by tying Lisa's pantyhose together, straining at the effort required to bind Zarela's hands and feet. He started to stuff a gag in Zarela's mouth, but thought better of it when he noticed that the man was breathing raggedly, his half-opened lips fluttering with each effort.

Mark searched through Lisa's files just to be sure that she'd been telling the truth when she told him that she'd taken all of his reports with her. He fiddled with the computer for a couple of minutes, then gave up and simply disconnected it from the screen and the keyboard. He would return it when he was sure it was safe to do so.

Gauguin was lying down, his nose inches from Zarela's, his big brown eyes staring at the spittle forming at the corners of Zarela's mouth.

Mark pinched Zarela's cheeks. "Wake up. Come on, wake up."

The only response was a series of chest-rattling wheezes.

Mark snapped his fingers, and Gauguin assumed a sitting position. He went through Zarela's pockets again, this time retrieving the key ring. Five keys: two narrow-bow car keys, two angularly bitted high-security keys, and one large old-fashioned iron barrel bit key, often mistakenly called a skeleton key. A very old key, made to fit a very old lock.

He traced both sides of all five keys on one of Lisa Cole's scratch pads, then returned the ring to Zarela's pocket.

"Thanks, pal," he said, as he stroked the dog's hair. Gauguin whimpered when he touched his ribs.

Mark silently thanked those FBI statistics. He knew that if he hadn't taken Gauguin into Lisa's apartment, he would be a dead man now.

Mark drove to a gas station and dialed the San Francisco Police Department's main number. "There's been a burglary at 545 Carolina Street," he said when the operator came on the line.

"Are you there now?" the operator asked in a nasally tranquil voice, as she clicked the address onto the computer screen situated directly in front of her.

"No. Someone is hurt. Hurry."

The operator sighed as the computer traced the call to a pay phone at least a mile from the reported burglary. She clicked some more keys and saw that a 911 call had been placed from the same Carolina Street address very early that morning. The code-3—emergency in progress—had found no one at home, according to the responding officers.

"Another wiseass," she said to herself as she assigned the call to code-1 status—officer to respond when available.

Victor Ganero gently fingered the five-hundred-year-old bronze statue, his eyes semiglazed, his tongue licking at his dry lips.

Harry Vlad had seen that same look before, on drug addicts seconds before they plunged a needle into their arms, and on prison gangbangers when they cornered a young, helpless newcomer in the shower or a secluded cell.

"It's wonderful," Ganero whispered. "Absolutely wonderful."

"Yes, sir," Harry agreed readily, though the statue, roughly the size of an Oscar, didn't look like much to Harry.

They were in what Harry assumed was Ganero's library. All four walls consisted of bookcases, the shelves overflowing with dusty, cracked leather-bound books. The ceiling and draperies were saffron-colored. Half-opened blinds gave a striped view of the garden. Sineo was outside, standing between two dark-haired, bare-chested men who were busily trimming a hedge.

None of the other items that Harry had stolen for

Ganero were in this room. He wondered just where the old man kept his treasures.

Ganero finally took his eyes off the statue and smiled at Harry. "You've done well. I have some good news for you. Mark Martel has turned up. In San Francisco."

"Yes, I figured that's where he was hiding out, sir."

"You figured correctly. You have my thanks, Harry. In fact, I believe I owe you some money, don't I?"

"Yes, sir. The statue. We—"

"Not the statue," Ganero cut in. "The reward for finding Martel. You do want the reward, don't you?"

"If you think I deserve it," Harry said tactfully.

Ganero nodded his approval of Harry's answer. "We wouldn't have found him without you. I expect Martel will be delivered here, to me. When he arrives, you'll receive your money. Until then, I want you to stay here, as my guest."

Harry shifted nervously from one foot to the other. "I don't want to be a bother. I've got a room at the Phoenician Hotel."

"You'll stay here," Ganero said, his tone leaving no room for argument. "You can assist Sineo until Big Soup comes back with Martel."

The man behind the counter at Eckstein Air Charter Services was wearing a tailored shirt that displayed his weight lifter's muscles to advantage. He introduced himself as Ken Eckstein, then repeated Mark's request.

"You want to go to Phoenix, huh?" He thumbed through a flight mileage manual. "Seven hundred ninety-six miles. Our charge would be $3,742."

"Round-trip?" Mark inquired.

"We have to fly down and back, so it's the same charge, one way or round-trip."

"It will be round-trip, but with a layover. A day. Two at the most."

"We charge five hundred dollars a night for layovers, plus you pay for the pilot's room and meals.

Listen. United Airlines can get you down there a lot cheaper."

"My dog can't handle those big planes. How long is the flight?"

"Three hours and forty minutes. That's in a prop plane. If you want to go first class, in a jet, we can get you down there in an hour and twenty-five minutes, but that'll cost you a little over thirteen thousand."

"I'm not in that big a hurry. When can we leave?"

Eckstein ran a hand through his dark, curly hair and frowned. "My pilots are all booked. I'd have to take you myself."

"When?" Mark inquired brusquely.

"How many passengers?"

"Just me. And my dog."

Eckstein pinched his lips together and made a clicking sound with his tongue. "Let me . . ."

Mark pulled out the roll of bills that he'd removed from Tony Zarela's wallet and began slapping hundred-dollar bills on the counter. "Yes or no?"

"I don't want to insult you, mister, but you wouldn't be carrying anything illegal, would you?"

"No. If you can't handle it, I'll get someone else."

Eckstein stared at the growing pile of hundred-dollar bills. "You sure must love your dog, pal."

Chapter 30

The kitchen door creaked open, and Harry turned away from the sink to see Victor Ganero enter the room. He was holding the Lorenzo Ghiberti statue.

"Where's Sineo?" Ganero wanted to know.

Harry turned off the running water and wiped his hands on his apron. "Checking on the gardeners, sir."

Ganero nodded his head, then said, "Send him to me when he's finished."

When the don was gone, Harry rolled a kitchen towel into a ball and threw it at the refrigerator. He felt like a goddamn houseboy. Washing dishes. Sineo even had him mopping the goddamn floor.

He opened the swinging door a crack and saw Ganero using a key to gain entry to a room down the hall.

Harry followed in Ganero's footsteps, pausing at the ornate door that led to what Sineo had described as "the boss's chapel. Keep the fuck out of there."

Harry couldn't resist checking out the door. He ran a hand across his mouth as if to wipe off a smile. He could pick the lock with a butter knife.

Ken Eckstein leveled the twin-engine Beech Baron off and pointed the nose of the plane in the direction of Phoenix. He turned to peer over his shoulder into the passenger compartment. The big dog stared back at him with soulful eyes.

Mark Verre was sprawled in the aisle, a sleep mask over his eyes, foam plugs in both ears. He flitted in and out of consciousness, occasionally glancing at his watch.

The sleep was sorely needed, as was the gun in his suitcase, which was the main reason for hiring Eckstein. There was no way to smuggle the weapon onto a commercial airplane, and if he drove to Arizona himself, he'd be exhausted by the time he arrived.

Mark had always feared that it would come down to this one day. That he would be found and identified, and then he would have to confront Victor Ganero and somehow convince Ganero that he'd had no part in his son's death.

At one time Mark had entertained thoughts of trying to find who *had* killed Junior Ganero and then turning that person over to the old Mafia don. But there was no way he could accomplish that without exposing himself. Mark figured that he'd been used as a patsy and that Junior's killer was most likely someone in the mob—someone who didn't want to see Junior take over his father's position when the old man finally retired.

If he couldn't reason with Victor Ganero, what was left? Kill him? Or make some kind of deal? Steal Ganero's treasured paintings and then barter with him? The paintings for the cancellation of the contract.

Mark knew that none of those options held much hope, but what else was there to do? Ganero was very close to him now. Sooner or later, Tony Zarela, Johnny Musso, or one of Ganero's other killers would find him.

At one time, Mark had had a workable plan to get into Victor Ganero's house. He'd known the time the mail was delivered, which meat market and grocery store supplied the house. The garage where Tony Zarela had the Cadillac serviced. The Catholic churches that Ganero attended in the morning. He had intermittently staked the house out for months, surveying the property from the nearby golf course. The eleventh tee allowed a view level with the front of the house. Once he'd spotted Victor Ganero on the front steps. Ganero looked old and feeble through the binoculars' lens.

It had been more than two years since Mark had been there. Ganero could have changed his security system or the perimeter fencing. That didn't discourage Mark. He was certain that the system's one major flaw would still be in effect: If anyone made entry to the property, the alarm worked internally. There was no hookup to the local police, no wailing sirens. Victor Ganero did not want the police responding to Casa Ganero under any circumstances.

Mark had purposely set off the alarm twice before. The cops never showed up, but Tony Zarela and another man had, prowling the grounds, armed with flashlights and machine pistols. Zarela had triggered off a silenced round of shots at a stray jackrabbit during the second false alarm, the startled animal unaware that he was being fired at until the bullets whined when they struck the iron fence.

Mark slipped the sleep mask back and checked his watch again. He yawned and pushed himself to a sitting position.

Gauguin gave a soft bark.

"Kenny," Mark called to the pilot, "how much longer to Phoenix?"

"About an hour. There's sandwiches and a thermos of coffee in the fridge behind your chair."

Mark poured himself a cup of coffee and one for the pilot and fed Gauguin a ham-and-cheese sandwich. He jangled the keys that he'd had made from tracings of those on Big Soup's key ring and began to give serious thought as to just how he was going to attack Victor Ganero's house.

Sineo answered the phone on the seventh ring. "Christ, when are you coming back, Big Soup?" he complained. "I'm going crazy. The boss is running me

ragged. I'm driving him to church and doing the cooking. I even gotta clean the house. You never should
have fired those Mexican broads."

"Put the boss on," Tony Zarela ordered.

"He's in the chapel. He don't wanna be disturbed,
Tony."

"Put him on the phone," Zarela roared loud enough
for Sineo to pull the phone back from his ear.

"Okay, okay. Hold on."

Zarela rolled the ice pack around the top of his
head and studied himself in the mirror while he
waited. His vision was still slightly blurred, as though
he were watching an out-of-focus television show. He
didn't know how long he'd been unconscious on the
floor of Lisa Cole's apartment, or how long it had
taken him to crawl over to the desk, inch his way up
to his knees, and use the edge of the metal desk to
saw through the bindings on his hands.

He moved the ice pack from his head to his groin.
The big dog's teeth had gone right through his pants
and shorts, but had only scraped his thigh and penis.
His butt hadn't been as lucky. The wounds were much
deeper and would need stitches.

"What?" Victor Ganero asked, the one word demand as sharp as a dagger.

"It's Tony, Boss. I saw Mark Martel today."

Zarela told Ganero exactly what had taken place.
He started to sit down as he spoke but jumped to his
feet when his buttocks made contact with the chair.

After he'd finished, Ganero admonished him. "You
had him and you let him get away."

Zarela cursed himself silently. He should have had
his bat, then he would have killed Martel and his
damn dog. But he hadn't thought he would need the
weapon for Lisa Cole. "It was the dog, Boss. I didn't
see the dog at first."

Ganero gave a grunt of contempt. "Where was
Johnny? Why wasn't he there to help?"

"He went to Boston. Remember Charlie Dwyer?"

"How could I forget that *testa di cazzo*?" Ganero swore, using Sicilian gutter language to describe Dwyer as a dickhead. "What has he got to do with Martel?"

"Didn't Johnny tell you, Boss? Dwyer quit the feds. He's working for Boston Insurance Company now."

"*Che cazzo*? So what? Make sense!"

Zarela began explaining how they'd found out about Dwyer and Lisa Cole from Bill Rangel. He swallowed hard, then told him how Lisa Cole had gained entry to Casa Ganero.

Not many things frightened Big Soup, but the receiver was slick with his sweat by the time Don Ganero spoke again.

"This woman, this investigator, came into *my* house and you didn't tell me?"

"I didn't know who she was, Boss. I didn't know until Harry Vlad broke into her place and found a photograph of her. Honest, I—"

"You didn't tell me," Ganero repeated, only this time it was an accusation.

Zarela stammered in trying to reply, finally saying, "I thought Johnny told you, Boss."

"He has told me nothing! I want you to find Martel. And the woman. Do you understand?"

"Yes, Boss. Do you want—"

"You stay there. I'll have to do this myself. I'm coming to San Francisco. Have Johnny call me. Right away!"

"Yes, Boss," Zarela said, biting off the rest of his response when he heard the line disconnect.

He winced and limped toward the bathroom, the movement causing the wounds on his buttocks to start bleeding again.

Chapter 31

Johnny Musso followed the slim young girl to a table on the patio. He listened to her spiel on the luncheon specials of the day, then said he'd finish his drink before ordering.

"A friend of mine recommended this place highly," Musso said as the youngster started to walk away. "Does Arlene Severi still own it?"

"Sure. That's my mom," the girl smiled. "She's in the kitchen. I'm Carrie. The waiter will be with you in a minute."

The restaurant impressed Musso. He'd expected some yokel mom's-cooking-type joint. Charlie Dwyer hadn't known much about the place, or Mark Martel's girlfriend, other than her name, Arlene Severi, and the name of her restaurant, La Cucina. The Kitchen. Judging from the menu and the prices on the wine list, it was more than just a kitchen.

He finished his martini, then scanned the wine list, grinning when he noted the numerous offerings from the Hatton Winery. When the waiter arrived, he ordered a bottle of Hatton's Viognier to go with penne pasta and duck confits, then leaned back in his chair and prepared to enjoy his food.

He was pleased with the way things were going. Killing Charlie Dwyer, the former federal agent, had been a risk, but a risk well worth taking. Dwyer had coughed up everything he knew about Mark Martel.

Musso's original plan was simple enough. If he ever found Martel, he'd kill him. Just as he'd killed Junior

Ganero. One shot in the eye. Junior had become a liability. Not only to Musso himself, but to the whole family. He was messing around with everything from cocaine to heroin. And when he was high, Junior would talk. Hell, he'd shout out his plans, how he was going to change things once his father retired. Bring the family into the twenty-first century, forge alliances with the blacks, the Asians, even the Irish punks who were strutting around Manhattan as if it were Belfast.

The night that he died, Junior had been yapping about his meeting with Red O'Leary, a loudmouth potatohead who claimed he'd killed forty-two British soldiers on the Old Sod. O'Leary had muscled his way into the labor unions, and Junior wanted the family to partner up with him. Partner up with a dumb Mick!

Musso had feigned interest in Junior's scheme. Enough so to lure him out to an alley where they wouldn't be overheard. The one shot in his eye had been a good move. He had gotten the idea the day that Mark Martel had threatened Junior in the courthouse. Everyone, including Victor Ganero, pegged Martel for the hit.

Musso had planned to whack Martel at the first opportunity, but that opportunity never came. Until now.

Now everything was falling into place.

Tony Zarela's loyalty to Ganero had always been the kicker in Musso's plans. Now Zarela was in deep shit for allowing a private investigator to con her way into Ganero's house and for letting Martel escape. Ganero was foaming at the mouth to get at Martel. Now all he had to do was coax Vic to come to California, to get him away from his mansion in Arizona. And that shouldn't be hard to do. Vic wanted to whack Martel himself.

Musso was tired of waiting for the old man to show enough class to step down. So, Mark Martel was going to perform one last favor for Musso. Kill Victor Ganero.

When Musso had polished off the meal and an espresso, he paid his bill, then poked his head through the kitchen's swinging doors. A short, attractive woman wearing an apron and a chef's hat turned to greet him.

"I just wanted to compliment the chef," Musso announced. "It was great."

Arlene waved the compliment aside with a chopping knife. "I hope you'll come back."

"Oh, you'll be seeing a lot more of me," Musso assured her.

Noel Field eased himself out of the tub of 104-degree mud and stood still while the muscular masseur hosed him off. He was given a fluffy white terry-cloth robe.

"The shower's right down the hall," the masseur indicated in a Scandinavian-accented voice. "I hope you're feeling better."

"I am, indeed," Field concurred. He soaped off the stench of the mineral-scented mud, then dressed in the casual clothes he'd purchased earlier in the day. The massage and mud bath had done wonders for his hip. He hadn't felt this good in years.

He tipped the masseur generously and vowed to return tomorrow. He inhaled deeply once he was out on the warm, sunny streets, fighting back the temptation to pound his chest and howl like Tarzan. God, it was good to have the pain gone, even for a short time.

Noel stopped at a newsstand to pick up a copy of the *Wall Street Journal* and a Jamaican cigar. It was only a two-minute transaction, but it was long enough for him to miss seeing Johnny Musso exit La Cucina.

The town hall was situated across from the restaurant, and Field selected the most comfortable-looking park bench with a view of La Cucina, leaned back, and began to whistle between his teeth.

"Good evening, Don Ganero."

"Musso. Where the hell are you?" Ganero demanded.

"In California."

"Did you hear what happened to Tony? He had Martel and let him get away! I can't trust anyone!"

Johnny Musso waited patiently for Ganero to cool down.

"I spoke to Tony. He wants to make it up to you, and I think I found a way for him to do it. I did do you some good in Boston. I found out where Mark Martel is living."

Victor Ganero's facial muscles relaxed. "From Charlie Dwyer, eh? He told you about Martel?"

"Yeah. He didn't want to, but he ended up telling me."

"Where is the *busone*?"

"Martel is living somewhere in the Napa Valley. It's about a hundred miles north of San Francisco. I'm still working on the exact address—"

"Then you don't know where he is," Ganero accused.

"I'll know by tomorrow," Musso answered confidently. "He's operating a winery."

"Then he shouldn't be hard to find."

"There are more than a hundred wineries in the area. But I'll get him, and when I do find him, I can waste him right by myself. A nice clean kill. I'll make it look like an accident, so no one will connect us to it. I can be in and out of here in a day."

"No," Ganero snapped. "You don't listen too good anymore, Johnny. I told you before, I want to be there. I'm going to carve his eye out. You find out just where the *cornuto* is, and Tony and I will take care of him."

"I'll know by the morning," Musso promised. "Tomorrow afternoon at the latest. But how will you—"

"I'll go to San Francisco and meet with Tony."

Musso smiled widely. Ganero was hooked. "I don't know if that's a good idea. I can send some people out tomorrow to—"

"I don't need anyone," Ganero said firmly. "We will all finish this together."

"What about the house? If you take Sineo there won't—"

"Sineo will stay here. You find out exactly where Martel is, *capisce*?"

"Yes, Don Ganero. I understand."

Musso severed the connection, then replaced the cell phone in its cradle on the dashboard.

"Boss, I don't know if you should do this," Sineo argued. "I mean, I can't let you go out there alone and—"

"*You* can't let me do this?" Victor Ganero shouted, the veins on his neck quivering under the withered skin. "You stay. Guard the house. See if you can do that without fucking up!"

Sineo picked up the don's suitcase. "But, Boss, a cab? Let me drive you to the airport. I don't—"

"*Zitto!* Keep your mouth shut and listen. The chartered jet plane is taking me to San Francisco. I'll meet Soup there. If you hear anything from Johnny Musso, call Tony right away! *Capisce?*"

"Yeah, Boss, sure. But what about Harry Vlad?"

Ganero pushed Sineo out of his way. "Keep him here. When I get back"—he turned and ran a thumb across his throat—"we'll take care of him."

Like Lisa Cole, private investigator Bonnie Nelson also worked out of her home, but Nelson's sprawling seven-room ranch house dwarfed Lisa's apartment.

One of the bedrooms had been converted into a mini-theater, complete with a row of comfortable chairs positioned in front of a large-screen TV. Nelson had salvaged the chairs from an old Phoenix movie theater that had been torn down.

She slid a videotape into the VCR and said, "This is today's footage." Bonnie handed Lisa the video control unit. "I'll get dinner started. Call me if you need help."

Lisa waited until Bonnie was out of the room before lighting up a cigarette.

She kept her thumb on the control's fast forward button. The static camera, which took a single frame of film every fifteen seconds, gave the viewer the feeling of watching an old silent movie. The disadvantage of watching the jerky photography was offset by the fact that an hour's viewing was cut down to four minutes, providing you didn't push the pause button too often.

Lisa admired the way that Bonnie had set up the filming. It was an automatic operation from sunrise to sunset. The home of one of Ganero's neighbors was unoccupied from July to October, since the owners chose to spend the oppressive summer months at their Montana ranch. Bonnie had negotiated an agreement with the caretaker to park the unmanned surveillance van in the driveway of the vacant home. The camera lens had an unobstructed view of the gated entrance to Victor Ganero's mansion.

Lisa leaned forward and hit the control's pause button when a taxi pulled up in front of Casa Ganero. She advanced the video in slow motion, bouncing to her feet when a short, muscular man with flaxen hair exited the cab. He had a small suitcase looped over his shoulder.

"Harry Vlad and the Ghiberti statue," Lisa said under her breath.

The cab made a U-turn, and Harry Vlad strolled to the entryway that was incorporated in the decorative wrought-iron gate.

A few frames later, Sineo appeared and ushered Harry in.

Bonnie Nelson returned carrying a tray that held a sweating silver cocktail shaker, two frosted glasses, and an array of olives and onions already speared onto toothpicks.

"That's Harry Vlad," Lisa informed Nelson. "The guy I filmed breaking into that house in Belvedere."

"I bet he's delivering the goods to Ganero," Bonnie said as she poured martinis.

Lisa pushed the forward button again. Another taxi arrived late in the evening. Sineo opened the gate and waved the vehicle into the grounds. Moments later the cab reappeared and Sineo locked the gates again.

"Your friend Harry must be leaving with his money," Bonnie Nelson observed.

"Good. I'm going to San Francisco and hit him over the head with the videotapes of him stealing the statue, and now delivering it to Victor Ganero."

The two women had drained the cocktail shaker by the time the day's filming was nearing its end.

"When are you going back to San Francisco?" Bonnie asked, rattling the melting ice in the shaker.

"As soon as I can. First I'll call Charlie Dwyer and—wait a minute!"

Bonnie's head twisted toward the TV screen. "What is it?"

"That dog," Lisa said frantically, rewinding and replaying the last frames of the videotape. "That monster dog. It looks like Gauguin."

Harry Vlad nervously paced the bedroom that Sineo had locked him in an hour earlier. It was almost as spartan as his prison cell: a single bed covered by a dismal gray corduroy spread, a clear pine dresser, an overstuffed chair situated in front of an old television set with rabbit ears bent outward like a turkey wishbone. He gazed out the windows at a thunderstorm and wished he was in an airplane, flying high above the storm, heading to South America. With the money Ganero owed him for the Ghiberti statue and the reward for flushing out Mark Martel.

Harry figured that if he did get any reward money from Ganero, Johnny Musso would see to it that it was dribbled out over a long time and a lot of it would be lost in the dribbling. He would much rather have made a deal with Martel, taken his art collection and whatever money Martel had left, and then maybe turned him over to Ganero.

The wall clock showed it was a little after eleven. According to Sineo, Victor Ganero had taken a business trip and would be gone for a day or two. When the don came back, Harry was supposed to get his money. Until then, Harry was going to help Sineo around the house.

Harry had assumed the cooking and cleaning duties for the day. He made sure his tasks took him past the chapel several times.

The chapel. That must be where all Ganero's stolen paintings were kept.

The storm had been playing havoc with the security alarm, and Sineo had to check the front gate when the soft chime of the alarm went off. Harry had worried that the cops might show up at any moment, but Sineo had informed him that the alarm system was strictly internal.

"Ain't no fuckin' cops coming in here—no way," Sineo had promised, all the while cursing the storm and Tony Zarela for leaving him there alone. Alone with Harry.

All of Harry's lock-picking tools were stored in a locker at the airport. The odd-shaped grapefruit knife he'd taken from the kitchen was sitting on top of the dresser. It would be all he'd need to jimmy the chapel lock. He had to see what was in there. He just had to.

He squatted down and examined the lock on the door to his room. It was an insult to his professional pride that Sineo thought he couldn't spring a lock like that in seconds. He used the grapefruit knife to slip the lock, then slid the knife into one of his socks and made his way to the chapel.

*   *   *

The temperature was hot, still in the high eighties, and the humid air pressed against Mark like a soft, clinging towel. Rolling crashes of thunder thudded over the crests of the McDowell Mountains to the east, tearing sheets of lightning into the ink-black sky.

He wiggled his hands into the thick leather gloves, then attached one end of a set of jumper cables to a twelve-volt truck battery. He waved Gauguin away from the iron fence, then clipped the opposite end of the jumpers to the fence rail. There was an angry spark that was quickly drowned out by a volleying clap of thunder.

He unhooked the cables and shoved them and the battery behind a towering umbrella pine that separated the golf course property from Ganero's land.

Gauguin loped alongside Mark as he wove his way through the forest and back to Casa Ganero's front gate.

Mark had set off the security alarm twice in the last hour. Each time just one man had come out of the house to investigate, a man he had never seen, but from the looks of him, Mark was sure it was Sineo, the one who had interrupted Zarela and saved Lisa from a beating by flashing the postcard from San Francisco.

He was fairly certain that Victor Ganero had just one bodyguard in the house. He hoped that Tony Zarela was either in jail or in the hospital in San Francisco.

The first key he tried from those he'd copied from Zarela's key ring slipped easily into the gate's entry lock. As he was turning the key an artillery of thunder rumbled overhead. A gust of wind whistled by like a blast from a jet engine. Seconds later the sky was veined with lightning.

Mark opened the gate, then gestured for Gauguin to follow. They settled into a cluster of citrus trees and waited.

The waving halo of a flashlight beam appeared minutes later. Sineo, the flashlight nestled in his left arm-pit, a short-barreled assault rifle in his right hand, widened his stride as he approached the front gate.

The wind blew his hair straight back, making it appear as if he'd been electrified. Sineo played the flashlight beam along the gate, then trudged back toward the house.

Mark signaled to Gauguin with an open hand across his right forearm, then pointed to Sineo. He tossed a rock toward the gate and when Sineo spun around, Mark snapped his fingers. The big dog leaped out, his jaws engulfing Sineo's arm. The assault rifle clattered to the cobblestone path.

Mark picked up the rifle and smashed it over Sineo's head. He dragged the body into the trees, where he bound Sineo's hands and feet with strips of black tradesman's tape. He placed a final strip of tape over Sineo's mouth, then commanded Gauguin to "stay" and guard the unconscious body.

He grabbed the flashlight, then moved silently and swiftly, hugging the contour of the house, the rifle at the ready.

The front door was open, casting a slice of yellow light out onto the tiled entryway.

He edged closer, then slipped inside, moving toward the living room. He crouched behind a large sofa. There was an eerie silence that was savagely shattered by another volley of thunder.

He had memorized Lisa's hand-drawn diagram of the house. The kitchen was off to his right.

He slithered from sofa to chair, progressing slowly, like a soldier advancing from foxhole to foxhole, pausing to listen, hearing nothing that sounded like human movement.

He nudged the kitchen door open. A plate holding a partially eaten steak and a mound of beans sat on the table. Only one plate, he noticed.

He made his way across the tiled floor to the opposite door and peered out to an empty hallway.

He moved swiftly to the massive oak door leading to the chapel. The iron-bit key rattled slightly as it entered the lock. Mark took a deep breath and turned the knob.

Chapter 32

A stab of lightning irradiated the stained-glass chapel windows for a split second. Mark flicked on the flashlight and played it around, the beam licking over the windows, then the walls. The room smelled of incense and candle wax.

Flickering alter candles bathed the space in a soft, pale glow.

Mark held his breath as he moved the flashlight beam from painting to painting, stopping when he came to Correggio's Madonna, the painting he'd delivered to the warehouse that fatal night in New York City.

"Don't move, Martel," a man's voice warned him.

Mark stiffened, then dropped the flashlight to the floor. It rolled around in a circle, spinning to a stop when it hit the altar pew, the beam fixed on a pair of shoes some fifteen feet to his right.

"Drop the gun," the voice commanded.

Mark's finger was tightening on the trigger, ready to spray the room, when the voice registered.

"Harry Vlad. I've been looking for you."

Vlad shuffled slowly toward the door.

"Hold it," Mark said, walking directly at Vlad. "You never carried a gun, Harry. I bet you don't have one now."

Vlad said nothing. Mark picked up the flashlight and focused it on Harry. He was standing perfectly still, a silly grin on his face, the Lorenzo Ghiberti statue clutched in his hand.

"The light switch is by the side of the door," Vlad said, his hand reaching in that direction.

"I don't think so, Harry. The door wasn't wired, but the switch probably is."

"I figured that, too. I've been using candles to find my way around."

Mark gestured with the gun, and Harry gently placed the statue at his feet.

"Where's Ganero?" Mark demanded.

"He took off on a business trip. I don't know where he went."

The air went out of Martel's chest and he felt the nausea in his head that often preceded a vertigo attack. He'd come all the way to Arizona to deal with Ganero, and now the old don had taken off.

"Where's Sineo?" Vlad asked.

"Resting outside. Who else is in the house?"

Harry paused, and Mark moved in close, sticking the tip of the gun into Vlad's ribs. "I haven't got a hell of a lot to lose, Harry. Ganero still has that contract out on me. Thanks to you, they've traced me to San Francisco. I met up with Big Soup Zarela yesterday. I'm running short of time. Who else is here?"

"Just Sineo." Vlad watched Martel's facial muscles twitch. He didn't want the same thing happening to his trigger finger. "If Sineo's taken care of I guess we can turn on the lights, huh?"

Martel sidestepped over to the wall and flicked the switch. "If anyone else is here, I'll kill you first, Harry."

"This is really something, isn't it?" Vlad said with a note of relief in his voice. "You ever see this much stuff in one room? Not even in a museum, right?"

"You're right," Mark validated. There were more than twenty old masters on the wall. Mark recognized the works of Botticelli, Canova, Mantegna, and Uccello. The portrait of Junior Ganero stood out like a decayed tooth in a string of lustrous pearls.

Harry pointed to a Piero della Francesca oil depicting Christ on the cross. "I took this from the Metropolitan warehouse four years ago. They may still not know it's missing. What do you think the insurance companies would pay if we turned them all in, Martel?"

"They're offering a hundred thousand for the Ghiberti statue you stole two days ago, Harry."

Vlad's hands clenched so tightly that the knuckles whitened. "How'd you find out about that so fast?"

"I was in a boat a hundred yards from the Belvedere house, Harry. With an insurance investigator. They have you on video. Breaking in, and coming out with your arms full, getting aboard *The Jakester,* and motoring back to the dock in Sausalito."

Harry swallowed hard. Martel wasn't kidding. He even knew the name of the rented boat. "What are you going to do now?"

"Where are Ganero and Zarela?"

"God's truth, I don't know," Vlad professed.

"Maybe they're in room 818 at the Bay Tower Apartments, Harry."

Vlad clenched his jaws. "You have been busy, wise guy. But you never should have killed Junior Ganero, Martel. That was a dumb move."

"I didn't kill him." Mark raised the gun to the ceiling and fired off half a dozen shots. Shards of ancient stained glass rained down on the two men. "I'll kill you. Right now, if you don't tell me where Ganero is!"

"I don't know," Vlad insisted. "I . . . I know that Johnny Musso and Zarela were staying at the Trent Hotel in Frisco a couple of days ago, and—"

"Johnny Musso was in San Francisco?"

"Yeah, sure. He and Big Soup. Musso took off, back to New York probably. I don't know."

"You broke into Lisa Cole's place, didn't you?" Mark accused. "What else did you do for Musso?"

"Nothing, really. I followed some old guy to his house out by the ocean. I don't know who he was."

"His name was Bill Rangel," Mark informed him.

"A Justice Department agent. Zarela and Musso beat him to death. That makes you an accessory, Harry."

"No, no. All I did was follow the guy," Vlad protested. He licked his lips. "Who has that video on me?"

"An insurance investigator."

Harry breathed a little easier. "But not the cops?"

"Not yet. Maybe we can work something out."

"We?" Vlad scoffed.

"I'm working with the investigator. I find you, turn you in, and they forget all about me."

Vlad furrowed his brow and clicked his tongue. "Maybe you didn't find me."

"What was the room number at the Trent Hotel?"

"Seventeen-eleven was Big Soup's room. Musso was next door."

Mark tapped the frame of Correggio's Madonna with the gun butt. "Okay. Start with this one."

"Start what with that one?"

"Packing. I want everything you've stolen since you started impersonating me."

Vlad moved slowly, hesitantly. "What are you going to do with them?"

"That's my business. Hurry!"

Harry carefully lifted the painting off the wall. "Ganero will blame me for this. He knows I'm here. He'll come after me."

"That's your problem."

Vlad shook his head as if it hurt. "Yeah. What about the cops? Are you turning me in?"

"No. But if I were you, I'd run to the insurance company, Harry. Make some kind of a deal with them. Maybe they can set you up in the witness protection program."

Tony Zarela waited until the Gulfstream's jet engines were turned off before gingerly hustling up to the aircraft. The plane's shiny aluminum skin opened, hydraulic stairs stretched to the tarmac, and the slim, stooped figure of Victor Ganero began descending the steps.

"Have you heard from Johnny?" Ganero said when Zarela held out a steadying hand to him.

"Not yet. You got luggage, Boss?"

"Yes."

Zarela boarded the plane. The male steward was struggling with a leather suitcase.

"What's he got in here?" the steward asked with a strained smile. "It feels like bricks."

Zarela's eyes turned to slits. The airplane wasn't the usual jet that they chartered for the don's infrequent trips to New York, and the crew member was unfamiliar to him. He jerked the bag out of the man's hand. "Mind your own fuckin' business."

The bag was heavy, and Big Soup rightly surmised that it held a variety of automatic weapons and ammunition.

"Where to, Boss?" he asked when he was beside the don again.

"Your hotel. We wait to hear from Johnny. Then we go take care of Martel."

"You are *not* going back to that house!" Bonnie Nelson declared. "Under no circumstances. No, no, no!"

"Goddamn it," Lisa Cole swore, "I'm going to find out what's going on."

Nelson folded her arms across her chest and spread her legs as wide as her skirt would allow. "No, Lisa. It's not going to happen."

Lisa's hand darted for the telephone. "If you won't drive me, then I'll call a cab!"

Bonnie grabbed Lisa's wrist and twisted it backward. "You go out that door, and I'll call the police. I swear it."

Lisa tugged her hand free and rubbed her wrist, surprised at Bonnie's strength.

"Call Charlie Dwyer," Bonnie urged. "Dump it in his lap."

Lisa bit down on her lower lip to keep from screaming. She had been calling Charlie for hours, at his office and at his home. The office was shut down and his home phone didn't answer. "Okay, okay. Then take me to the airport. I'm not doing any good here."

Victor Ganero waved Tony Zarela away from the phone in the hotel room. He picked up the receiver and said, "Johnny. Where is he?"

"This ain't Johnny, Boss. It's Sineo. I got some bad news."

Big Soup watched as the don sank slowly into a chair, his face turning into a gargoyle of rage.

After several minutes of listening in silence, Ganero said, "You take the rest of the paintings. Behind the altar is a door leading to a crypt. Put the paintings there. And don't let anyone in the house. Anyone!"

He lowered a finger, breaking the connection, then slammed the receiver into its cradle. "Somebody came to my house. They knocked out that *figlio di puttana* Sineo. They took my paintings." His voice raised several octaves with each word as he repeated, "They took my paintings!"

"Who, Boss? Harry Vlad don't have the guts to—"

"Vlad is gone!" He waved his arms wildly in the air. "*Volatizzare.* He vanished, into thin air."

"I don't think that Harry Vlad could—" Zarela stood stock-still as Ganero approached him with wild eyes. Ganero reached up and grabbed Zarela's cheeks kneading them in his hands as if they were cookie dough. "Sineo didn't see the man, but he saw a dog, Tony. A big, ugly *cagna.* You understand? Like the one that bit your fucking ass!"

Chapter 33

Gauguin appeared to be as exhausted as Mark. As soon as he got into the rented van, the dog buried his head in his paws and started snoring.

Mark was anxious to get back to Calistoga, but the adrenaline that had been driving him for the last few days had finally dissipated. He pulled in at the first hotel he could find along the highway and rented a room.

The paintings that he'd taken from Victor Ganero's chapel were tucked in the back of the van. After taking Gauguin for a walk, he herded the dog back into the vehicle and nuzzled his face close. "Stay," he whispered. "Guard."

He left a wake-up call for eight o'clock and was asleep as soon as his head hit the pillow.

After taking a shower and relieving Gauguin of his guard duties, Mark used the cell phone to call Lisa Cole's apartment. He left a brief message on her machine. "Call me."

He then called Arlene in Calistoga. "I'll be back by this afternoon," he told her.

Arlene's response was just what he had hoped for. "Great! I love you. Hurry back."

His next call was to Victor Ganero at the Trent Hotel in San Francisco.

Tony Zarela answered the phone anxiously, hoping it was Johnny Musso.

"Let me speak to Victor Ganero," Mark said.

"Who's this?"

"Mark Martel. How's your ass, Tony?"

Zarela kicked out savagely at the small cabinet next to the bed. "Listen, you prick, I'm going to—"

"Shut up and put your boss on the phone."

Zarela cupped the phone with his hand and bellowed over his shoulder. "Boss, it's Martel!"

Victor Ganero picked up the receiver in the bedroom.

"How did you know where I am?"

"What does it matter?" Mark said. "I have some things of yours. Do you want to do a deal?"

"Listen, you *picio*. I'm going to find you and pull out your other eye," Ganero threatened. "With my fingers, I'm going to gouge it out with my very own fingers!"

"You're wasting your vengeance. I didn't murder your son. I certainly thought about it. If I had, I would have killed Zarela and Johnny Musso, too. I had the chance to kill Zarela yesterday. Look at those marks on his neck. They're from my hands. I'm not a killer. You've been chasing the wrong man."

"*Stronzo!*"

"No, it's not bullshit," Mark said patiently. "You should start looking elsewhere for your son's murderer. If the police thought I had killed him, they would have prosecuted me. They didn't, because I had an alibi. I was under police protection, in a federal safe house in Jersey at the time your son was killed."

Ganero shook his head slowly from side to side. "You think I'm stupid, huh? We checked you out. Checked you out real good, mister. You weren't in no safe house. You killed my boy."

"No. And whoever checked on me lied."

"My paintings. Where are they?"

"I took five, including the Correggio Madonna, and the Ghiberti statue."

"What do you want?" Ganero said, his voice quivering with rage. "What are you going to do with my paintings?"

"Destroy them. Poor lighter fluid over the paintings and set them on fire. And the Ghiberti will go into the ocean."

"If you do that, I will kill you," Ganero promised.

"You can only kill me once. Or maybe I'll turn everything over to the police and tell them about everything else that's in your chapel. Both the police and the insurance companies would love to hear about it."

"Don't threaten me," Ganero rasped.

"Maybe you can save what's still there. Unless Harry Vlad took off with them. You'd have to hide them somewhere. Build a new house, a new chapel. That would take time. How many years do you have left?"

"What do you want?"

"To be left alone. Then you get everything back."

The scowl faded slowly from Victor Ganero's face. "Your life, is that it? My possessions for your life."

"That's it. I'll be in touch," Mark said, then there was a click and the buzz of a disconnected line.

"What did Martel say?" Tony Zarela asked when the don sank heavily into a chair.

"He said he wants to trade. The things he stole from me for his life."

"So what are you going to do, Boss?"

"What do you think I'm going to do?" Ganero snarled. "I'm going to get my paintings back, then kill that *figlio di puttana*."

Tony Zarela was feeling edgy. He didn't like seeing the don like this. Out of control. When word of what had taken place at the Carefree mansion leaked back to New York, there would be rumblings about getting rid of the don. And Johnny Musso would be the first to start the movement.

"What about Johnny?" he asked, mopping up the last morsel of the room service breakfast. "You want me to try and get in touch with him, Boss?"

"No." Ganero paused for a moment, as if marshaling his thoughts. "We wait." He padded slowly toward Zarela. "Take off your shirt."

Zarela hesitated for a moment, then began unfastening his shirt buttons.

"Enough, enough," Ganero said. He reached up for Zarela's head, twisting it so he could see the bruising on his neck. "Martel. He could have killed you, eh, Tony?"

Zarela gave a lopsided smile. "He knocked me out, Boss. With a lamp. Like I said, if it wasn't for the dog, I—"

"But he could have strangled you, *si*? Why do you think he let you live?"

"I don't know, Boss."

Ganero gently pressed the tips of his fingers into Zarela's neck. "I will rest. Wake me when Johnny calls."

Johnny Musso slouched down in the front seat of his rented car. He'd been up since six in the morning, first checking at the Hatton Winery and then at Arlene Severi's house and restaurant.

There'd been no sign of Martel at his house on the winery property last night or this morning, and although the lights in Severi's house went on before eight, so far there was no sign of her, either.

At nine-forty the screen door to the house swung open and Carrie came out. She was dressed in shorts and a man's blue work shirt tied high at the waist. A backpack was hooked over her shoulders.

She strode over to a bicycle, hopped on, and pedaled away.

Musso pulled out behind her, his eyes fastened on her tight butt, hovering over the bicycle seat.

Her braid trailed straight down her back. She had long, strong legs that propelled the bicycle with little visible effort.

Carrie biked up Lincoln, then turned south on the

Silverado Trail. Probably heading in the direction of Martel's place.

Musso kept Carrie in sight, pulling over to the side of the road every so often so that he wouldn't be noticed. He goosed the engine when the bike made a left turn. Where the hell was she going? The entrance to Martel's house was a good quarter mile down the road.

He caught sight of her head flashing through the rows of grapes. A shortcut to the house! That's where she was going. Martel's house.

Musso approached the house slowly, searching for Martel or the big dog that Tony Zarela claimed had taken a chunk out of his butt. There were no cars in the parking area, just the girl's bike. The sliding glass door leading to the house was open, the drapes fluttering in the soft wind.

Carrie was in the pool, working on her breath control, trying to swim a length without taking her head out of the water. She reached the deep end and paused, gulping in air. She swallowed some water when she saw a hawk-faced man staring at her.

"Who are you?" she shouted.

"Don't you remember me, Carrie? I was in the restaurant yesterday. I'm looking for Mark Verre," Musso said, crouching down to talk to her. "Where is he?"

"Mark's not here."

"I haven't seen Mark for a while. How's he doing?"

"Fine," Carrie answered, breaststroking down to the shallow end of the pool. "What's your name?"

Musso straightened up and looked at the house. When he turned back, the girl was climbing out of the pool. She was young, very tall and willowy. She seemed nervous and unsure of herself.

"When will he be back?"

"I don't know." Carrie pulled her swimming cap free and tossed her hair.

She edged away when the man approached her,

ready to either push him in the pool or start running.
But he didn't come near her, veering off to the house,
peering in through the sliding glass doors.

"I've got a business proposition for Mark. I've got
to see him soon, kid." Musso tried to smile. "Mark
told me about you. And your mom."

Carrie wiggled her feet into her sandals. If she was
going to have to run, she didn't want to be barefoot.

"I'm glad Mark recommended your mom's restaurant to me. It was terrific."

"Where do you know Mark from?"

"Back East. We were in business together."

"What kind of business?" Carrie asked as she shuffled backward toward the house.

"The art business," Musso laughed. "Mark knows
a lot about art. Hey, look out!"

Carrie dropped her eyes to the ground and Musso's
hand snaked out and grabbed her by the throat. He
ran a knife blade slowly before her eyes. "Who else
is here? Who else!"

"No . . . no one," Carrie rasped.

Musso effortlessly dragged the girl into the house,
releasing her neck as he closed the glass door and
yanked the drapes closed.

Carrie was shaking, her body out of control, her
face paling under her tan as her eyes fixed on the
knife.

Musso rapped the blade against his open palm and
approached her confidently. Knives. Women feared
knives more than men feared Big Soup's baseball bat.
He slapped her across the face, grabbed her braid and
cut it off with one slash.

Carrie began sobbing.

Musso waved the braid in front of her. "Tell me
where Mark is, kid. Tell me."

"I . . . I don't . . . know," Carrie stuttered.

"If you want to get out of this alive, you better
come up with an answer," Musso threatened.

Carrie swallowed hard. "Mark called. He talked to

my mom. He's coming back today, but . . . I don't know when." She tried swallowing again, but it felt as if her tongue was glued to the roof of her mouth. "Honest," she croaked. "That's all I know."

"You did some shopping, I see," pilot Ken Eckstein said as he helped Mark load the packages containing the paintings and statue into the Beech Baron's cargo hold.

"I guess you could say that," Mark said.

Gauguin growled a little when Mark bent down to help him into the plane's cabin.

"I don't think he's a happy flyer," Eckstein observed.

Mark nodded his agreement. "It's the only thing I've ever seen him really frightened of."

Chapter 34

Noel Field found he had to control himself to keep from breaking into a jog. The second spa treatment had him feeling, literally, in the pink. His entire body was a glowing rose hue from the hot mud and vigorous massage. He saw that Arlene Severi was already preparing for the evening meal. The pungent aromas coming from the restaurant kitchen were divine.

"Top of the afternoon," he boomed loudly as he poked his head in through the swinging door to the kitchen.

To his delight, Arlene gave him a wide smile. "Mark called. He'll be home this afternoon. He asked me to tell you to stick around here and wait for him."

Noel rubbed his hands together briskly. "Well, as long as I'm sticking, I might as well be of use. Can I help with the sauces or baking?"

"Thanks," Arlene said sincerely. "Maybe you could start on the dishes?"

Noel turned to the overflowing sink and the yawning door of the dishwasher. Wisdom does not come with age, he rebuked himself. He'd violated a hard-earned forty-year-old lesson he'd learned in the service—never volunteer.

He rolled up his sleeves and turned on the hot water.

"Mr. Field," Arlene said to his back, "why did you become a thief?"

"It's not a chosen profession. I just sort of drifted into it."

Arlene began inserting wafer-thin slices of lemon under the chicken skins. "What about Mark? Why did you drag him into that kind of life?"

Noel turned to face her, his wet hands held up in front of him like a doctor waiting for a nurse to rubber-glove his hands before surgery.

"I don't think 'drag' is quite the right word, Arlene. The art world is . . . intoxicating, addicting, and brimming with scoundrels of every possible variety. I started out, much like Mark, as an artist. However, I lacked the talent to succeed. I was quite a competent forger until these"—he wiggled his fingers—"began betraying me. By my late thirties, I realized I had no other marketable skills, so I more or less drifted into what became, quite frankly, a lucrative occupation. Risk and reward, of course, like everything else, but the rewards were quite high indeed, and actually the thefts required very little time. Two, three weeks at the most to handle one job, and I seldom found it necessary to take on more than two jobs a year."

"Stealing art or robbing a bank, there doesn't seem to be much of a difference to me," Arlene argued.

"My dear lady, I'm not apologizing for what I did. And if I had ever been arrested, I would have been quite rightly deposited in jail with the likes of those nasty bank robbers." He turned back to the sink. "The trick is not getting caught."

Johnny Musso walked over and chucked Carrie under the chin. She was bound to a kitchen chair at the ankles, her arms twisted around to the back of the chair, her mouth gagged with a handkerchief.

Musso grabbed the strap of her swimming suit, stretched it away from her shoulder, then let it snap back. "Now we just have to wait for Martel and my friends to show up. You're too young for me, kid, but you better be right about Martel coming home today, or I'll let Big Soup have a go at you." He patted her head. "Don't breathe so fast. Relax. Take it easy or you'll swallow the gag and kill yourself."

"I have to talk to Charlie Dwyer," Lisa Cole asserted.

"I'm sorry, Miss Cole, but Mr. Dwyer is not in."

"Listen. This is urgent. I've been calling Charlie at his home and there's no answer. Did he say he was leaving town? Where is he?"

"I'm sure I don't know," the Boston Insurance secretary answered coolly.

"Mr. Dwyer is my uncle. And I'm working for him on a case in San Francisco. Please have him call me as soon as you hear from him."

"I'll leave a message," the cool voice acknowledged.

Lisa pocketed her cell phone. She had been stalling for time the last hour or so in the Double Play, an old-time sports bar and restaurant located temptingly close to her apartment. She didn't even want to drive by her place until she had talked to Uncle Charlie.

Her answering machine had several messages from Mark Martel, all with the same request. "Call me." The last message had an added statement: "I've got them."

She went back to the bar. An aging, curly-haired Lothario wearing a shirt with "Oroweat Bakery" monogrammed across the chest had commandeered the stool next to hers.

"Hey, something wrong? You look upset. Can I buy you a drink, pretty lady?" he asked when Lisa climbed onto her stool.

Lisa gave him what she hoped was a sad smile. "My husband and I had a fight. I'm afraid to go back to our apartment."

The bread driver stiffened his back and straightened his shoulders. "Did he push you around?"

"Not this time. But—"

"Where do you live?"

*   *   *

Lisa parked in the driveway leading to her apartment. The bread truck driver double-parked alongside her.

"Just let me see if he's there," Lisa said over her shoulder as she walked cautiously up the front steps.

She took a deep breath, ready to let out a loud scream as the door swung open. She stood transfixed in the doorway, stunned by the mess that greeted her. A chair overturned, broken glass on the floor, her desk out of position. Her computer. Shit! The computer was gone. The thudding of footsteps on the stairs brought her out of her trance.

"You okay?" The bread driver asked, sticking his head over her shoulder. "Jesus. He really busted up the place."

Once Lisa was sure there was no one in the apartment, she asked him to stand guard at the door while she picked up a few things. The bread man advised her to call the police.

The sight of her bedroom froze her for a moment: the drawers of the chests open, her undergarments spilling to the floor, a nightgown neatly laid out on the bed pillows.

She dropped to her knees and reached under the mattress, searching for the gun that her father had given her years ago.

"You okay?" the bread driver asked.

"I'm not sure," Lisa said. "I'm really not sure."

"Soup. Martel is at 4991 Silverado Trail, Calistoga. The name of his place is the Hatton Winery. Go north past the main entry for about half a mile. There's a small road. Turn right. Martel lives in a house with a swimming pool up the road. The nearest neighbor is another winery a couple of miles away."

"Hey, Johnny. Good stuff. I'll tell the boss. He's taking a nap. Hold on."

Moments later the sleepy voice of Victor Ganero came on the line. "Tony tells me you've found Martel."

"I found where he lives."

"Where are you now?"

"In Martel's house," Musso replied, looking out at the swimming pool. "He's got to come back to his house sooner or later."

Ganero affirmed his agreement with a nod of his head. "Yes. What about the police?"

"They won't be a problem," Musso predicted. "Calistoga is too small to have its own department, and the sheriff's cars patrol all over the county."

"You did well, Johnny. We're on our way. You told Tony where the house is?"

"Right. I'll be here waiting."

"Yes. That's what I want," Ganero said before he hung up the phone.

Tony Zarela adjusted the shoulder holster chafing at his armpit. "Johnny done good, huh, Boss?"

Ganero slid the Glock pistol out of Zarela's holster. It felt light in his hand, because it was made almost entirely from plastic. Nothing like the weapons he'd used when he was a *soldata*. Half the time he was worried that a shotgun would blow up in his face or that a pistol would jam. "Crazy Vic" Ganero had been the first shooter to attain the level of *capo-de-capo*. He'd been the Mafia's number one hit man in the '50s and '60s. Previous dons had all participated in their share of killings, but not in the wholesale fashion that Ganero had. He clicked off the gun's safety and jacked a round into the chamber. "Tony. After my son was killed, did you help Johnny look for Martel?"

"Yeah, Boss, sure," Zarela answered, trying to keep the nervousness out of his voice.

Ganero sighted the weapon in on the TV set, then slowly brought the barrel around until it was centered on Zarela's ample stomach.

"Johnny is positive that Martel killed my son. Positive."

"Sure, Boss. It was Martel. It had to be Martel. Johnny checked it out. Who else could it be?"

Ganero lowered the gun and clicked on the safety. "Let's go," he said, casually tossing the weapon in Zarela's direction.

Chapter 35

After collecting his Jeep Cherokee from the San Francisco International Airport parking lot, Mark loaded Gauguin and the paintings and the Ghiberti statue into the vehicle and drove north toward San Francisco.

He called Lisa Cole twice en route, frustrated at once again connecting only with her answering machine.

He took the Vermont Street freeway exit and cruised by her apartment. There was no sign of her car, or of anything that looked like an unmarked police vehicle in the area.

He tried the cell phone one more time, but the batteries had given out.

Perhaps Lisa had smartened up. Her encounter with Tony Zarela in Arizona, then the break-in at her apartment, should have sent her scurrying to safety.

The aftermath of his fight with Zarela, the broken lamp, damaged furniture, and missing computer in her place would no doubt have sent her into a panic.

He hadn't had the chance to tell her about that, and it wasn't a message he wanted to leave on her answering machine.

Mark's original plan had been to have Cole film and record him returning the paintings and statue he'd taken from the chapel to Victor Ganero. But he wondered now if Lisa would balk at that. She just might demand that he turn over the paintings to her. That way she'd get her finder's fee. And he'd be left with Victor Ganero coming after him.

Would it be better to talk to the police? To Dan

Heller? Heller was going to learn Mark's identity sooner or later anyway, and the big policeman would be a better ally than enemy. A lifetime of wariness toward policemen made that the last choice. And Heller might just take the opportunity to throw him in jail for taking the paintings from Ganero's house.

Every time he did something that appeared to help him climb out of the dangerous hole he was in, someone came along and shoveled dirt back in his face.

Gauguin seemed happy to be back in comfortable surroundings. He clawed around on the passenger seat, then sighed deeply as he settled down, his head in Mark's lap.

Mark scratched him behind the ears, and Gauguin let out a soft, satisfied murmur.

"Don't relax too much," Mark advised him. "We've got a lot of work left."

They had chosen different routes. Martel drove up Highway 101, then across the Bay Bridge and through Vallejo before joining the Silverado Trail at Napa.

Big Soup Zarela traveled via the Golden Gate Bridge, bypassing Sonoma before taking Highway 29 into Calistoga.

Victor Ganero sat stiffly in the backseat, consulting a map and making phone calls to New York City.

Zarela shifted uncomfortably behind the wheel. The two pillows under his rump helped, but they didn't eliminate the pain from the dog bites.

"This is Calistoga, Boss. Where do we go now?"

Ganero lobbed the cell phone up to the front of the car. "Find me a phone booth. This damn thing isn't working."

Zarela was gazing at the storefronts, searching for a restaurant, or a delicatessen, so he didn't notice the white Jeep Cherokee pass them by.

"You getting hungry, Boss?"

"No," Ganero responded in a tone that made it all

too clear he didn't want to stop to eat. "Just find a phone."

Tony spotted a pay phone on the street in front of a small market with a hand-printed ICE COLD BEER sign on the window.

He pulled into the parking lot and waited until Ganero had climbed out of the car and started his phone call before venturing into the market.

It was that quiet time in the restaurant business: after lunch and before dinner.

Gauguin nearly knocked Arlene Severi over in his excitement. Mark pushed the dog out of the way and gave Arlene his own greeting.

Noel Field's polite cough caused them to break up their kiss.

"I'm glad you made it back," Noel said solemnly. "Did you bring any souvenirs?"

Mark tossed him the car keys. "The white Jeep Cherokee down the block." He signaled Gauguin to follow Field. "I'll be with you in a minute."

Noel led the dog outside. Once there, Gauguin took over and sprinted to the Jeep, which was parked under a lacy weeping willow tree.

Field opened the cargo door and gently unrolled the first canvas. When he saw it was a Caravaggio, he gasped, "Oh, my God," loud enough to attract the attention of a passing mailman.

"Are you okay?" the postman inquired.

"Never better," Field assured him as he put on a pair of thin leather driving gloves in order to examine the second canvas.

Field didn't know how long he stood there, in utter awe of what Martel had taken from Ganero's private museum.

He jumped when a finger poked him in the back, and his head hit the Jeep's headliner.

"What do you think?" Martel asked calmly.

"I think you'll give an old man a heart attack leaving these unguarded in the street. What are you going to do with them?"

"I wish I knew," Martel answered sincerely. He went over his options with Field, who had ducked his head back into the cargo area and was studiously scrutinizing the paintings.

"I told Ganero that I'd trade him. The paintings for my life."

"You know that Ganero will kill you as soon as you return these to him."

"Oh, yes. I know."

"And you can't get hold of Lisa Cole."

"No. She may have gone back to Boston."

"Then call Charlie Dwyer," Field suggested.

"Dwyer and I never got along very well."

"Yes, but you've got the crown jewels now. Use them. First let's find them a place of safety. I can't bear leaving them unguarded in the car."

"I think I have just the spot," Mark said. "You want to come along for the ride?"

Field looked lovingly at the canvases. "I don't know if you can trust me with them, son. I really don't know about that."

Tony Zarela was popping open his third Budweiser when Victor Ganero finally finished his phone calls.

He chugged the beer, then jumped out to open the door for Ganero.

Ganero settled in the back of the limousine and, despite the heat, pulled a knit blanket over his lap. He held up a map to the window. "Get going. Straight ahead for a few blocks, then turn right on Silverado."

Big Soup followed orders. As he slowed down to make his turn, Ganero crawled forward, his head resting on the back of the driver's seat, so that his lips were inches from Zarela's ear.

"Tony, I know you don't like it out here with me."

"Hey, Boss. That's not true," Zarela protested.

"Soon you can go back. To New York. I've decided to retire. For good. So I won't need you. I just talked to Louie Licarto. He has my backing, Tony. He'll take care of you."

Zarela felt a mixture of relief and fear. Relief at being able to go back to New York. But fear that the don might be thinking of sending him home in a box. He knew too much. About Junior's crypt. About the stolen paintings.

"I like Louie," Zarela said. "We get along okay. But what about Johnny Musso? I thought that was—"

"I don't want anything to happen to Martel until I find out where my treasures are. If Musso tries to interfere, shoot him."

Big Soup's entire body twitched, causing the car to cross over the yellow dividing line momentarily.

"Hey, Boss. You sure you want me to shoot Johnny?"

"You never questioned me before, Antonio."

Antonio. The boss had never called him by his formal name before. "I ain't questioning you, Boss. Never."

"I don't think it will be necessary. But be ready. *Capisce?*"

"Yeah, sure, Boss," Zarela said, though he didn't understand any of it. Whack Musso. What the fuck was going on? Louie Licarto was a *segaiolo,* an empty holster, a skinny little runt who had always hung back when there was heavy work to do. He'd sat in the car more than once when Tony was working a hit. The boys wold not like him jumping over Musso. They wouldn't like it at all.

"Slow down," Ganero commanded. "I think we're getting close."

Mark bypassed the road to his house and turned in at the main gate of Hatton Winery.

"This is impressive," Noel Field said, swiveling his head back and forth to take in the acres of vines.

"It's a lot of work is what it is," Mark replied. "That big brick building to your right is the office and visitors' tasting room. Over there, behind that stand of Italian cypress, is where we do the pressing and store the wine, in three-thousand-gallon stainless-steel tanks."

A swirl of dust preceded by a battered pickup truck was coming at them from between the rows of vines. Pete Altes beeped the horn, and Mark pulled over and put the Jeep in neutral.

"Hey, welcome back," Altes said through his open window.

"Hi, Pete. This is a friend of mine, Noel Field."

Altes tipped his hat. "Howdy. I haven't seen anything of that black van lately, Mark."

"I don't think we have to worry about him anymore. Any other strangers been around?"

"Just those tourists that come in for the tastings."

"Where's Joan?"

"At the tasting room. We've got a full afternoon of buses on the way." Altes tipped his hat again at Noel and said, "Glad you're back, Mark."

"Altes is the foreman," Mark explained as he drove up the narrow road, veering off to the right and pulling up in front of a carbonized steel door set into the hillside.

"This is it," Mark said. "We barrel and age the wine in the cave."

Once again, Noel Field was impressed as Mark told him how a small natural cave had been hollowed out and expanded to house the thousands of barrels of fermenting wine.

The floor was poured concrete; the irregular ceiling height fluctuated between ten and twenty feet. Wine barrels were neatly stacked and labeled along the limestone walls.

Noel inhaled the incomparable aroma of fermenting wine: the pungent combination of grapes, yeast, sugar, oak barrels, and the musty smell of the cave.

He watched in admiration as Mark wheeled a fork-lift back and forth among the six-high stacks of fifty-gallon wine barrels.

The paintings had been carefully inserted into three empty barrels, whose tops Mark had removed. Then he stacked those barrels on the wall of barrels stamped "Cabernet Sauvignon." The Ghiberti statue was tucked into Mark's waistband.

"Four rows up, four casks over from the south wall," Martel called from the forklift. "Don't forget."

"I have my senior moments," Field confessed, "but that is something I'll never forget."

The forklift's engine sputtered to a stop, and Mark used the storage facility's telephone to call Boston Insurance. It was too late to worry about calls being traced back to him.

"Charlie Dwyer, please."

"Who's calling?"

Mark hesitated for a moment. "Mark Martel."

"Who are you with, sir?"

"The Justice Department. I worked with Charlie when he was in our New York Office. Just give him my name. I'm sure he'll want to talk to me."

The woman's speech thickened and Mark heard a sob. "Mr. Dwyer is . . . dead."

"When? How?"

"I'm afraid I can't say."

"Then put me through to someone who can."

Mark gnawed at his lower lip. Dwyer dead. Lisa not answering her phone. Damn. It could all—

"I understand you're with the Justice Department, Mr. Martel?"

"That's right. The New York office."

"I'm Merle Iverson, chief investigating agent here. Will you be working with the local police on this?"

"That depends. How did Charlie die?"

"The preliminary word I have is that death was caused by a sharp object inserted into his ear. Proba-

bly an ice pick. The Coast Guard fished him out of
the bay late last night. He was naked and wasn't ID'd
until they ran his fingerprints. Now, are you coming
to Boston?''

Chapter 36

"You drove too far," Don Victor Ganero complained. "We missed the road."

Tony Zarela turned left into the entrance of the Hatton Winery, then backed out and continued slowly in a northerly direction until he found the cutoff.

"Over there. By those trees," Ganero directed. "I see a house. That's got to be Martel's place."

"Okay, Boss." Zarela unbuttoned his coat. The silenced Glock was in his shoulder holster. His cement-filled baseball bat nestled between his legs.

He rolled the sedan to a stop. "What now, Boss?"

"What now? What do you think?" Ganero reached for the door latch. "We do business."

Zarela led the way, Ganero trailing safely behind in the big man's shadow. Tony held the Glock down at his side, the baseball bat dangling from his other hand. The boss said not to whack Martel until they had the paintings, but if he sighted the damn dog, he was going to plug him.

Zarela, unable to swim, hugged the cement path away from the pool. One of his heavy thighs bumped into a plastic table and knocked a Coke can to the ground. The can clattered and rolled into the pool.

The sliding glass door to the house opened, and Johnny Musso stepped outside, his hands in front of him, palms upward in a welcoming gesture. It also signified that he had no weapons.

"Don Ganero. Good to see you. And Tony. Have I got a present for you. Come on inside."

"Where's Martel?" Victor Ganero demanded once they were inside the house.

"He's on his way," Musso said. "He should be here any minute."

Ganero's eyes flicked around the room. "How do you know this?"

"Martel's girlfriend has a daughter. She told me." He gestured toward the door leading to Martel's studio. "She's in there, all tied up and waiting for you, Big Soup."

Zarela opened the door with a slap, causing Carrie to jerk around in the chair.

"Well, well, well," Zarela said in a husky voice. "Look at you." He holstered the gun, dropped the bat to the floor, and approached Carrie, who squirmed backward in the chair, nearly tipping it over.

"You can have her later," Musso said. "First we get Martel."

Victor Ganero beckoned Zarela with his finger. "*Un brava ragazza.* She's a little girl. I don't hurt little girls."

Big Soup gave him an embarrassed look. "Hey, Boss, I was just gonna—"

"You better move the car, Tony," Musso said. "We don't want Martel to see anything but the kid's bike. Park down on Silverado and hike back, like I did."

Zarela reluctantly pulled his eyes away from Carrie and looked at Ganero, who gave him an affirmative nod. "Go. Hurry back." He turned to Musso. "Make me some coffee. We have to talk."

Noel Field felt a sudden twinge in his hip, trying to keep up with Mark as they hurried from the cave to the Jeep. "An ice pick in the ear. Sounds like something that one of Ganero's men would have some familiarity with."

Martel yanked open the Jeep's door. "Noel, I want you to go back to Arlene's place. Tell her to call her ex-husband and—"

"The policeman?"

"Right. Charlie Dwyer knew everything about me. The winery, where I live, and about Arlene. Stay with her until Dan Heller shows up."

"And then what?"

"Bring Heller out here, but leave Gauguin with Arlene."

Noel looked nervously back at the storage cave. "You're not going to tell him where the paintings are hidden?"

"That's the least of my worries." Mark snapped his fingers and Gauguin leaped into the Jeep. "Go on. Get going."

Noel slipped awkwardly behind the wheel. His hip was back to its normal condition of pain and stiffness. "What about you? Where are you going?"

"To my house," Mark said. He patted the car's roof. "Get going."

"But that's the first place Ganero's men will look for you. Surely you can't—"

"I'm safe as long as he doesn't know where the paintings are." He reached through the window and squeezed Field's shoulder. "Take off, Noel."

"I'll drop you at the—"

"No. It's quicker for me to cut through the vineyards. Get going!"

Noel fumbled with the car keys, and they fell to the floorboard. By the time he picked them up and looked out the car windows, Martel had disappeared.

Mark slowed his pace when he saw Carrie's bicycle leaning next to the stairs leading to the swimming pool.

He kept to the shadows and slowly traversed the area. There were towels drying on the chaise lounge, and Carrie's backpack was sitting on the patio table. A Coke can bobbed in the swimming pool. Carrie would never throw a can into the pool.

The radio was playing progressive jazz. Carrie was

no jazz fan. Her tastes ran to heavy metal, and she always turnd the radio to one of her stations when she was at the house.

He backtracked to the parking area and cut around the rear of the house, using his key to gain entrance to the back door. He crept down the hall. He could hear loud, angry voices coming from the kitchen. Men's voices. He eased open the door to his studio.

Carrie gave a muffled response when he approached her and began squirming in the chair.

Mark put his finger to his lips and undid her gag. Carrie spat and then sucked air into her lungs.

"Easy," Mark whispered. "Easy. You're all right now, Carrie. Relax. I'll get you out of here." He worked on her bindings, but the knots had tightened from her efforts to free herself.

He foraged through the cabinet, searching for the gun he knew was there. But it wasn't! He now cursed himself for not taking the revolver from the Jeep. He found a hook-shaped knife that he used to score canvases. The blade was dull, and it took precious minutes to cut through Carrie's bindings. When her hands were free, she reached out and pulled Mark to her, trying to hold back a sob.

"You're all right," he said softly into her ear. "You're all right now, Carrie."

As Carrie's cramped arms dropped back to her lap, one hand grazed an easel and it toppled to the floor.

Victor Ganero's voice dropped to a dangerous low. "You dare to talk to me like that?"

"You've got to face the times," Johnny Musso said. "New York is not happy, Vic. When they hear what happened at your house, they're going to be pissed. A *busone* like Martel breaking in, taking out Sineo, walking away with your paintings, it doesn't look good for you. Not good at all."

Ganero fought to keep his temper under control. He set his coffee cup down on the kitchen sink, aware that it made a rattling noise. "I spoke to Louie Licarto today, Johnny. I have decided that *he* is going to head the family."

"You decided!" Musso protested. He thumped his thumb against his chest. "I'm the one who has been running things in New York. Not Licarto. I'm next in line."

"Louie and I had a long discussion," Ganero continued in a conversational tone. "We talked of many things. The death of my son, for one."

"That's why we're here. I found Martel for you. We waste him, then it's over. You will go back to Arizona." Musso paused dramatically, then said, "For good, Vic."

"Yes," Ganero continued as if he hadn't been interrupted, "Louie did some checking for me. Martel was locked up when my son was killed. In Jersey, Johnny. You didn't find that out, did you? No, you told me that Martel killed my son, and I believed you."

"Martel did kill Junior, for Christ's sake. Licarto doesn't know what he's talking about."

The sound of a crash coming from Martel's studio cut off Ganero's reply.

Musso shoved Ganero out of the way, almost knocking him to the floor. He pulled out a gun and yanked the door open.

Mark Martel was on his knees, desperately working on Carrie's leg bindings.

Musso snarled something unintelligible and took careful aim at Martel.

Ganero bumped Musso's shoulder as the gun went off. The bullet whizzed by Martel's head.

"*Basta!*" Ganero screamed. "Enough. Put the gun away!"

Musso's reply was to turn and point the barrel at Victor Ganero. He lowered the weapon when Tony Zarela thundered into the room, the baseball bat gripped in one hand. He was red-faced, out of breath. There were saddlebags of sweat under each arm.

"What's going on, Boss?" he gasped.

"Take Johnny's gun," Ganero ordered.

Big Soup hesitated and Ganero screamed out at him. "Take it!"

Zarela cocked the bat with his right hand and extended his left to Musso. "Better do what the boss wants, Johnny."

Musso's response was a bitter laugh. He tossed his weapon onto a table holding several bare canvases. "You've got Martel, Vic. Finish him off, let Tony have the girl, and we can get out of this dump."

Martel spoke up. "If any of you so much as touches her, you'll never see your paintings again, Ganero."

"Is that right?" Ganero asked, moving slowly toward Martel. He smiled at Carrie, who was hanging on to Mark's hand with both of hers.

Ganero looked at the statue in Mark's belt. He wiggled his fingers. "Give it to me."

Mark pulled the statue free and passed it to Ganero, who stroked it fondly for several seconds. "And the paintings. Where are they?"

Martel shook his head firmly. "Not until I have your word that you'll leave me and my friends alone."

"Hey, Boss, let me work him over," Zarela said.

Musso rapped Zarela's arm with his knuckles. "I've got a better idea. Let Martel watch Tony work the kid over. He missed the action last time."

"I'm serious," Mark snapped. "Touch either of us, you'll never see your paintings, Ganero."

"Where are they? They are not harmed?"

"I have them. They're safe. But if I don't show up tonight, they'll all be destroyed." Mark stared at Musso. "The actual paintings. Not like the fake you burned in the Brooklyn warehouse."

Musso coughed, phlegm rattling in his throat. "He's bluffing, Vic. Go and wait in the kitchen. Tony and I will find out where the goddamn paintings are."

Zarela's hand tightened on his bat. He had never

heard Johnny Musso, or anyone else, talk to the don in that manner.

Ganero gently laid the statue down and picked up the gun Musso had thrown down. He pointed the barrel at Musso. "You murdered my son. You! Tony, *sterminare lui.*"

Johnny Musso pulled the trigger of his backup pistol. The bullet hit its target squarely in the forehead. Victor Ganero crumpled to the floor, knocking over the table holding the Ghiberti statue.

Musso casually pointed the gun at Zarela. "You don't think I'd be stupid enough to carry just one gun, huh, Soup? Vic was crazy, you can see that. Senile. I didn't kill Junior." He lowered the gun to his side. "Well? Are you with me? Or . . . ?"

Zarela squeezed his eyes shut for a moment. When he opened them, he bowed his head at Musso. "I'm with you, Johnny."

"No more Johnny. Don Musso from now on." He patted Zarela on one meaty shoulder. "You're a good soldier. I'll take care of you, Tony."

"What about the don . . . I . . . made a promise. That he'd be buried in the chapel. I gotta do that."

"Sure, sure. No problem. Get the car. We'll take him back to Arizona. Whack Martel. But don't shoot him. Use your bat. I want him to suffer."

That brought a smile to Zarela's homely face. "Yeah. What about the girl?"

"She's yours. And find out where Martel hid those paintings. We might as well pick them up. I'm going back to the Mountain View Hotel in Calistoga and get my stuff. Meet me there when you've finished." He smiled broadly at Martel. "Maybe I'll have dinner at your girlfriend's place again." He pursed his lips and blew a kiss at Carrie. *"Ciao, bambina."*

Chapter 37

Tony Zarela pried the gun out of Victor Ganero's hand, slipped it into his pocket, then slapped the fat part of the baseball bat against an open palm as he approached Mark Martel.

"Okay, pretty boy. You tell me where the paintings are. Tell me, and I'll take it easy on you."

He turned and slammed the bat into an orange-hued painting on the wall, ripping though the canvas and gouging a hole out of the Sheetrocked wall.

"You tell me where the paintings are, and I take you out quick. One pop." Again the bat banged into the wall, this time ripping open a jagged hole the size of a watermelon. "One pop right on the head, and you're gone. Otherwise, I start on your arms, then your legs. One at a time. You know how many bones there are in a guy's body? I read about it once. A couple of hundred." He whirled the bat around in the air, like a cowboy with a lasso. "Where are they?"

Mark brought his mouth to Carrie's ear. "There's a knife on the floor. By your feet. I'll get him out of the room. You get free and run."

Zarela rapped the bat on the floor, making a loud pinging noise. "You saying good-bye to your girl-friend, Martel? She's cute. Real cute. I'm gonna have a lot of fun with her when you're gone, pretty boy."

Mark edged away from Carrie, backing into the cabinet that held his paint supplies. "Did you ever make it with a girl that wasn't tied up, Big Soup? Or beat up? Or already dead? Do you have a problem? Is that why you use the big bat? To make up for your shortcomings?"

Zarela halted, his face twisting into a frown for several seconds until he understood what Martel meant. *"Rompere le palle a qualcuno,"* he swore, promising to break Mark's balls.

Mark's hands groped blindly behind his back, coming up with a tube of paint. "Maybe you don't really like women, huh? *Tony vuole sempre scopare di pecorina?* Maybe you should stick to sheep."

Zarela lunged forward, swinging wildly. Mark ducked as the aluminum bat whistled over his head before plowing into the cabinets.

Mark picked up a canister of paintbrushes and hurled it at Zarela, who swatted it away and laughed. "Come on, pretty boy. Come on."

Out of the corner of his eye Mark could see Carrie reaching down for the knife. He backpedaled away from the door, afraid that Zarela would drop his bat and use the gun if he got too close to an exit.

Zarela was sweating profusely and breathing heavily through his mouth. "Maybe I'll let you watch me and your girl, Martel. Maybe you'd like that."

Mark's heel caught on Victor Ganero's leg and he fell backward, stumbling to the floor.

Zarela was on him in a flash, the bat raised over his head, poised for a chopping blow, like a lumberman ready to bury his axe in a log. Mark rolled Ganero's body over his own, and the bat hit the dead gangster's chest with a sickening *thwack*.

Mark scrambled free. Zarela was confident now. Mark could see it in the big man's eyes, the way he moved, the way he tapped the bat against his palm.

It was now or never. Zarela cocked the bat, baseball style, but instead of running away, Mark ran straight at him, taking a heavy blow from Zarela's arms, but not the weighted bat. He jabbed the tube of paint into Zarela's face, squeezing it tightly, causing the fiery red acrylic to squirt into Zarela's nose and eyes.

Zarela dropped the bat and grabbed Mark in a bear hug, as he grunted angrily.

Mark was lifted off the ground. He howled in pain as Zarela choked the air out of his lungs and threatened to break his ribs. Mark's thumbs slid around Zarela's paint-smeared face, searching for his eyes.

Zarela screamed wildly and spun around the room, Mark clutched to his chest. He twisted his knuckles into Mark's backbone, vowing to break him in two.

Mark dipped his head and fastened his teeth on Zarela's nose, biting as hard as he could, hanging on like a bird with a fish in its beak as Zarela careened into the wall, the paint burning his eyes. He tried to wipe it away with his sleeve, releasing his grip on Mark.

Mark sank to the ground, gasping, trying to catch his breath. It felt as if his chest had been crushed. He scrambled to his feet as Zarela spun out of control, banging into furniture and the wall.

Carrie was on her feet. "Run, Carrie. Run!" He pointed to the back door. "That way. Keep running."

Mark picked up the nearest solid object, the Ghiberti statue, and hurled it at Zarela before darting out to the kitchen.

Lisa Cole circled the gravel parking lot before stopping near the stairs leading to Mark Martel's house. There was no sign of Martel's white Jeep, or any other vehicle, except a girl's bicycle leaning against the railing.

She could see the swimming pool through a curtain of flowering rosebushes. It appeared to be empty. She sat patiently, listening to the car's engine ticking away its heat, the smell of burning oil wafting into the late-summer air.

She rolled down the window, then placed her hand back into her purse, her fingers on the grip of the pistol, a gift from her father to celebrate the day she'd received her private investigator's license. She had no permit for the gun, and had only fired it once, the day her dad had taken her to an indoor shooting range in South San Francisco.

She eased her way out of the car, her purse slung over her shoulder, her hand still on the gun.

Lisa had no set plan, other than to confront Mark Martel. She didn't think that Mark had trashed her apartment, but he had been worried about the information on her computer. If she had to break into his place to find out what was going on, then so be it.

There were damp towels spread across a chaise lounge alongside the pool. A canvas backpack with a paperback novel sticking out of one flap was sitting on a plastic table.

The radio was on, the outdoor speakers blaring loud jazz.

The sliding glass door leading to Martel's kitchen was open a crack. The hem of the curtain flicked in and out with the breeze. Someone was in there. Martel's girlfriend had a teenage daughter. Lisa had worn her swimsuit the day she'd talked to Mark in the pool. What was her name? Arlene was the mother's name, and the daughter was . . . Carrie. That was it. Carrie.

She approached the door cautiously, her fingers tightening on the gun in her purse.

"Hello," she called out. "Anyone home?"

Mark Martel burst out of the kitchen and streaked toward the sliding glass door. He collided with Lisa Cole. She went sprawling, her purse sailing backward over her head and plopping into the swimming pool.

Zarela had found his gun and now fired off three shots. The door suddenly exploded into thousands of fragments.

"What the hell—" Lisa shouted, rolling onto her knees.

"Run, damn it!" Mark shouted, grabbing her arm and pulling her to her feet.

Tony Zarela barged through the shattered glass

frame, his burning eyes searching for Mark. He blinked rapidly when he saw Lisa. The private eye bitch! He jabbed the gun at her.

Mark crouched down and hurled himself at Zarela, plowing into his knees.

Zarela tottered momentarily from one foot to the other, and Mark hit him again, sending both of them into the swimming pool.

Zarela dropped his gun as he hit the water. Mark struck out with both hands, pummeling Zarela's face.

Zarela retaliated by securing one hand around Mark's neck, his sharp nails threatening to sever Mark's carotid artery.

Mark wrapped his legs around Zarela's hips and pulled him under the water. The pressure on his neck ceased as Zarela's arms flailed ineffectively through the water.

Mark hung on tight, carrying Zarela to the bottom of the pool. The gangster was goggle-eyed. He opened his mouth as if to scream. Mark tightened his grip. The big man's strength advantage disappeared under the water, and Mark rolled him into the deep end of the pool.

Zarela thrashed around like a fish on dry ground. He gave a sudden, final convulsion, then was motionless. Mark continued to hold him under until his own lungs felt as if they were ready to burst. He released his grip and surged upward, gulping in air as he broke the surface.

Zarela's lifeless body rose slowly and floated alongside Mark.

"Jesus Christ," Lisa Cole shouted. "I thought he was going to kill you. What the hell is going on?"

Mark splashed water in his face and tried to regain his breath before replying. "Go in the house. Make sure Carrie got away."

He waded to the end of the pool, unbuttoning his soaking shirt. "Then call the sheriff. Victor Ganero's inside. Dead."

Lisa gave him a questioning look, then turned on her heel and ran into the house. Mark was right behind her, taking the steps to his bedroom two at a time, pulling a dry shirt out of the closet and then retrieving a pistol from the nightstand.

Lisa was waiting for him at the bottom of the stairs. "Carrie's gone. What happened?"

"Can't tell you now," Mark panted. "Where's your car?"

"In the lot. But—"

"Give me the keys."

"They're in my purse," Lisa said, angrily pointing to the swimming pool.

Mark waded back into the pool. Tony Zarela was floating facedown, legs together, arms outstretched as if he were nailed to a cross. Mark pushed the body out of the way, snatched up the purse, upended it on the tile pool coving, and picked out the keys.

"Call the sheriff, Lisa," he repeated.

"Where the hell are you going?"

"Calistoga," Mark said, already trotting toward the parking lot. "By the way, I've got your paintings," he called over his shoulder before bolting up the patio stairs.

Chapter 38

"Thank you for spending time with us, Mr. Johnson," the desk clerk at the Mountain View Hotel said with a professional smile. "I hope you'll stay with us again."

"Sure, sure," Johnny Musso mumbled as he paid his bill. He shot his cuff and looked at his watch. Big Soup probably wouldn't be back for an hour or so. He wandered across the antique-laden lobby to the hotel saloon.

An oversized oil painting of a strange-looking animal hung above the bar. A brochure racked between bowls of peanuts and pretzels identified it as a Catahoula hound dog, the official dog of the State of Louisiana, a cross between the Spanish war dog and the Native American red wolf, with webbed feet that it used to paddle around the Bayou Country.

The Catahoula made Musso think about Martel's dog. Zarela had described it as big, ugly, and mean. Why hadn't the beast been with him at his house?

The bartender, a round-faced man with nutmeg-colored skin and a Zapata mustache, was pouring drinks as fast as he could work to satisfy a crowd of thirsty tourists.

Musso waved a ten-dollar bill at him and said, "Jack Daniel's on the rocks."

He settled comfortably on a stool and took stock of what had happened a short time earlier. Victor Ganero was dead. Finally. Martel was dead by now. Tony Zarela had been his only worry, but Big Soup had fallen right in line, and Musso had no doubt that Tony would remain loyal to him. He desperately wanted to get back to New York City, and there was more than enough work to go around back home.

Louie Licarto wasn't going to be a problem. Without Ganero around to back him, he had no chance of taking over the family.

Vic's precious paintings would be a bonus. He'd peddle them through that wimp art dealer, George Alvord. And the Arizona mansion. That should bring a good price, too.

The drink arrived and he pushed the ice cubes around with his manicured forefinger. He was about to take a sip when the grating sound of a siren distracted him.

Musso carried the glass over to the window and saw a tan-and-white sheriff's car, red lights flashing, bull its way down the town's main street.

He strolled back to the bar. It could be anything, he reasoned. A car accident, somebody hitting a deer, a family fight, you name it. Still, if Zarela didn't show up in half an hour, he'd go on and leave without him. The big slob was no doubt enjoying himself with Martel and the kid.

Mark Martel kept the accelerator of Lisa Cole's Toyota on the floor, his foot grazing the brake only when absolutely necessary.

He made a careening turn onto the Silverado Trail, his eye flicking from the road to the hillside, constantly checking for Carrie Severi.

He spotted her head weaving through a row of vines, slammed on the brakes and jumped out of the car, waving his arms.

"Carrie! It's me. It's okay!"

Carrie stood still for a moment, then began running toward him with an awkward gait. She was obviously in shock. Mark helped her into the passenger seat, noticing that the bottoms of her feet were scraped and bloody.

"It's okay," Mark repeated, once he was back behind the wheel. He reached out a hand and patted her on her bare leg. "Are you all right?"

"I . . . I think so." She gulped and swallowed, then stuck her head out the window and vomited.

Mark squeezed her leg. "I'm taking you home, Carrie. You'll be all right."

A sheriff's car was coming at them from the opposite direction. The uniformed driver gave Mark a hard look as he whizzed by.

Mark eased down on the brake pedal as they neared town. He took a back road to Carrie's house. Arlene was standing out in front, talking with Noel Field, her hands chopping the air as if she were an orchestra conductor.

Gauguin bounded down from the porch as Mark picked Carrie up and carried her into the house, shaking his head at Arlene's string of questions. "Call a doctor," Mark advised. "She's in shock." He put Carrie gently down on a sofa and covered her with a bright-colored blanket.

"What happened?" Arlene's voice had a shrill edge to it.

Mark grabbed her by both shoulders. "She's had a bad scare. Call a doctor. And get the police over here. Did you call Dan Heller?"

"Yes," she answered gruffly, pushing him away, dropping to her knees and caressing Carrie's face. She stiffened when she felt the back of her daughter's head. "Who cut her hair? What the hell is happening?"

"Carrie's safe now. You're safe. I'll explain everything later."

Mark ordered Gauguin, "Stay," then grabbed Noel Field by the elbow. "Victor Ganero and Tony Zarela are both dead. They're at my house. Lisa Cole is there now. She called the cops. Johnny Musso is here. In town. I'm going after him. You stay here and—"

Arlene Severi stood up and slammed her fist into

Mark's chest with as much force as she could muster. "God damn you. What is going on? Who did this to Carrie?"

"Noel will fill you in," Mark said, hurrying to the door.

Shoppers and tourists quickly sidestepped as the wild-eyed man in wet clothing barged past them.

Mark made sure his shirt covered the pistol in his waistband as he drew near to the Mountain View Hotel.

The hotel purchased a lot of Hatton wines and the desk clerk recognized Mark. His eyes narrowed when he saw Mark's condition: soggy pants and damp, uncombed hair.

"Mr. Verre. Are you all right?"

"Fine," Mark answered, trying to catch his breath. "I'm looking for one of your guests. He's about forty—with a big nose, and he has a New York accent. He was wearing a brown sport coat. His name is Johnny Musso, but I doubt if he—"

"You must mean Mr. Johnson. He checked out a short time ago. I believe I saw him go into the saloon."

Mark raced into the bar, scanning the crowd. He waved Joely, the bartender, over and described Musso.

"You missed him by a couple of minutes, Mark." He jerked a thumb over his shoulder. "He went thataway."

Thataway was to the rear of the hotel, where guests parked their cars.

Mark hurried to the parking lot. A silver Ford Mustang was backing out of a stall. The driver was a dark-haired male. As the car turned to the left, Mark recognized Musso.

Johnny Musso saw Martel at the same moment. The Mustang's engine snarled, the tires spun as he straightened out the steering wheel and gunned it, heading directly for Martel.

Mark tried to jump to safety, but the Mustang's fender clipped his leg and he was thrown to the ground. As he lay flat on the asphalt, he cradled the revolver in both hands and fired off four shots at the speeding car's tires.

Musso felt the Mustang momentarily slew out of control. He stepped on the gas and veered around the corner, narrowly missing a trio of elderly men crossing the street. He could feel a tire go. The car lurched to the right and there was a whining screech as the steel rims furrowed a trail along the pavement.

He jammed on the brakes, but the out-of-control car didn't respond and slammed into a corner fire hydrant. The air bag activated with a loud cracking sound, knocking Musso backward. He flailed wildly for the door handle. The air bag had him pinned to the seat. He managed to free his gun from its ankle holster and pull the trigger twice. The punctured bag wheezed and began to collapse.

Musso kicked and elbowed his way out of the car. The broken hydrant was spraying a geyser of water fifteen feet into the air. He shouldered his way through the knot of onlookers that had formed around the vehicle.

Mark thought that his leg was broken. He stood gingerly and grimaced as he hopped on one foot from car to car. The pain gradually decreased, and he was able to limp down the street. He reached the smashed Mustang. Joely, the hotel's bartender, was standing among the onlookers.

"The driver. Where'd he go, Joely?"

"I don't know. I just heard the crash and came out for a look." He skirted the hydrant spray and peered into the car. "The air bag probably saved his life. Who was he, Mark?"

Mark put two fingers into his mouth and gave a loud whistle. When he had the crowd's attention, he said, "Did anyone see where the driver went?"

A heavy-shouldered man in shorts and a red Stanford T-shirt, holding a wriggling infant in his arms, said, "He was headed over there, by where the gliders are. He didn't appear to be hurt."

No one else had an opinion, or was willing to share it with Mark, who still held the gun in his hand.

"What's going on?" Joely wanted to know. "What's doing with the gun, Mark?"

Mark pocketed the revolver. "Call the sheriff, Joely. The man's a killer." He pushed through the crowd and limped toward the glider concession.

Johnny Musso eyed the small airport nervously. There was just one biplane, sitting near a row of useless gliders, at an angle to the lone runway.

Ten to twelve people were waiting for glider rides. He took off his sport coat and melted in with the crush of pedestrians. He saw Mark Martel limping toward the smashed Mustang. Damn Martel. The bastard was indestructible. Dumb-shit Junior Ganero had shot him point-blank in the eye, and it hadn't killed him, and now Big Soup had somehow let him get away.

He found a store that sold everything from gardening supplies to casual clothing. He purchased a straw cowboy hat, a blue neckerchief, and a faded denim jacket, then disposed of his sport coat in a street-side garbage bin.

He tilted the hat low over his eyes and scouted the area for a likely car to steal. A police car screamed down the street. He watched the whirling red light for two blocks. The vehicle turned sideways, effectively blocking traffic. Musso ventured out into the street and looked eastward. Two more police cars had formed a barricade at the Silverado Trail turnoff, effectively sealing off the entire town.

So much for stealing a car. He slipped in among a group of well-dressed and, from the sound of their laughter, well-lubricated middle-aged couples. One henna-haired woman with a wineglass in hand said something about a train. "I love trains. I could just ride back and forth all day."

He looked over her shoulder and spotted the inviting sight of a turn-of-the-century Pullman coach.

Mark searched frantically all along Lincoln Avenue for Musso. Someone grabbed his shoulder, and he spun around, ready to strike out.

"Easy, son," Noel Field admonished. "What happened to your leg?"

"Johnny Musso tried to run me down. He's here somewhere."

"So is Inspector Heller. He is not at all pleased with you, Mark."

"I bet. Just the same, I'm glad he's here." A sheriff's car cruised by. "Though it seems there're more than enough cops to go around." Mark gave Field the rundown on Musso's car crash. "He's got a gun, Noel, so be careful."

"I intend to. May I make a suggestion?"

Mark peered into an ice cream parlor. "Sure."

"You say his car crashed. The police have cordoned off the area, but I'm afraid it's you they're looking for, not Musso. If he wants to leave, there's one obvious choice. The train."

Mark leaned against a light post and rubbed his injured leg with both hands. The California Wine Train. Four elegant dining cars that traveled at a leisurely pace through the vineyards, from Napa to Calistoga and back, the thirty-six-mile round-trip taking three hours. Passengers sipped fine California wines and champagne in the glass-topped Vista Dome car, then settled down to elaborately prepared four-course dinners. He'd taken the ride once when Arlene had been the guest chef.

"It's a good possibility," Mark admitted. "Let's check it out."

Someone walking behind the two of them might have wondered which was in the worse shape. The younger, rather disheveled man with the dragging limp, or the older, distinguished gentleman with the rolling gait.

The train station was surrounded by a barnlike building that housed several shops and arcades.

A portly man in an old-fashioned conductor's uniform and hat was checking his pocket watch. "They're boarding," Noel observed.

Mark walked along the vintage Pullman. The shades shielding the etched-glass windows had been pulled down halfway.

The conductor waved his hand over his head toward the engineer, who was leaning out of the cab. A long blast on the whistle followed and the conductor shouted, "All aboard. Five minutes. We leave in five minutes, please."

Mark grabbed the Pullman railing and was about to hoist himself up when someone grabbed his shoulder and slung him back to the ground.

"You're not going anywhere," Dan Heller said defiantly.

Mark jabbed a finger into Heller's chest. "I'm going on that train. Johnny Musso may be on board."

Heller reached for Mark's shoulder again and Mark knocked his hand away. "Listen, Dan. You've heard of Johnny Musso, haven't you?"

Heller's jaw bunched. "No, and I don't give a damn—"

"He is—or was—Victor Ganero's right-hand man. He killed Ganero, at my house. Carrie was there when it happened."

Heller bunched his fist and looked as if he was ready to punch Mark's jaw.

Noel Field moved in between them, like a boxing referee. "Gentlemen, let's not forget our priority for the moment, which is finding Johnny Musso."

Heller pushed Field away and kept his fist cocked.

"Victor Ganero is a New York Mafia don. What the hell has he got to do with you, Verre?"

"His son shot my eye out and killed my fiancée. Ganero thought that I killed Junior. I didn't. Musso did."

Heller slowly lowered his hand and frowned as the information registered. San Francisco policemen don't have much to do with New York mobsters, but Heller vaguely remembered reading something about some guy having his eye shot out and later testifying against Junior Ganero. Verre's glass eye. Jesus Christ.

The train whistle blared again and the conductor shouted, "Last call, all aboard."

"I'll go with you," Heller said.

"No. I'm not sure Musso's on the train. If he's not, I'll hop off down the track. Noel knows what Musso looks like. He'll help you here in town."

Heller gave Field a suspicious look. "You were at Arlene's house."

"Indeed I was, Inspector. I suggest we start checking the side streets. Musso may be looking for a car."

Mark climbed onto the train. The guests were just settling in for the trip back to Napa.

The Pullman bar was open for business and waitresses dressed up like western saloon girls were wandering about with linen-wrapped bottles of champagne.

Mark moved through the dining car. The well-appointed tables featuring fine china, lead crystal, and damask linen were all full of chatting passengers waiting for their gourmet meal.

There was a long whistle and the train chugged away from the station.

Martel checked the observation car and the men's rest room. There was no sign of Musso.

He was about to jump off the slow-moving train when he caught a glimpse of a man in a straw cowboy hat opening the door leading to the engine compartment. The cowboy hat and denim jacket worked together, but not the pants and shoes—dark-blue mohair and tasseled loafers.

"Musso!" Martel shouted.

Johnny Musso turned quickly, then disappeared through the door.

The conductor approached Martel with a stern look. "If you don't have a ticket, I'm afraid you'll have to leave, sir."

"Stop the train," Mark said. He shook the engine compartment door, but it wouldn't budge. "Stop the train right now!"

Chapter 39

There was a loud hissing noise as the engineer, Ronnie Black, released the air brake. He yawned as he nudged the throttle forward and the eighty-ton locomotive edged away from the Calistoga station. He shouldn't complain, he advised himself. The job was steady work, but chugging back and forth on the same boring tracks day after day at a speed of seven miles an hour was not exactly an exciting way to make a living. He often thought back to the trips from Denver to Chicago on the *Zephyr*—1,015 miles through the Sierra Nevada Mountains, across the plains at an average speed of seventy-eight miles an hour, with a string of fifty to sixty boxcars, along with a dozen or more passenger cars and a caboose well stocked with rotgut whiskey and poker-playing trainmen. Now that was railroading.

He leaned his head out the cab and gave the whistle chain a pull, which was just about the highlight of his day, scattering stray dogs and an occasional horse and rider.

He'd lost a good deal of his hearing years ago, somewhere along the tracks between Denver and Chicago, so he wasn't aware of the man behind him until something was jammed into his ribs.

"Crank it up, old-timer," Johnny Musso commanded, twisting the gun barrel into Black's striped coveralls. "Crank it up."

*   *   *

Mark Martel wrestled with the doorknob leading to the engine compartment while the conductor berated him.

"You can't do that! You can't—"

A sudden lurch of the train sent the conductor flying backward, landing him on the carpeted floor with a thud.

There were howls of protests as standing passengers bumped into each other, spilling glasses of champagne onto their seated companions.

Martel hung on to the doorknob to keep from falling.

The conductor struggled to his knees. "Old Ronnie must be drunk," he shouted. "He's going to get us all killed!"

Martel kicked at the door. "Help me open this damn thing."

The conductor crawled over beside Martel, key chain in hand. "It's busted," he said, after several attempts at turning the lock.

Martel had seen numerous movies in which the hero shot the lock to break open a door. In real life, however, the bullet would often ricochet back and hit the shooter, or do nothing more than jam the lock further.

He pulled the fire extinguisher off the wall and pounded the blunt end against the polished-mahogany door paneling. After several hits the wood shattered. Martel reached in and cast about for the interior lock.

The train picked up speed, rocking back and forth on the tracks.

Johnny Musso clamped his fingers around the train engineer's hand. "Faster, pal, faster."

"This ain't no sports car," Ronnie Black protested, his head hanging out the side cabin window. "There's a crossing up ahead. Could be cars, trucks, or people coming across."

"That's their tough luck," Musso responded harshly, pushing the brass throttle handle forward.

Black wrenched his hand free and jerked on the whistle cable. "I got to warn those people."

Musso saw the speedometer tickle up to forty-five, then fifty. He turned over his shoulder in time to see that the door had been broken and a hand was grasping at the lock.

He snapped off two shots in the general direction of the door.

"I got a crossing coming!" Black howled against the deafening hammer of the diesel engine. "We got to slow down."

Musso dug the gun barrel back into Black's ribs, then pressed his mouth to Black's ear. "Where's the emergency brake?"

Mark peered cautiously through the hole in the door. The train was wobbling on the tracks and he could barely make out the locomotive cab. There was a sudden blast of the whistle followed by the agonizing screech of metal on metal as the brake shoes clamped onto the drive wheels. Mark lost his balance and did a back step, his arms windmilling as if he were in water, before crashing into the conductor and sprawling to the floor, the gun falling from his hand and skidding down the aisle.

There was a chorus of screams and shouts from the passengers as the train screeched along the tracks before coming to a jolting stop.

After a moment of relieved silence, the passengers began hollering and running toward the exits in an every-man-for-himself panic. Mark kicked in the door leading to the locomotive cab. The engineer was slumped against the cockpit controls, his head at an awkward angle. Mark gently fingered the bloody contusion behind the man's right ear. Black emitted a muffled moan.

Mark swung down from the cab and surveyed the terrain. The train had come to rest in an area thick with trees and low-growing brush. The ground sloped away sharply to a shallow-running creek. He couldn't

see Musso, but he could hear someone moving through
the brush in the direction of the creek.

He slithered between clumps of thorny brush, his
feet kicking through a carpet of orangey poison oak
and wild manzanita. He splashed across the knee-deep
creek and approached a grove of oak, bay, and pine
trees. So thick were the trees that their long branches
interlocked like linked hands, crowding out the afternoon sunlight.

He leaned against a thick-trunked oak and listened.
There was still a lot of noise coming from the train.
The engineer must have regained consciousness, because the blasts from the train whistle were in the
recognizable three-beat rhythm of the SOS disaster
signal.

He heard movement coming from his right. Someone cursed, and the branches of a low-growing tree
waved, then snapped back into position.

Johnny Musso was pulling his feet out of a patch of
jellylike mud. The muck had oozed into his shoes and
he was having trouble keeping his balance.

He saw a shadow coming toward him and raised his
gun and fired. The bullet plucked at the ground a yard
from the tree Mark was crouched behind. A pair of
blue jays flew past Musso's face, blocking his view for
a moment, then there was a sound like cats screaming.
Suddenly a flock of huge feathered creatures broke
from the brush and whooshed toward him. Musso fired
wildly, pulling the trigger until he heard the click of
the hammer striking an empty chamber. He'd hit one
of them. It fluttered to a stop, its seven-foot wingspan
flapping in a final dance of death.

"Shit," Musso cursed. Turkeys. Wild goddamn turkeys!

He swung the gun around when he heard footsteps.

Mark Martel launched himself in a headlong dive,
smashing into Musso's chest. The impact of the fall
knocked the breath out of Musso. His hands clawed
desperately for his knife. He kneed Martel between

the legs and rolled over, freeing the knife from his pocket and snapping the blade open.

Mark got to one knee as Musso circled him, waving the knife in a right arc, crouched low in an alley fighter's stance.

There was no sound now, except for the heavy breathing coming from both men. Mark picked up a wrist-thick oak branch and jabbed it at Musso as if it was a sword.

"That stick ain't going to help you," Musso said between gasping breaths. "I'm going to teach you a lesson, pal."

Mark had survived his share of street fights in New York City and had three years of armed-combat training while in the Marines.

"Tony Zarela tried teaching me a lesson. He's dead now. Drop the knife or you'll be joining him."

Mark feinted with the tree branch and Musso blocked it with one arm, then drove in, the knife blade flashing up, aiming for Martel's stomach.

The tip of the blade slit Mark's shirt and drew blood. Musso pulled the knife back, swiveling his hips, ready to deliver a death blow.

Rather than backing away, Mark crowded in, his hands anchoring around Musso's arm, his foot lashing out at Musso's legs. They tumbled to the ground, Musso landing awkwardly. His left wrist broke under the impact and his face went white for an instant. The knife skittered into a clump of poison oak.

Mark drove his extended knuckles into Musso's neck, aiming for his Adam's apple.

Musso's right hand clawed at Mark's face, his fingers digging into Mark's skin. Searching for his eyes. He twisted his fingers, a surge of strength pushing away his pain as he yanked his opponent's flesh. He roared in triumph as his fingers came away with an eye. Martel's eye! He twisted around, bucking his hips, waiting for Martel to scream, to stop hitting him. Then he squeezed the eye in his hand. It was glass!

Mark felt Musso's strength sag. He aimed again at Musso's neck. This time the tip of his elbow caught its target, driving the cartilage into Musso's anterior jugular vein.

Musso made a harsh strangling sound, then his body quivered for several seconds before stiffening and giving one final shudder.

Chapter 40

George Alvord dismissed his assistant, Gerald Nerbert, with a sharp wave of his hand when he saw Harry Vlad approach the office door. "Go. Go," Alvord ordered.

Nerbert gave Harry a curious look as he passed him.

"You've got a lot of nerve showing up here," Alvord said once Vlad had closed the door. "After what happened in Arizona, I would think you'd be hiding in Brazil or some other god-awful place."

"Hiding from who?" Harry smiled. "Don't you watch the news? Read the papers? They're all dead, except for Mark Martel."

"What about the police? And the insurance people?"

"Nothing to worry about there," Harry answered breezily, hoping that Alvord hadn't heard about the videotape of him breaking into the Belvedere house. He had to peddle the paintings he'd swiped from Ganero's place after Martel had taken off. Peddle them fast, then take Alvord's advice and hide out for a while. Maybe not in Brazil, but somewhere warm, sunny, and far away. He produced a rolled canvas from behind his back with the flourish of a skilled magician.

Alvord's eyes widened as Harry unrolled the canvas across the desk.

"That's a Uccello," Alvord said in a reverent whisper. "You must have taken it from—"

"George. Don't ask, I won't tell. And I've got two

Mantegna Crucifixions that will make you weep. Are we still in business?"

Alvord wiped his sweating palms on his trousers.

"Why not, Harry? Why not?"

Mark Martel was sprawled on Arlene Severi's porch swing, a cup of coffee in hand, Gauguin at his feet. A dust-coated sheriff's car was parked under the nearby weeping willow. The uniformed driver slumped in the front seat, his fingers locked under his chin as if he might be praying.

"I'm under house arrest," he explained to Noel Field.

"Does the house include Arlene's restaurant?"

"Yes."

"Then you'll be attending the dinner tonight."

"Definitely," Mark assured him. "Have the police given up on you?"

Field rubbed his aching hip. "Oh, yes. I was never a major player in this drama. I'm going home."

Arlene Severi bumped open the screen door with her hip and brought a tray of fresh-baked croissants and a thermos of coffee out to the porch.

"How's Carrie doing?" Mark asked.

"Just fine." She settled the tray onto a redwood bench. "Youth is wonderful, isn't it? Carrie can't wait for school to start now so that she can tell all her friends about what happened." She reached out a hand to Mark and settled on the swing next to him.

Noel gave them both a choppy salute, then said, "I have another mud bath appointment, then I have to make my flight arrangements, but I'll see you at dinner." He shook Mark's hand and gave Arlene a fatherly hug. "Take care, children."

Arlene planted her feet on the ground and pushed the swing into action. They watched Noel hobble out of sight. "What happens next?"

"More interviews," Mark sighed. The FBI had commandeered his house and was using it as a center of operations for the duration of their investigation. "They're coming by again this afternoon."

She took his hand and pulled it to her lips. "Is it over now, Mark? Really over?"

"Yes. It's over." Ganero was dead. Tony Zarela was dead. Johnny Musso was in the hospital. He was going to survive, but it would be some time before he'd be able to talk to the police. His larynx, the *pomum Adami,* was ruptured.

So far Mark had given statements to the Napa County district attorney, the sheriff's office, the Justice Department, and the FBI. Dan Heller had sat in on all of the interrogations.

Heller had surprised Mark by backing him up and taking personal responsibility for his not fleeing the area. The original FBI plan was for Mark to be taken to the county jail until the investigation was completed.

Mark knew that that could stretch out for weeks or months. Heller had escorted him from the D.A.'s office to a bar in downtown Napa.

"Carrie told me what happened. What you did for her."

"I never meant to involve Carrie. Or Arlene," Mark swore.

"Maybe you never meant to, but it happened. You can stay at Arlene's house." The big policeman looked at his hands, twisting his thin wedding band slowly. "This is Arlene's idea. I'm going along with it. You sleep downstairs. In the front room. Alone. Get it?"

"Got it," Mark said.

"Good. Because I'm going to be right down the street. You do anything funny, you try and get away, and I'll come after you, Verre, so help me."

That had been two days ago. Two days of incessant interrogations and avoiding the press.

"Here's Carrie," Arlene said when she spotted Dan Heller's car pulling into the driveway.

Gauguin jumped to his feet to greet Carrie. She

rubbed his face with both hands, then gave her mother a kiss. She twirled in front of Mark, fluffing up her new short haircut.

"Like it?"

"It makes you look younger," Mark said.

She stuck her tongue out at him. "No, it doesn't!"

Heller beeped the horn and waved Martel over. It was then that Mark noticed Lisa Cole was in the backseat.

"This lady says you've got something that belongs to her," Heller said, sliding back behind the wheel. "Let's go get those paintings."

Mark slid in beside Lisa. She gave him an appraising glance. "I hope you feel better than you look."

His leg was in a soft cast and there were splotches of pink-colored medicine on his face and hands.

"Where to?" Heller wanted to know.

"The winery. The cave cellars. I'll tell you where to turn."

Lisa fidgeted in her seat. "The Arizona police went to Ganero's mansion. I was there. The house was empty. We found more paintings, in a tomb under the chapel. And something else was there. Victor Ganero, Jr.'s coffin."

"And who gets the finder's fee, Lisa?"

"Not me," Cole answered gloomily. "At least not yet."

"I was sorry to hear about Charlie Dwyer."

"Were you really?" Lisa said tightly. "Uncle Charlie thought you were in on the thefts right to the end."

"Turn here," Mark directed Dan Heller. "Up this road about half a mile."

Mark could see Joan Hatton, Pete Altes, and the picking crew working a section of Cabernet Sauvignon grapes. He longed for the time when he would be able to join them and go back to the simple life of helping Joan with the winery.

"This is it."

Heller pulled the car up to the cave doors and

turned off the engine. He leaned across the front seat, directing his comments at Lisa Cole.

"Remember our agreement. The paintings go to the FBI first. You can fight all you want with them for possession, but they have first shot."

Lisa was already half out of the car before she responded. "Okay, okay. Let's see them, Mark."

Martel unlocked the doors, snapped on the switch, and the fluorescents flickered to life.

"Where are they?" Lisa asked anxiously.

"In the barrels on the—" Mark cut himself off. The forklift was parked directly in front of the row of barrels where he'd stored the paintings. But the three barrels, starting with the fourth from the left in the fourth row, were no longer in place. They sat upright alongside the forklift.

Lisa could wait no longer. She ran to the barrels, her heels sounding like pistol shots on the concrete floor. She pulled a canvas from one barrel and let out a happy yelp. "It's the Botticelli!"

Dan Heller helped her retreive and carefully unroll the other two paintings.

"They're wonderful!" Lisa raved. "Really wonderful."

She got to her feet and peered back into the barrels. "Where's the Correggio? *The Assumption of the Madonna*. The one that started all of this. I thought you said it was here."

"I must have been mistaken."

Lisa reached deep into the barrel. "There's a scrap of paper." She held it up to the light. "It's a cocktail napkin. From the Oak Bar at the Plaza Hotel. How'd that get in there?"

"I wonder." Mark answered with an amused grin, knowing full well that Noel Field wouldn't be there for dinner tonight.

ONYX

Michael Slade

"A GENUINE RIVAL TO STEPHEN KING."
—*Book Magazine*

❏ **BURNT BONES**   0-451-19969-3 / $6.99
Meet Mephisto—he buries his victims alive, just for the fun of it.
No real harm . . . yet. He's waiting for the two detectives who are
on his trail. Waiting for the real fun to begin....

❏ **EVIL EYE**   0-451-40695-8 / $6.99
Someone has murderously targeted the elite members of Canada's
Royal Mounted Police, and it's up to two veteran investigators of
the Special X division to unravel the most horrifying case of their
careers. But this killer, with mystical, supernatural ties half a
world away, has vengeance on his mind and death in his heart.
And with each step taken toward the truth, he watches, and
patiently waits.

Also available:

❏ **GHOUL**   0-451-15959-4 / $6.99